MOONSTONE SHADOWS

CRYSTAL MAGIC, BOOK 7

PATRICIA RICE

Book View
Café

Moonstone Shadows
Patricia Rice

Copyright © 2019, Patricia Rice
Book View Cafe, July 9, 2019
First Publication: 2019

Published by Rice Enterprises, Dana Point, CA, an affiliate of Book View Café Publishing Cooperative
Cover design by Kim Killion
Book View Café Publishing Cooperative
P.O. Box 1624, Cedar Crest, NM 87008-1624
http://bookviewcafe.com
Ebook 978-1-61138-810-7
Print 978-1-61138-811-4

ACKNOWLEDGMENTS

As every author since the beginning of time has acknowledged—a book cannot be written without the help of a village or tribe of people willing to contribute knowledge, ideas, and a sympathetic ear. After all these years, my tribe is enormous. I love you all dearly, although I'm usually too reticent to say so.

In no particular order, I offer gratitude to: My fellow wenches—their support and brainstorming skills are par none. My BVC partners—without their skill and expertise these books are never likely to happen. To my cover designer—without whom this cover would be a green rectangle with a title. And to my family—who allow me to drift off into my head without warning and give me the space I need to work. Hugs to all of you!

And last, but certainly not least, I thank my readers for following me from the wild West, through the misty murk of revolutions, to the tearooms of the Regency, and into the living rooms of today. I love you all!

HILLVALE

~

The following is a purely directional map, not proportional or representative, but just for the sheer fun of it. Enjoy!

~

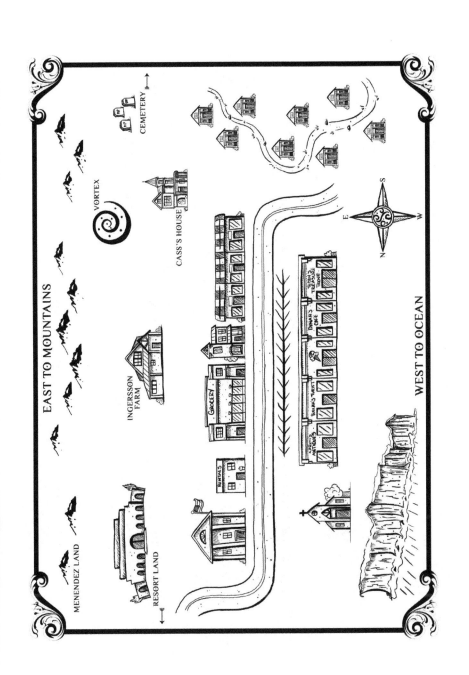

ONE

HEARING *LOOK AWAY, LOOK AWAY. . .*IN HIS HEAD, AARON IGNORED THE mental admonition and swept his walking stick across the path. The expression *whistling Dixie* took on another whole level of meaning when roaming Hillvale's haunted hills.

Except *Dixieland* wasn't the word coming to mind—Fairyland, maybe. *Evil* land made more sense, even in the original song, he realized sardonically. His subconscious was working overtime.

If he could only find and destroy the source of the evil. . . He'd feel free to abandon this isolated town, maybe travel again, visit his child-hood home in the Shetlands.

Except his hand-carved staff had yet to locate any of the new vibra-tions the women had reported. They were now calling their crystal-knobbed staffs *Lucy sticks* after a Hollywood fantasy director had referred to them that way. Aaron preferred *staff* as in "Thy rod and thy staff, they comfort me."

The thick walnut killed snakes too.

Ah, there it was. The stick twitched in his hand, and the crystal eyes of the eagle handle glowed hot against his palm.

He'd done many wrong things in his checkered career. Too much knowledge jaded the mind and blurred the line between right and wrong. It could be that his attempt to right old wrongs by guarding this mountain was as perverted as the people who initially bled evil into the dirt.

But he could only act on what he knew, and he could feel the evil rising in agitation. The Force had awakened, as his renter, Harvey, had claimed, in his own inimitable way.

The late afternoon shadows were growing longer as Aaron followed the vibrations through the old pines on this shadier side of the mountain. This wasn't old growth by any means. Centuries of native slaves, settlers, farmers, and miners had cleared the original forest—until everyone died, often unpleasantly. The dirt beneath Aaron's feet reeked of centuries of torment—and the evil that had been interred here.

A clearing opened ahead—the consecrated ground of an old church. Spanish missionaries had attempted to establish a mission in the early 1700s, long before the miners and the farmers. Nothing grew on that ground these days but native grasses, brown after a dry summer.

Something disturbed the grasses now—or *someone*.

In surprise, Aaron halted at the clearing's edge. Although the land was owned by the local resort, even tourists steered clear of this side of the mountain. The darkness was that bad. Could this be the cause of the disturbance?

He'd almost start believing in fairies if the figure sprawled on a blanket in the patch of sunlight wasn't so obviously human. A spill of honey-blond hair fell over her shoulder and a shaggy fringe hid her forehead as she slept on her side. This was August, so she'd apparently shed her hiking gear in the heat and used it as a pillow. Pale ivory skin revealed her unfamiliarity with California's perpetual sunshine. Her incandescent pink t-shirt outlined nice but not large breasts and a too-slender waist.

He'd never seen her before. Sooner or later, every tourist who visited Hillvale traipsed through his antiques store, drawn by the whimsical and the historical in his display windows. He'd have remembered this visitor.

Look away, look away. . .

He couldn't. Why, by all that was holy, had the woman chosen the only safe patch of ground on the mountain to sleep? No rattlesnake or spider would bother her there. The evil in the woods wouldn't touch her, but it sure the hell knew she was present.

"Back off, Aaron," he told himself, even as he took a step forward. "You know she has to be a Lucy. You don't mess with Lucys," he reminded himself. "They cling like limpets."

But it was his self-imposed duty to keep Hillvale safe from the evil lurking in these hills, and this sleeping princess was agitating the spirits.

Of course, he could just be crazy, but that was part of the territory.

He would just touch the backpack, then decide whether it was safe to leave her there. He'd mastered the nuances of psychometry—the ability to read the past on objects—better than he had human nature.

The army-green canvas was old and tattered. The memories on it might go deep. Summoning his concentration, he let his right hand hover over the backpack. Detecting nothing dangerous, he skimmed his fingertips over the surface—

And conjured a faint vision of someone weeping as she added an old diary and a fountain pen to the empty bag.

The fairy-woman on the ground abruptly sat up and stared at him. Her eyes were the color of the forest in autumn, a honey gold like the hair nearly falling into them, only darker. Framed by long dark lashes and round cheeks, her eyes were nearly oblong, more so as she narrowed them.

"Not you again," she cried. "Not while I'm dying!"

As abruptly as she'd woken, she lay down and fell back to sleep.

Dying? Stunned, Aaron backed away. "Not again," he muttered, unconsciously repeating her warning. "Not ever again." He'd barely survived the last time.

Standing to his full height, he marched in the direction of the road. Not his problem, he told himself sternly. She was perfectly safe where she was.

Upon reaching the gravel road to civilization, he discovered Cassandra waiting for him—of course. Cass never set foot on this ground unless it was an emergency. *Faex*, shit—the Latin curse was as familiar to him as the English.

Silver-haired, slim, and erect as any professional model, the omniscient witch waited for him to speak first—even though she had to be here because she knew something he didn't.

Angry at himself, angry at the sleeping woman for sucking him in like that, he stopped only to announce, "She's one of yours. Keep her away from me."

Not waiting to hear Cass's warnings, Aaron whacked his stick against the hard ground and increased his stride toward town.

"WAKE UP, CHILD, IT'S LATE AND THE AIR IS COOLING. YOU'LL CATCH pneumonia or lure predators."

A hand shook Hannah's shoulder. Stretching, slowly awakening from what felt like the first good sleep she'd had in years, Hannah let peace fill her before responding.

Had she dreamed the striking man in black with the sexy goatee? Of course she had. Ever since she'd encountered the painting in Keegan's castle, she'd been dreaming of a tall dark knight with a neat chin beard. In this past year, the dreams had become so insistent that she'd been forced to question her sanity. Eventually, those dreams, and the fainting spells that ensued, had caused her to seek medical assistance.

Perhaps if she'd heeded the warning of the painting sooner—but it was too late now.

She rubbed her eyes and sat up. The sun was gone from the clearing. The pine shadows were long. She'd slept the hours away instead of calling Keegan! What was wrong with her?

Frowning down at her was a fairy godmother, or a woman quite magical to behold, at least.

"Sorry, am I trespassing?" she asked, scrambling to pull on the jacket she'd worn on the plane. The woman watching her wore a sleeveless linen ankle-length dress—maybe she was a druid emerging from the pines.

"You're not trespassing if you're a guest of the lodge. But we have mountain lions and rattlesnakes here. You're better off sleeping in your bed."

Apparently, fairy godmothers sounded like every disapproving school teacher she'd ever had.

Hannah stood and folded her blanket. "I didn't mean to sleep so long. I'd only meant to take a quick look at my new home. I'm jet-lagged, and this place is so peaceful. Sorry if I worried you. Thank you for warning me. I'll be fine. I'm pretty sure I know how to get back."

"You're not fine," she said severely. "I'm Cassandra Tolliver. I assume you're the librarian Keegan said would be visiting."

Ah, small town, right. She knew how that worked. "Librarian, historian, teacher, jack of all trades." Hannah shoved the blanket into her backpack and started toward the path she remembered following. "Good to meet you, Mrs. Tolliver. I'm Hannah Simon."

She didn't intend to follow up that line about not being fine. Hannah knew she wasn't fine. From communication with her Cousin Keegan and his wife, Mariah, Hannah knew the old lady was the self-appointed leader of the prescient *Lucys*. Lucys didn't really know anything more than she did, which was next to nothing. They just made educated guesses, as she did.

"People here call me Cass. Keegan said you might be interested in teaching in the school we're starting." Cass strode with a long-legged confidence that belied her silver-haired status.

"Or perhaps I could help setting up your history museum. I'm not sure I can teach a one-room school."

Cassandra nodded. "Thanks to several wealthy donors, our school will be better equipped than you're thinking. We'll have computers connected to teachers from around the state. We've hired an elementary grade teacher. As of now, you'd only have one student above that level."

"Wow. The mind boggles." Hannah hesitated, not eager to explain her predicament. She might have a year or ten years. She had to support herself while she searched for the painting that might hold clues to a cure. A museum director just sounded nicely isolated and less emotionally involved.

She really didn't want to fall down dead in front of little kids.

"You have time to think about it," Cassandra said, as if reading her mind, which she might very well be doing. "I trust the Kennedys are offering you a decent rental rate to encourage you to stay?"

"I just got in today. I've not talked to anyone but the desk clerk, not even Keegan. I didn't know if Mariah had her baby yet. I was supposed to call." She checked her watch but it was still on UK time.

"We're still anxiously awaiting the first child born here in over thirty years. Give them a call once you reach your room. It's early yet." Cassandra stopped outside the timber lodge where it appeared a limo was disgorging a bridal party. Women in gauzy gowns laughed and clung to wilting bouquets. Undisturbed by the clamor, Cass continued, "I'll leave you here. Call on me anytime. Everyone knows where I live."

Hannah held out her hand to shake Cass's. "Thank you. I appreciate that. I hope I'll be able to stay in Hillvale." If she didn't find the painting, couldn't find a cure, she didn't know how to plan a nonexistent future.

A shadow stepped down from the enormous lodge veranda. "What the hell are you doing on my property, you old witch? Didn't I make it clear I'd have you arrested if you came near what's mine?"

Even the noisy wedding party hesitated at the angry cry.

"Oh dear," Cassandra said with a sigh, dropping Hannah's hand. "No good deed goes unpunished."

Hannah watched in puzzlement as a lovely, tawny-haired woman dressed in bronze and gold stepped into the light beyond the aging stone porch. She looked like a sun goddess—and screeched like an owl.

The goddess glared at Hannah. "You, whoever you are, take your trash and leave with her. I'll not have more of your kind polluting my property."

Having utterly no clue what *kind* she was—mutt?—Hannah felt more embarrassed for the screecher than for herself. The bridal party hurried for the open doors to escape the unpleasant scene.

"Me?" Hannah pointed at herself. "I'm a paying guest here. You don't want guests?"

"It's only partly her property, dear. She can't throw you out. Carmel, may I introduce you to our new teacher, Hannah Simon? I don't believe your sons would appreciate you throwing her out, not if they expect to raise children here."

Hannah refrained from mentioning that she hadn't agreed to teaching yet. Cass had apparently spoken the magic words to stop the squawking.

The golden lady stiffened, and her mouth worked, but nothing emerged. Cool.

"Carmel has been ill, dear, and it appears she's off her medications again." Cass took Hannah's arm and strolled toward an open air shuttle waiting in the drive. "She could make life unpleasant for you if you stay at the lodge. Why don't we explore alternatives?"

"All our properties are taken!" Carmel shouted as they turned their backs on her.

Keegan had said Hillvale was weird. He hadn't mentioned how weird.

"What *kind* am I?" she whispered out of curiosity, climbing in the cart with her companion. "Is she a racist?" Hannah's distant Asian heritage wasn't overtly evident, but racists might note the shape of her eyes and conclude she wasn't like them.

"You're a Lucy, dear. Carmel is a *witchist*, if I may coin a word."

"She can tell I'm a Malcolm librarian?" Hannah had grown up knowing she was a Malcolm—or a *Lucy* as Hillvale called the psychically endowed. Her talent was a minor one for finding family journals and categorizing them, not exactly a gift that was obvious to anyone except herself.

"I think Carmel simply associates anyone with me as not her kind—unless. . ." Cass pursed her lips and fell into a study.

Just as Hannah thought she wouldn't hear the rest of that speculation, the older woman shrugged and completed her sentence.

"Unless the evil in her recognizes the good in you. I'd rather hope she's not possessed by demons. Here we are. Let's talk to Aaron, shall we? He has a spare room."

Demons? That was the first Hannah had heard of demons.

Cass climbed off the shuttle in front of an antique store displaying a splendidly ornamental medieval cuirass—*just like the one the knight wore in Hannah's dream.*

In shock, she couldn't flee but only stare.

TWO

A<small>T THE RINGING CHIME OVER THE SHOP DOOR</small>, A<small>ARON DIDN'T LOOK UP FROM</small> the clock he was repairing. He knew who had entered. Cassandra managed to emanate disapproval and anger without speaking. The odd. . . serenity. . . entering with her could only be the new Lucy. Both women created recognizable vibrations.

Gritting his teeth, he continued tinkering. "No," he said before Cass could phrase the question. "I'm using the room for storage. Let her sleep at your place."

"Josh is still using my apartment for his studio. Amber may not be happy if Hannah moves in with him. Amber needs security right now as she rebuilds her career, and having the schoolteacher living in her husband's office isn't conducive to that."

Using delicate tweezers, Aaron twisted the pin into a gear. "Then she can stay at the lodge until she finds a place."

Schoolteacher! Of course the new Lucy was a schoolteacher—innocent, childlike, everything he was not and never would be. Given her lack of negative vibrations, she was probably a guardian angel or some weirdness like that. The Lucys had a never-ending supply of talents.

"Since it seems Carmel is off her medication and has taken a dislike to Miss Simon, that might not be the wisest choice," Cassandra said patiently. "Let us have the key to the spare room, and we'll move boxes. It's not as if she arrived with a house full of furniture."

"Excuse me." A firm voice that did not sound particularly angelic spoke up. "I'm not a dog bone. I come from a long line of warriors and druids and know how to speak for myself. I'll be fine at the lodge until I decide if I'm staying in Hillvale. I just wanted to visit my cousin, give him news of his home, and meet Mariah in person."

Rolling his eyes, Aaron set down his tools and stood to lean over his counter. Damned if the woodland fairy wasn't even more enchanting awake than asleep. She'd donned an atrocious camouflage jacket over her bright pink shirt. Her khaki pants were wrinkled and grass-stained. But her honey hair framed a delicate chin and porcelain features, and her heavy-lidded eyes were much too discerning beneath the messy bangs.

"You're a Lucy. Of course you'll be staying. Cass has a house large enough to hide an army. She doesn't like sharing any more than Carmel does. Play the two old witches against each other, and they'll find you a place soon enough." Aaron turned his glare on Cass. "I am not one of your minions to be played like a chess piece."

"I don't go where I'm not wanted, but at least I'm a paying guest at the lodge. I'll be fine there." The teacher stalked out, defying Cass and scorning Aaron.

He was good with that.

Cass glared. "No man is an island. You cannot live like this forever." She marched out after her newest protégée.

Oh yeah, he could live like this forever and eternity. He was happy like this, with no one demanding his time and attention and devotion. He'd made himself a damned wealthy man now that his time was his own.

The phone rang as the women walked out. Expecting a call from a supplier, he grabbed it.

"The baby's coming," Keegan growled into his ear. "Word is that Cass has my cousin at your place. Send them up." The call abruptly shut off.

The Scot geologist was a sound man and a good friend who generally left Aaron alone, as he liked it. Aaron couldn't return the favor by ignoring the plea of a panicked new father.

Crossing the crowded shop in a few strides, Aaron shouted out the door at the women walking away. "Baby's coming. Command performance."

Cass turned with a regal nod of acknowledgement. Miss Simon pretended he didn't exist. Being ignored by the newcomer might almost work—if he didn't have to hear the faint lilt of home in her voice.

HANNAH'S INSIDES WERE IN SUCH KNOTS THAT SHE'D FEAR THE SICKNESS WAS in her gut and not her head if she hadn't just undergone a complete physical—

And recognized the reason the antiques dealer and criminal fraud churned her insides. Tall, lean, exuding muscular strength and assurance, the man had near-black hair, a neat goatee, a Roman nose, and a mellow baritone to melt her bones—the modern equivalent of the knight in the painting and in her dreams, despite the expensive blazer and designer knit shirt. A *modern* knight—with a medieval cuirass in his window.

A normal person would simply assume she'd seen him before—he had the faint accent of the Shetlands, a place of few inhabitants. Her American parents had lived there when she was quite young. She supposed it was logical to believe the familiarity was because she'd met him as a child.

But she wasn't normal or logical. She was a Malcolm—and she'd been studying Malcolm texts since birth. Weird coincidences *dinnae* happen, as the old stories told. Besides, he would have been a child, too, when she'd last been in the Shetlands, and no child would sport a goatee. Could the knot in her brain conjure coincidence?

How had her dream knight become twisted together with a criminal who had gone to prison for selling fraudulent art? She'd come here looking for *Aaron Townsend*, the conman who had stolen the painting the journals had spoken about. Now that she'd found him—she needed to treat him with extreme wariness and not like a dream knight.

Lost in thought, Hannah instinctively followed Cass down the street. She looked up now to see if they were heading for a hospital or a bus to take them to wherever Mariah was giving birth.

Instead, they were hurrying down Hillvale's main street, picking up a procession of chattering, excited followers. As they passed the café, a slight woman in an overlarge apron waved and closed the shutters over the café's window. She leaned out the door to call, "I'll be right there. Let me take the baby cakes out of the oven."

"Baby cakes," a short, heavy woman with glorious sunset hair repeated with a laugh. "Mariah would ask if she's baking babies now."

"They're like biscuits, aren't they?" Hannah asked. "Hi, I'm Hannah Simon, Keegan's cousin, and I have no idea what's happening."

"Amber Gabriel née Abercrombie. The name is still new to me." She flashed an amber wedding band set with pearls and diamonds. "And we're holding a birthing circle, I believe. Cass told us about it, although I've never attended one."

"A birthing circle? It's a Malcolm tradition." Thrilled to have arrived in time for the birth of her newest cousin, comfortable with the role of historian and teacher, Hannah fell in stride with her friendly companion. "We call on the spirits of our ancestors to look after the mother and the spirit taking residence in the unborn child. Traditionally, it was done in ancient Malcolm castles—there's a whole story behind how we lost our original home. But we're so widespread now, that tradition has become what we make of it. I'm fascinated to learn how Hillvale does it."

"Oh, you're the new teacher!" Amber chirruped in joy. "My nephew will love you. And Teddy's sister has just moved in with her two little ones, although you won't have them for a few more years. It's just so exciting to see the town grow like this. Welcome."

"Mariah told me there was a museum director's position?" Hannah asked, sticking to her goal as the growing procession of women walked up a narrow lane of cottages nearly hidden by lush, exotic foliage. After her parents returned home from the UK, she'd grown up in the San Francisco area where most of her family resided. She'd returned to Scotland to work in Keegan's castle these last years, but it was good to be back in California again, she thought.

Amber waved plump fingers adorned with rings. "I think the director's job will mostly be a volunteer position until we start collecting actual artifacts besides what we find in our attics. Your expertise will be welcome, but it's the school that's vital."

Hannah wasn't the type to waste energy on curses, but she considered a few expressive epithets. Then the procession turned up the drive of a small house eccentrically adorned with what appeared to be silvery computer disks hanging from the eaves, twinkling in the fading rays of sun, and she let the future go in favor of the present. A birthing circle, for her cousin's first child!

A tall woman with a head of platinum dandelion-fluff hair, who appeared to be in the first stages of pregnancy, joined them. "This is so exciting! Hi, I'm Samantha Walker. You must be the new teacher. Mariah usually helps Cass lead our ceremonies. She's the strongest among us, but she's otherwise occupied today," she added with a laugh. "I hope you know the ceremony."

So, it looked as if she was the new teacher—if she found a room. Keegan was right, though. Hannah thought she'd like it here. Arriving in time to sing a welcoming song for her new cousin seemed an auspicious opening for this last stage of her life.

"Hannah, if you'll start the chant, I think it will help connect the child to Keegan's heritage. I'm closer to Mariah's," Cass commanded.

The older cousin she knew and respected had been talking more than usual if strangers were acquainted with her background. She supposed new fathers could be excused for seeking aid. "We don't usually form a circle until the child is about to arrive. Is the midwife here?"

"Brenda's been in there since before noon," an auburn-haired woman called from the other side of the circle. "Mariah's sending out pretty strong signals now."

The only signals Hannah picked up were from books, but she knew many of her ancestors and their descendants had psychic abilities far greater than hers. "A twilight birth is special," she exclaimed, understanding the growing excitement. "Is Brenda a physician?" she asked Amber as they joined hands.

"A nurse practitioner and healer. Mariah said the child wants to be born here, not down the mountain in a hospital. I'm a little terrified at the idea of being dictated to by an unborn child," Amber said with a half-laugh. "I want drugs."

"Not modern drugs," Hannah warned. "They're not good for those with psychic abilities. Modern medicine might be responsible for diluting our numbers and talents over the years. It's not possible to prove that, though. Genetic failure for marrying outside our ancestral boundaries could also explain it."

"Hannah!" Cass said sharply. "Mariah needs us."

Unused to group participation, Hannah had to remember she wasn't sitting in her lonely library. She'd never led a chant either, but the words were in her head, just as the many texts in the library lurked there, ready to be called upon as needed.

Clasping the hands of Amber and Samantha, with the sun's final rays fading behind the trees, Hannah spoke the ancient words asking for the blessings of mother earth and the ancestors who came before, asking for protection for the new child and her mother. She started in the old tongue of her druidic forebears, proceeded into the Gaelic of Keegan's family, added the Mandarin of her maternal family, and worked her way to English.

An older gentleman with a long, graying braid kept time on a leather and wood drum, chanting in an unfamiliar tongue similar to the one Cass took up now. Hannah assumed the language belonged to Mariah's Native American ancestors. They both followed up with Spanish. A tall black woman Hannah hadn't met added an African and a Jamaican blessing. In repetition, the chants blended, droning through the night air after the sun descended, welcoming the spirit child from wherever it came.

Once upon a time, birthing circles had been held in castle keeps with extended family present, Hannah knew. Here, where tiny cottages replaced towering halls, and far-flung families couldn't unite, this coming together of many hereditary lines offered a similar security. Even though these women were strangers, the warmth and excitement of bringing new life into the world connected them to each other and beyond the veil of the spirit world. Hannah could almost feel their long-gone ancestors gathering.

With the sun vanished below the horizon, the squall of a newborn cut through the drone of their chant. A clear soprano broke into joyous song. Hannah located the refrain coming from a tall woman, clad in black and wearing a veil, whom she had noticed earlier. Recognizing the song, she joined in, as did Cass and several of the others.

The babe's cries quieted. The front door opened, letting out a slash of golden light, before Keegan, a giant of a man, blocked the glow with broad shoulders while holding a swaddled infant. "A girl, meet Daphne Daisy Ives, nine pounds, ten ounces. Mariah is doing fine, thank you all."

A cheer echoed through the dark.

"Daisy!" Samantha whispered excitedly. "Mariah thought she felt Daisy's spirit. I guess we won't know until Daphne's old enough to show if she has a creative talent."

"Look at Daisy's lamassu," Amber whispered back, pointing out the absurd little stacks of wired stones scattered about the yard. "Their eyes are glowing."

The crystals attached to the top stones did seem to be catching the lamplight. "What does that mean?" Hannah asked. She'd learned about Hillvale's inhabitants and their abilities from Keegan and Mariah's communications, but she wanted to absorb her surroundings through all eyes.

"Daisy was one of the original Hillvale commune artists. She was Mariah's mentor and created those sculptures to protect us against evil. She was murdered last year, and Mariah misses her. So she could just be engaged in wishful thinking, but Daisy's spirit could be present!" Amber said in excitement.

Even Hannah felt a little thrill at thinking the text in the old journals hadn't lied about the spirits of ancestors entering the womb. Surrounded by all this estrogen, she was sorry that she would never experience the initiation of new life. But she wouldn't leave any child of hers motherless, and so would never know this thrill for herself. Her excitement was for the women around her.

She would not think of dark knights making babies. That was the knot in her brain talking.

After the little cook handed out her soft, sugary cookies, the circle broke up, with people drifting in different directions. Most of the women appeared to live on this enchanting lane and drifted to their cottages, one by one. By the time she traipsed into town, Hannah was alone except for the auburn-haired woman she'd heard called Teddy.

"You'll fit right in here," Teddy said happily. "I don't know that my niece and nephew have any gifts, they're still young, but a gifted teacher can only be a benefit. Keegan says you carry a library in your head. Oh, and hi, I'm Teddy Kennedy. I own that jewelry store." She nodded at a building on the corner of the main street and the highway.

Hannah introduced herself and wondered if the lodge shuttle ran after dark.

"Don't worry," Teddy said, as if reading her mind. "Harvey can take you back to the lodge in the golf cart if the shuttle has quit running. Since we closed town early for the birthing, it probably has. Oops."

"Ah, you're the empath Keegan mentioned." Hannah studied the dark town lit only by a single light pole. "Who is Harvey? Is he the musician?"

"Among other things. He's a Lucy, too, although he and Aaron and Keegan hate being called Lucys."

"Understandably," Hannah said with a laugh. "Keegan is more Ives than Malcolm, so he hates being called a Malcolm too, since most of us are female."

"You sound too American to be Scots, although I know you just came from Keegan's home. Have you lived here before?" The auburn-haired jeweler stood with Hannah beneath the street lamp, apparently confident that a ride would magically appear.

"I was born in the Shetlands, but my parents returned to their families in San Francisco when I was little. So I went to school in California, completed university courses in the UK, and felt called to help Keegan with his library and their local school after that." Hannah was glad that her family wasn't the type to hover. She'd always been a loner, and they accepted that. She could visit occasionally and hope they wouldn't notice any changes.

"I should travel more," Teddy said. "But I'm always too busy. Huh, that's Aaron's van coming down the street. I wonder where Harvey is?"

"Maybe he's driving the van," Hannah said with hope, not wanting to face the angry man with a criminal past after the beautiful evening. "Aaron doesn't like me."

"Aaron avoids everyone. He's very good at closing himself off so even I can't tell what he's feeling. But once he gets involved, he's passionate about pursuing what's right. Ask Fee sometime. You're safe in his hands."

Hannah was having difficulty processing all the names and people, but she believed Fee was the cook who had passed around baby cakes. She didn't have time to question before the van halted and the passenger door opened. The light inside only revealed the shadow of the driver against the darkened windows.

"There could be a serial killer in there," she said weakly.

"Nah, only Aaron would open the door without speaking. Stop by my store any time. I'm always eager for a coffee break and a chat." Teddy walked off with a wave.

Reluctantly, Hannah climbed into the passenger seat. Her dark knight with the criminal past grimly gripped the steering wheel.

"They had a baby girl," she said, trying not to sound frightened. "Daphne Daisy they're calling her."

"Am I picking up your luggage and delivering you anywhere?" he asked without comment on the happy news.

"I'll be fine at the lodge. Keegan wouldn't have recommended it if it was unsafe," she said with an assurance she wasn't certain she felt. The roaring lioness had been pretty unbalanced.

"I'll go in with you. If Carmel has another fit, I'll take you to Walker's place. They have a spare room. Samantha just fills it with seedlings and crap." He drove the large van up the narrow lodge drive with the expertise of a knight on his steed.

She had to stop thinking like that. Noble knights didn't go to jail for selling fake art.

It wasn't dreadfully late. The lodge parking lot was filled with cars, and people strolled the walks and spilled from the well-lit restaurant and bar.

"I appreciate the ride, but I'll be fine," Hannah assured him. "If you let me out here, you won't have to find a parking space. I can go in the back door without notice."

Ignoring her, he drove around to the rear of the lodge and parked. He climbed out, came around, and held out his hand to help her before she could step down on her own.

The minute Aaron's palm closed over Hannah's, she knew her mistake.

THREE

AARON CLUTCHED THE THRICE-DAMNED WOMAN'S FINGERS AS SHE CRUMPLED.

"*Deodamnatus,*" he muttered in his schoolboy Latin, catching the teacher's other arm to prevent her from hitting the pavement. She slumped against him like a rag doll. "*Faex.*" Now what did he do?

Cell phones didn't work in Hillvale, or he'd call the lodge desk for help. "*Futue deodamnatus faex.*" He despised helplessness—and he was damned scared she'd die on him.

He heaved her unconscious form back in the van so he could rummage through her backpack for the room key.

The instant he released her, she stirred.

"That was awkward," she muttered, eyes still closed against the dim interior light of the van.

"Tell me about it," he retorted, relieved beyond measure that she was still alive. "Or better yet, don't. Just find your key so I can see you inside, where you need to call a doctor or I will."

"They can't do anything. Just don't touch me, and I'll be fine." She opened her eyes but wouldn't look at him.

Anger followed terror. "Seems to me you say that a lot—*I'll be fine*—when you obviously aren't," he said in disgust. "Give me your backpack. Can you climb down without my help?"

She handed him the heavy pack and rewarded him with a look of scorn.

The look did his jaded heart good. Scorn he could handle.

He stood back and let her use the door as crutch to climb down again.

She tried to retrieve the backpack, but he shouldered it. "I'm seeing you to your door. If you want to collapse and die once you're inside, that's on you."

He didn't ask if she only fainted on him or if she made a practice of it. She'd said she'd seen doctors. He didn't want to know anything more personal or intimate than that. But for a very brief moment there, his damned psychometry had kicked in and he'd seen. . . something. He'd trained himself to block any impressions he didn't want, or shaking hands could raise some really ugly, and occasionally lewd, mental pictures. He didn't know how she'd broken through his block even for that brief second.

But she'd left him wondering if the Malcolm librarian had the gift of psychometry too. That could be awkward if she started poking around his store. Because, yeah, he'd figured out that this was the librarian Keegan had brought to Hillvale, curse the damned geologist's generous heart.

"I'm not usually given to collapsing," she said tartly, marching down the dark sidewalk at the rear of the lodge. "But then, I don't normally meet men with the gift of psychometry either. I'm receptive. I can be affected by psychic gifts but cannot reflect or employ them."

"Good to know," he said curtly, relieved that his touch hadn't set off a brain bomb. Then he processed the sentence beyond himself and scowled. "There are people who can reflect or employ my gift if I touch them?"

And how the hell would that work? They saw what he did when he touched an object? Or they could see what was inside his head? That gave him mental shudders.

"It's been reported, yes, but passive agents tend to be villains and not journal writers, so I have no firsthand reports, just observations from ancestors." She entered the brightly lit hall of hotel rooms and stalked down the carpet.

His need for knowledge warred with his desire to avoid a woman who represented everything he never wanted in his life again.

She unlocked her door and Aaron held it open so he could throw her backpack in. Before he could think better of it, he asked, "If I buy you a drink, will you tell me more of these villains?"

She hesitated, casting him a wary look, before shaking her head. "No, I think not. Thank you for the ride. Good night." She took the door and waited for him to leave.

Perversely, he didn't want to be denied. "As librarian, aren't you supposed to offer us any information to be found in our ancestors' journals?"

"Give me your card with your email address, and I'll send you the volumes and pages referencing the villainy. It's obscure and not very helpful." Stone-faced, she continued to wait for him to back off from the door he held open.

Grumpily, he produced a slim mahogany card case from his jacket and handed her the cream-colored card for his store. "I'd appreciate that."

He stalked off, leaving the obstinate female to her brain fits. Deciding he'd check the bar for more congenial company, he headed into the interior. Since Hillvale had started hosting weddings in the garden Samantha had created at the vortex, the lodge often accommodated loud bachelor and bachelorette parties. It sounded as if one occupied the bar now.

The Kennedy brothers waved him over from one of the more private booths. As partial owners of the corporation controlling the lodge and most of the rental property in Hillvale, the Kennedys had privileges that allowed them to claim prime real estate in the dark, heavily masculine tavern. The low roar dimmed considerably in this sheltered corner.

"The babe was safely delivered. You can go home now," Aaron said wryly as he slid into the booth. Their wives had been part of the birthing circle. Well, Fee and Monty weren't married yet, but the little cook wore the mayor's ring. Close enough.

"We've been warned," Kurt Kennedy acknowledged. The taller, darker, more lean of the two brothers, he sipped his drink with an air of resignation. "Once one of the women has a kid, they all want one.

Samantha was a natural, of course. She grows things, so growing babies was the next step. Walker is on board with that."

"But Kurt and I are still knee-deep in debt and not ready for baby formula and diapers," Monty said morosely. His muscled bulk reflected the football career he'd abandoned to step in as mayor of the deteriorating town the Kennedys owned. "We'll have to build a hospital just to handle the population explosion."

"Our resident nurse wants an urgent care center." Aaron ordered a beer and sat back, relaxing. The Kennedys weren't Lucys, just mortal men with mundane problems. "Can your Hollywood director swing for some fancy equipment? The Lucys won't willingly go down the mountain to a real hospital."

Kurt nodded. "We've planned one for the shopping area of the new development. But these things take time. We'll have to set one up in one of the empty buildings in town, which means complete rewiring and plumbing."

"Fee was hoping to expand the café into the building next door, but that's the most convenient one for an urgent care center. The others are long and narrow or two stories." Monty's gloom didn't lift.

Their problems weren't his. Aaron sipped the beer the waiter delivered, then cautiously delved into the newcomer. "Where are you putting the school now that the new teacher has arrived?"

"We can use one of the two story buildings for the school, no problem. We thought the old place next to the ice cream shop would be good until the new school is built. We'll have to run cable and stronger electric boxes for the computers, but there aren't enough kids for the plumbing to be a problem yet." Kurt sketched idly on a napkin. "We'll need to talk to the teachers, but it seems logical to put the young ones downstairs and the older students upstairs for now."

"You'll need to find a place for the new teacher," Aaron warned. "Your mother has taken an instant dislike to her. I understand there was an altercation involving Cass earlier."

In identical gestures, both Kennedys ran their hands through their hair and rubbed their temples. That was their usual reaction to their mother's volatile behavior.

"Her docs won't talk to us," Kurt explained. "After Fee forced her into the hospital, Mom claimed the doctors found lumps. But she checked out and went to our condo in Hawaii. If she had any medical procedures done while she was there, we don't know about it."

"Personally, I think the lumps are in her head," Monty growled. "But we'd have to go to court to claim her incompetent so we can take control of the corporation and obtain power of attorney to talk to her doctors. How do you do that to your mother?"

Aaron shrugged. "Mine's long dead, so I wouldn't know. What does Fiona say? She's the one diagnosing her as ill."

"Fee says she smells decay, which isn't exactly useful. I swear, Lucys make life more difficult," Monty complained. "They can point out something wrong but can't fix it."

Aaron refrained from mentioning that he was one of the Lucys. The Kennedys knew, but he generally didn't discuss his psychometric knowledge. "That's why we have the librarian. Fee needs to ask our newcomer if there have ever been any references in the journals to smells of decay. Hannah will be able to refer her to the right books. Whether or not they've been scanned and are accessible may be another problem."

"Thanks. Fee knows nothing of her heritage, so it's good for her to have a cookbook of sorts to follow instead of relying entirely on her own observations. I wish I knew a property convenient for our new teacher, but the cottages are all booked through most of the year. I guess we can offer a discount on her room at the lodge—or include it as part of her salary." Monty pulled out a notebook to jot down the thought.

"That won't solve the problem if your mother doesn't want her here," Aaron warned. "You'll have to tell Cass to open her doors for a change." He finished his beer and stood up.

"Have you ever been inside Cass's place?" Kurt asked with a wry intonation. "You do not want to send our new teacher into a different dimension."

There was that, Aaron supposed, but he wasn't interested in Cass and her machinations, not any more than he was interested in Carmel and her brain rot. He simply did not want the new teacher moving into the empty room above his shop. "You don't want her polluted with evil, either," he warned. "We found her wandering in your woods earlier. She apparently doesn't have the Lucy ability to sense evil."

He walked away before the Kennedys protested. As Nulls, they simply didn't understand—or believe—in the spiritual. They'd accept the danger of lions, bears, and snakes as well as landslides, earthquakes, and sinkholes to which the area was susceptible. They might even believe the ground was chemically polluted. They would not believe in the blood of innocents or souls of evil polluting dirt.

Aaron did. He'd felt the grip of *malum* before.

He'd better do a quick patrol of the lodge, just to be certain the new teacher was safe.

HANNAH TOOK A HOT SHOWER AND TRIED TO SCRUB AWAY THE INTERPOSED images of dark knight and sophisticated crook twisting in her deformed synapses. Just touching Aaron's palm had nearly allowed her to slip away again. The doctors hadn't been able to explain the brain lapses. She knew of nothing in Malcolm journals that fit them. She simply had to accept that the inoperable mass in her head was creating hallucinations.

How could she teach when she never knew if she'd have another fit?

Which was why she needed to find the painting showing the Healing Stone—the artwork Aaron had stolen and presumably sold to some unidentified customer, if he hadn't kept it for himself.

She wrapped her hair in a towel and, wearing a hotel bathrobe, padded out to the tiny desk beside her bed where she'd set up her laptop. She should let her family know that she'd arrived safely. She didn't know if she was strong enough to face a huge family gathering, so she'd just have to let them think she was buried in work setting up the new school. Not that she had a clue as to how to start a school, but she ought to be able to manage a classroom of one.

After sending emails, she remembered Aaron's card. She looked up his website—it rivaled anything she'd ever seen in the UK, where priceless antiques cluttered warehouses across the countryside. Judging by the images he seemed to specialize in furniture and paintings, although from what she'd seen of his cluttered shop, he had a lot more than that. He was definitely no flea market dealer. If they were genuine, the value on some of these pieces. . . would buy a mansion or three, even in California, where real estate was ridiculous. Of course, he'd have to sell them first, so cash flow might be a problem , hence the art fraud. That had been years ago.

She entered the Malcolm website she and Mariah had been working on, looked up the passages she'd promised, and sent him the links. Mariah's generous gift of an expensive scanning machine had made Hannah's job immensely easier. Keegan's hiring of an expert to scan the delicate older books had given her freedom. With a solid understanding of the library, she no longer needed the actual volumes—but she needed to do *something*.

She'd loved hiking in the wide-open spaces of Scotland, away from the pressures of family and expectations. She'd always wanted to be a librarian and teacher, not the university professor her family had expected. She was good with that. *Fine*, she added defiantly, remembering Aaron's contempt.

Completing her correspondence and still feeling restless, she debated whether she could sleep after spending half the day napping. She needed to adjust to the time change somehow. Maybe she could use the pool.

She stuck a clasp in her damp hair, pulled on her bathing suit, and covered it with a sarong and loose knit top. Donning sandals, she slipped down the hall, following the direction of the signs. To her disappointment, a sign said the pool closed at ten, but she heard laughter emerging from behind the curtained windows. She peered through a slit between frame and cloth and saw the voluptuous, sunset-haired, tarot reader climbing out of the water. With her was a movie-star handsome male who watched Amber with such obvious adoration that he had to be her new husband.

Hannah felt the pull of melancholy, probably brought on by the birthing earlier. She normally thrived on her lonely book life. She was too boring and plain to attract serious boyfriends. Her head had always been too full of duties to see if her occasional hook-ups could develop into more. And now it was too late for that as well—probably for the good of all.

Music played in the bar, so she turned in that direction. Perhaps she could ease into her new time zone gradually. As she walked through the sprawling lodge, she stopped to admire the ghostcatchers Mariah created. Hanging near the ceiling, the stringy nets dangling with crystals and feathers swung and spun even when there was no breeze. Mariah claimed they halted the poltergeists who haunted the area.

Hannah wasn't certain that ghosts were any better than loud wedding parties, but the one in the bar had mostly broken up and gone to their rooms by the time she arrived. A few well-dressed members of the group were getting snockered together. The music apparently came from loudspeakers. She didn't see any musicians. Oh well. She couldn't really expect a pub experience here.

She probably shouldn't tempt fate by wandering the halls where Carmel might see her. Maybe she should study on how to set up a school. She'd had too much stimulation for one evening anyway.

She turned away from the bar, took the corridor back to the lobby, and headed down the back hall to her room—where she heard loud voices raised in fury. Shoot. Maybe the walls of her room would block out the racket?

A woman's furious screech cut through the empty hall. Hannah panicked, freezing where she was. Another loud cry abruptly cut off. . . and then, silence.

Were those running footsteps?

She swung around and fled for the front desk. She'd recognized that ugly screech.

Carmel.

Hannah felt like a fool telling the desk clerk someone was being murdered. Carmel wasn't rational, she recalled, so she simply told the employee that she heard screams. The clerk started making calls. Clenching her fists, feeling helpless, Hannah watched as uniformed security raced from outside in response to the calls. An older, portly man in a business suit strode from a side hall, looking grim at the security rushing past. He nodded curtly at Hannah, then followed in their path. Several people who had entered the lobby from a side door seemed confused and lingered. A handsome younger man emerged from the bar, walking rapidly. Deciding he looked wealthy and worried enough to be Carmel's son and one of the lodge owners, Hannah followed.

Murder on her first night in town would *not* be auspicious.

FOUR

Patrolling the grounds of the lodge, Aaron nodded briefly at neighbors he recognized strolling the walks. His walking stick lurched abruptly as he approached Carmel's suite, indicating a violent change in the resort's vibrations. Alarmed, he increased his pace.

Reaching the lighted pathway to Carmel's private entrance, he lifted his staff to test the air—and saw a body spilling golden hair sprawled across the threshold.

Aaron hated approaching. He had no particular reason to despise Carmel Kennedy. She'd been a beautiful woman any red-blooded man could appreciate, even at twice his age. He ought to take her pulse, verify what his stick had already told him. But even when she'd been vibrantly alive, Carmel had oozed a malevolence that could be seeking a new victim as her dying breath departed.

Running footsteps approached.

Standing above a dead woman holding a knobbed walking stick didn't look good, but Aaron saw no reason to cast his staff into the bushes. Everyone knew it belonged to him.

When Harvey arrived, Aaron was forced to act. He held out his walnut staff to stop the younger musician. "No. I'll do it. Aim your crystal toward us and call up any prayers you know."

Raising his staff, Harvey began a Latin prayer reflecting his half-Catholic origins. The long-haired musician could play any instrument, but he had a voice like a frog, Aaron noted as he approached the body in the half-lit doorway.

Kneeling near Carmel's sprawled arm, Aaron verified she had no pulse. Voices and pounding feet approached from around the outside corner.

Someone was already knocking on the interior door.

Blood seeped from the tawny hair of the Kennedy matriarch. Whoever had done this hadn't removed the fortune in gold she always wore draped on her neck, wrists, and fingers. This had not been a robbery but an act of rage.

Satisfied there was nothing he could do, Aaron stepped away as a uniformed security guard ran up swinging his flashlight. Lights flipped on inside the suite a moment later as one of the Kennedy brothers shouted, "Mom?"

Aaron wondered if her sons would suffer grief or relief that someone had taken a decision out of their hands—until he caught a glimpse inside of the schoolteacher arriving like an avenging angel in the company of Kurt and the lodge manager. *Faex.*

What the hell was the damned woman wearing? She looked like an exotic dancer with that sarong hanging on her narrow hips and her pale belly partially bared beneath a top that revealed more cleavage than he'd expected. He forced his gaze upward, which didn't help.

Her big autumn eyes widened as she took in the scene of Carmel bleeding on her own doorstep, with Aaron and Harvey standing over the body, wielding heavy staffs.

Aaron waited for the condemnation, the disgust, and the accusations.

"I heard heavy feet running," was all she said as Kurt fell to his knees beside his mother. "Did you see anyone?"

The question was directed at him, and possibly Harvey and the security guard. Sensible, Aaron supposed, since she really didn't know any of them, and the innocent would assume the guilty would flee.

"We heard screams. You may have heard us running toward them. I haven't seen anyone else." Aaron turned to Kurt, who'd hidden any emotion beyond shock as he sat back on his heels. "You need to call

Walker. I didn't sense any vibrations while touching her. I probably need the murder weapon to pick up anything useful. I don't want to touch anything without Walker's permission."

Kurt knew about Aaron's psychometry, that he could possibly read the killer's thoughts on a weapon. That didn't mean the Null fully grasped what Aaron was telling him.

Roper, the lodge manager, helped Carmel's stricken son to return to his feet. Behind them, Hannah appeared to have taken Aaron's comment as a request to hunt for a murder weapon. Strange woman. Shouldn't she be having one of her fainting fits?

"I don't see anything in here," she said, staying inside the lighted room. "I'm not a sensitive. Do you have anyone who can lay her spirit to rest?"

Harvey had stayed in the shadows, lowering his chant to a mumble. The Hispanic security guard appeared to accept the prayers for what they were. The city boy manager did not. Fred Roper and Carmel had been much alike. Roper was accustomed to dealing with the wealthy and pampered and considered Lucys as little more than practitioners of voodoo.

Walking the line between superstition and reality required balance and wording his reply carefully. "In this case, a spirit circle could be dangerous, especially for women," Aaron told her, keeping it vague. "You need to stay back. Harvey and I will hold the fort. Call Cass and Keegan, maybe."

Hannah's eyes narrowed as she processed what he didn't say aloud. He was calling for men and a woman past the age of fertility. If the schoolteacher knew as much as she claimed, she'd work it out. The teacher had seen Carmel in action and had to suspect the evil behind the madness, right? He didn't want evil finding an unborn child.

To his relief, the teacher intelligently left the room. Aaron was pretty certain they were all disturbing a crime scene. Walker would have to sort it out.

Hillvale's chief of police arrived in company with Cass not long after. The prescient old woman had probably called Walker before security had. Keegan arrived a few moments after them. That Val, their self-proclaimed death goddess, hadn't arrived said more about the hatred between her and Carmel than her failure to recognize a death.

With his weird mix of Asian and Irish pragmatism and superstition, Walker gestured for everyone to move away to allow the ritual. While the Lucys gathered, Roper led Kurt deeper into the room and out of sight. Aaron hoped he was leading Hannah away as well.

Even though Cass and Carmel had despised each other, sorrow shadowed Cass's eyes as she passed her walking stick over the body. "There is nothing here," she said with a hint of grimness. "Her soul is long gone. Aaron, what do you feel?"

He and Harvey held up their crystal-knobbed sticks. Spirits were drawn to the crystal, but no light glimmered from within.

"I think whoever did this was angry." Aaron didn't want to theorize in front of disbelievers. Walker was married to a Lucy and accepted weirdness, but there was no point in pushing his credulity.

Raising his stick to meet the others, the big Scot studied the bushes providing privacy to Carmel's back door. Honest to a fault and oblivious to the security guards, he spoke what he thought. "I'm not any more sensitive than Hannah. But if evil exists, as you say, I can see where Mrs. Kennedy could have spontaneously invoked it in anyone to whom she spoke. Perhaps we should look for someone weeping and shaking with fear at what they've done."

At least he hadn't mentioned the possibility of evil spirits escaping Carmel.

Finished with taping off the crime scene, their chief of police intervened. "I know you clowns mean well, but you really are not a psychic detective agency. Dispel the spirits and go home. I know where to find you if I need you."

"We should give her a respectful farewell," Cass suggested. "She raised two good men and held this place together on nothing for years."

Carmel might have been arrogant, selfish to the point of narcissism, and half-mad, but she'd been a survivor. Aaron agreed that her sons deserved to see her treated with respect.

To his relief, Hannah appeared on the sidewalk behind them, keeping her distance. The librarian's voice lifted with Cass's, making it easier for Aaron to mumble his way through the words.

Kurt arrived, accompanied by Monty, apparently having gone around the building like Hannah, so as not to disturb the suite. As Nulls, the brothers didn't participate. But they bowed their heads as if they were in church, offering respect to Cass as well as their mother.

For this moment of sorrow, accusations didn't fly. That would happen in the clear light of day, Aaron knew, once the shock had evaporated and grief and fear took over.

~

HANNAH CRADLED HER ELBOWS AND CLUNG TO THE RHYTHM OF ANCIENT rituals, closing her eyes to the dimly lit scene.

In his dark blazer, carrying a heavy walking staff, standing strong and imperious against the night sky, Aaron appeared capable of bringing down stars. That much power was frightening, and she pushed away any thought of how he might wield it to remove dangerous spirits like Carmel's.

Birth and death in one day had shaken her to the core, leaving her raw and exposed, even though she barely knew the people involved.

Carmel might have been half mad, but she'd been vibrantly alive a few hours ago. Now, she was no more than empty flesh adorned with gold.

The Lucys drifted away as more policemen and a man she assumed was the coroner arrived. The musician slipped into the woods, apparently as uncomfortable with company as a skittish deer. Hannah stuck close to her cousin Keegan, not wanting to return to her room. Aaron stalked ahead of them, a black cloud practically circling his dark head.

After speaking with the Kennedys, Cass joined them. "This happened on our doorstep," she said crisply. "We cannot leave it to outsiders."

"You're not the law, Cass," Aaron said heavily. "Walker might listen to us, but the sheriff won't. He'll follow procedures."

"Which will point to all of us. I'm not a doddering old fool who doesn't understand how the world works. Everyone knew Carmel hated Lucys, mostly because of me. Monty and Kurt are living with Lucys, so even they are suspect. We must employ all our abilities."

"My gift isn't useful for your purpose, but if you need Mariah, I'll sit with the baby while she works," Keegan offered.

"Everyone will sit with the baby if needed," Cass said with a hint of humor. "But we'll need suspects before Mariah can investigate them."

"We'll need suspects before *any* of us can investigate," Aaron said dryly. "It's not as if you can run everyone in the lodge through Amber's tarot shop, Teddy's empathy, or past Fee's nose. I'll test Carmel's room when Walker says it's safe to go in, but usually it is emotional overload that imprints most clearly on objects. I need the murder weapon—which you will note, could very well have been a Lucy stick."

"I'm not very useful," Hannah said quietly. "But I know organization. If you feed me everything you find, I can set up a system where you might start making connections."

"Samantha will let us know what Walker finds. Mariah can dig out anything the sheriff keeps from him. We'll start there," Cass said with confidence. "I don't think any Lucy is capable of such violence, but let's keep a low profile around the Nulls."

Did Hannah imagine it, or had Aaron's wide shoulders just relaxed a trifle? And why was she noticing?

They reached the front of the lodge where the drive was filled with official vehicles, their lights turned off so as not to disturb the guests.

"I'll take you home, Cass," Keegan offered. "Hannah, I don't know if it's safe for you to stay if the killer knows you turned in the alarm. Aaron, can you store her in your place for tonight?"

"I don't want to be stored anywhere," she said with annoyance. "I'm sure half a dozen people reported screaming before I did. Besides, my luggage is here."

"You're *fine*," Aaron mocked. "But as we have already established, you're not fine. Give me your key. Stay here with Keegan, and I'll fetch your bags."

"You will do no such thing," she objected. "For all I know, you have a fetish for women's undies. I managed to travel all the way here without anyone's aid. I'll be *fine*."

"Hannah, there is a killer loose in the lodge. We'll all sleep better tonight if our librarian is not under the same roof as evil," Cass said patiently. "Aaron does not sleep in his shop. You'll be. . . *fine*," she added, her amusement more pronounced than earlier.

Oh, crap, even she knew better than to argue with the town's doyenne. Resentfully, Hannah stalked up the front walk toward the lobby with Aaron on her heels.

Men in uniform were interviewing guests and employees in the conference room and business office. One stopped them on the way through, checking off their names on a list. Hannah heard Aaron mutter, but the chief had been efficient in gathering names and addresses. Hannah didn't recognize the address listed for her, but it was local, so they were allowed to proceed.

"You gave my address as your shop?" she guessed as she unlocked her room, wishing she'd never left it.

Aaron shrugged and waited for her to gather her possessions. "Walker probably did. He and the county sheriff have a working agreement. The sheriff doesn't touch Walker's people because he knows Hillvale residents are weird. Hillvale can't afford a forensic team, so Walker calls in the sheriff for major crime. But Walker has as much experience or more than the sheriff. He owns a fancy corporate detective agency in LA and has services at his beck and call that the sheriff doesn't—provided someone pays for them."

"Symbiotic," Hannah said with grudging approval. "Thank you for explaining. And thank you for allowing me to stay in your place even though you don't want me there."

His eyes were shuttered as he took the rolling suitcase from her hand. "You'd be better off in Cass's bright and airy studio. I'll talk Josh into moving out in the morning."

"Not if he's the millionaire paying for the school. I'll be. . . content. . . with a roof over my head." She added her backpack to her smaller carry-on bag and followed him down the hall.

He snorted. "You might be *content*, if you're not a sensitive. Otherwise, you'll want out soon enough. Maybe Kurt can add a room for you at the school. It's not as if you'll need the whole top floor for one student."

The contents of his store didn't appeal to sensitives? But *he*, apparently, knew how to block their unpleasantness. She almost wanted to have the gift of psychometry so she could find out what he was hiding. Could she hope the Healing Stone painting was there?

She kept her reply light. "I might like that—no commute. I was starting to wonder how I would get up and down the mountain every day if I stayed here." She walked beside him, keeping her hands engaged and resisting touching him. She was raw and afraid and she simply didn't need her dark knight walking out of her head and into her life.

Apparently exhausting his communicative limits, Aaron silently led the way back to his vehicle. From the high seat of the van driving down the mountain, Hannah could see an occasional light in the creases and crevasses surrounding town. Could she make her home here, become part of these people? Keegan had done it.

She'd wait until she met Mariah and toured the schoolroom before becoming too comfortable. She could always go back to her family in San Francisco, but she really didn't want them hovering over her as if she were an invalid. If the knot in her head didn't grow, she could live quite a long while. Only time would tell.

FIVE

Aaron parked his van in the town lot and opened the back to remove Hannah's suitcases. Most of the shopping district was dark at this hour, but a light streamed from beneath the gallery doors. Once an old church, it had been turned into a community center and art gallery—which Lance Brooks, Carmel's brother operated. *Deodamnatus.* Had anyone told Lance?

As Hannah lifted out her smaller suitcase, Aaron nodded at the lit doors they'd have to pass. "I need to check on Carmel's brother. He's had problems in the past and might need someone with him."

"Yes, Keegan has mentioned him. He's sort of a lost soul, an architect who lost his heart and head to drugs during the commune days, right?" She lifted her bag so it didn't roll noisily down the boardwalk.

"He's been doing reasonably well these last years. I'm uncertain how much he relied on Carmel." Aaron eased open the broad church door.

Benches lined the center of the gallery. A track light had been placed to illuminate the triptych of Hillvale, displayed in what once would have been the apse behind an altar. It took a moment before his eyes adjusted to find Lance's gray-blond hair. The tall artist was seated on one of the benches—next to the equally tall woman who called herself the Death Goddess.

Val had gone to Lance instead of singing over Carmel's missing soul. Interesting. Val always knew when someone died in Hillvale. She'd have told Lance.

Aaron backed out and closed the door. "He's in good hands," was all he said.

Hannah appeared to take his word for it and quietly followed him down the boardwalk. He liked people who didn't chatter and question everything he said or did.

It would be better if she chattered so he could despise her.

He didn't turn on the shop overheads as he led the librarian through his crowded store. There were night lights scattered about, enough to see familiar paths through the clutter to the stairway in the rear. If she taught all day maybe her presence here at night wouldn't bother him. He had his own home elsewhere. It could work—for a while.

He held his breath as she ran her fingers over an inlaid coffee table he'd stacked on top of one with a tiled top. The tiled one had been created by an old man dying of cancer. The inlaid one had held a gun used to murder a young mother. He assumed both had been sold by grieving families. He didn't like letting that level of tragedy into the universe, so he stored it here until he figured out what to do with it.

She didn't react to the tables. Impatiently, he waited as she glanced longingly at the walls of books along the perimeter—until she aimed straight for the two large wardrobes on those same walls. Maybe she thought they contained books. The wardrobes were rosewood and mahogany works of art, exuding happiness that concealed the plain black frame between them from Lucy sensitivities.

Not from Hannah. Her hand reached in the direction of the damned hidden work, but he'd stacked too much furniture in front of it. Shaking her head in puzzlement, she stepped away and continued toward the back of the shop.

Crap. Now he'd have to move it again. If the thing was so strong even non-sensitives could feel it, it might need a lead box.

She didn't say anything as he took her upstairs and introduced her to a room not much larger than the one she'd had at the lodge. Dressed in that ridiculously inappropriate sarong, she simply pointed at a place to put her suitcases. He admired the way the light fabric swayed with her hips, revealing well-proportioned legs, but she wasn't his type. He preferred glamorous women, ones who drew attention when he took them out to dinner. Trapped as he was up here, he needed that occasional dip into the world he'd left behind.

Fortunately, Hannah was as plain as her name, appropriate for a teacher and a librarian, so he could steer his course away. Obviously, she was a female, with curves in all the right places, but she'd be back in her practical baggy khakis in the morning. He'd be. . . fine.

"This is perfect, thank you," she told him politely. "I'll try to find another place as soon as possible."

"Kurt and Monty own most of the town. They'll know what's best. You won't be afraid here alone?" The vibrations on some of his inventory were so strong that even he was reluctant to spend the night here.

She looked surprised. "Of course not. I've slept quite comfortably in drafty castles populated with ghosts. I'm simply not aware of the spirits as you are."

It was almost a relief to think ridiculous things and have someone understand. "All right, good. I come in around nine-thirty and open the shop at ten. I can't promise quiet after that. I have internet. The password and the spare shop keys are in the desk. Good-night." He handed over the room key and backed out quickly.

Was it his imagination, or did that damned evil painting hum in anticipation as he walked out and locked up? He'd order a lead box in the morning.

Having napped half the day, Hannah slept restlessly that night. Images of Aaron with his sparkling walking stick held high blended with those of the golden woman sprawled across her doorstep with blood trickling from her hair.

Could a single blow kill a woman?

She woke with that question in mind, followed by—wouldn't a body fall forward if struck from behind? In which case, Carmel must have been leaving her suite when someone inside hit her. Aaron had been outside.

But as the chief had said, she was no detective. She'd leave speculation to those who knew what they were doing. It was bad enough sleeping under the roof of a convicted felon without suspecting Aaron to also be a ruthless killer.

The room was cozy and well designed for her purposes. She showered and checked her email. The wall of books and the strange light in the wardrobes below called to her, but first, she needed sustenance. She couldn't remember when she'd eaten anything except Fee's biscuits.

With that thought of Fee and the little café, Hannah stepped out just as the morning sun sent its first rays beneath the boardwalk roof.

The café was packed. She hesitated, especially after heads turned to stare at her entrance. She almost backed out until Fee gestured at her with a coffee mug. Petite, with short-cropped brown hair and the small chin of an elf or fairy, the cook pointed at a booth toward the far end of the room.

A beringed hand waved—Amber. Relieved, Hannah smiled at a few familiar faces from yesterday and slid into a booth across from the tarot reader and Teddy, the jeweler.

"Sam's helping Mariah with the baby. As the police chief's wife, she's our best news source," Teddy immediately announced. "So now you have to be our substitute. Kurt said you were at the lodge last night. He's too shocked to talk about it. What did you see?"

Carmel's son, Kurt Kennedy, was Teddy's husband, Hannah recalled. "I'm sorry for your loss," she said, although from the excited hum around the café, she thought not too many were grieving.

"Carmel has been lost to her sons for decades." Teddy lifted her coffee cup and grimaced. "She was their mother. Kurt and Monty respected that, and that she'd saved their inheritance from the debacle their father left. But apparently she did so at the cost of her soul. I think they would rather have been poor and had a human mother."

"Carmel was an emotional vampire," Amber explained as Fee brought over a menu.

"She smelled of rot," the petite cook agreed sadly. "She was ill, but no one should have to die like that. Tea, coffee, or juice?"

"Tea, please, and if you have a juice smoothie, that's enough for me."

Hannah scanned the menu but didn't see smoothies on it, although the machines were right behind them.

"You could use mango," Fee decided for her, removing the menu. "The machines are Monty's idea. I'd rather bake. But I'm learning to appreciate the nutritional value of mush."

She departed, filling coffee cups along the way.

Hannah turned back to Amber. "An emotional vampire draws from those around her." She tried not to sound like a teacher, but providing information was her purpose in life. "Did she harm her sons? Others?"

"Yes," Teddy said flatly. "She drained the entire town lifeless until Cass dragged Samantha back here to nourish us. Things have been picking up ever since. It's a kind of synergy, I think. We're all building and creating and supporting each other, filling the empty well, diminishing Carmel's power. It's even better now that we've drawn Kurt and Monty away from the polluted lodge."

"Was Carmel the cause of the pollution?" Hannah asked, trying to understand her new home.

"You get it! You'll fit right in here," Amber crowed in delight. "I need to read your cards. Come over later and we'll see how your arrival relates to the witch's death."

Humming the tune to *ding dong, the witch is dead*, Amber took the sack of food a waitress handed her. "Thanks, Sally. I need to feed the hungry before they eat the TV. Sally will be our new elementary teacher."

Young, round-faced, and smiling, Sally nodded a greeting and flitted away to help another customer.

Hannah remembered—Amber's new husband was paying for the new school, and Amber's nephew was to be Hannah's lone middle-school student. She needed to learn all she could and not say too much about herself. "I thought Lucys are the witches, and the Kennedys are Nulls."

"Define witch, and then sort white magic from black." Amber squeezed out of the booth, stopping to chat with other customers as she worked her way through the crowd.

"We really don't do magic, and Amber doesn't read futures," Teddy warned. "She's psychic to a degree, but she needs cards or powerful emotion to focus. If you have secrets, avoid Amber. We never knew how dangerous she was until she collapsed a couple of corrupt Hollywood film studios."

Duly warned. "Says the empath who kills ghosts," Hannah said dryly. "I'm not sure secrets are possible in this town. Keegan has obligingly written down everything he's learned so I can record it for the library."

"But Keegan is a man and a scientist and accepts nothing unless it's proven. He didn't tell you that Carmel was an emotional vampire, did he?"

"He mentioned evil crystals, because he's experimented with those he found here. But I thought evil was in the crystal paint used in the commune. Carmel didn't strike me as artistic." Hannah sipped her tea. Fragrant and delicious—she took a moment to savor it. Fee had known exactly which blend she preferred.

Across the table, Teddy shrugged. "The commune was a huge deal back in the day. Everyone visited—musicians, politicians, rich college kids by the droves. I think that's how Carmel met her husband. Her brother is an artist and lived there a while. But we have no way of knowing if crystals affected her."

"It stands to reason that if Kennedy Senior was polluted with greed, Carmel would be eventually," Hannah said. Having spent a lifetime absorbing ancient Malcolm journals, she had no problem discussing arcane philosophies like evil. "We just don't know how or why they were infected. It could have been their nature, the crystals, or the land itself. Or all of the above."

Harvey slid into the empty seat beside Teddy. The lean, long-haired musician wore a guitar case over his back, a dark beard stubble, and carried a carved walking stick.

He handed the stick to Hannah. "There's no question who you are. I had it ready before you arrived. I just needed to choose the stones after we met."

Polished cherry, the stick felt light and soothing against her palm. "Nice, thank you! This is marvelous work." Hannah studied the handle —a vengeful angel with agate eyes. Most of the sticks she'd noticed had Harvey's idea of protectors on them—dragons and lions and so forth.

"You found the stones in Hillvale?" She admired the way they flashed in the sunlight through the window.

"Part of my grandfather's collection. Keegan can probably tell you their origin. He's already paid for it. We wanted to welcome the new teacher a little more pleasantly than last night."

Harvey was one of the most attractive men she'd ever met, with soulful dark eyes and cheekbones to die for. Hannah wanted to learn more, but he slid from the booth almost as quickly as he'd arrived.

"Teach well," he said with a half smile, before slipping through the crowd and out again.

"He's what the old folks would call elven, isn't he?" Hannah asked in amusement.

"Maybe in Scotland. Here, he's just an itinerant busker and some relation to the family who owns the mountain above the lodge. He's also a concert pianist but he's ruining his hands carving those sticks."

Hannah ran her palms over the polished stick. "Or he's soaking the wood with his music and storing it there. He doesn't belong in concert halls, does he?"

Teddy rubbed the head of her own staff. "No. As you say, he's like a forest creature, shy of people until he knows them. Or perhaps I should say, distrustful. Harvey isn't exactly shy."

"Elven," Hannah repeated, accepting the smoothie she was handed. "Fiercely guarding his homeland, I suspect. Is there any way Carmel could have threatened him or the land. . . ?" She raised a querying eyebrow.

Teddy shook her auburn curls. "Nope. Not believing any Lucy has the capacity to kill. Kurt and Monty are Nulls and have more reason than most to want Carmel dead—she was draining the company resources and hampering progress. But I sense no violence in them either."

"So the suspects are everyone in the lodge except the people who knew her best?" Hannah sipped the perfect mango smoothie and regarded her new acquaintance innocently.

Teddy shook her head again and slid from the booth. "Nope. Not playing that game. For all I know, the devil came to claim his own."

Well, yeah, there was always that, Hannah supposed. If Hillvale could have ghosts and elves and psychics, why not the devil himself?

And speak of the devil. . . She should get back to Aaron's shop before he came in. That faint translucence in between those wardrobes drew her imagination like iron to lodestone. He was the last known person to own the painting of the moonstone. Outside the comfort zone of her library, did she have the courage to explore?

SIX

Accompanied by Xavier, the rental agent who knew all the available properties in Hillvale, Aaron unlocked his shop door early, determined to move the schoolteacher out. He thought he might be a little irrational on the subject. No Lucy had ever paid attention to his inventory. He had no reason to believe Hannah would notice, but he relied on instinct as much as his psychometry. Hannah Simon was a danger to his peace of mind.

Opening the door, he sensed wrongness and instantly hit the overhead light switch, filling the shop with light and shadows.

The wardrobes were stored on the far end of the shop—near the stairs. He could see the tops of them from the door, but not the area where the painting was stored. He had hoped the good vibrations on the two wardrobes would neutralize the painting, but he should have shoved the damned thing *behind* the wardrobes. Unfortunately, it took two people to move them, and he didn't want to explain why.

Now he was not only irrational but obsessively focused on the painting. He tried to be sensible, but he took the shortest path through the clutter, leaving Xavier behind.

The schoolteacher lay crumpled in the small space in front of the wardrobes, her arm stretched to reach between them. She'd shoved a Victorian settee out of the way to clear the opening.

"Call Brenda," he shouted at Xavier, while dropping to his knees to check her pulse. Two women in two days. . . the sheriff would have good reason to lock him up if this one was dead too.

He had to jumpstart his heart after he found her strong pulse.

Too damned many people had died on his watch—and too often they had connections to this infernal scrap of canvas. He had good reason for his paranoia.

Releasing her wrist, he tugged at the teacher's arm, pulling her hand off the damned painting. He ought to just burn the thing, but he couldn't help sensing the artist's urgency in wanting to pass on valuable information. He'd just never seen anything in the oil to be acted on.

With the removal of the painting from her touch, Hannah's eyelids fluttered—but closed again as soon as he touched her. He yanked his hand away.

What the damned hell had caused the teacher to hunt down the one piece he didn't display?

Satisfied that she was alive, he sat back on his heels to see if she'd moved anything else around.

She moaned and stirred again. Holding her hand to her head, she tried to sit up. Aaron didn't dare touch her again. He seemed to fry her neurons every time he tried. That should teach him to keep his hands off.

"We have a nurse coming. You should lie down or the next time you fall, you're likely to crack your head. It's a wonder you didn't this time." He knew he sounded cold. He couldn't help it. She'd terrified him in ways he didn't want to explore ever again.

"A nurse can't help me. Don't waste her time." Color slowly returned to her cheeks as she sat up. She leaned against one of the wardrobes, not looking at him.

This morning she'd dressed in khaki shorts and a bright red t-shirt, nothing clingy but enough to reveal slender curves. He topped six feet, and her head came to his shoulder, so she might be slim, but she wasn't petite. She still seemed frail.

"You always have fits and collapse without reason?" he asked sarcastically.

"With reason, but that's none of your business." She shifted enough to peer between the wardrobes where he'd shoved the painting. "That thing is almost luminous. What is it?"

"Luminous?" That startled him out of his frustration enough to avoid the actual question. "The wardrobes are works of art, but they're hardly luminous."

After finishing his phone calls, Xavier weaved his way around crystal chandeliers and rusted armor. A skeleton of a man with receding gray hair that he'd recently taken to having styled, Xavier dressed vaguely like the lawyer he'd once been. In the heat, he'd discarded his usual suit coat and wore a pressed short-sleeve shirt with collar and tie. "Brenda's on her way from the café."

"I'll pay for the breakfast she's probably missing, but don't call her again, please." The teacher started to reach between the wardrobes.

Aaron grabbed her arm to stop her. She started to topple. "*Stultissime*," he growled and released her.

She bobbed up again like a damned jack-in-the-box.

"I'm hoping I remember enough Latin to believe that was directed at yourself," Xavier said sternly, stepping between the damned intrusive schoolteacher and the apparently *luminous* painting hidden between the wardrobes.

"*Total idiot*, masculine, singular," the teacher translated Aaron's curse, rubbing her arm where he'd touched her. "But unless you knew I was susceptible to your touch, I don't believe you're a *total* idiot. So far, no one can explain what sets me off, not even the most learned men of science or any ancestor in any journal in any of the libraries I've searched."

"But they have theories, don't they?" he asked harshly, knowing from just brief touches that she hid secrets.

"As do we all. Now please explain that luminous painting. I believe I passed out when I touched it." She inched away from him and the wardrobe but gazed steadily between the two towering pieces.

Xavier reached in before Aaron could stop him and tilted the frame so he could yank it out.

They all studied the ugly oil of red and blue blotches framed in cheap black-painted pine.

"Not that thing," she said, reaching for the frame, then drawing back as if it were a hot poker. "I'm afraid to touch it. What's behind the ugly canvas?"

Aaron grabbed the frame, opened a wardrobe, and heaved the oil on the top shelf. "If it causes you harm just by touching the frame, then it's nothing you want to see."

In relief, he watched sturdy, no-nonsense Brenda enter. The nurse practitioner was somewhere in her forties, he guessed, and already dying her hair to an unnatural red. But she was good at what she did.

He left Brenda to argue with her recalcitrant patient while he stepped away, out of range of the damned painting he hadn't wanted to touch and the woman he *shouldn't* touch.

"You see why I need to move her out of here?" he asked in a low voice.

Xavier shrugged. "Won't be easy. Monty and Fee have claimed the old Adams' place, so I've quit booking it, but it still won't be empty for a month. Most everything else is rented until Christmas."

A month, *crap*, but even a month was better than forever. "Then can she use the cabin Monty's living in now? It's not too far out of town."

"They're building an RV park next to it for the workmen on the new development. You really want your teacher living down there in the mud with the contractors and their crew? Take her and Kurt over to the old drugstore, see if the upstairs can be divided off. I told Kurt that's the best place for a schoolroom."

The old drugstore was near city hall and right across the street from him. Hillvale was small. Aaron supposed he couldn't hope for better than that.

Done with checking her patient, Brenda stood and dusted off her jeans. "Nothing wrong with her that a little nourishment wouldn't help. She's probably just allergic to you, Aaron."

With that cryptic comment, the nurse headed for the door.

ALLERGIC TO AARON? HANNAH DECIDED THAT DIDN'T EVEN BEGIN TO MAKE sense. She fainted when he touched her because she was allergic? That's not how allergies worked.

After she'd had time to recover from her embarrassing ineptitude at spying, Xavier returned with his boss to show her across the street to the building they hoped might house the school.

Leaving the men to talk with each other, Hannah crossed the rough wooden floors of the old drugstore attic, her sandals clapping noisily. The place needed carpet. With slanted ceilings, it really couldn't be called a second story. She could feel the heat pouring in through the roof—only a sheet of plasterboard and a few boards away. Insulation apparently hadn't been invented when the place was built.

It was probably best to take a place of her own. She might not be accustomed to heat, but she had lived in worse places. Besides, the lodge was too expensive, if not just creepy.

"There's enough space for a schoolroom and a studio apartment," she acknowledged. "The back half is already walled off, as is the bathroom. That leaves a front area large enough for several students and desks."

"You shouldn't have to share a bathroom with your students." Kurt Kennedy, architect and owner, frowned as he studied the layout. "We could add extensions to the piping and create a second bathroom without a shower for the students. I'm just not certain how long we'll be using the place. The permits for the new development are starting to line up, and the utilities up there are almost in. We can start building a real school before long."

"You can rent this place out then," Aaron pointed out. "*En suite* master bedroom and powder room."

Allergies or not, Hannah stayed on the opposite side of the room from the antique dealer. The damned man exuded too much assurance and more pheromones than she could handle.

And he was hiding that painting from her. What if it was the one she needed?

"I hate to mention this, but most schools would not allow a single teacher and student alone, unsupervised. It's a liability issue. Maybe we should just look at dividing the downstairs into two schoolrooms." Hannah started for the stairs. She didn't much care where she lived. Her only goal right now was a good look at that painting.

That wouldn't be easy if she passed out every time she touched it.

She wasn't a sensitive. Why would the painting affect her like that?

And if it was the one she sought, what was there about it that had made Aaron go to jail rather than give it up?

Before she could escape his presence to better examine the lower floor, heavy feet pounded up the stairway, and a golden god with a slight resemblance to Kurt emerged. Tall, with jock shoulders, and dressed as if he were on the way to a ball game, he nodded at Hannah. "The new schoolteacher," he said in approval.

Looked like she was the new teacher then. She was pretty certain this was Kurt's brother, the mayor.

"Monty!" Kurt called from his measurement of the bathroom wall, sounding concerned. "What's wrong?"

The mayor's pleasant charm instantly disappeared. "Uh. . . the cops are letting us into Mom's room." He looked uncomfortable, a state so outside the normal that even Hannah sensed the difference. "They want some kind of. . . inventory to see if anything is missing."

Kurt's shoulders sagged as he zipped up his measuring tape. "Do we have to? We told them last night that we couldn't see anything missing. It's not as if we have a list."

Even Hannah could sense the grief and confusion in their voices and body language. The brothers didn't know how to handle their mother's death.

"Will they let *me* inside?" Aaron asked quietly. He didn't push, didn't mention his talent, but distracted the Kennedys enough to offer them a little breathing space.

Hannah hadn't thought the icy antique dealer possessed that much compassion. Maybe he didn't. Maybe he just had experience in getting what he wanted.

But the Kennedys responded with relief. "You might help," Kurt admitted, reluctantly heading for the stairs. "Maybe you can tell what she was thinking. We never could."

With no talent to offer, Hannah trailed behind the men and down the stairs. She supposed she should stay here and figure out how to set up a schoolroom, if the rental agent didn't have to lock up immediately.

They emerged into the sunlight to find Teddy and Fee waiting for them. Hannah glanced at the café to see if Monty's fiancée had shut it up for the day, but business appeared to be booming as usual.

"Dinah and Sam are covering for me," Fee said, noticing the direction of her gaze. "Teddy's sister is covering the jewelry shop. Come with us for moral support. Maybe you'll add fresh perspective."

Hannah wanted to say she had nothing to add, but curiosity won out. Leaving Xavier to lock up, they swept her into the open-air shuttle waiting in front of city hall.

She ended up sitting on the last seat—with Aaron. They both edged to the far ends of the metal bench. She squirmed a little watching the two couples in front offering each other love and understanding. She'd never been part of a pair and now she probably never would be. Aaron simply twirled his walking stick. Hannah hadn't thought to bring hers.

The shuttle let them out at the front of the lodge, where tourists waited to take it back to town. Hannah followed the Kennedys as they traipsed down pathways to the rear of the lodge where Carmel had her suite. Even Fee and Teddy refrained from chattering once they reached the yellow crime scene tape. Walker, the police chief, waited for them.

He looked askance at Aaron and Hannah—the chief was a Null, she knew. But like the Kennedys, he was married to a Lucy and apparently understood that they might help more than harm.

Hannah hesitated, feeling like a voyeur, but Teddy grasped her arm and tugged her forward.

"Neutral party," she murmured. "The emotions are over the top right now, pushing my empathy into overdrive. You and Aaron provide a calming blanket that keeps everyone from boiling over."

"I'll take your word for it," Hannah murmured back. "I just don't want to be in the way."

Fee stepped back to listen, then sniffed the air. "Your scent reminds me of the canyon on a sunlit day—serenity and sage."

"Or boulders," Teddy added with a low laugh. "Hannah is whatever the opposite of tightly wound is."

"A rolling stone?" Hannah suggested, choosing to linger by the door to study the suite where they'd found Carmel just last night.

Carmel had lived in quiet opulence: linen and silk, in oatmeal and subdued gold colors. Mahogany and rosewood accent tables added contrast to a bed and dresser in a blond custom lacquer finish with gold leaf. A silk Persian rug over a thick ivory carpet completed an interior fit for any design magazine.

Kurt and Monty stood helplessly among their mother's feminine accouterments. Like Hannah, Walker stayed near the door, simply keeping an eye on the proceedings.

"Let me touch first," Aaron suggested. "You're likely to imprint grief or anger over anything else."

"Start with the valuables," Kurt said. "Maybe an expert thief would lift a few of the more expensive pieces, figuring we wouldn't notice."

"Which we wouldn't," Monty added honestly. "She has a bank vault full of jewelry from her family that might be on an estate list. Otherwise, we have no clue what she bought on her own."

Aaron passed his hand back and forth over a large jewelry cabinet, and then opened the drawers to study the contents. "A few heirloom pieces here but mostly modern designer. She has one of your crystal pieces, Teddy."

"I'm guessing not the one with honesty stones." Teddy crossed the carpet to check the drawers after Aaron was finished examining them. She raised her expressive eyebrows. "No other crystals. She preferred gold. I can't do math on figures this large, but you can probably make the down payment on a new house reselling these."

"She had nothing else to spend money on," Kurt said, glancing around. "She had free room and board and a chauffeured limo. And she still insisted on receiving dividends even when the corporation had no cash. She'd go to the bank and sweet talk her old buddies into writing loans that Monty and I had to figure out how to pay. If you can sell all that crap, we might finally pay off some of them."

"I know good wholesalers." Teddy sorted through the gold. "They'll buy the lot. Or I can set up a page on my website and sell direct for twice as much. It would just take longer."

The conversation reminded Hannah that it was what one accomplished while still alive that mattered more than what one left behind. For all intents and purposes, Carmel had vanished from this world, sadly, leaving few fond memories, only gold to be sold. Hannah wanted to hug the Kennedys and make the emptiness go away, but they had people who could do that better than she could.

She had never given it much thought, but she had always wanted to be a teacher and librarian. Her instincts leaned toward improving the world rather than accumulating wealth. Removing Carmel's killer seemed a good place to make improvements, so she reluctantly followed the antique dealer/psychometrist. After dismissing the jewelry, Aaron had vanished inside a walk-in closet. She edged over to peer in.

He'd turned on a track of overhead lights revealing rows of tailored outfits, neatly organized by color. A fancy closet system at the back held evening gowns and furs, with pull-out racks for shoes and purses. Aaron didn't touch anything, just moved his palm steadily up and down, searching for whatever it was that he felt.

"I'm only sensing Carmel in here," he said as he approached the far end. "The closet excited her. Suppressed emotion is almost as powerful as expressed. It's more concentrated."

Hannah thought that might be more words than he'd spoken to her since they met. She was afraid to break the spell by commenting. Maybe he assumed she was Kurt.

"Here it is. Call the Kennedys." He crouched down at the rear of the closet and poked his staff beneath the evening gowns.

All right, he knew she wasn't Kurt. Hannah gestured at Teddy, who abandoned the jewelry cabinet to catch Kurt's arm. Hannah stepped aside so the brothers could crowd in behind Aaron. Fee and Teddy slipped inside while Hannah and Walker waited in the double doorway.

"She loved whatever was behind this wall," Aaron explained, pushing aside the gowns with his stick. "Everything back here is permeated with her anticipation. She's been here recently. The impressions are clear and strong."

Aaron ran his hands over what appeared to be a blank wall beneath the gowns. Within seconds, he'd located a latch that opened under pressure. An opening in the wall swung out, and he backed away so everyone could see.

"She spent a fortune remodeling this closet," Kurt said in disgust. "Now I see why."

Hannah had to strain to look past the brothers—a safe! Beside her, Teddy and Fee snorted in disdain. Believing anyone needed protection against theft in a small town like Hillvale bordered on paranoia. How much more gold could Carmel have stored in a safe than was already in the jewelry cabinet? Hoarding so much wealth while a town suffered. . . It happened, Hannah knew, for a variety of reasons, not all of them rational.

"Some people think only of themselves," Fee whispered, almost angrily.

"But whatever she stored in there may be how she kept the lodge going for those years her sons were young," Walker corrected without inflection.

"In her head, that might easily have justified hiding funds," Hannah murmured, sad for the woman who had never known the freedom to be generous or giving.

"We don't know the combination," Monty protested in impatience, crouching beside Aaron. "Can we blow it up?"

Hannah caught a flicker of amusement in Aaron's dark gaze as he glanced back at the honest mayor. Without a word, he turned to the safe and set his skillful fingers on the dial. It clicked open in three spins. His psychometry had apparently picked up Carmel's thoughts as she'd turned the dial.

"You would have made a great bank robber," Hannah muttered, unable to tolerate the suspense.

"Thank you." Aaron opened the safe door, then sat back so the brothers could access it first.

"Just an old metal box." In disappointment, Kurt pulled out a heavy object Hannah couldn't quite see.

"Filled with cash?" Fee asked hopefully.

"This damned thing is locked too. We need a key." Kurt dragged the heavy, ornate box to the center of the closet where they could all surround it.

Before Hannah could exclaim at the familiar item, Monty applied his boot heel to the trunk's rounded top.

"No. . . damned. . . way." He underscored each word by applying his heel to the lock.

On the third stomp, the metal caved.

SEVEN

LOOSENING THE CASKET LID RELEASED A. . . AARON DIDN'T HAVE A WORD for it, but the emanation was strong. He caught Monty's hand before the mayor could open it. "*Don't.* Stand back. Whatever is in there isn't normal. Maybe you should all back out. I'll use my stick to pop it open."

The librarian watched him with suspicion. He had the feeling that she knew his history and had good reason to distrust him.

She was the Malcolm librarian; of course she knew his history. Chances were good Walker had investigated him as well, but the police chief kept his own counsel. Walker had a habit of unobtrusively listening and watching, gathering information until his formidable mind had formed the right questions.

Aaron had spent this last decade staying above suspicion, and he wasn't changing now, even if Monty's rage and grief had just crushed a medieval jewel casket. Maybe it needed crushing. Carmel's overriding excitement left impressions on the ornate surface that were all negative in his mind. Lust for objects never had pleasant connotations.

They all reluctantly gave him space.

"If evil demons are about to pop out, you might want to gather a few holy relics first," the librarian suggested.

She was an oasis of calm in a torrent of emotions. He couldn't tell if she was being facetious.

"At least bring it out here where you have more room," Walker suggested.

"I'd rather keep it contained," Aaron explained. "I don't sense anything living, just strong vibrations."

"No zombies," Hannah murmured, definitely tongue in cheek.

Aaron shot her a look that she met with amusement. He couldn't tell if she was being brave or stupid by ignoring his warning.

"There's an identical casket in a medieval painting hanging in Keegan's library," she explained. "That's either a very good imitation, or the original, in which case it's quite possibly a Malcolm artifact."

A Malcolm relic would explain a lot—except for why Carmel had it. Everyone tried to push closer. Aaron was forced to shove it out of the shadows so they could all see.

She was right, damn her. He recognized the box as well, but it hadn't been in a medieval painting. It was in the painting he'd hidden in the top of the wardrobe. He couldn't even call it coincidence. Malcolm artifacts had a habit of turning up around Malcolm descendants.

While everyone watched, Aaron pried at the lid with his stick. It wouldn't budge. Cursing under his breath, he crouched down. Objects this old were dangerous and often excruciatingly painful to touch, especially ones exuding such strong emanations. Calculating the right pressure point to open the lock, he pressed two fingers to the metal.

Excitement. Greed. Spite. Anxiety. Fear. Flashes of countless blurred images. That last might have knocked him over, except the intensity of Carmel's greed buried the earlier impressions. He was afraid that meant Carmel hadn't known what she had or hadn't possessed the sense to respect its power.

The lock still didn't give. He yanked his fingers away. If Monty hadn't smashed it, he might have been able to pick the lock. Under the cold eyes of the law, he was almost grateful he had an excuse not to exhibit his expertise.

"I don't think anyone has touched this except your mother in a long time." Aaron didn't see any way of opening the box without force. The metal had twisted beneath Monty's frustration and the lid needed to be pried.

"Could it be the source of the lodge's pollution?" Hannah asked.

Good question, one he couldn't answer except to say that Malcolm artifacts were usually more helpful than dangerous. Reluctantly, he pulled out his pocket knife and pried at the metal. He didn't want to harm anyone, but his audience wouldn't leave until they saw the contents.

"Stay back," he warned as the latch gave.

The opening was almost a let-down. The frayed, velvet-lined interior contained what appeared to be rough stones or raw gems. They'd all seen the crude crystal rocks Keegan had mined from the cave up the mountain, and the polished jewels Teddy ordered for her store. This wasn't Aladdin's glittering treasure trove by any means.

The stones still emanated energy similar to the vibrations surrounding Hillvale.

"There was a bigger object in the center," Teddy observed, looking over his shoulder. "Someone added a bed of padded satin to protect the stones. There's a dent in that lining where something heavy must have been stored for a long time."

Aaron pressed his finger into the indentation. "The impressions are muddied but powerful." He glanced up at the stoic police chief. "I know you have no reason to believe me, but this may be what the thief stole."

"Stand back, let me take pictures and measurements." Walker snapped photos of the interior and measured the indentation. "I don't see how a thief had time to tuck all this back in place after killing Carmel. The stone may have been gone for a while."

"May I touch them?" Teddy asked warily.

"I think you'd better let Keegan see them first. These might be like the crystals the artists in the commune ground into their pigments. Some of them may be the almandine garnets that reflected evil." Aaron was pretty sure that was exactly what this trove was—the missing gems that had been brought here no one knew how long ago—from the collection of Keegan's Malcolm ancestors. In other words, weird and dangerous rocks that had been experimented with by alchemists or who-knew-what over the centuries. Had they originally arrived in this casket?

Hannah was silent, but she didn't disagree with him. She'd seen the painting in the castle and probably some of Keegan's stones. Aaron respected her silence on a subject that wasn't hers to comment on.

Which was what librarians did, he realized—stored and provided information without commenting on the contents, leaving people to read and decide for themselves.

"The missing piece is almost a tennis-ball sized rock," Walker said, standing up.

"The murder weapon?" Aaron asked.

Walker shoved his phone back in his pocket and shrugged, before turning back to the Kennedys. "The coroner hasn't done a full report, but he did say your mother had an unusually thin occipital bone. Many people can take a blow to the back of the head and come away unharmed or with a mild concussion. Not your mother. The blow crushed her skull. Bone fragments pierced the part connecting with her spine, killing her pretty quickly. It's possible that our killer only meant to knock her out."

Fee and Teddy hugged their significant others. Their sympathy for the brothers was almost tangible.

In frustration, Aaron returned to running his hands over the tables and other objects in the room. He had no reason to hate Carmel but every reason to want his hands on the contents of that jewel casket. But protocol required that Walker lock them up as evidence. Finally, he had a clue to what the painting might be trying to say—and he couldn't read it.

"Let's find Keegan," the librarian said in low tones while Walker and the Kennedys argued over the disposal of the stones.

"Won't do any good if Walker locks up the stones as evidence," Aaron muttered back, casting a longing glance at the casket.

Hannah held open her slender palm to reveal a small grayish raw garnet.

AARON SAT IN STONY SILENCE BESIDE HER AS THE SHUTTLE HAULED THEM back to town. Amused, Hannah kept her distance, just in case she really was allergic to him. The stones had belonged to her ancestors. The police had no idea what they were. She saw no good reason why she shouldn't take a small, rather inexpensive rock for an expert to examine. But her amusement was because Aaron objected to her thievery, yet hadn't made her put it back. The man's morals were definitely bent, but then, apparently so were hers.

When the shuttle let them off in front of the café, Hannah waited for Aaron to decide if he wanted to go with her to Keegan's house. She had yet to speak with her cousin, meet his wife in person, or see the new baby, and she was eager to do so.

Aaron rolled his fingers into fists in an evident internal argument. She waited patiently. At some point, he would have to actually talk to her.

Not yet, she noted as he stalked toward the lane of cottages. She thought she could find the house without his help. She recalled the hanging computer discs from last night—so much had happened since she'd arrived!

Her towering geologist of a cousin was waiting for them. "It's about time. The Lucy grapevine is buzzing. Mariah is about to come after you." He stepped back to let them in.

"And hello to you, too, Cousin," Hannah said wryly, stepping into the small front room made smaller by outsized furniture.

Aaron was as tall as Keegan, but leaner. Keegan came from a line of sturdy miners and had spent the better part of his life swinging pickaxes and toting boxes of rocks, building impressive muscles in already thick limbs. Aaron's strength was more sinewy. But they both sported the patrician noses and dark hair of their Ives ancestors.

The woman emerging from the back hall wasn't any kind of Malcolm she recognized. Hannah appreciated the furniture size after seeing her cousin and his wife together. Mariah was tall and sturdily built, with Hispanic or Native American heritage, not fair like the American part of Hannah's family.

She'd already been informed that Mariah wasn't a hugger, but neither was Hannah. They'd spent a lot of time together over the internet these last months, so it was as if visiting an old friend.

"At last!" Mariah cried. "It's good to finally meet you somewhere besides Skype. Daphne is sleeping. Do you want to peek in at her? But then you need to tell us everything." She led the way back to a bedroom where an infant slept in a rocking cradle.

Awestruck by the tiny bundle of life, Hannah stroked Daphne's tawny-soft cheek and watched, teary-eyed, as the infant's little pink mouth puckered. She blamed hormones for the sudden urge to have one of these for her own. Wiping back the moisture, she stepped aside so Aaron could look.

"Cute," he muttered, staring as hard as Hannah. "I'm polishing some silver spoons for her. I'll bring them up later, when our schoolteacher isn't stealing garnets."

Mariah socked his shoulder and shoved him out of the room. "*Tell.* I hate being kept out of everything."

"I'm trying to tame her," Keegan said in amusement, leading the way back to the front room. "But if you don't feed Mariah constant information, she'll be digging bunny trails into your computers to siphon them."

Hannah held out the stone she'd confiscated. "We found a stash of these and others in Carmel's safe. It appears a very large stone is missing."

Keegan grabbed a towel from the kitchen just off the front room, snatched the stone from her hand, and deposited it in a glass bowl. "If this is one of our ancestor's rocks, you shouldn't touch it. He experimented with some pretty dangerous stuff. Wash your hands."

"Do we need to call Walker and tell him to put them in a lead box?" Aaron headed for the landline.

While Mariah hovered anxiously, Keegan ran his hand over the top of the bowl, not touching the rock itself. "Yes, for safety's sake, lock them up. I'm picking up some of the same vibrations we found in Daisy's art hoard."

Muttering Latin curses, Aaron punched numbers into the phone while Hannah scrubbed.

"Could the evil in those rocks have polluted Carmel over the years?" Mariah demanded. "That would explain a lot."

"Without knowing what else was in that box, we can't make that assumption yet." Keegan found a lid for the glass bowl. "We know how to neutralize the paint the artists made from these things, but we still know almost nothing of what our ancestors did to them or where they found them."

"These were in a medieval jewel casket, the same one as in that painting in your study at home," Hannah told him. She glared at Aaron and waited for him to finish leaving a message on Walker's voice mail before continuing with a hint of spite, "I suspect it's the same casket as in that painting Aaron went to jail for, although that was a different era and set in Hillvale."

Silence descended. When Aaron didn't immediately respond, Mariah gestured at the living room. "I think we need to sit down and work this out sensibly."

"I'll fix coffee." Keegan rummaged for the beans.

Hannah settled into the smallest chair in the room, leaving the large leather ones that were obviously their hosts' favorites. Aaron looked longingly at the door.

"Hannah is our librarian," Keegan called over his shoulder as he filled the coffee machine. "You know damned well that position comes with the knowledge of everything about who we are."

Recognizing her knowledge didn't appear to appease Aaron. He started to pace.

"Because of Keegan's discoveries, I had reason to study Hillvale," Hannah explained. "Most of my knowledge is innate—it isn't active. It's just there to be called on as needed. But I have a photographic memory. I sought the original journals on the gems and read them once Keegan started asking questions about crystals. Then I followed every lead I found on Hillvale. Mariah isn't in our library, but Aaron is."

Settled into a recliner, Mariah chortled and began rewrapping her long black braid. "I'm special."

"There are people with special gifts who aren't Malcolms," Hannah acknowledged. "But you're married now to a Malcolm descendant, and you should start recording your discoveries and teach Daphne to do the same. Knowledge is half our power."

Aaron glared at the stone, out the window, and anywhere but at Hannah. She silenced, allowing him to let off steam and gather his thoughts. She didn't enjoy being interrogated by a furious man, but this wouldn't be the first time. She'd been surrounded by powerful men like

Aaron and Keegan since birth. The Ives strain of the family had bossiness down to a science.

"I found the damned painting in a thrift store when I was just a kid," Aaron finally said in disgruntlement. "I'm originally from the Shetlands, but at the time, my father was working in Oxford, and my mother was doing research for her doctorate. I was missing the hills of home and didn't know what to do with myself in a city. Because of my gift, I was naturally drawn to antique stores and the like."

"I'm thinking of putting radio signals and chains on Daphne," Mariah said knowingly. "Our gifts are dangerous when not moderated."

"The reason for our journals," Hannah reminded them. "As soon as you discover Daphne's abilities, I'll find the books she needs."

Aaron disregarded their exchange. He grabbed a mug from a shelf the instant Keegan's coffeemaker indicated the caffeinated fuel was ready.

Fortified, he leaned against a cabinet rather than sit down. He looked like a sophisticated Parisian art dealer, Hannah decided. His camel blazer was tailored to good effect on his wide shoulders, falling open to reveal a black silk t-shirt clinging to impressive pectorals. Tight black jeans just needed a codpiece to resemble the leggings of her medieval knight—the one in Keegan's painting.

"I didn't have your Malcolm background," Aaron said dismissively. "My father was a Null, and my mother pretended she was too. I explored my ability on my own. I had no good way of explaining why I was so excited by the rather ugly piece of American art I brought home. I could tell them it was compelling, but they couldn't feel what I felt. I just knew the artist had a message he was desperately attempting to pass on, and it called to me."

"Even though they didn't understand, my parents helped me hang it on my wall. My mother wanted me to take art classes. I had absolutely no interest in any art except this piece, which told a story I needed to decipher."

"Describe it, please," Mariah insisted. "Why would American art be in a Brit thrift shop?"

He shrugged. "The artist is Malcolm Eversham, a contemporary of Lars Ingersson, one of the commune artists who went on to great fame.

Apparently the oil and frame didn't make enough of an impression for former owners to leave their thoughts on it for me to read. I'd say someone inherited it from the original purchaser, thought it was boring, and gave it away. That's the usual path."

Which, as an antique dealer, he had the experience to know. But that part was irrelevant. Hannah recited from her encyclopedia of knowledge. "Malcolm Eversham was a descendant of the British Malcolms, a distant American cousin to Keegan's branch, and not along legitimate lines. There are probably some connections to the famous artist Lucinda Malcolm. He was never as well known as some of the other commune artists, but he gained a quiet fame for his historically accurate western paintings. He was one of the commune artists who didn't die in abject poverty or from unnatural causes."

"Eversham must have been a Lucy," Mariah breathed, almost happily. "A Lucy smart enough not to use the evil stones the others were using."

"One who didn't need drugs to enhance his natural talent," Hannah agreed. "He didn't leave a journal, but his work was so accurate that some of his family speculated that he could *see* the past."

Aaron didn't take a seat. Neither did Keegan. He handed mugs of coffee to Mariah and Hannah, then leaned against the counter between kitchen and front room. "So, Aaron, what did our bastard cousin paint that excited your juvenile soul? Naked ladies?"

Aaron scowled, drained his cup, and went back for more. "He painted a priest, a Spanish soldier, and a dozen half-naked Native Americans. It wasn't the subject matter that excited me, but the vibrations left by the artist. He thought the subject matter extremely important and was frustrated that no one listened to him. I'd not received such a strong message before. To a lonely child, it was rather like talking to an adult."

"Before you explain what this exotic group was doing, please explain why you've hidden the painting?" Hannah asked politely, concealing her own frustration.

Still holding his steaming mug, Aaron crossed his arms in a classic defensive position. "Because it killed my parents and my wife."

EIGHT

KEEGAN BROUGHT OUT A BOTTLE OF SCOTCH AND ADDED A LARGE DOLLOP TO Aaron's coffee cup. It was a hot August day with no air conditioning, but the heat of the whiskey warmed the coldness inside him as he faced the tale he had to tell. Aaron despised explaining himself, but at least this audience was receptive. He'd not had that benefit in the past.

"Your parents died in a plane crash," the librarian said for him. "Your wife died of cancer. It was during her illness that you sold the fraudulent Eversham."

There was no condemnation in her recitation, although there ought to be. Going to jail hadn't been one of his finer moments, even if his intent had been altruistic. "That's not the whole tale."

He refilled his cup and sank down into one of Keegan's plush leather chairs. Or Mariah's. The computer genius had money before she moved up here. Her former home must have been immense to hold furniture on this scale.

He was procrastinating. "It was right after my parents hung the painting that my father got an offer for a position in New York. He needed to go over for an interview, so they left me with one of my father's assistants and hired a local pilot to take them to Manchester airport. The plane had mechanical failure and went down in a field."

In a way, part of him had perished with his parents—his innocence perhaps. They'd been his entire world, and then he'd learned his world could be crushed in an eye blink. He'd been devastated. And lost. It had taken him years to trust close relationships again. Even when he'd finally married, there had always been the sensation of waiting for the next blow to fall that had put a distance between him and Natalie. Despite insulating himself with distance, her death had flattened him all over again.

He waited out the protests that the plane crash was mere coincidence. The librarian didn't say a word, he noticed. She just waited, absorbing and processing. The woman was damned dangerous. No one had ever exposed his secrets as she had, and she had done it with the precision and thoroughness of a surgeon excising a tumor.

He resented the interference but admired her ability. "After my parents died, I was sent to my maternal aunt in Boston. I took the canvas out of the frame and rolled it up to fit it in my suitcase. At least Nan was more in touch with her roots than her sister. She had a small gift for healing, nothing dramatic, but she acknowledged my psychometry and encouraged it. I left the painting rolled up because the memories of my parents' pride in me were too fresh and too painful."

Mariah got up and began slicing cheese, her knife hitting the cutting board a little too forcefully. She had bad memories in her past as well, Aaron knew.

The librarian with her secrets was the enigma here. Maybe Keegan knew them.

"My parents left some insurance and a small trust fund, enough to help Nan raise me on her nurse's salary. Mostly, I got by on scholarships, but I had no real vocation. Psychometry is a hard talent to sell. I met Keegan in Oxford, and he was the one who mentioned the Malcolm library and suggested I see if it would give me any ideas."

"Psychometry is a rare gift even among Malcolms," Hannah said. "It's often painful, if you don't learn to control it. You may be descended from Felicity and Ewen Ives. She had to wear gloves all the time because she was so sensitive to the pain on objects."

"The journals helped me learn control," Aaron admitted. "I've kept my own journal since then. And I began to appreciate the history I discovered in museums. When I returned to Boston, I volunteered at the museum and began working in an antique store, learning more about American history and how it related to my British one."

"And you kept the painting rolled up?" Mariah asked.

"Eventually, I almost forgot about it. I'd stored it in Nan's attic when I left for Oxford. When I opened my first store specializing in American antiques, Nan reminded me of it. Natalie and I had been married less than a year. We were decorating an apartment on a meager budget, so Natalie happily took the painting and had it framed and hung over our mantel as a gift to me."

Aaron knew the rest of his story rested on his peculiar gift and not reality as others understood it. He glared at Hannah, who serenely crossed her hands and waited. Her innocent disguise didn't deceive him. The fool woman would climb into the wardrobe and take the damned thing out if he didn't make this convincing.

"I spent a lot of time traveling. Natalie was a writer who worked from home and occasionally did research for me. She's the one who identified the Eversham and the history of Hillvale, to what extent it's available. The Spaniards and Ohlone portrayed in the painting didn't leave much in the way of written records. She took the painting to a western historian and to an art expert. She learned its value but not much else. At the time, western art was hot, and she got a really good offer for it, money we could use."

Natalie had been brilliant and loving, and she hadn't deserved to be saddled with an unfeeling cad like him. Her loss was still an ache in Aaron's heart that would never heal. Good people shouldn't die young. The world needed their goodness more than it needed his cynicism. He didn't think he could explain the beauty of Natalie's soul.

"You don't have to do this," Hannah said suddenly. "Maybe we could just look at what you have and learn what we need from it."

Aaron wanted to let relief roll over him and cave to her suggestion. Instead, he glared. "I'm telling this tale once and once only. Eversham was a real artist, a Lucy with weird abilities. I went to prison for selling a *forgery*. What do you think is in that wardrobe?"

"I think your wife let a museum copyist reproduce the painting so she could sell the original," Hannah promptly replied. "Did the copyist die too?"

"He did." Aaron sank deeper into his chair. "Fell off a ladder and broke his neck shortly after he handed both oils back to Natalie. She fretted over the incident, but by that time, we had even more reason to need the money. She had stage three breast cancer and the cost of treatment would break us."

"So she sold the painting for a nice sum, hung the fake on your wall, and then died anyway?"

Hannah's soft query eased him past the horror of memories of Natalie curled up and shivering from treatments, her beautiful hair falling out, her chest scarred—and then sucker punched with learning the cancer still grew elsewhere.

Aaron shut out the pain and nodded. "At the time, her illness had knocked me to my knees. I didn't *care* how we were paying for the treatment. I didn't start putting two and two together until the doctors told me the treatments weren't working. When Natalie knew she was dying, she confessed she'd sold my painting and hung the copy. That's when I learned of the death of the copyist. I was almost glad the damned original was out of our house, but once Natalie died, I was compelled to check on the purchaser. He'd died of a heart attack shortly after hanging the painting in his collection."

"So you believe contact with the painting caused their deaths?" This time, it was Keegan speaking, his formidable brow drawn into a frown. "So why haven't *you* died?"

"It apparently has a use for me." Aaron knew he sounded gruff, but he'd been over this ground in his head too many times. "Natalie was ill, but we don't know if it started before or after hanging the painting or if she might have recovered had the painting not been involved. I can't bring her back with speculation."

"So why did you go to jail?" Hannah asked, pushing. "She didn't sell a fake."

"Because a twelve-year-old little girl inherited the collection. She was the same age I'd been when my parents died. At that point, I'd decided to burn the damned thing. So I told her family it had sentimental value, asked if I could hang it at Natalie's funeral, and switched it out. I didn't want another death on my conscience."

"You were grief-stricken and half-crazed," Hannah translated for him.

"Yeah, that, too." Aaron got up to pour more coffee but the machine was empty. He dumped another shot of Scotch into the mug instead. "The collection was appraised and the fraud uncovered. I refused to reveal the whereabouts of the original, and I had no money to repay the estate. I went to jail. Used the time to get a doctorate. The painting didn't get burned. By the time I got out, I decided Natalie shouldn't have died for nothing. The painting had to have some purpose. I'm still looking."

"And you won't let anyone else touch it because you fear we'll die." Hannah rose from her chair. "But I have reason to believe the painting holds a clue to stopping the evil polluting Hillvale, and that it can *save* lives too."

∼

HANNAH HELPED HERSELF TO A SWALLOW OF THE SCOTCH. SHE HAD NEVER meant to tell her tale, but *Dr.* Aaron Townsend had just stripped himself bare in front of her, a complete stranger. She could see the suffering in his dark eyes. He'd deeply loved his wife and her death still tortured him. She had to word her story carefully, so he might see hope.

That was a bit hard to do with Carmel's body lying on a slab and evil haunting the hills.

She weighed whether Aaron could be lying, but Keegan and Mariah seemed to trust him. They had gifts far greater than hers. Her knowledge was of the written page, no more. For the most part, lies and emotions escaped her.

She looked for a kettle for tea, but apparently her hosts were coffee drinkers. Unable to leave everyone hanging any longer, she took her sip of Scotch back to her chair. "I researched the painting hanging in Keegan's study." She didn't have to tell them why. "There's a knight with a jewel casket at his side, with his hand out to a lady. They're standing in front of a stone well. He's wearing a sword with an enormous ruby in the hilt, but he's handing her what appears to be a rock. I've compared it to other images, and I think it may be a moonstone."

Everyone listened without helping her along here. Keegan knew the painting. For all she knew, so did Mariah. Photos were in the Malcolm files. Anyone could look it up.

"Anyway, I found a Malcolm journal related to the scene. The painting depicts what appears to be late medieval era, probably the 1400s, judging by the knight's rounded sabots and etched mail, similar to the cuirass in Aaron's window." She cast a quick glance at Aaron but he seemed lost in black thought.

She continued. "There's a tiny sketch of the knight in a Malcolm journal from that period. The journal is in Latin. There's no mention of the lady, just a note that Sir Geoffrey retrieved the Healing Stone, and the plague had been conquered."

"Healing Stone?" Mariah had produced a laptop from a hidden pocket in her chair and was already cruising through files.

"You won't find much in the journals," Hannah warned. "Women were called witches and killed back then. A literate woman in the 1400s would be instantly considered suspect. So any notes were limited, and an artifact that might be called magic would be concealed by innocuous terms—in between recipes, in this case."

Hannah finished her sip of whiskey and heard the infant stirring. She needed to speak quickly. "The tiny sketch of the knight and the note were from the 1400s, but the painting itself wasn't completed until much later, in the 1600s, by another Malcolm ancestor who apparently painted her dreams." Vivid dreams, like hers had been lately. Except Hannah couldn't paint. "The artist's notes about the painting are equally limited, but she appeared to know where the Healing Stone was located, so it might have generated the dreams."

"A touch of psychometry involved, perhaps?" Aaron asked, apparently riveted by her tale. "A powerful object would leave strong impressions."

"There were still gifted male Malcolms at the time," Hannah said. "And yes, one had your talent. He was in the same household as the lady painter. He seems to be a priest who used the stone to combat what they called *evil* in his parish, so the painter would have been familiar with the stone. The priest's mentions were brief. He was less likely to be burned at the stake, but healing stones and the like are pagan, a relic of our Celtic origins. He probably told no one else but his journal—and the painter who had dreams about it."

"Or dreams about him," Mariah said with a snort, apparently finding the painting in their online library. "That's one hunky knight. I wonder if the painting looks like the priest or the original knight."

Hannah didn't look at Aaron. If no one else saw the resemblance, she wouldn't draw attention to it. She might be the only one dreaming of a knight in shining armor carrying a stone that healed—a stone she prayed might heal *her*.

"What does this have to do with *my* painting?" Aaron demanded, still focused on his goal.

Hannah curled up in her chair. "The stone was mentioned again in the 1800s, by a Victorian spiritualist who claimed to have sent the family's famous Healing Stone with her sister to the Americas. That was circa the 1870s. If the sister kept a journal, it's been lost."

"None of these journals mentioned how the stone was used or if it actually worked?" Keegan asked, rising and heading in the direction of his mewling daughter.

"With no written instructions from the original time periods, that information is lost too," Hannah admitted. "The spiritualist who left the journal wasn't a healer. She talked to ghosts and acted as a medium. Her sister wanted to take it to Lily Dale, the spiritualist colony in New York, to see if anyone knew how to activate it. Unless you count the description of the Eversham painting, there was only one more mention of the stone—one of the Lily Dale psychics decided to take it with her when she took the train to California."

She stared pointedly at Aaron, who grimaced. Even Keegan halted in the doorway and waited.

"There is no stone in the Eversham that could be held in the hand," he protested.

"But in his journal, Eversham specifically said he'd painted a *Healing Stone*, and he was a Lucy painting a vision of the past," Hannah insisted. "It's far-fetched as a coincidence, unless there was an oral tradition we don't know about, and he was painting what he'd been told."

"There are no photos of the Eversham painting online," Mariah said in disappointment, typing rapidly on her keyboard.

"Because it's in Aaron's shop hidden by an ugly piece of kindergarten paint," Hannah declared, making a not-so-wild guess.

"I promise, the only stone depicted in that scene *did not kill Carmel*," Aaron said, standing. "If I show it to you, and you take a photograph to show the others, will you leave it alone?"

Thank all that was holy, he gave in before she had to reveal the reason why she wanted to see that painting.

Even she knew it was insane to believe she'd find a stone that could heal the walnut in her brain.

NINE

THE LIBRARIAN'S FACE LIT WITH SUCH HOPE AND EXCITEMENT THAT AARON didn't have the heart to point out the fallacy in their fairy tale. The oil he hid represented the Americas in the early 1700s. The Healing Stone they talked about had been in England in the 1600s and 1800s. The casket and the stone had obviously parted ways at some point.

He had other reasons to doubt his painting had anything to do with the stone in Carmel's box, but he'd let them see for themselves.

He was grateful Hannah didn't seem eager to hang around for infant feeding time. After admiring the wailing infant one more time, they said their farewells and headed back to town.

"Thank you for trusting me," Hannah said, hurrying down the dusty lane. "I understand the date discrepancy, believe me."

Well, *faex*, there went that hope that he could persuade her to leave the painting alone.

"I've studied this," she continued relentlessly. "It's possible, unlikely, perhaps, but possible. Ships crossed the Atlantic regularly. The Spanish and British were at war most of the time, but we're talking about Malcolms and maybe Ives. They used to get along way back when."

"You're more steeped in family history than I am," he reluctantly agreed. "But I think even you'll give up when you see the painting."

Aaron had left Harvey in charge of the shop while he'd shepherded the librarian around all morning. The musician gratefully fled once they returned. Harvey wasn't much of a salesman, but he knew how to operate the cash register, which was all that really mattered. Hillvale didn't provide much of Aaron's income. The objects stored here were mostly his private neurosis and not worth a lot of salesmanship.

Aaron assisted a tourist in opening the locked drawer of a bureau using one of the skeleton keys he kept for the purpose, while keeping his eye on Hannah. She was poking around his inventory, studiously avoiding the wardrobes. It was apparent she didn't have any feel for the objects she touched.

So why did the painting set her off? And *him*, apparently.

She'd fainted every time he'd touched her. For reasons he didn't understand, that annoyed the hell out of him. He had a "friend with benefits" in the city. He didn't need to obsess about sex. It was just that— there was just something. . . *ethereal*. . . about the librarian that brought out his protective streak, he supposed. That was foolish. She seemed quite sturdy.

She'd told him she'd seen a doctor, and there wasn't anything they could do. *Damnatio et infernum*. He wanted no more sick or dying women in his life. He needed her gone soon, if not sooner.

Once the customer left, Aaron crossed to the wardrobes. Hannah left the bookshelves she'd been perusing to produce her cell phone and warily watch as he opened the wardrobe doors.

"You might want a better camera," he warned. "This is the one and only time I'll do this."

"I'm a librarian, not a photographer. This is all I have. Do you have better?"

Muttering curses, Aaron returned to his desk and produced the miniature camera he carried with him when assessing an estate. "You'll have to trust me to send the photo to you," he reminded her.

"I'll have mine," she said complacently.

Nothing disturbed the damned woman. Shoving the camera in his coat pocket, he took the frame from the top of the wardrobe. Flipping it over, he used a screwdriver to pry off the glued paper concealing the hidden canvas. He'd mounted the aging canvas on a treated board that removed easily.

He swallowed hard as he lay the oil face up on the settee.

The painting was riveting in its simplicity. A Spanish knight in bloody armor, a Franciscan priest in a tattered brown robe, and half a dozen dark-skinned natives kneeling, standing, watching as one native carved a rock with a chisel-like tool. The figures surrounded what appeared to be a crumbling well. In the distance, smoke rose and clouded the sky. In the foreground, the medieval casket rested near the native carver.

The expressions of anger, pain, and despair on their various features told a horrifying story.

Even without touching it, the painting of Hillvale's past compelled him.

"I see what you mean," she said softly. "There is something in the stance of the natives—"

She reached to touch the oil. Instinctively, Aaron caught her hand. For a moment, both their fingers brushed the canvas. A moment was all it took.

Nighttime. Stars high above on a crisp cool evening. Smoke from a wood fire mixed with the mouth-watering scent of grilling meat. People—everywhere. Some stoned, sitting around the fire. Others molding clay. Painters packing away their brushes for the day. The farmhouse glowed from candles behind the windows.

A small hand clutched his. Blinking, not understanding, Aaron glanced down at the woman beside him—the Librarian. She was almost transparent. For all that mattered, so was he. He studied his translucent hand in disbelief where it held hers.

She was staring at their joined hands in equal shock. And then her eyes widened, and she eagerly scanned the setting. He didn't need to study it to know they were on the commune property above Hillvale, with the mountain looming over them and the redwoods lining the bluff in the distance. And the bearded young hippy artist packing up his paint was Eversham.

Aaron yanked his hand from Hannah's, fearing she'd faint in this weird scene where he had no one to help her.

The painting slid off the settee and hit the floor. Aaron glanced hurriedly at Hannah, but she was still standing, still staring at her hand in shock. "Can we do it again?" she asked, reaching for the oil.

He used his stick to shove the frame from her grasping hand. "That's what got us in trouble last time. Are you insane?"

"We weren't in trouble," she said primly, exactly like a spinster schoolteacher, crossing her hands in front of her. "We were observing." But another thought worried her, he could tell. Her pale brow puckered in a frown.

"We just had an out-of-body experience," he practically shouted. He didn't usually lose control like that, not anymore. He bit his tongue and tried to analyze what he'd seen. *They'd* seen. Apparently it wasn't just him, which was weirdly reassuring. "And you want to risk it again?"

"Like time travel?" she asked uncertainly. "Because that wasn't here and now. That looked like. . ." She hesitated. "A commune? Beards and long hair and vests and bell bottoms—the seventies, maybe? I don't have out-of-body experiences. But. . ."

Too much hung on that one word, and she was too close to nailing it on the head. "Tea?" he suggested, remembering she'd not drunk the coffee earlier.

She nodded doubtfully and stared at the canvas on the floor, which had landed face up.

"Don't touch it," he warned. "Get pictures. Study the stone and see why it isn't what you want."

≈

SNAPPING PICTURES TO COVER HER INTENSE DISAPPOINTMENT OVER THE subject matter, Hannah considered the strange painting and the scene she'd just. . . *experienced*. Dreamed? She saw no link between this scene from the distant past and the weird one she'd shared with Aaron. If he had seen it too, it couldn't be a dream or a brain lapse, could it?

Malcolm abilities didn't normally manifest so late in life. Did she dare hope that she was a late bloomer and not dying? Or maybe the walnut in her head had stimulated a previously unknown gift—or she was groping for hope now that there was none. She was pretty certain that Aaron had inspired this particular adventure.

The Spanish soldier in the Eversham painting looked dutifully authoritative. The priest appeared downtrodden, upset, not in the least happy as he laid his hands on what appeared to be a round, rough boulder, the one the native carver worked on. The brown natives crouched in the shadows of an even larger rock, watching intently.

The jewel casket sat in the dust between the priest and the soldier. It was open but the contents weren't visible at this angle. She saw nothing that resembled the stones they'd seen in Carmel's box or the ones in the knight painting. Maybe jewel caskets like this one were a dime a dozen back then, who knew?

The tale of the healing moonstone was apparently just that—a good tale.

Determinedly maintaining her focus so she didn't collapse and weep, she snapped photos from every angle, making certain she got a good shot of the artist's signature. She had no way of knowing if this was the original. She was no expert. But if the weird scene they'd experienced meant anything at all, she'd have to say there was a strong association between the work and the artist.

Which probably meant that she'd enhanced Aaron's normal psychometric abilities to see what the artist was seeing and nothing more.

Aaron returned with a tea tray. He'd been raised by British parents. He must recognize that tea was better than Valium. She drank hers black. Her hand shook as she took a cup and saucer, so she sat on the settee to steady herself. She hadn't realized she was so rattled.

"I have no Malcolm gifts other than carrying a library in my head," she said as firmly as she could, if only to reassure herself that she was in the here and now and capable of speech.

He leaned his hip against a heavy carved game table and drank from a large handcrafted ceramic mug. With his neat goatee and tailored jacket, he gave the appearance of elegance and assurance. But his dark eyebrows drew together over his formidable roman nose, and his chocolate-brown eyes looked troubled. "We saw *Eversham*," he said bluntly. "I never see more than impressions, usually generated by strong emotions. I have never seen the person leaving the impressions."

"We had a joint hallucination?" she asked. "Perhaps there was something in Keegan's whiskey we responded to? Should we experiment?"

She really wanted to experience that moment again. It might have been the most exciting event of her entire lonely life. If she had to die young, then shouldn't she cram as many experiences in as she could?

"That was *not* whiskey. That was the cursed damned painting. Burning may be necessary." He glowered at the painting and sipped his tea. "You have to admit that neither the boulder or the rock depicted can be the Healing Stone some Victorian lady transported across an ocean and a continent."

"Why can the stone not be in the jewel casket?" she argued. "If we could speak with Eversham—"

"*That* is not happening." The bell rung over his door, and he turned his formidable glower on the tourists daring to venture in.

They hastily backed out.

"We time traveled," she insisted. "There are incidences in the Malcolm records." Incidences in her own family, but if she told him about those. . . He really would burn the painting.

"More likely, something in that damned painting sucked us in. It won't happen again," he said with finality, setting down his mug and rummaging in a chest of drawers until he'd produced heavy-duty work gloves. "I'm wrapping this thing up and locking it away."

She had the photos. She didn't need the painting any longer—unless she wanted to be sucked in. And she did, so very *very* badly. . . "What if I'm a magnifier?" she asked. "Maybe it's not the painting. Maybe it's the two of us together."

"Magnifier?" In irritation, as if she'd said a bad word, he glanced over his shoulder but didn't halt his steps toward the back room. "Don't be ridiculous."

But she heard the. . . alarm? . . . in his tone. Aaron wasn't dense. If that painting had an impression he could feel, he knew what they'd done.

She knew how to dig down to get what she wanted. "I told you earlier, some of us have the ability to enhance the gifts of others. If the painting speaks to you, maybe I'm helping you access those impressions better." She searched her memory for passages of description about how magnifying worked.

"You faint every time we touch," he said in scorn, reaching the door between the shop and his storage room. "You probably just fainted and sucked me into *your* dream world."

"That's an outright lie," she shouted after him.

Huh, she never shouted. But her hand was steadier for having done so. She could hear him unrolling wrapping paper or bubble wrap or whatever he had back there that crackled. She studied the image on her phone. She needed it on a bigger screen.

She needed to see inside that damned jewel box.

She could still smell the wood smoke and hear the whisper of the wind in the trees. It had been a beautiful night. Had she ever sat outside and simply enjoyed the beauty of nature and companionship?

Quite definitely not. For one thing, it was damned cold at night in Keegan's lonely outpost. She'd have to have gone to the pub for companionship, and she wasn't much of a drinker or conversationalist. She preferred the company of books.

She was making excuses. She'd had opportunities. She simply hadn't been interested. Her head was too full of books to allow in anything extra, like people. She needed to experience more of life.

Aaron returned without the painting. She felt a deep, abiding disappointment—in herself as much as in the missing art.

"Tell me about magnification," he demanded.

She shrugged. "Like all else, it works differently for each individual. Generally, there has to be an element of closeness, if only to discover the ability. One sibling might interfere when another is accessing their gift, and bang, something super exciting happens. It's not always a welcome perception. Try to imagine some of the impressions you've encountered over the years, and then magnify them ten times."

"What we just experienced was sensation enough not to want to do it again," he said grimly, picking up the tea tray.

"Coward," she murmured into her cup. She wasn't a bold sort of person, but he aggravated her in ways she couldn't explain. And if she was to set a new course of experiences, she really *needed* to do it again.

Grimly, he held out the tray for her empty cup and stalked to the back room again.

So, she'd seen the painting. It hadn't told her how to find the stone—

her one and only hope that there was a way of surviving whatever was eating her brain. Now what?

The shop door opened and Tullah, the tall voodoo queen from the thrift store, stalked in, radiating energy. Wearing a bright red and orange halter dress that emphasized her muscular shoulders and arms, she strode with hip-swinging grace through Aaron's inventory in Hannah's direction. "You're playing with fire, Librarian."

The vibrations they'd been giving off must have been powerful enough to reach the psychic. Hannah knew that no one completely understood how Tullah's mind worked. Tullah never explained. She let Cass rule the Lucys, but from what she'd read, Hannah was fairly certain Tullah was equally receptive.

Before Hannah could respond, Aaron returned carrying a ragged sock monkey. His chiseled face was cold as stone. "Magnify this," he demanded, nodding at Tullah but glaring at Hannah. "Tullah will see that we return."

She didn't want to touch a dirty stuffed creature. It probably held nightmares. But if Aaron could hold it. . . If her time here on earth was short, she wanted to experience more than books in her head.

Fortifying herself with a deep breath, she wrapped her fingers around a torn paw.

Nothing.

Aaron's hard brown hand covered hers.

Pain, anguish, toxic chemicals stinking in the hospital air. The agony of helplessness.

TEN

Clutching Money Monkey, her once ivory skin sunken into shadows beneath her cheekbones, Natalie whispered, "Let me die."

ANGRILY, AARON SHOOK OFF THE TRANSPARENT HAND CLINGING TO HIS.

Instantly, the heart-shattering episode vanished, returning them to the dim, dusty shop where the librarian stood, stunned and blinking.

He'd seen Natalie again and not died of anguish. Maybe he was healing. Maybe.

Refusing to be called *coward* again, he shoved the stupid stuffed monkey into a dresser drawer and glared at Tullah. "Well, what happened?"

Hannah dropped down on the settee again. If the prim-and-proper teacher could see what Aaron saw on that velvet-covered cushion, she wouldn't sit there so readily.

If he took her hand, she would apparently see what he saw. *Deodamnatus.* He resisted.

"You both froze," Tullah said succinctly. "Your souls, your ectoplasm, your life force, whatever you want to call it, departed your bodies, but you didn't fall. Very interesting. I hope it was worth it because that way lies madness. I have a store to tend. Quit acting like children and do not summon me that way again. You disturb the universe."

She turned around and marched out.

"And *that's* why I don't need a magnifier." Aaron refused to feel sympathy for Hannah's pale face and shocked expression. He'd needed to make her understand why he would never get personally involved again.

"I'm so sorry," she said abjectly. "She was so beautiful and in such terrible pain! I thought they gave pain medication to make the end easier. No one should suffer like that."

"She saved the pills and took them all at once. It wasn't pretty. She begged and pleaded until I had to read the books and tell her how to do it. I am not a *coward*. If I were a coward, I would have taken the pills myself and never have to remember that moment again. I do *not* want to remember it ever again. So you need to go play schoolteacher and leave me alone. There will be no more magnifying anything."

Because, judging from those brief interludes they'd shared, he was damned certain that transporting themselves back in time would create psychic bonds he didn't want.

"We'll have to solve Mrs. Kennedy's murder without your help," she said sadly. "I don't know how you live like that. I'm so sorry I pushed you. I don't know what came over me. I just wanted to be *useful* for a change."

She stood up and headed for the front door, shoulders slumped.

He felt like a rat. He'd felt worse. He watched her go. The sooner she moved out, the better off they both would be.

They'd traveled back in time. He didn't doubt it for a minute. The impressions had been too vivid, beyond anything he'd ever experienced.

The images he received from objects never contained smells or sounds or anything other than a vivid impression of emotion and an act, usually violent. He had a few pieces that reflected passion, like the loveseat, or the happiness of a new mother with her infant, or a man on the brink of proposal, but happiness was usually like water or perfume that spread thin and evaporated so he could only sense the emotion.

Unpleasant scenes, however, were corrosive acid, so destructive that they etched the object with the memories of the hatred and violence that caused a finger to pull a trigger or a hammer to hit a skull.

With Hannah, he not only saw but *sensed* the whole memory—and it didn't have to involve violence or any other emotion. Probably not real time travel, but as she said, a magnification of the vibrations he picked up. And in Natalie's case, he had the memory to accompany it.

Could they solve murders that way?

No, quite definitely *no*. He didn't take Tullah's warning lightly. He'd almost lost his soul when Natalie died. Prison had leached the life out of him. He was just now starting to find his feet again, to feel as if he might build what passed for a normal life. He wouldn't jeopardize that *or* the strange female whose shadowed eyes spoke of the mysteries of the northern isles he'd once called home.

Needing normality, Aaron sat at his desk to update his website. Before he had time to immerse himself, Walker called to warn him that the sheriff was sending a man to question him about last night.

So much for feeling as if he might have a normal life. Aaron flung his keyboard in his desk drawer. Anyone with a prison record had a target on his back, no matter how respectable he made himself. Walker might understand that Aaron would never kill a woman. A deputy steeped in law enforcement tradition only knew what he saw on paper.

He welled with resentment when the uniformed officer finally entered. Quelling the negativity, Aaron finished dealing with a customer, then turned to the uniformed intruder. He refused to offer his hand to shake. He didn't want to know where the deputy's hand had been last.

The cop went through the usual list of identifying questions, leaving the best for last. "You served time in prison for art fraud and theft?"

"I did. I don't believe that has anything to do with Mrs. Kennedy, since I assume that's why you're here." Deliberately dismissive, Aaron sat down again and removed his keyboard from the drawer.

"Not much difference in art theft and jewelry theft, is there?" the deputy asked. "I'll need a time line of your activities between ten and eleven last night and the names of witnesses."

"I was with Monty and Kurt Kennedy in the bar at the lodge, as I'm sure they told you." He hadn't been looking at his watch, but he knew there was a time gap between the time he'd left them and the time he'd found Carmel.

"They said you left before eleven," the deputy persisted.

The bell over the shop door rang. A wind carried in the fresh scent of sunshine and evergreens. He'd never noticed that before. Aaron looked up to see the librarian bearing down on them with golden fire lighting her eyes. Interesting. Most of the time, she looked so bland as to be invisible, but there was a dragon princess in there somewhere, if her expression now was any indication.

"They don't believe my whereabouts when Mrs. Kennedy was killed," she said in a tone of cold steel. "*We're* the ones who reported her screams and called the police, and *they don't believe me!*"

Aaron refrained from lifting a questioning eyebrow. There had been no "we" to it. She'd apparently run to the reception desk to fetch Roper and the Kennedys. He'd been outside, looking for evil demons. Apparently, he hadn't known what one looked like, because he'd passed half a dozen people and not one appeared to be a killer.

"You're saying this gentleman was with you before the call was placed?" the deputy asked, rightfully dubious.

"I stopped at the bar just as he was leaving. I'd wanted to go swimming, but the pool closes at ten, so I thought I'd have a drink. Aaron persuaded me otherwise. He was escorting me back to my room when we heard the screams. I heard running footsteps but saw no one. I'm not that familiar with the lodge," she stated indignantly. "So it's not as if I knew where to go except back to the lobby."

As much as he hated being defended by a woman, Aaron saw Lucy connivance for what it was. They were circling the wagons against outsiders. Since he knew he hadn't murdered Carmel and neither had the librarian, he didn't correct her take on things.

"There are two halls crossing the main one," Aaron said, drawing out the explanation to see where it would lead. "And outside doors at the end of every corridor, including Carmel's."

"But *you* went looking anyway," she said accusingly. "You could have been killed!"

She was a pretty good liar for looking so guileless. What the hell had driven her to defend him? He was sure he'd find out in due time.

"I didn't know anyone was being murdered. I just assumed that someone so weak they made an old woman scream wouldn't be difficult to tackle," he said, as if he'd ever tackled anyone in his life. "But I only saw people sticking their heads out to see what the racket was about."

"You'll have to talk to the people in those rooms," Hannah told the deputy, still looking huffy. "And look for someone who actually *needs* to steal things, if indeed, anything was stolen. I'm new here, and even I know Mrs. Kennedy was not liked by many people."

"You're the one she was yelling at in front of a whole party of people, aren't you?" the deputy asked, accusation in his voice. "Maybe you took a dislike to being thrown out of the lodge. Maybe she saw you and started yelling again."

Ah, now Aaron got it. She'd been wandering the halls alone when the deed was done. She needed his alibi as much as he did hers. Fair enough.

"The Kennedys assured me that I wouldn't be thrown out, that their mother could be irrational. Besides, I have plenty of other places to go. I wasn't in the least worried. But knowing there's a killer at large, I'm concerned about finding him, and that won't happen if you're focusing on innocent people just because they're easy targets. Surely you have forensic evidence that can provide more information than we can. Would you like some tea?" She turned her big fairy eyes to Aaron.

He assumed she wanted tea, so he nodded. "Please. Officer, would you care for tea?" He could feel generous now that Hannah had verbally slapped the poor man around a bit.

"No, thank you," the officer said grumpily. "And forensics has found evidence of the entire lot of you all over the room, so none of you are off the hook." He shoved his notepad in his belt, nodded, and strode out.

"Mariah send you?" Aaron asked, rising from his desk chair and following Hannah back to his electric kettle.

"Just about everyone in town sent me," she said with a half laugh. "And the other detective was even more obnoxious than this poor man. They really do think they can find a killer just by accusing us of being there. Thank all that's holy that Mariah just had the baby and wasn't there too. If they'd discovered who she really is, they'd hound her out of spite."

"And you're so sure that I didn't do it?" he asked, adding leaves to his teapot while she ran the water.

She flicked on the kettle switch and shot him an impatient look. "You proved you could have robbed the woman blind any time she left her room. You didn't have to kill her. And you had less reason to want to kill her than I did. So unless you happened to be in her room while she shouted at someone outside, and decided you were tired of listening to her, I'm just not seeing you as killer, no."

"Under your scenario, there should be two people who know what happened—one outside and one in. Since I was outside, maybe I'm covering for the person inside." He poured the boiling water over the leaves in the pot. "Lunch? I can call Fee and have someone deliver it."

He must be out of his mind, but her performance just now had left him gobsmacked. People didn't come to his rescue often. The librarian had hidden depths behind the round cheeks and flat expression.

"Maybe you thought Carmel deserved what she got and that her killer shouldn't suffer? Why do I feel as if that's unlikely? And Fee said she was sending over sandwiches." She washed out their cups in the small sink.

"Maybe I'm not likely to let a killer go, but I can think of a few dozen people around here who'd be quite happy to see Carmel dead and believe whoever did it had been well-intentioned. I probably saw half a dozen locals roaming the grounds as I circled the lodge."

"Have you told Walker who you saw?" she demanded.

"I did, and it's none of your business."

Aaron left her to contemplate that while he rummaged in his desk drawer for cash and met the café's runner at the door. The kid was the one Hannah had been brought in to teach. Zeke beamed at the tip and ran off again. Amber's nephew was an ambitious brat.

Hannah had set up his poker table with cups, teapot, and napkins by the time he returned with the brown bag. He'd given up telling the café's cook what he wanted within days of Fee's arrival. She always knew what he needed better than he did.

The way he felt right now, he hoped the sandwich was raw bloody meat.

"It's happening anyway, isn't it?" he said gloomily, removing the sandwiches and identifying his by the rare roast beef. Damn, the cook was good.

Hannah looked up questioningly from her bean sprouts.

"We're stuck working together in hopes of getting the law off our backs. It's not a big deal for you. I'm pretty sure no one will believe you arrived from Scotland to murder Carmel. But it's a pretty damned big deal to me. I've spent the last decade re-establishing my reputation. Even if they can't convict me, they can ruin my business with suspicion. I don't want to drag you into this, but if you can magnify or enhance what I feel. . ."

"We need some way of doing it without actually leaving our bodies," she said, sipping her tea with a delicate pinkie lifted, for all the world as if she were a Regency countess. "I was hasty in my eagerness to try again, I apologize. I've never been gifted, and the experience was rather thrilling."

"More thrills than you'd like if we happened to see a murder," he said gloomily. "Is there a means of enhancing my psychometry without getting ourselves trapped in another dimension?"

"I don't recall anything specific to our cases. Ives occasionally nulli-fied some of the worst aspects of Malcolm gifts, but I'd say Ives DNA is in your blood already, and it didn't help."

"Ives DNA? What makes you think that? I know I'm distantly related to Keegan somehow, but I don't know from which side." Aaron had known Keegan was related to the Marquess of Ashford, Earl of Ives and Wystan, but he'd assumed the connection was distant.

"Besides the genealogies, you have an Ives' nose, very patrician, just like Keegan's. From my reading, I think the original Ives descended from the engineering Romans, and the original Malcolms were descendants of druids, but that's all irrelevant in this day and age, isn't it? My Malcolm ancestor was part Mandarin. Tullah and Mariah are apparently different lineages entirely, so there may even be Chinese druids or Jamaican witches we don't know about. Our journal library only follows British Malcolm descendants and can't encompass everything there is to know. We may be venturing on unknown waters."

"There be dragons," he muttered. "What's the point of having weird talents if they can't be used for good purpose?"

She nibbled at her focaccia sandwich as she thought about it. "It depends entirely on the individual, of course. Some are risk takers, willing to do whatever it takes to achieve their goals. I'm afraid I'm more of a student, preferring to learn and teach, but that's because I've had no other opportunity. If we record everything we learn, then it's all for good purpose, isn't it?"

"But no one has recorded time travel, or whatever it is we did, have they?" He ripped off a hunk of roast beef and tried not to think murderous thoughts.

The lecturing teacher was silent a little too long. Aaron regarded her with suspicion.

A wayward sunbeam caught a strand of her gold bangs as she studiously avoided his gaze. Her velvet brown lashes brushed her pale cheeks as she picked at her bread. The librarian liked to give out her knowledge. Why was she reluctant now?

"Now you're worrying me," he admitted. "Has someone reported traveling back in time?"

"My great-great aunt," she murmured. "Her journals are in Mandarin. I think her daughters sent them to me because they couldn't read them."

"But you can read Mandarin, of course." Chilled, Aaron poured more tea.

She nodded without looking up. "My gift is knowledge. I have a good idea what's in all our books, even if I don't speak the language. But I learned Mandarin at my mother's knee. She insisted that I know because quite a few of our family journals are in that language."

"Walker's mother will love you," Aaron said sardonically. "I don't think she's a Lucy though. Shouldn't there be Chinese librarians?"

She shrugged. "There probably are more librarians than me. But my knowledge is of the British Malcolm branch, despite my distant heritage. Or because British Malcolms lived in China for generations."

"Quit pussyfooting around the question at hand," he said impatiently. "What aren't you telling me?"

She looked up and grimaced wryly at whatever she must have seen in his face. "My time-traveling great-great aunt lives in San Francisco. She's in her nineties now. She's quite insane."

ELEVEN

HANNAH HAD DINNER WITH KEEGAN AND MARIAH THAT EVENING. THE BABY was heart-meltingly delightful, but not a mind-reader, and Hannah had serious matters whirling in her head.

"Didn't persuade Aaron to come with you, did you?" Mariah taunted as they sipped coffee over a fruit tart from Fee's café.

"He's resistant to people," Hannah replied. "I understand why, but he must be lonely if he won't even make male friends."

"You're dealing with a town of alpha males. They'll never bond the way women do." Looking the picture of health with her shiny black braid hanging over her shoulder and her naturally bronzed skin glowing, Mariah pushed back from the table.

"We communicate," Keegan said, unperturbed by her classification and rising to clear the table. "You just don't always know about it. We'd do better if we had shared interests, but musty furniture does nothing for me. Grubbing in dirt doesn't excite Aaron. And Harvey. . . now there's your real loner."

"We know all about your beef-grilling manly get-togethers," Mariah said, checking on the rocking cradle they'd carried into the front room. "But discussing how to build a school is not the same as discussing feelings. All of you could be dying of cancer and not one of you would admit it."

Hannah hid her expression behind her coffee cup. She wasn't likely to discuss the walnut either. "The problem here is that we're all under suspicion over Carmel's death, and Aaron won't share what he knows. He's afraid *sharing* means communication, which means relationships."

Her landlord had more problems than that, but she wasn't ready to reveal their time traveling experience just yet either. Like Aaron, she was too accustomed to keeping to herself. She'd like that to change, but she wasn't entirely certain how to go about it.

"Let me see the image of that painting again." Deciding little Daphne wasn't waking yet, Mariah held out her hand for Hannah's phone. "I'll put it on the big screen. Maybe we're missing details."

Hannah handed over the phone and got up to dry the dishes that Keegan was washing. "The jewel box is there, but we can't see inside it. Maybe all jewel boxes looked like that back then."

"I tested the stone from Carmel's collection." Keegan wiped the last pan and set it in the drainer. "It's raw alexandrite, a particularly rare example from Tanzania. Alexandrite wasn't even discovered until the 1800s—which leads me to wonder if maybe I had more than one predecessor who collected stones, except he hid his discoveries so the world didn't know about them."

"Or if the collection has been added to over the centuries since your knight brought them home?" Hannah asked.

Keegan shrugged. "Rocks are eons old. I can't judge age. Given the vibrations I'm picking up from this one, I'd say it's been stored with a collection of equally rare stones."

"Sounds like the collection from your ancestor's jewel box, although how Carmel ended up with it is hard to imagine." Mariah switched on the wide screen TV and hit her keyboard. "There's the painting in Keegan's library, showing his knightly forebear presenting a box of raw gems to whoever the woman is."

Hanging the towel to dry, Hannah entered the front room to look more closely at the painting she remembered much too well. The knight didn't seem to have a goatee like the one who haunted her dreams. But he had the roman nose, bronzed complexion, and dark eyes of Keegan's family. The stones in the box looked like rough pebbles to her. "How does anyone recognize a gemstone when it's in that state?"

"Experience. And my gift helps. I assume my ancestor had something similar." Keegan leaned over the cradle to adjust the blanket around his sleeping daughter. "Many in my family do. I had one relation who could actually smell mineral deposits."

The domestic scene made Hannah want to weep in longing, but bent on learning as much as she could, she continued questioning. "If the police would let you touch that jewel box, could you tell how old it is?"

"That's Aaron's bailiwick. He may not always see clear images, but he's working on some method of judging time from the layers of memories on an object. Let's see Hannah's image of the Eversham." Keegan settled into his recliner to study the photographs Mariah flashed on the screen.

That sounded like Aaron, putting his gift to use to make money, although knowing an oil painting was an original was probably valuable knowledge for museums.

Hannah stood near the TV to study the images detail by detail. The Spanish knight could be an Ives, but the distinctive characteristics were shadowed by his helmet. He *did* sport a goatee, however. Interesting.

"I think I know where that is," Mariah said with interest. "My granny told me the stories about the old church on Kennedy property. There was a well in the same vicinity. She called the area evil and haunted. But Cass says the church is consecrated ground and safe. It's the area *outside* the church that is polluted. What she didn't say was that there are usually cemeteries outside churches."

"So the polluted area could be riddled with bodies?" Keegan asked in distaste.

"Given that the Victorian spiritualists began a new cemetery up by Cass and far from the old church, it's possible they abandoned an older one for reasons unknown." Mariah played with the image on the screen.

Hannah flipped through her mental index of Hillvale and American spiritualists, but as always, very little came up. Shipping journals to England would have been a precarious business from California until after the Gold Rush opened travel routes. Even then, the trip was hazardous.

"Many of the spiritualists in the late 1800s were charlatans. Given the number of gifted living here now, I assume there were also some real spiritualists, but they left no record. Is that when the church was built?"

"One of them. My gran said the one on resort property was built on the foundation of an older church, as usually happens. There's nothing there now but the evil vibrations surrounding it. The legends about Hillvale hauntings centered on the ranch where the lodge is now. After the ranch burned and the spiritualists told them the land was haunted, they moved down the hill and built the town instead. I'm guessing the gallery was once the Victorian church, and that they just abandoned the old one and started the new graveyard on Cass's land." Mariah expanded both images to show the jewel box.

"Looks like the same box to me." Keegan got up and pointed at initials etched among the elaborate engravings in both paintings. "AD 1453 and a crude Ives coat of arms. Over the centuries, the Ives shield got more elaborate than this one. Someone would have had to exactly duplicate those ancient details if the Spanish box is a copy."

Mariah picked up the phone and punched a button. "Walker, who has Carmel's jewel box? Can you ask them if there's a coat of arms and the date 1453 on it?" She hung up. "He's checking. I'll send him a screenshot."

"I wish Ives had kept journals," Hannah said fretfully. "Men were allowed to write back then without being deemed witches."

"They had their hands full slaying dragons," Keegan said with a snort. "And persuading recalcitrant witches to marry them, if this early painting is to be believed. I don't think the lady is impressed with the rocks though."

"Not if they're evil. But the Malcolm journal from that period calls one of them a healing stone. I wonder how they knew?" Restlessly, Hannah paced the small room stuffed with overlarge furniture. "I wish we could see inside that other box. If only one is a healing stone, why would they carry around a box of rocks?"

"The whole box was full in the medieval painting," Keegan pointed out. "From what I'm hearing, Carmel's cache was considerably lighter, with one large stone that's gone missing."

Hannah sighed. "This is hopeless. Would it help to have Lucys gather near that spot on the Eversham painting if you know where it is?"

Mariah grimaced and shook her head. "That's the center of the evil *malum* as Aaron calls it. We avoid it for fear it might pollute us. Both Aaron and Harvey can show you. Take your stick though."

"I was on an archeological dig one summer." Suddenly inspired, Hannah perked up. "I'm not a sensitive, so bad vibrations won't affect me. I want to dig that area where they're standing, see if the painting really is telling us something. There's a well and a boulder. It shouldn't be hard to find."

Mariah looked dubious. "It's probably one immense graveyard dating back to the first missionaries or earlier. The original inhabitants probably came over before Christ was born. Just because you don't feel the evil, doesn't mean it isn't there. We're convinced Carmel was affected, and she's not even a Lucy."

But if Hannah's time was limited, that didn't matter. She'd find it. Finally, she had a purpose. She waved aside Mariah's objections and changed the subject.

"Aaron said he saw a number of locals near the lodge the night Carmel died. One of them could be a witness. Have you heard anyone mention being there?" Hannah returned to the kitchen to refill her teacup.

"Watch out," Keegan warned. "That's Hannah being devious."

"But it's a good question." Mariah disconnected the TV images and played her keyboard like a piano. "I've been distracted and not keeping up."

"I can't imagine why," Hannah said jestingly, hovering over the cradle to watch Daphne squirm. "I'd rather cuddle babies than look up crime scenes too."

"And walk the floor when they scream, and feed and diaper them at every bloody hour of the night and day," Keegan said with parental pride.

"Here it is." Mariah focused on her mission. "The police have been interviewing everyone at the lodge. Their notes are pretty brief."

"You're sitting there looking at the sheriff's report?" Hannah asked, still amazed that such a thing was possible.

"Men," Mariah said in disgust. "They're territorial and competitive. The sheriff won't tell Walker what he's doing, and Walker doesn't tell anyone anything. Someone has to communicate."

"Mundanes have no way of knowing who to trust," Keegan pointed out reasonably.

Mariah acknowledged that excuse with a shrug. "It takes time to file paperwork. But here's Aaron's report to Walker. Orval the vet was there with Brenda, the nurse—two healers, nice. He said he saw Lance—that's Carmel's brother. Lance has a cabin right there, so that's expected."

Hannah typed text notes on her phone. Her memory was visual, not auditory. "We saw Lance with Val in the gallery not long after we left the crime scene. That's quite a hike for him to be there so quickly. Does he drive?"

"Carmel has a chauffeur. He might have taken Lance down. The chauffeur is on Aaron's list too, so that's a good possibility. He lives at the lodge."

"Francois is about to be fired, if I heard Kurt correctly," Keegan interjected. "The Kennedys were cutting back on their mother's extravagances, and her chauffeur was on the list."

Mariah grimaced. "Francois is a shiftless, blackmailing sycophant. Carmel would have found some way to keep him because he worshipped her. Here's an interesting bit—Pasquale and Wan Hai were there together!"

"Good for them," Keegan said. "They've been yelling at each other for ages. It's time to get it out of their system. Maybe this wedding business is turning Hillvale into a lover's nest."

Hannah had no idea who these names were but she dutifully added the information to her phone.

Mariah's silence was telling. Hannah waited. Keegan didn't. He confiscated the laptop. "Xavier? Why shouldn't an old bachelor like him be at the lodge? He likes to eat and drink the same as anyone else."

Keegan turned to Hannah to explain. "Have you met Xavier? Older guy, acts as the Kennedy rental agent. Used to be a lawyer until he started hanging out in the commune and got into drugs."

Hannah remembered Xavier showing her around the new school house. He seemed businesslike and nice enough.

"There was a competition between Carmel and Cass over Xavier back in the day," Mariah said quietly. "I think that's why Cass married a man she didn't love and never married again after her first husband died. I think Cass and Xavier both have reason to hate Carmel."

She wouldn't say more. Daphne began to whimper, and Hannah excused herself, figuring the new parents needed time alone with their infant.

So, Xavier and Cass. . . Maybe Xavier wouldn't *kill* Carmel, but if he'd been a witness, he might not tell who had. Interesting.

~

AARON CLEANED UP THE REMAINS OF HIS DINNER, THEN SETTLED AT HIS DESK to update his inventory list. He did this occasionally, when Harvey was entertaining at the house. He refused to admit that he was lingering, waiting for his renter to return.

Hannah had been unhappy with him for not sharing the names of potential witnesses. He'd been less than happy with her when she'd refused to tell him more about her time-traveling relative. He was used to keeping his own counsel.

But she'd been the one to come to rescue him from the law, not any of the other Lucys.

Yeah, she had a reason for that, but once Walker had warned them the sheriff's men were in town, the Lucys could have invented any number of alibis. He'd never worried about his position in Hillvale. The place crawled with empaths and psychics who knew he was honest. He could have lived anywhere in the world, but Hillvale offered him acceptance, and he was grateful.

He heard a key in the back-door lock. His renters always preferred to enter through the storage area rather than the maze of his main shop. She should see his light on.

He hadn't really expected her to seek him out, but, he heard her turn toward his office. He glanced up. In the shadows of the storage area's lone nightlight, Hannah possessed that ethereal air again. She wore her hair up tonight, with a few curled ringlets to soften the effect. The simple sun dress emphasized the paleness of her skin and firm, youthful curves.

"Mariah says you know the spot where the Spaniard and the priest stood in the Eversham painting. Could you take me there?"

His first reaction was an irritable *don't be a bampot*. The idea didn't even deserve a Latin curse but one from his childhood. But he had to remember that Hannah *knew* things. And weigh it with his own desire to know more.

"It's not safe," he warned, because he wasn't capable of letting her trot off without understanding.

"It's evil, yadda yadda," she said with an irritating wave of dismissal. "It might even be an old burying ground and the natives won't want it disturbed. Got that too. But Eversham painted that scene for a reason, and I doubt that it was so we could dig up the Spaniard's bones. He included that jewel box deliberately."

"Because it was in the scene he saw in his dreams." In equal irritation, Aaron shut down his computer. "Evil is real. For all we know, in that image they'd just buried the devil and rolled a boulder over him."

"Oh, I hadn't thought of that!" She actually brightened in anticipation. "The boulder might be concealing the Healing Stone. Is it still there? Will it be impossible to move?"

If he didn't show her where it was, she'd traipse all over creation in search of it. Aaron stood and loomed over her, testing his ability to intimidate.

She glared back defiantly and didn't budge. So much for that hope.

"I'll show you the boulder—if you'll take me to meet your insane great-great-aunt."

He'd had all evening to work out that demand. He still wasn't entirely certain why instinct said he had to meet a time traveler.

He had the horrifying notion now that it was because he wanted to know more about the stubborn, aggravating, *glowing* gold leprechaun who'd landed on his doorstep.

Natalie had promised to send him angels. He was pretty certain, despite her unearthly innocence, that Hannah wasn't one.

TWELVE

"I DON'T KNOW WHY YOU WANT TO WASTE YOUR TIME VISITING A NINETY-three-year-old mental patient," Hannah griped as Aaron drove his van down the highway the next morning.

She had a nervous feeling that she did understand, but she didn't want him to take an interest in her or her near-to-nonexistent abilities. And she really wasn't ready to tackle her family just yet, although she supposed she should. That was the only reason she was in his van right now. She had no other means of visiting the city.

"I don't either." Brown hand on the steering wheel, he fiddled with the audio. "But you're hell-bent on learning things you know nothing about, and that isn't healthy."

She could explain why nothing she did was healthy, but that wasn't any of his damned business. "This won't help find Carmel's killer."

"Let Walker find a killer. That's not our job. We'll go in, have a nice visit, eat lunch somewhere that doesn't include bean sprouts, and then map out a plan on the way home." He tuned in a classical station from his phone.

Her mouth watered at the thought of good Chinese, or maybe Thai. Positive—she should think positively. "It won't be a nice visit for you. The home will call my parents. Every relative available on short notice will descend on us. You'll hate every minute." That thought made her smile—see that was positive.

"Charming. You could have warned me sooner." He didn't turn the van around.

"Tell me more about this plan we're to map out," she suggested, cheering up by the minute.

"Not until we see if I come out of this alive," he muttered. "Do you have a plan for telling your family why you're visiting a mental patient?"

She grinned at the dozen replies immediately coming to mind. She settled on the easiest one. "I'll tell them I'm thinking of having myself committed."

"Oh good, that will do it," he said sardonically. "I'll tell them I'm your doctor, and you've been behaving irrationally. I'm guessing your family will be happy to agree."

"They won't care one way or another," she said with a dismissive wave. "I've been on my own since fifteen. My family accepted that I have an encyclopedia for a brain, and that there isn't much they can tell me. I have a small trust fund that financed my education and travels. They all have their own interests, so it works out."

He apparently stewed over that the rest of the way into the city. Hannah directed him to the small, exclusive home Aunt Jia had chosen to live out the rest of her days. Time travel had some benefits. Aunt Jia was not a poor woman.

Aaron said nothing as they presented ID at the gate, parked in the landscaped lot, and wandered a garden path back to a private courtyard where a keypad allowed her to type in her password.

"As the song goes, Aunt Jia can check out any time she likes." Hannah tried for cheerful, but losing one's mind wasn't a cheerful business.

"But she can never leave?" He finished the refrain, showing he was paying attention.

"I'm not certain she knows how any longer. You'll see." It had been several years since she'd last visited family. Her great aunt had been spry and bright and had called her Mei.

Hannah opened the gate into her aunt's cement yard. Potted plants thrived, evidence that her aunt still maintained her gardening skills. A small round table and two chairs offered a place to sit in the sun. The door was open as if they were expected. Hannah pushed a button that emitted the music of wind chimes.

"Come in, come in, I have your teacakes ready," a faint voice called from the interior. "Your mother is in Portland this week but she sends her love. I believe some of the cousins are coming to make certain you aren't here to talk me out of my fortune."

Hannah grinned. "Having one of your mean days, Aunt Jia, are you?" She led the way to the tiny gallery kitchen.

She hadn't called to tell her aunt they were coming.

Jia may have once been five-feet, at most. Bent and shrunken with age, she didn't reach that any longer. Still, her gnarled hands reached for the teapot with steady confidence. "Sorry, it happens sometimes. Your cousins don't seem able to comprehend just how much I know and see."

Her aunt looked up, and her long, narrow eyes widened. "Ah, your prince has come! It was only a matter of time. I'm so glad you've finally found him again. This time, don't let him slip through your fingers."

Aaron offered a courtly bow. If he was nonplussed by Jia's reaction, he didn't show it. "My lady, it is a pleasure to meet you."

Jia laughed. "I like this one. Come along, Mei, let us wait for your cousins. Bring the tea tray, please."

Mei, the name Jia had called her last time. Hannah couldn't explain any of this to Aaron, so he'd have to just observe.

"We've come to pick your brain, *Ayi.*" Hannah used the easiest term for aunt, to remind Jia who she was. "How did you learn to return from your time travels?"

She didn't look at Aaron as she set the tea tray on the low table beside her aunt's chair. Although Jia seemed to accept him as someone she knew, he wasn't family. He didn't get to interfere.

"I just do, dear. I'm there, then I'm not. That's the last of the lotus blossom. Drink while it's hot." She poured the tea—which had been made from teabags and not lotus blossoms.

"Don't eat or drink anything," Hannah whispered to Aaron, before setting her cup to one side.

"Your tea is always delicious, *Ayi.* So you simply touch an object and see another time?"

"The missionary is late," Jia replied. "Check with the maid to see if she can see them."

Which probably meant her cousins were on the way. Unruffled, Hannah accepted a hard cookie her aunt passed to her. "I am sure they're coming up the road. Give them a few minutes. What era do these cups represent?" She examined the delicate porcelain adorned with the tiny brushstrokes of hand painting.

"Oh, I just bought these from. . ." Her eyes narrowed and she pushed the cup to one side of her tray. "I don't remember. You must return to England with the missionaries. It's not safe here any longer. Your prince will find you there."

"I shall, *Ayi*. I think I hear my cousins now. Shall I refill the teapot?" Without waiting for an answer, Hannah confiscated the tea tray and collected the cups. She'd rather not poison anyone if her aunt had decided to medicate the teapot.

The doorbell chimed as she turned on the kettle. She heard Aaron's rumbling voice, and breathed a little in relief that he seemed to accept the Looking Glass world he'd plunged into.

"I brought tea and cakes," her cousin called. "We don't want to poison you just yet."

"Frannie, I haven't seen you in ages." Hannah cleaned out the teapot and heated it with hot water. "Bring me the tea. I'm just preparing a fresh pot."

Considerably older than Hannah, Francesca was a lithe, athletic airplane pilot—and a psychic, dangerous to be around.

"He's gorgeous," her cousin whispered. "Where'd you find him? Will you keep him?"

"That would be akin to caging a wild cougar, don't be silly."

"Then may I try? You're too young for that one."

"Experience counts?" Hannah snorted. "Open the cakes and pass them around before someone attempts Jia's biscuits. I hope the home is providing her meals or she'll poison herself one day." Hannah accepted the tea Francesca handed her and filled the strainer.

"They're getting better at learning her plants," Frannie admitted. "And they confiscate her grocery deliveries before they arrive to be certain they don't include rat poison. What are you doing here? Couldn't you call your parents and arrange a real visit?"

"It's complicated." She filled the pot with boiling water and carried the newly prepared tray back to the front, where her cousin Jack leaned against a wall. Sturdy, with more Asian DNA than Hannah, he saluted her with a middle finger. Hannah stuck her tongue out at him.

Aaron had abandoned his seat, leaving the chair for Francesca. Hannah made hasty introductions while she set the tea tray beside her aunt.

"I hope you have come to take Mei Ling to the village," Jia said fretfully. "The king's men will take her if you do not. Her future is not here."

"She's safe with us, *Ayi*," Jack assured her. "Let us have our tea, and we'll take her away."

"Good. Don't let her go back to the mountains. Evil lurks there." Jia bit into her cake.

Hannah grimaced at Aaron's pointed look. "She can be talking a mountain in China a thousand years ago," she reminded him.

"And it's not *evil* you fear, is it?" Frannie asked.

"Keep your nosy mind to yourself, big cousin." There were few secrets she could keep from a psychic, but Hannah could hide her walnut. "I have come here to learn from Aunt Jia, not to entertain you. Aaron, was there a specific question you wished to ask?"

"Were you ever in danger when you traveled outside your body?" he asked politely.

Jia snorted. "Of course. Try grabbing a runaway horse and losing yourself in a palace at the same time. You ask foolish questions, my lord."

Aaron picked up a jade elephant from the bookshelf, blinked in surprise, then put it back. "You were very fortunate to escape when you did. I am sorry your father did not make it with you."

Hannah refrained from rolling her eyes. Just what she needed, another freak in her freaky family to keep the conversation on cosmic levels. Aaron was reading her aunt's most treasured possessions. Her British-raised aunt had escaped China at a time of revolution.

Her cousins waited as expectantly as she did. Jia's wrinkled face expressed confusion, then resignation as she set down her cup.

"He saved us, all of us. None of us would be here today if he had not acted when he did. I go back to see him from time to time." She nodded her white-haired head and seemed to fall asleep.

Francesca picked up the tea tray this time. "Lunch? There's a good restaurant right down the road."

~

IT HAD NOT BEEN AARON'S INTENTION TO SHARE HANNAH OVER LUNCH. Nor had he intended to eat at another rabbit food restaurant. But Hannah and her family intrigued him, and he hoped to learn more, especially after perusing the wine menu. Rabbit food came with a nice selection of alcohol to anesthetize the taste of grass.

"Are you back for good then?" Francesca asked after placing her order.

"Who knows?" Hannah replied gracelessly. Apparently unaccustomed to the choices in a San Francisco restaurant as compared to a pub in the islands, she was still working her way through the menu.

Aaron ordered a bottle of wine and leaned over to point out a selection, catching a whiff of sunshine cologne that stirred senses better left unstirred. "This will work well with the bottle I just ordered. I like to work backward from the wine."

Hannah intelligently accepted his suggestion and handed her menu back to the waiter. She wore earrings today, apparently her idea of dressing up. Otherwise her outfit merely consisted of jeans and a blue tank top. The swingy little turquoise pendants peeked from beneath strands of silky gold hair and brushed her slender throat—the one he'd probably strangle before the meal ended, if only to put him out of his misery.

"Need a little alcoholic help to imagine holding on to a horse while your spirit inhabits a palace?" she asked tauntingly.

"If I was inclined to imagination, I'd consider much more interesting possibilities," he said smoothly, before turning to her cousins. "Has your aunt always talked in circles or was there a time when she was more lucid?"

"We were infants when she was still fully functional," Jack said.

"We've only known her slow deterioration. But she's always been able to take care of herself, so it's no normal disease."

"She simply inhabits several worlds and times," Francesca said with nonchalance. "We don't know how she originally slipped back and forth. Everyone from her youth is gone now."

"We can't even know if she's talking of memories or if she's still slipping through time." Hannah tasted the wine the waiter poured and nodded approvingly. "*Mei* is apparently someone she knew in some life or another. She often mistakes me for her."

"You planning on time traveling?" Francesca asked perceptively. "Don't think we failed to notice your connection to the jade elephant, Aaron. Jia brought that piece from China. The story is that her father gave it to her as a symbol of his love the night they fled."

"I'm a psychometrist, that's all. I'm not planning anything. I simply want to stay informed." Unaccustomed to this level of perceptiveness outside of Hillvale, Aaron preferred to keep his thoughts to himself—as much as was possible with a psychic even stronger than Amber.

"Don't let him touch your ring, Frannie," Hannah warned, sniffing the soup that had just been delivered. "You really don't want Aaron to know who you are. Jack is the one you want to know, Aaron. He can find anything. Bit of a nuisance, actually, if one doesn't wish something found."

The very normal librarian seemed to fit right into Aaron's weird world, as his parents and friends never had. The cousins teased and quarreled just as any family might, and he settled in to appreciate the phenomenon.

If he hadn't appointed himself guardian against Hillvale's evil, he might enjoy building a world-wide network of eccentrics like himself. It might be even more useful than Hannah's ancient journals.

Later, edgy and frustrated after parting from the cousins after lunch, Aaron considered helping Hannah into his van just to see what happened when he touched her.

She sensibly grabbed the door and hoisted herself inside. Now that they had cell transmission, she was buckled in and reading her phone by the time he climbed into his seat.

"Keegan says the jewel box from Carmel's closet has the same date and shield on it as the one in the paintings," she reported. "How did Carmel get her hands on that box? And why?"

"A box that old has dangerous levels of memories, so I didn't dare open myself to it. Carmel's greed overrode everything in that closet. Chances are good that prior owners may have considered it no more than an old box of rocks. But it is peculiar that *Carmel* would recognize them as valuable." Aaron studied the road signs and wondered what it would be like to be normal and simply take a route to the beach and a quiet hotel with an interesting woman at his side.

He'd lost all that with Natalie.

Hannah put her phone away and frowned at the road ahead. "Would it take too long to make a quick side trip to Pacifica so I could dip my toes in the ocean again? It's been a long time since I've done that."

Aaron narrowed his eyes and wondered if she was taking up her cousin's habit of mind reading, but her request was perfectly reasonable. Even *he* was feeling the effect of a relaxed meal and sunshine. He followed the road sign that had caught his attention.

"Tide's in. Doesn't leave much beach," he observed as they located a parking spot and wandered the beach trail.

She threw back her head to absorb the sun on her face, letting her golden hair cascade over her shoulders. Her hair was thicker than it was long, he observed, just right for burying his hands in. He clenched said hands behind his back as they walked.

"I just needed to be reminded of the ordinary world," she said. "Sometimes, living inside one's head is stultifying."

"*Stultifying*, good word. We become numb to the real world around us when we're forced to spend so much time dealing with our paranormal abilities." He'd never really had anyone to discuss this with. Keegan and Harvey were the only other men he knew with odd gifts, and they weren't exactly communicative.

She took off her shoes, rolled up her jeans, and ran through the sand to let waves splash her feet. Aaron had no particular urge to bare his feet and chill them to the bone, but he enjoyed watching Hannah play with the surf. It struck him that she was considerably younger than he, in more ways than physical age. Or maybe he just felt old.

He bought her an ice cream while she let her feet dry off. "This was a nice break," he said. "I probably should do this more often."

"You'd need a better cashier than Harvey or you'd go broke." She laughed and licked her cone. "Couldn't you hire help from the next town down? It's not that bad a commute."

"Yes, I could hire someone. And no, I probably won't." They ambled back to the van. Aaron checked his watch. "We won't be back until closing. I can't remember a time when I took a whole day off. It's a good thing you'll be teaching soon so you don't infect me with your bad habits."

"You're planning on spending the next thirty-plus years of your life huddled behind a desk in that gloomy cave? You'll turn into a vampire. Tell me your master plan." She wiped off her hands with a tissue from her purse.

It took him a moment to remember their morning conversation. "I have no master plan. We're supposed to discuss your insane desire to dig up evil, and my desire to keep you from doing so." That put him on firm, familiar ground. He let the sunshine laziness dissipate.

"Well, we could look for whoever stole Carmel's stone, I suppose," she said with what sounded like sincerity. "But that means looking for a killer, and you said to leave that to Walker."

"Why don't you just help set up the school?" he asked in exasperation. They were right back where they'd started.

"Because the real teacher they hired to teach the little kids knows far more than I do. I will be little more than a glorified babysitter. I have a massive *encyclopedia* in my head, but Google will be more useful to Zeke than I am. I am *tired* of collecting dust. You should be too." She glared out the windshield.

"There have to be ten thousand better ways of shaking off dust than directly defying evil," he grumbled. She was making him feel older by the minute. "You have your entire life ahead of you. Learn to be a teacher. Help kids."

She sulked in silence for a few blessed minutes. Or maybe she was just plotting.

"I don't want to drop dead in front of kids." She broke the silence with a bombshell.

"I knew it." Aaron pounded the wheel in frustration. "When I first saw you, you said you were dying and told me to go away, so I did. But you haven't said anything since, so I assumed you were dreaming."

"As if *you* would mention it if it were you," she scoffed. "I don't want people pulling the poor, poor, pitiful Hannah act. I'm fine. I could live to be a hundred. But I apparently have a time bomb in my brain."

"An aneurysm? Can't they fix that?" he asked in alarm.

"They don't know what it is. They can't touch it. It's apparently smack in the middle of neuron central or something. If they operate, I could turn into a turnip. Not being fond of turnips, I refused to let them probe. I get weird spells, big deal. But living with a time bomb means I want to accomplish what I can *now*. Why should I be superstitious and refrain from researching the Eversham painting if I might die tomorrow? It's patently ridiculous."

She was quite vehement in her argument. Aaron could understand that. He was just too shattered for a comeback. She was so damned *alive*. For a few hours, he'd entertained notions he hadn't entertained in years. And now. . .

He cursed loud and long and apparently effectively because she shut up.

When he wound down, she looked at him with interest.

"Huh, even my Latin couldn't keep up with all that. You've had practice. Re-living our Roman ancestry, are we?"

Only Hannah would consider that. He sighed and beat his fist against the wheel again before speaking.

"I collected Roman artifacts when I was a kid, along with roaming the antique stores. I picked up strong impressions from the soldiers, including words. That made me want to know what they were saying or thinking. It gave me something to do while I sat around the house waiting for my parents to come home."

There, he'd said that without screaming curses at the universe.

"Did you ever figure out what the coins were saying?"

She looked sad as she leaned her head against the window. He wanted her laughing and turning her face to the sun again. He understood why that wouldn't happen.

"Mostly, the soldiers were counting the days and the coins until they could go home. As an adult, I would have figured that out on my own. Back then, I was still learning. How did you learn about the brain thing?"

She shrugged. "I was having dreams or visions, even in daylight. They had a very real quality different from any other kind of dream I've ever had. I went to a neurologist who called for an MRI. I'm almost sorry I did."

"That explains why you faint on me occasionally?"

She frowned as they pulled into the Hillvale parking lot. "Maybe. It's never happened when I touched anyone else."

He climbed out and deliberately walked around to help her down, holding up his hand in challenge.

She took it, and he fell into her dream.

THIRTEEN

Her bare fingers held the rough grip of a knight in dusty metal. Hannah glanced down. Their touching hands didn't seem translucent. She looked up again, into a face so much like Aaron's that she searched for the small mole he had near his ear. If it was there, she couldn't tell because of the helmet.

He seemed a little stunned as well. He traced a rough brown hand down her cheek, brushing her headpiece back to study her hair.

The touch was brief, too brief. A small brown dog ran up, barking. She turned to hush it, and the spell broke.

She was leaning against Aaron's van, no longer holding his hand. She clung to the moment, hoping for that simple caress one more time. It didn't happen.

"You didn't faint." He closed the door and locked it, not giving any indication he'd shared the vision.

"I might yet. This time was different." She didn't let go of the van just yet but refused to let him get away with stonewalling. "What did you see?"

"You fell into Keegan's medieval knight painting," he stated coldly.

"No dog in the painting." Idiotically relieved that she hadn't been the only one suffering that weird vision, she straightened to test her balance. Deciding she wouldn't fall over, she headed for the antique store.

He followed her across the lot as if she might tumble over at any strong breeze.

"The painting started the visions, I think. It hung right over my desk. I had to get out of there." She needed to re-orient her universe.

"You need to get out of Hillvale," he muttered.

Yeah, maybe that, too, but not yet. "I'll ask Mariah how to find the boulder. Or look for it myself."

Still shaken, Hannah waved at Harvey as she entered the gloom of the antique shop. If she was going to end up like Aunt Jia anyway, she may as well attempt to accomplish the impossible.

Aaron was on her heels as she climbed the stairs. She ignored him as much as she was able.

If she wanted to believe a dream or a painting, they'd *known* each other in some prior life, and she thought it might have been a Biblical knowing. She could feel him in more ways that she thought credible.

She pulled her hiking boots out of her backpack, put them on, and tied a flannel shirt around her waist in case she stayed out until dark.

Aaron glowered. He'd probably pace, if there'd been room for it. She couldn't honestly blame him. She'd sucked him into her world.

"You should relieve Harvey," she told him, picking up her walking stick. "If he was up wandering all night as usual, he's probably operating on two hours sleep."

Aaron eyed the walking stick, then set out down the stairs. "Harv, close up for me, will you? Miss Persistence wants to play with the devil."

"I want to play archeologist," she corrected, following him down. "Where can I find shovels and gloves?"

"You'll lose light before you can dig. Stake where you want to dig first." Aaron disappeared into his back room, returning with short sticks and a mallet.

Harvey watched as if they were an entertaining TV show.

Aaron unhooked his walking stick from the wall. "If we're not back by dark, search the old church. And if we glow after we return, stake us."

Harvey's lips twitched as he handed Hannah a pair of work gloves. "Irritate him some more. I like it."

"He's too easy," she scoffed. "Just tell him *no.*"

"You didn't tell me no," Aaron shouted from the front of the—fortunately—empty shop. "You just insist on getting yourself killed."

"He's a guardian," Harvey said. "He can't help himself."

Guardian? Hannah ran that word through her extensive library as she hurried to follow Aaron. Knight—lord—soldier—all showed up with some frequency in Malcolm annals, not always in congenial terms. Women taking risks attracted a certain masculine element, apparently.

Aaron might be the modern equivalent—with the added twist of paranormal DNA. Dangerous.

Instead of taking the steep drive up the hill to the lodge, he took a beaten path out of town and down the mountain. Hannah actually needed her stick for balance to keep up with his long strides. Aaron was obviously familiar with the path. She wasn't.

Just as the trail veered out of rocks and boulders and toward a stand of evergreens, Aaron pointed at a side track. "My place."

He walked on. Hannah halted to study the wood-sided and glass structure hidden behind a grove of trees that appeared to have been deliberately planted to conceal. "Nice," she called after him.

He didn't acknowledge the compliment.

Aaron had channeled his talent into wealth, she remembered. He could have built a palace in the woods. It appeared as if he'd remodeled a sprawling 70's style California ranch house instead.

Using her stick, she hurried to catch up. The ground here was a little more level, but she could sense it was climbing again. The lodge sat on top of the bluff overlooking the town valley. They seemed to be circling around it from the opposite direction of the public entrance.

They crossed more dust, rocks, and sage. "Have you told Samantha about this path? It could use a few roses."

He grunted. Maybe she could smack him across the back of the skull with her stick.

Of course, she'd revealed her death warrant to him pretty crudely. She wasn't entirely certain why she'd told him at all.

Yeah, she did—because she'd wanted to warn him. Their day had been too pleasant. They'd been in semi-danger of falling in like. With his history, he deserved better.

He had a really rotten history if he was the rejected knight in the painting. She must have been a nun in a prior life. No, that wasn't right, not if she'd known the knight intimately. Maybe she imagined that part. Maybe she imagined everything.

They passed a clump of cottonwood that seemed better suited to valleys than a place where cactus grew. How did she know that was cottonwood?

Rummaging through her memories for trees, she nearly ran into Aaron's back when he abruptly halted.

Dry grass rippled in a breeze across a clearing—she remembered this place. She'd fallen asleep here—right in the middle of an evil cemetery?

The boulder was on the left of the grassy clearing. The cottonwood grew on higher ground to the right.

Cottonwood—she finally found the reference. It grew where there was water—the well.

"Harvey thinks water gathers up the mountain and flows underground through here. He's been trying to find the source, hoping it's clear of whatever pollutes this area." Aaron held his stick up over the trail. "The *malum* is strong today. I'm not sure we should continue."

Hannah examined the crystal-eyed guardian angel knob on her stick and waited for the signal other Lucys experienced. "I don't feel anything." Accustomed to disappointment on the magical end of things, she studied the shady grove where the well must once have been, and its distance from the sun-drenched boulder. This had to be the area from the painting. If the rock the priest had been blessing was still around, she couldn't tell from this angle. "Where was the church, can you tell?"

He pointed uphill from the cottonwood grove. "Right where you were sleeping. Until you woke up, I had to wonder if you were an angel fallen from the sky."

"Fanciful. Angels wear backpacks? I was jetlagged and looked like hell." Dismissing his superstition, Hannah set off toward the cottonwoods.

"I was tired and the sun was setting." He loped alongside her, keeping pace. "I'm entitled to hope the veil had spit out a little heavenly help in beating back whatever pollutes this ground. Personally, I'm thinking the old well was a portal to hell."

"I don't believe in angels and demons," she said flatly. "I can believe in Mariah's ectoplasm theories easier than I can believe in evil and benevolent beings who aren't just us."

"Live here long enough and you'll broaden your horizons." He halted again, this time grabbing her arm to hold her back.

She weaved, feeling the air go blurry again. With resolution, she yanked her arm from his grip. Aaron looked a bit dazed as well, but he shook it off as she did.

"Sorry. I wasn't thinking. Look." He pointed his staff in the direction of the cottonwoods.

Crumpled navy lay among the long grasses. A homeless person all the way out here? She caught a glint of gold on the rags. She instinctively took a step to see better. Aaron shoved his stick in front of her.

"Don't. With our luck, we'll be disturbing a crime scene. I need to see if he's alive."

Hannah widened her eyes and stood on tip-toe as Aaron walked closer, waving his staff in the direction of the blue. Was that a shovel sticking out from under the blue? And over-turned dirt? She covered her mouth and tried not to shout at Aaron to get back here *now*.

He stooped down, touched the shovel, but didn't linger over the crumpled blue. Looking as angry as he did sad, he got up and marched past her, back down the path, evidently expecting her to keep up. She did, half-running to match his pace.

"What?" she demanded.

"Francois, Carmel's chauffeur. He loved his gaudy uniform."

"Her chauffeur? Was that a shovel? Was he digging at the *well*?" Hannah couldn't decipher the mix of horror and shock whirling her around. She'd never met the man. He was nothing more than blue rags to her. But he was *dead*? Right where she'd wanted to dig?

"Could have been a heart attack," Aaron said. "As far as I'm aware, the man never lifted a hand to so much as change a tire. It's *where* he dropped dead that concerns me."

And her. This was not a normal coincidence. "And you know for certain he's dead?" she asked in horror. "Couldn't we try CPR?"

"Flies are buzzing," he said curtly. "He's been there a while."

She wanted to vomit. "We need cell phone towers," she muttered instead.

"Not in Hillvale. Watch. I'm amazed they're not here already. Cell towers would interfere." He hurried up the trail, looking determined.

Hannah heard them before she saw them—a low humming chant, a dirge, like the one the Lucys had sung over Carmel. "How?" she demanded.

Aaron shrugged. "Val says she knows when a spirit departs the body. She should have been here hours ago. The others—hell if I know. I figure it's Cass. Maybe it's our sticks. But I triggered it the second I waved my staff near the body."

"Val didn't come when Carmel died," Hannah reminded him. "Wasn't there something about Carmel having no soul?"

"I'd like to say superstitious poppycock, but there could very well be something to it. But first you'd have to believe in selling souls to the devil." He stopped in a narrow place along the trail, placing himself between the approaching women and the body on the other side of the hill.

Cass led the way. Tullah was close behind her, along with Brenda the nurse. Samantha, Teddy, and Fee held back, ambling along with Mariah, who probably shouldn't be out of the house at all. Val drifted off to one side, through the evergreen shadows.

"It's Francois, and it's too late," Aaron told them. "Someone needs to call Walker. If you want a ceremony, do it here. The *malum* is agitated."

Cass glared at him before ordering her troops. "Hannah, if you'll lead the way, take Mariah and her friends to Aaron's place to make your calls. The rest of us will stay here to properly send off any lingering spirit. Even if he has departed across the veil, he could be lingering in confusion. All souls deserve a farewell."

Hannah glanced at Aaron for approval of this authoritarian command.

He merely handed her his keys and continued blocking Cass. "Do you remember the trail?" he asked, keeping his eye on Val in the distance.

"I think so." She pushed past him, thinking Mariah should be sitting down and not out here singing at missing spirits.

The others didn't argue over Cass's command. More Hannah's age, the ones told to turn around possessed Hannah's skepticism, she could tell from their murmurs as they hiked back the way they'd come.

"I can't imagine Francois ever had a soul," Mariah said. "I could hang ghostcatchers all over the clearing and they'd come up empty."

"Cass isn't taking chances with us," Samantha said serenely. "I'm carrying a child who could be affected, much as you may have been affected by Daisy."

"Affected or infected?" Teddy asked with decided irreverence for Malcolm beliefs.

Val's soaring soprano rose over the low conversation. Hannah wanted to stop and admire the beauty of her song, but the others hurried on.

"Walker is still with the sheriff down the mountain," Sam said worriedly. "His phone works there, but it will take time for him to drive up."

Hannah indicated the less battered trail leading toward Aaron's house. "Aaron said Francois could have died of a heart attack. There's no urgency in that case."

"Aaron sent us all back together and is standing out there guarding Cass," Teddy pointed out. "He's afraid there's a killer lurking."

"The air reeks of must and mildew," Fee said sadly, finally speaking up. "Some of that is Francois. He smelled like a dead rat who dried up in the walls."

The usually unobtrusive cook drew looks of shock and disgust as they hiked through the stand of trees concealing Aaron's house. Hannah shuddered and tried to concentrate on the beauty of the architecture hidden from public view.

"You think there's a killer out there who reeks of mildew?" Mariah asked.

Fee shrugged. "I don't know. But the smell is stronger than Francois in life."

Hannah listened as she applied the keys to an expansive glass patio door. Finding the right one, she unlocked it and slid the panel back to let everyone in.

"I didn't even know this was here," Sam admitted, looking around as she entered. "Aaron never brings anyone home."

"Except Harvey," Teddy reminded her. The jeweler immediately gravitated toward a crystal chandelier—not the Victorian kind but a modern-art design.

Hannah admired the dark hardwood floor, the mid-century modern furniture in what appeared to be a family room and study, and the open, stainless-steel kitchen that seemed to fill the center of the house. An air conditioner whirred quietly, keeping out the hot August heat and humidity—a rarity in Hillvale, she knew.

Seeing a refrigerator, she opened that while Sam called her husband, the police chief.

"He has beer, wine, and some fancy bottled water," she called. "Mariah, sit *down*."

"I don't dare," the computer expert cried. "This sofa looks like a high-end designer piece, probably listed in Antiques-R-Us."

"So do the chairs," Hannah agreed. "But you know Aaron uses them. *Sit*."

"Dang, these are first editions!" Teddy said, opening volumes on the bookcase. "Where's Harvey?"

"Closing up the antique shop." Fee appeared beside Hannah, opened a few refrigerator drawers, and removed lemons and limes. "Mariah and Sam need vitamins, not beer. You and Teddy are on your own."

"Wine," Teddy called. "Chilled, preferably."

Hannah had already had enough wine for one day. She settled for water. "Will Harvey know we're here or will we scare him to death?" She peered around the wall of cabinets and found stairs. Apparently there was another level that hadn't been obvious through the trees. The house was huge.

Teddy, not being as polite as Hannah, ventured into the front room and peered out the front door. "There's a separate entrance at the end. If Harvey doesn't want to speak to us, he can sneak in."

After serving drinks all around, petite Fee perched on a counter stool and spun around. "So, do we talk about who would want Francois dead, or why Aaron is showing his house to Hannah when he never showed it to anyone else?"

~

AARON'S PATIENCE HAD BEEN TESTED ALMOST BEYOND ENDURANCE BY THE time Walker arrived. Val kept wandering off, presumably in search of lost souls. Brenda refused to leave Francois alone until she'd verified his death. Tullah and Cass fell into their medium and stooge act—he assumed to consult with any invisible entities in the area.

And he was left fretting over Hannah and the others left vulnerable to whatever evil lurked. But he couldn't follow them until he was certain the rest of the Lucys were kept off haunted killing fields.

A sensible Null like Walker was a relief. He came accompanied by men with a stretcher, the coroner, and a deputy.

"He's probably been dead since before noon," the red-haired nurse practitioner told them. "I didn't want to touch the body but I saw no contusions or abrasions, no sign of violent death. Francois was a man in his fifties who smoked and drank too much and led an inactive life."

"No signs of struggle?" the coroner asked as the others followed the trail Aaron indicated.

Aaron kept his eye on the Lucys rather than follow Walker. He didn't give a damn about the blackmailing SOB lying in the field, but everyone knew Francois never acted on his own initiative. Who had ordered him to dig up what? Or bury it, for all that mattered.

Once the law officers departed, Brenda spoke again. "Digitalis toxicity," she said with certainty. "He was probably on medication. Someone pushed him over the edge with an overdose. It could have been done in any number of ways, but foxglove is the favorite of mystery readers. We don't grow any other digitalis herbs here."

"Samantha planted foxgloves in the city garden," Cass said.

The Lucys instantly left for town. Aaron assumed that they'd decided Francois had left nothing of interest exposed by his digging. He had a feeling Hannah wouldn't leave it at that.

Walker stopped beside Aaron to watch the body carried out. "No sign of violence, but Sam says Fee smells mildew and must."

Aaron bit back a groan. "That means she's suspicious. Brenda says digitalis poisoning. I suppose it would be too easy for him to have the missing stone on him."

Walker didn't even question but jotted a note. "He hadn't dug far. Found an arrowhead and possibly a femur. Coroner said it was ancient."

"It's a graveyard," Aaron said. He hesitated, uncertain whether to explain why they were here. But Sam would tell him eventually. "That's the site of an old well, one depicted in the Eversham painting I was accused of stealing."

Walker nodded. "Makes no sense, like every other damned Lucy episode. Are you certain Carmel wasn't a Lucy?"

"Not that I'm aware. Hannah carries a genealogy in her head. You might ask her." Aaron finally unstuck his feet and started toward home —a home invaded by the women he'd hoped to keep out.

The sun had gone behind the evergreens when they reached the shortcut to his yard. The women were already pouring out to greet him —all except Hannah.

Carmel and Tullah had gone ahead on their own. The younger ones peppered Walker with questions. The chief led them away, offering mostly assurances. Aaron let them go. He opened his patio door to find Hannah washing and drying glasses and putting them away.

"You don't have to do that. You should follow the others back to town. It will be dark soon." He glanced around, noting changes in the furniture, a book lying on the table. He was unused to anyone disturbing his environment.

"I don't know where I fit in," she said, gathering citrus peels from the sink. "Do you have a compost can?"

"I doubt you'll fit into it," he said dryly. "It's under the sink."

But he knew what she meant. The Lucys were a tight knit group, like family. Hannah had that sort of connection with her cousins—the kind where she had shared history. With the Lucys—it was shared gifts, and Hannah didn't feel as if she had any. Until Hillvale, he'd been on the outside looking in for most of his life. He'd adjusted to the loneliness.

She dumped the peels and washed her hands. "I'll leave you alone. I just wanted to thank you for letting us in. Mariah tried to do too much and needed the rest."

He shrugged. "It was the closest place with a landline. I'm not a complete hermit."

"You are the next best thing to a recluse, and you know it." She put away the misplaced book. "You'll get worse with age."

"I just prefer to take my personal business out of town," he countered, opening the refrigerator to see if he had any beer left.

She headed for the door. "The Lucys agree that you have a woman in every town you visit. That isn't the same as having a life."

Worked for him.

She headed out the door—as he'd told her to do, three verses back.

He took a gulp of his beer and considered letting her go. He'd done that the other day. It hadn't helped. It had just made him feel like a callous beast.

He might live with feeling like a beast, but he'd never live with himself if there was a killer out there, and he let her go alone.

FOURTEEN

"Stay," Aaron told her.

Hannah hesitated with her hand on the door latch. "I don't think I'm likely to be attacked by a killer with a bottle of digitalis. Brenda told us what happened."

"Someone sent Francois to dig. I touched his shovel." Aaron reached for the beer, then remembered neither of them had eaten dinner. Getting drunk might be appealing when he was alone, but not a good idea around a Lucy. He rummaged in his freezer for anything he could nuke.

She flipped a light switch, found a dimmer, and lowered the glare— as if she were right at home. Then she pulled the blinds. "And?"

Aaron supposed with her travels, Hannah was accustomed to making herself at home anywhere.

"Francois had just argued with someone and was angry. He had visions of riches to show someone up, although in his muddled head, wealth seemed to be mixed up with Carmel's box. So he'd seen it at some point, suspected the contents were valuable, and maybe thought he could find more. There was so much rage and fear that I couldn't get a clear reading." Aaron found a frozen lasagna and stuck it in the microwave. Meat and carbs, his favorite food groups. Tomato sauce counted as a vegetable, right?

"But he didn't know the police have the box? Or he thought Carmel buried it?" Hannah opened his refrigerator and pulled out wilted lettuce, then searched fruitlessly for other salad makings.

"I use lettuce for sandwiches to say I eat healthy. You'll not find anything else, including dressing." He set out plates and wondered if he'd lost his mind. He didn't even share dinner with Harvey, who'd rented a room here for years.

"And the limes and lemons are for mixed drinks? Figures." She opened his freezer and located an ancient package of frozen broccoli. "That was all you got on Francois? That he was a lazy idiot?"

"I got the impression that his thoughts were on the night Carmel died, that he was angry someone had taken his meal ticket, and that the cops had taken the box. He was also angry because he'd been locked out of her suite, where presumably he could have helped himself to the jewelry." He poured wine. "I wasn't clear on who the anger was directed at. Half Hillvale, I suspect."

"So we know Francois didn't murder Carmel, one suspect off the list, if you're reading the shovel right. Did the police take the shovel?" She poured broccoli in a colander and set it over a pot of water to steam, then rummaged in his cabinets to produce olive oil and an old bottle of vinegar.

"They did." He sipped his wine and watched her hunt. Natalie used to produce feasts out of nothing. He'd forgotten that. He needed to forget it again. He turned his back to fill Hannah's glass and let her search. "I need to go through his things and see if I can find out who told him that digging would bring him gold. Francois wasn't much inclined toward hard work."

"His room will be roped off. We need to simply dig where Francois did, as I originally intended. Eversham wanted us to see that well and boulder for a reason."

His late wife had never been this stubborn. She'd always listened and let him lead the way.

Natalie had only been an inexperienced twenty-two-year-old. Hannah was probably the virtuous lady in the painting stubbornly rejecting the knight, even after he'd returned from the Crusades with a Healing Stone.

Where the hell had that thought come from?

From their shared vision earlier, the one he'd deliberately shut out? Double *deodamnatus*.

He didn't believe in reincarnation, did he?

The Lucys did. That's essentially what their whole spirit world was about. Just kill him now.

By the time the lasagna was done, Hannah had tossed a salad with wilted lettuce, broccoli, the mushrooms he used for steaks, and a dressing made from whatever ancient herbs cluttered his cabinets. It was even edible, he discovered, when they sat down and ate.

"We need to experiment," she said when they were done.

He was feeling relaxed and on strong ground again. "No, we don't." He picked up their plates and set them in the dishwasher.

She took the plates out, rinsed them, and returned them to the dishwasher. "There's a killer on the loose. Evil has saturated the land. And the killer may have the stone needed to heal Hillvale. I can dig on my own, but you hold the key to interpreting what I find."

"Ask one of your psychic family to do it. I'm not for hire." He rinsed the crystal wine glasses and set them in the drying rack.

Hannah rummaged until she found a drop of dishwashing liquid and a sponge to soap the crystal. "My family would not let me out of their sight if I they could read my mind. I understand you don't want to see me drop dead any more than I want my students to see it. I get that, honest, I do. But what we want and what we must do are often different."

"You don't know the half of it," he muttered. "I'll walk you home before you start polishing the granite."

She dried off her hands and gave him a piercing golden glare. "I don't particularly want to die. I cherish a ridiculous notion that a healing stone might actually heal. So, yes, I have ulterior motives in wanting to find a killer. But if you have a chance to heal this land with a magical stone, shouldn't you jump at it?"

She damned well had him there. Killing the evil would set him free.

~

HANNAH HAD HARBORED VAGUE HOPES THAT AARON WOULD LET DOWN HIS walls and take her to bed, but he walked her back to the store instead. Probably for the best, but if she was going to die, she'd like to go having great sex.

She was uncertain if Aaron had any interest in the same. A handsome, confident man who could have any woman he wanted wouldn't necessarily want a plain one who came with a lot of baggage. She had to quit reliving that damned painting—or making up stories to go with it.

Aaron verified the shop wasn't inhabited by digitalis killers or ghosts, said good-night, and left her there, alone.

To hell with that. She let herself back out again and wandered over to the café. It was closed, but a nice contingent of the younger Lucys had congregated in the restaurant next door. They waved her over to join them.

"Kurt still doesn't have a bartender, so we're limited to wine," Teddy said as Hannah pulled up a chair. "We could repair to the lodge bar, but that's where the men are."

"Dinah doesn't object to us filling up one of her tables?" Hannah checked and the restaurant was bustling.

"Not us," Amber, the sunset-haired tarot reader said with laughter. "We're like the special groups in history—the Algonquin Round Table, the Rat Pack. . . We need our own name."

"*Lucys* ought to be enough," Fee said dryly. "People stare at us as it is."

Hannah glanced around. Fee was right. Several of the customers watched them and whispered among themselves. Not many, just enough to know the town's reputation for weird was spreading.

"Tell us what you found out from Aaron," Teddy said eagerly.

"There's no private conversation among Lucys?" Hannah asked doubtfully, uncertain of the unwritten rules.

"The men want us to think like that, but communication is key to solving problems, and a killer is a real problem. We're developing a bad reputation that will destroy the momentum we've developed over the past year." As a successful jewelry designer, Teddy had business experience and the confidence to use it. As wife of the owner of half the town, she also had influence.

"Well, the reporters keep my café busy," Fee said wryly. "But I can see brides might be reluctant to hold weddings with murderers around."

Hannah had communicated enough with these women recently to know them fairly well, but she was naturally reticent about herself. And somehow, Aaron had become part of that reticence. She sorted through what little she knew and told them about Francois and the shovel.

"So you think we need an archeological dig?" Amber looked dubious. "We'd better bring in Sam and Mariah on that, they have more understanding of what's out there. I'd love to use the golf cart and take a look though. Until I get this bum knee worked on, I don't want to walk all the way there, then have to run from crazed killers."

"Ha, Hollywood movie star," Fee teased. "You don't want to mess your pretty hair. Besides, don't you have a recording schedule?"

Amber wrinkled her nose and sipped at her bubbly water as if it were wine. "I don't want to miss out on any Lucy fun. I can reschedule if needed."

"I'm supposed to be setting up a school," Hannah reminded them. "So this gets complicated."

"Kurt is bringing in workmen to convert the upstairs for your apartment and to start painting and whatnot in the schoolrooms. Sally is asking for chalkboard paint and a bulletin board divider for the classrooms. You'll probably need to tell them what you need." Teddy waved at Brenda, the nurse, as she hovered in the entrance.

A woman in her late forties or early fifties, with dyed red hair, Brenda was petite and wiry and always seemed to be in a hurry, Hannah noticed.

"Samantha can't tell if the foxgloves have been disturbed," Brenda announced. "Any part of the plant can be dangerous. He could have drunk tea from the leaves or someone could have put flowers in his salad or pounded seeds into his coffee. . . I have no idea what that would taste like."

"Do we know for certain that he was taking digitalis?" Hannah asked.

"Mariah checked the sheriff's report. The coroner hasn't done an autopsy yet but they found prescription bottles in his room, so yes, digitalis poison is very possible. Did Aaron say anything useful?" Brenda asked.

"He said Francois was angry, and that he's pretty sure he wasn't Carmel's killer. He thinks maybe someone sent Francois out there. He also said the evil was stronger than usual today. Combined with what Fee said about the smell of must and mildew, is there any chance the killer was with Francois when he dropped?" Hannah hadn't drunk much of her wine, but she took a gulp now, waiting for the verdict of the other Lucys on her theory.

"We need to get into Francois's room," was the conclusion Teddy reached.

"*Aaron* needs to get into it," Hannah corrected.

"And Mariah needs to research Francois," Fee added worriedly.

"The cops probably have his pill bottles, so I'm no more help here. Let me know if you need anything else." The nurse departed without sitting down.

"Aaron won't go near Francois's room unless Walker lets him in." Hannah was pretty sure she'd correctly read his reluctance to break the law. He'd even been upset about her removing a pebble.

"Divide and conquer," Teddy crowed, draining her glass. "Sam can persuade Walker to take Aaron around Francois's bedroom. I'll go with Hannah and Kurt to the schoolroom tomorrow, ostensibly to inspect the place where my niece and nephew will be educated. Afterward, Hannah and I will go off to discuss plans—and just happen to wander down to the old well. I'm not Keegan. I can't sense crystal mother lodes. But if there are crystals anywhere around there, maybe I can sense something that will lead us to the right area for digging."

"I can't contribute much, but I know how to use a shovel," Hannah agreed. "I think we need more evidence than sensing evil or the smell of mildew to convince Keegan to join us."

"Let me know when you need a psychic," Amber said cheerfully. "Shall I hand out free tarot reading flyers to all our suspects?"

"That might not be a bad idea." Fee stood up. "And then you send the guilty ones to me."

"No poisoning of suspects," Teddy admonished. "But you're free to make them sick for a week."

Hannah laughed and rose with the rest of them. Following the example of the others, she left cash on the table for her drink. She'd need to find a bank soon, but right now, she had no paycheck to deposit in it.

She was almost glad she didn't *feel* evil or any other weirdness as the others did. Strolling down the boardwalk under the single light from the parking lot, she enjoyed the warm night. She thought it might be fun to spend the night under the stars without shivering, but not tonight. The day had been draining.

Letting herself in the front door of the antique shop, Hannah wandered through the shroud of shadows illuminated only by nightlights.

She almost wished the Eversham painting were still there. That brief glimpse of the commune hadn't been enough. She wanted the thrill of traveling back in time.

Losing her mind wouldn't be fun though. What if she had already lost it? Except Aaron had seen what she had, she was positive.

So mostly, she wanted an active gift as the others had. She would have to be content being an encyclopedia.

She was halfway across the shop before she saw the glowing crystal of a Lucy staff.

At the same time as she noticed it, a shadow rose from the stairs. "Before you hunt crystals, Library Girl, you need to know what you're looking for."

FIFTEEN

AARON WASN'T CERTAIN IF HE FELT RELIEF OR DISAPPOINTMENT WHEN HE unlocked his shop the next morning and knew Hannah had already left.

He'd slept restlessly, reliving those odd episodes inside Hannah's head—or his own. He was unclear how just touching her could set off a trip down someone else's memories.

If Hannah the Encyclopedia couldn't find similar examples, they really were up a creek.

He got caught up on his bookkeeping, sold a lamp, and was working on his website when Walker entered.

"I need you to go with me to search Francois's room before the Lucys do it," Walker said sourly. "Wan Hai said she could cover for you, but she'll probably arrange the whole shop under the principles of *feng shui* before we return."

"It would be worth it." Aaron closed out the computer.

He hadn't realized he'd been bored out of his skull until Walker entered. Hannah was right. He'd turn to dust here. Guardians should guard, not be shopkeepers.

Walker's *feng shui* expert arrived not long after. A neighbor of Walker's mother, Wan Hai had offered her services to Hillvale as a wedding gift to Sam and Walker. So far, she'd only succeeded in rearranging

Walker and Sam out of one home and into another and persuading Pasquale to organize his grocery store.

"The women are conspiring?" Aaron asked as Walker drove his official vehicle up to the lodge.

"You had any doubt? The sheriff knows damned well about Mariah's hacking skills, half the western world does. But he's taken no action on protecting his network, so I've washed my hands of it. I can keep her out of my head, but that's my limit. Even having a baby can't slow her down." Walker parked at the rear of the lodge, near the kitchen.

"And what has Mariah learned from the sheriff that has the women wanting to search the room of a dead man?" Aaron unfolded from the SUV and tested the energy with his staff. The lodge always vibrated with unpleasantness, but Mariah's ghostcatchers had settled most of the restless spirits. He didn't detect an elevation of forces.

"She apparently didn't learn enough," Walker said grimly. "Hence, the search. The coroner hasn't done his job yet, so we have no way of knowing that Francois was even murdered. But the Lucys are right. If anyone knew anything about Carmel, it was her toady."

The lodge manager, Fred Roper, met them at the door to Francois's room. Slightly balding, with a middle-aged spread unconcealed by his tailored suit, he'd taken over the management of the lodge after Kurt Kennedy decided to return to architecture. Aaron knew Roper came with impressive credentials for managing high-end resorts—and that he conducted a shady side business for a few of the lodge's privileged guests. Carmel had liked the man, however, and finding someone she liked had been a requirement.

"I'm keeping the key code for this room and Mrs. Kennedy's under my own password," Roper said, unlocking the outside entrance with his key card. "As you requested, the maids aren't able to access them. Do you have any idea when we'll be able to open them up again?"

"Up to the sheriff at this point," Walker said noncommittally, ducking under the police tape. "I'll take it up with him after we're done here."

Roper sniffed at the odor emanating from the room and grimaced. "The sooner, the better. I'm afraid there may be mice in the walls."

Aaron ducked under the tape without commenting. The room did smell musty, and he wasn't particularly sensitive to smells. "Mildew in the walls?" he asked.

"Mr. Kennedy said he'd have the place cleaned out so workmen can look for leaks," Roper acknowledged from the other side of the tape. "Lock it up when you leave, please." He strode off.

Walker stood back, leaving Aaron to drift around the room in search of the strongest vibrations. "I'm inclined to believe Fee and think it just smells of Francois," Walker said. "The man was scum. I won't give you a dossier until you have a look around."

The bed had been made by the lodge's maids the day Francois had died and looked untouched now. The carpet had probably been vacuumed at the same time. Francois took good care of his fancy livery, which hung in an orderly fashion in the small closet. A heavy scent of fresh marijuana emanated from the desk. Ancient avarice clung to the dresser. Wearing gloves, Aaron pulled open a few drawers. Thin gloves were no protection against the slime coating the furniture. "Sheriff take any diaries or anything from here?"

"Yup. Francois did a little blackmail on the side. He kept notebooks of potential victims, along with photos, stolen letters, and whatnot. He had access to the entire lodge and all Carmel's wealthy city friends. The word *unsavory* was invented for him. I've made a few calls. The only reason he's never been caught is that his demands were small and easily paid off like a generous tip—in cash, of course." Using gloves, Walker checked behind picture frames.

"Just enough to pay for the weed and his gold buttons and not cause complaint, I'm guessing. Is the sheriff looking at Francois as a suspect in Carmel's death?" Aaron pulled out a drawer and turned it over. An envelope was taped to the underside.

Walker snapped pictures of the drawer before prying off the envelope. "Of course. They can wrap up both cases with no further effort, as long as the coroner rules no foul play."

"Life would be simpler that way. That envelope has Lance's impressions on it. You probably don't want to open it. The guy's life has already been ruined. Doesn't help to drag him into his own sister's murder." Aaron backed off, wishing he'd searched this place on his own, without officialdom breathing down his neck.

He didn't do illegal these days.

He kept searching while Walker pried open the ancient paper. The vibrations in the room were so thick with. . . Aaron didn't know if he could call it *malum*. Francois had been too lazy for evil. *Ugly* was the best word he could summon. But there was evil here. The crystal in his staff flickered with it.

"It's a love letter to Val, written decades ago. Must have happened right after she was disfigured. She may even have been in the hospital. Sounds like she was refusing to see him." Walker tucked the paper back in the envelope. "Doesn't look like the letter ever reached her."

"Carmel probably intervened. At the time, Val was a bankrupt Ingersson and a scarred actress with no future, not high on the list of wealthy and powerful Carmel favored." Aaron crouched down beside the bed. Surely the cops had searched the mattress? He was really, really reluctant to touch it with his senses open.

"Francois was with Carmel that long? And he kept this letter why?" Walker sounded disgusted.

"Ammunition would be my guess. Against Lance or Carmel or maybe even Val, should an occasion rise for its use. Will you turn over this mattress? I don't want to touch it, even with gloves." Aaron stood back, away from the vileness he sensed.

Insensitive Null that he was, Walker flung the top mattress, comforter and all, to the far side of the bed.

They both studied the box springs. Francois had covered them with newspapers and a yellowing sheet.

"I'm guessing the maids don't vacuum the mattresses," Aaron said.

"Or Francois told them to leave it alone. You want me to lift the papers too?" Walker leaned over to read the dates and articles. "They don't look relevant to anything."

Aaron reluctantly touched the top layer, then removed a glove to pick up the folded pages from a San Francisco newssheet dated a dozen years ago. "Not picking up anything useful. At best, it could mean he laid this nest back then and hasn't added to it."

They carefully sorted through the layer, stacking the newspapers in order of date, until the yellowed linen was uncovered.

"If he's hidden anything under here, he's not touched it in years," Aaron warned. "It's what's in here that's giving off the bad vibrations."

"I'm still disgusted the sheriff's men didn't uncover it. Go ahead, rip it off." Walker caught one corner of the sheet and tugged.

"The deputy thought he had a heart attack victim. He was only after the prescription bottle." Aaron tugged off the other end of the sheet. Together, they flung it to join the top mattress and comforter on the far side of the bed.

Reluctantly, Aaron touched the box spring cover. It produced no distinct images other than avarice, much like Carmel's closet. Feeling safer, he ran his hands over every square inch. When he reached the side, he hit the jackpot. "Here." He removed a penknife from his pocket and cut threads. "Francois mended his own uniforms?"

"Probably. He once worked for a clothing designer, got fired for getting high and molesting a clothing dummy," Walker said in disgust. "Francois was never the brightest light in the fixture."

"Not if he fried his brains. He should have been born twenty years sooner so he could have joined the hippies at the commune." The seam of the box spring opened. Aaron continued cutting at the neat, almost invisible threads. "Although I think most of the hippies actually had brains and talent before they fried them."

"We all do dumb things when we're young. It's not learning from our mistakes that's the dividing line between ignorant and stupid. Francois had a history of stupid, until Carmel took him in. His mother was an old family servant. Kurt says Francois worshipped Carmel and would do anything for her, hence, the long tenure." Walker snapped pictures of the opening in the box spring.

"If she hadn't taken him in, he'd have ended up OD'd in a homeless camp. Not sure which finale is preferable." Aaron reached cautiously into the interior, finding a thick 8x10 envelope, testing it before drawing it out. "Francois's retirement plan, if I'm not mistaken."

Walker muttered something in Chinese that Aaron was glad Hannah couldn't hear. He thought a few Latin obscenities himself as he tugged the envelope out and presented it to the chief of police. "I can feel enough of the contents to know I don't want to acknowledge their existence. I can only hope Francois was a really bad photographer and used bad paper to print the shots."

Unfazed, Walker pulled out a handful of professionally printed photographs. "Jeez, the man was a real sleaze ball. And Carmel wasn't a sight better."

"I think I'll go home and take a shower now." Aaron stood up and headed for the door.

He didn't want to be in Walker's shoes. How did one show pornography of a dead woman and her lovers to her grieving sons?

Yawning after too few hours of sleep, Hannah followed Teddy down the trail toward the old church and well. She'd hung her staff on her backpack, carried a shovel, and wore her practical hiking boots and jeans.

Teddy had pulled her thick auburn hair in a knot and topped it with a ball cap covered in sequins. In deference to the heat, she accented her curves with a bright yellow halter top, blue jean shorts, and high platform sandals. Hannah felt like a pencil stump beside her. Or a nun.

"So Harvey showed you his hoard?" Teddy asked as they passed the track to Aaron's place. "Are they all polished gems or uncut ones?"

"Polished by his predecessors, apparently. Some, he buys. I don't think he knows how to cut them. And they're mostly quartz as far as I can determine, nothing valuable. But I can't feel anything on them." Hannah reined in her frustration. How was she supposed to identify evil or good when she only saw pieces of glittery rock?

Harvey had been as disappointed in her as she was with herself.

"He let me see them once. I wasn't certain if that was all he had. Harvey's secretive. What made him trust you?" Teddy stopped to pull a weed from between her toes.

"He doesn't journal. I think he wanted me to write up what he does with them. I told him I couldn't write what I didn't know, and it was his responsibility. Maybe he hoped I could identify their source since I've seen Keegan's collection, but that's on Keegan, not me. They're all rocks to me." Another source of frustration. She ought to be able to actively *do* something useful besides spouting what anyone could look up.

"Let's hope Walker is too busy at the lodge to rope off the well yet. Maybe we can all pretend Francois died of heart failure so reporters won't be all over us again. I really want to lay this evil business to rest once and for all." Teddy marched on through the dusty sage and up the back hill.

Hannah snickered. "Right. Let's just mutter a few chants and drive a stake through the heart of whoever is buried there and declare the land cured."

Teddy bestowed an evil look on her and continued on. "I have far better things to do than deal with a non-believer. A Null Lucy just does not compute."

"Librarian," Hannah corrected. "I am supposed to observe and remain neutral. Even digging is probably against the rules, had anyone thought to write rules."

The wind whispered across the grasses as they reached the old cemetery, which is what Hannah called the land in her head. She pictured the Eversham painting as they approached. There was the shoulder-high boulder where several of the natives had crouched. The priest and the soldier had stood near an old stone well, against a backdrop of cottonwood. There had been no grass then, just dust and pebbles and the rock the priest was blessing.

She hunted the spot where she'd slept the other day—higher up the bank in a level field.

"Presumably, they wouldn't have buried people by the well, right?" Hannah asked, studying the peaceful scene. A man's body had lain there yesterday. The dry grass was crushed from gurney wheels and boots, leaving no other sign that Francois had existed.

"As I understand it, an earthquake buried the well in the early 1800s, a century after the scene the Eversham depicts." Teddy gestured in the direction of the old church. "The bluff crumbled and slid downhill, probably taking out any burial ground." She crouched down to examine the soil. "Maybe the gold rushers or the ranchers didn't know the history and planted their dead and built their church in the soft soil from the quake."

"The cottonwoods are a dead giveaway of the well." Hannah examined the sunny boulder, wishing for markings or a map. In this dry heat, even moss didn't cling to the rock's rough surface. If anything had ever been carved in the stone, it had weathered away.

"My crystal is reacting to something," Teddy said worriedly, holding up her staff, which was visibly vibrating.

Hannah studied hers. Nothing. "Can you tell if it vibrates more strongly in one place than another?"

Teddy waved the stick much as Aaron had the other day. "Maybe more strong near the boulder than where you found Francois. What are the chances he was burying something rather than digging it up?"

Hannah crouched by the newly-dug shallow hole in the hard ground. "He didn't get far either way. Maybe we're going about this all wrong. Maybe we need a bulldozer."

She got out her hand shovel and peeled a layer of hard-packed earth from the edge of the hole. "Do you want to work on this one while I use the shovel over there where you feel it more?"

"If I don't need to be archeologically neat about it." Teddy twirled her staff into the ground, indicating where she wanted to dig. "Mostly, I want to see if I can find any crystals, any indicator that the contents of that box were buried here."

"Good goal. Digging up bones isn't high on my list." Hannah switched places with Teddy, leaving her the hand tool while she shouldered the shovel.

They worked silently for a while, then stopped to drink from their water bottles. Hannah eyed the bottle, then the shallow hole she'd pried from the ground. "This would be a damned sight easier if we had water to wet the dirt."

"It won't rain until winter. Want to wait that long?" Teddy poured a little water in her hole and tried digging again. "Bulldozer," she said in discouragement.

"Magic wands. Why can't we have real magic?" Hannah jabbed the shovel into the ground again, hitting more rocks. She hoped they were rocks. Bones should be deeper, right? She dug around the obstacle some more, then crouched down to see how far out the rock stretched.

"Buried treasure?" Teddy called, glancing up from her own dig.

Hannah sat down and used her work-glove-covered hands to dig around the gray mass. "It's rock, but it's sort of round. Is that natural?"

"Sure, why not?" Teddy came over with her hand shovel to dig around it.

"Because it takes water to round a rock. Keegan said the ocean once flowed through the canyon, which is why they found round rocks there. If this is debris from the earthquake, shouldn't it be chipped shards? Or flat slabs? I want to take back something that will force Keegan to come out and help us." Hannah stood and jabbed her shovel in again.

"Wait, wait," Teddy said excitedly. "Archeological methods, please. I sense. . . something similar to crystal. It's not deep. Let's do the surface."

They were sweaty and filthy and digging excitedly in a shallow trough by the time Kurt and Aaron found them.

SIXTEEN

Aaron held his staff over the hole the women were digging, cursed at the strong vibrations, and shoved the wood into Kurt's manicured hands. Without thinking, he crouched down to pry loose the dirt remaining around the set of stones already uncovered.

The instant he brushed the stone Hannah was touching, he disconnected.

"If setting the stones brings peace, let them cover the whole cursed graveyard." The sour thought curdled his stomach in the same way the bloody battlefield had.

The woman inhabiting his head replied by whispering prayers to the ill and slaughtered, both soldiers and natives alike. He hated when she did that, but he would have hated having her here even worse. The land was a killing field.

In the distance, smoke boiled up from the remains of the mission.

"Add the crystals," she commanded. "They will absorb the evil that has been done here so later generations will not be affected."

She was gone from this life, but not gone from his heart—or his head. In this, he would heed the voice of the angel and not the hardened doubt of his battered soul.

He crouched to take crystals from the trunk for the shaman to add to the rock guardians he was creating. Touching the shiny rock. . .

Aaron jerked backed as if burned.

Beside him, Hannah looked pale as death. She braced herself with one hand on the ground. He'd been dreaming in Spanish? Had Hannah heard what he heard? She looked shell-shocked enough to have seen something.

"You two okay?" Kurt asked with concern. "Maybe it's time to go back and get some lunch. We don't want you suffering heatstroke. You're looking dehydrated."

Aaron had no reason to be dehydrated, but Hannah's pale skin was showing signs of sunburn. He handed his bottle of water to her, and she swigged gratefully. "You've uncovered a *lamassu*," he said. He waited for her to confirm it.

She nodded. "That vision was *really* weird. I wasn't even there." She glanced into the hole. "This just looks like a pile of rocks, nothing remotely like Daisy's guardians. Does anything look like a crystal?"

So she'd not only heard the voice, but understood. Intrigued despite himself, he worried about Hannah and how any of this affected the knot in her brain.

Teddy sat back on her heels. "Explanation, please? You two go all weird, and now you're hunting crystals?" She drank from the bottle Kurt handed her.

"I apparently enhance. . ." Hannah glanced at him. ". . .or aggravate, Aaron's psychometry. Apparently I'm too weak to hold up for long though."

Without explaining how she'd been inside his head, Aaron scraped at the rounded stack of rocks they'd uncovered. "I think the natives buried stone guardians, maybe *lamassu* like Daisy's, only larger. And the Spanish soldier used crystals from his box to absorb evil. This was in mission days. And the reason a mission was never established here was because the natives fought back rather than be enslaved. Or that's the impression I'm getting. A lot of people died of illness, blood was shed, Spanish and native, and the mission was burning while they raised these stones on top of the dead. Or their ancestors. They could have been adding to an ancient burial ground or battlefield. It's not clear."

"Keegan told me Mariah's story about Daisy." Hannah sat back, her expression sad as she surveyed the rocky field. "He said when Daisy time-walked, she talked about native women waiting for warriors who never came home. We could be digging in a burial ground."

"We need to find that crystal," Teddy insisted, ignoring history for their current dilemma. "Crystals that *absorb* evil are damned scary. Keegan should be here."

"There could be a whole field of *lamassu* here," Hannah warned.

"Full of crystals absorbing evil?" Kurt sounded dubious. "Teddy, do you sense any crystals?"

"I sense *wrong* vibrations." Teddy ran her hand over the round rocks. "Plus the *absence* of crystal? That doesn't even make sense to me."

"Sit back," Aaron ordered Hannah, who intelligently scooted away. The original statue had evidently toppled, possibly during the earthquake. The ones in his vision had been standing, but this was mostly flat. He couldn't tell front from back.

He ran his hands over the uncovered granite, seeking anything unusual. The images his other sense picked up were ancient and fading. Hannah's ability to enhance his vision was disturbing. Why had he seen the soldier and not the shaman who had placed the stones?

There, the indentation on the smallest stone. The soldier had touched it there, saying a prayer, although he apparently believed his *angel* more than the power of words. Aaron scraped off more dirt. "The stones were evidently bound with vines, the way Daisy used to bind them with wire. She used to put crystals on the top stone for eyes. Here's where they were secured." He pointed out the two shallow indentations—now lacking crystals.

"Someone took them?" Hannah asked, worry in her voice.

Aaron gauged the stone figure as roughly three feet in height, had it been standing. Daisy's statues were measured in mere inches. Perhaps her time-walking had shown her these local guardians? "Floods over the years, as well as the earthquake, may have toppled the statues. Running water could have buried and unburied the stones dozens of times over the centuries."

"Leaving the crystals uncovered for scavengers to find," Teddy finished for him. "But I can still sense the *power* of those crystals, even in their absence. Those weren't any ordinary stones." She traced her fingers over the empty holes.

"Raw crystals?" Hannah asked hesitantly. "Like sparkly quartz rocks, not gems?"

"Like the ones Keegan is digging out of his cave or the ones in the medieval painting, yes," Aaron said.

"Do we know how many of these statues might be buried here?" Kurt asked. "And why Francois was digging around?"

Aaron looked at Hannah. She shrugged. There had been nothing in their shared vision except the one statue the shaman worked on. The ceremony could have gone on for days. There could have been other statues not visible in their vision. Or they could have dreamed the whole thing.

He grimaced and shook his head. "No notion." He got up to examine the hole Teddy had been enlarging, the one Francois had been working on. Holding his hand over the dirt, he opened his extra sense. "I'm picking up desperation and seeing rocks. I might get more if I had his shovel."

"May I?" Hannah asked, quietly crouching beside him and holding out her hand. "Francois isn't the same deal as the paintings. And I haven't fainted recently. Maybe I'm becoming accustomed to your ability."

Aaron's first instinct was to reject her offer. But logically, it made sense. Francois's memories were too recent to cause *time-walking*. And if Hannah was right, what they did together wasn't time travel, but *enhanced* psychometry. He didn't want to hope or get excited about this expansion of his ability. It was still dangerous on too many levels.

Deliberately allowing Hannah inside his head. . . was a step well beyond anything he was prepared to accept. But the urgency of the situation caused for desperate measures. If they had the ability to trace guardian rocks. . .

"Sit down so you won't fall," he instructed. "Brace yourself. Shut out your own thoughts and center your mind on the wind or the hard ground or anything neutral."

She sat cross-legged next to him, closed her eyes, and turned her palms upward.

Aaron placed his left hand on the dirt Francois had been digging, then lay his right palm across Hannah's.

Visions crumbled like the dirt he touched. *The shovel hitting rock. Tearing excitedly at the hole with his hands. Disgust at uncovering the bone. An image of Carmel's box and the stones inside. Then pain, great pain.*

Aaron yanked his hand back.

Hannah was staring at her own hand in incredulity.

"Not liking this," he muttered, shoving upright.

Kurt and Teddy waited expectantly. He shook his head at them. He wanted to hold out his hand to help Hannah up but figured that was a really bad idea. She stood and dusted herself off.

"Francois was most likely delusional," he said. "I get the impression that someone had told him that Carmel found her rocks here, and he meant to find his own."

Aaron bit his tongue and waited for Hannah to spill the rest. She said nothing. Had she felt what he had? She merely picked up her water bottle and guzzled—a portrait of non-engagement.

The impression of *Lance*, Carmel's brother—and Kurt's uncle—had been strong in Francois's muddled mind as he dug.

To Aaron's relief, they all agreed it was time for lunch. Aaron shouldered Hannah's heavy pack, and without looking at the face of an angel, led the way back to town.

HANNAH HADN'T RECOGNIZED THE LANKY, PONY-TAILED MAN IN AARON'S vision of Francois's thoughts. Her habit of noninvolvement won out when Aaron didn't mention him either. She was still processing her frightening ability to *aid* Aaron's psychometry.

She had a gift besides lugging a library inside her head? Was it her task to communicate what Aaron saw or was she only there to help? What else might she do—if this wasn't really time travel?

She was beginning to realize the limitations of her library—every gift was individual and unpredictable, molded by DNA and the environment, in the same manner that shaped their bodies and other talents.

Could she help Keegan or Teddy with their crystals? Not that she knew anything about crystal energy or how it worked. Maybe she could enhance Amber's psychic readings? Hannah had difficulty imagining hiding under the table, touching Amber's toes while she read tarot cards for her customers—but she ought to try.

Kurt spoke as they reached town. "I need to pick up Uncle Lance and take him to the city. The lawyer is reading Mom's will, and she apparently did something right for him for a change."

Aaron squeezed Hannah's arm—briefly. Not long enough to get dizzy but enough to know she shouldn't speak. *Lance?* Was that the man she'd seen in his vision?

Teddy returned to her jewelry shop. That left Hannah to pick up something at the café or the grocery—alone.

"We need to talk." Aaron didn't walk off as expected.

"I need to shower," she countered in self-defense. This seeing inside the heads of others was a little too intimate and left her vaguely queasy —and understanding why gifted people questioned their abilities or abandoned them entirely. With great gifts came great responsibility—and utter confusion.

Aaron's responsibility scared her half to death.

"I'll pick up lunch at the café." As if she'd agreed to share it with him, he strode off and left her to enter the antique shop alone.

Already shaken, she almost backed out as soon as she opened the door, fearing she'd entered another time zone.

Sunlight caught on the sparkle of water and the pleasant bubble of a fountain that hadn't been there earlier. A thick, zebra-striped rug welcomed her feet to trod on it. A rainbow of prisms beckoned the eye to the right, where the now-empty shop window spilled more light.

She missed the medieval cuirass, but the prisms were enchanting.

Soft light glowed in every corner of the high-ceilinged shop from fixtures that had once sat empty.

The magic fairy dispelling the gloom sat on a stepladder, dusting a fiery red porcelain teapot and humming. Wan Hai didn't even look over at the opening door. Hannah could have been a thief and robbed the place blind for all the *feng shui* expert would notice.

She wanted to see Aaron's face when he entered his cave, but she really needed that shower too. Greeting Wan Hai, who just vaguely waved, Hannah hastened up the stairs.

She showered, donned a denim dress that hit just above her knees—

probably her sexiest outfit—and was sitting on Aaron's desk, facing the door, drinking a refreshing glass of iced tea by the time he returned.

She waited expectantly. He halted just inside as she had done. Hands full with bags redolent of Fee's cooking, he glanced down at the rug and over at the window, just as she had. His brow drew down in a glower. He studied the gleaming light fixtures, then glanced over at Hannah. His gaze instantly dropped to her swinging legs, then deliberately swerved back to scowl at the rest of her.

She rather liked the interest, and the scowl put her in a better humor. She was tired of His Arrogance ignoring her.

He stalked toward his desk. "Hai, get down from there and eat some lunch."

"In one moment," Hai said contentedly. "I am to meet Pasquale at one."

"Hai, didn't I hear you and Pasquale were at the lodge when Carmel died?" Hannah asked, watching Aaron squirm with impatience. "Who else did you see that night?"

Wan Hai frowned down at her. "Many people. We had dinner with the dog doctor and Nurse Brenda. Mr. Roper gave us discount. Mr. Aaron was there with the Kennedys. Everyone there."

"Even I was there," Hannah said with a shrug. "Way too many people."

Enjoying Omniscient Man's discomfort a little too much, she leaned forward to take one of his sacks. "Tell her the shop looks fabulous," she whispered.

His dark eyebrows raised. He frowned at the brightly lit shop. Then with visible effort, he said, "Wan Hai, you've done a great job in here, thank you. I feel better already."

The *feng shui* master beamed and returned to polishing.

He rolled his eyes and hissed, "Satisfied?"

Hannah grinned and hopped off the desk. "I'll wager you didn't have a single sale all morning." She took the other bag from him and carried both to the back while he checked the register.

"It's a good thing I don't have to live off shop sales," he muttered a moment later, joining her and helping to unpack the bags.

"She's a fabulous housekeeper." Hannah retrieved a cold beer from his small refrigerator and handed it to him. "And if you had a real sales person, you might make a living. People need jobs."

"No one else knows what I do about my inventory. Nor would they want to." He took cartons and napkins out of the bags. "Utensils in the third drawer down."

Okay, from the way he said that, she probably didn't want to know either. She regarded what appeared to be a filing cabinet of shallow drawers, selected the third, and revealed a mismatched collection of real silverware. It was her turn to roll her eyes.

She was comfortable like this, rummaging through old drawers, doling out meals, conversing casually.

She was distinctly uncomfortable—make that terrified—of crawling around in other people's heads. Especially Aaron's. How did she communicate that?

"I am a librarian," she announced in the only way she knew how, directly.

"Yeah, like I'm an antiques dealer." Aaron swigged his beer and propped his hip against a secretary desk, looking sexier than 007. "You just keep telling yourself that, kid, leave the hard work to the rest of us."

She flung a napkin at him. It fluttered to the floor. She wanted to be able to levitate it back to the counter, make it disappear into another dimension, something *useful*, like in the journals. She picked up the trash and debated walking out, but she was hungry, and Fee's food shouldn't be wasted.

And maybe just a little of her fear was of Aaron's attractiveness—not just physical, although that was a given. But if being inside his head told her anything at all, the man really did believe he stood between Hillvale and evil. How did one deal with that kind of magical thinking?

Not well, if the painting visions were to be believed. Knights and soldiers made bad domestic companions.

"Go ahead," he taunted. "Whine that you don't like fainting, that you don't know anything, that you might die any minute. Let it all out."

"You really are the most obnoxious toad on the face of the earth." She gnawed her way through the delicious lamb-stuffed pita bread. Apparently Fee thought she needed spice and protein today.

"And I like it that way. If I'm supposed to find a killer, it's probably best if I'm not a charming salesman." He bit into his steak sandwich, after peeling off the tomatoes.

Damn, but he had a way of cutting to the chase. "You don't think that gray-haired man is the killer, do you? Did it feel as if Francois was afraid of him?"

"That gray-haired old man is Lance Brooks, Carmel's brother, the one Kurt was taking to the lawyer's office because she left him something in the will." Aaron swigged his beer, looking thoughtful. "Speculation will get us nowhere. Francois was a disgusting excuse for a human being, a sniveling worm lost without Carmel to protect him. He could have been afraid Lance would heave him out. I don't want to imagine how his mind worked."

"What did you find in Francois's room?" Reluctantly dragged back into the mystery, Hannah listened as Aaron explained, not in detail, what they'd uncovered.

"So Lance might have had motive for killing the worm," Hannah concluded thoughtfully. "And I can't say I'd blame him a lot. But I gather Carmel was not alone in those photos and Francois could have black-mailed half the state's married male population of a certain age."

"That's one way of looking at it. Did Francois panic after Carmel died and increase his blackmail demands? Or did he know something about Carmel's killer that made him dangerous? And how does any of this tie into the rocks we found in her closet and that Francois apparently wanted to dig up?" Finishing his sandwich, Aaron crossed his arms and waited.

Hannah lined up all the instances she'd researched about the rocks in Keegan's possession, the ones found in Keegan's caves, the ones used in paint for the commune, and those in assorted collections. "We know too much and too little," she concluded. "Hillvale is near a cave with a streak of malleable crystals Keegan can turn into diamonds, if he wants, but the process is destabilizing for him as well as the crystals. Keegan, Teddy, and Harvey all possess old rocks from their families, rocks that are not quite normal. We have a painting of a jewel casket containing rocks and mention of a healing stone. Lucinda Malcolm's journal and an earlier geologist theorize the crystals reflect the intent of the user and help access talent. We have the geologist's journal with some of the experiments that have been done on those old rocks, but it contains nothing conclusive."

"Because the man who wrote it was a scientist and would not conclude anything without evidence," Aaron added. "But all of us in Hillvale are aware that the older crystals Harvey adds to our walking sticks pick up energy vibrations, and they have also absorbed particularly strong spirits. Keegan isn't ready to let us play with the new crystals he's found until he's certain they won't cause harm. Teddy has locked up the rocks she considers evil."

"None of that explains why Carmel thought her raw crystals were *valuable*. Yes, the artists in the commune believed when they were ground into their paints, they enhanced their talents. And apparently they were right, since most were extremely successful before they self-destructed. But Carmel wasn't an artist. Neither was Francois." Hannah picked at the remaining crumbs of her sandwich.

Aaron rummaged in the freezer of his small refrigerator and produced two ice cream bars, handing her one. "And no one in any of your immense library mentioned crystal stones that absorbed evil?"

And there it was—their shared vision. Hannah opened the ice cream bar rather than meet his eyes.

"Did you hear the voice inside the soldier's head?" he demanded.

"I *was* the voice inside his head," she whispered.

SEVENTEEN

Instead of returning his shop to the gloomy cave he preferred, Aaron left the lights on and spent the afternoon sinking into the first-edition classics lining his walls. He dusted the books, then sampled favorite scenes, while trying to block out the disturbing idea of Hannah *talking* inside his head three centuries ago. Or that he might once have been a Spanish soldier. Thinking like that was a sure road to Aunt Jia's madness.

He spent the evening telling himself that his gift was for objects, not people. But even as he dug into his steak, he knew he was lying to himself. He'd simply learned to *block* people. He would never survive otherwise. Opening his mind to a living human being blasted him with thoughts, images, and emotions more powerful than having a bomb dropped on him. He did not want to go there, ever.

But even using his blocking ability, he could read Hannah. Or she read him. Hell if he knew.

It was becoming agonizingly clear that he couldn't stop evil with a walking stick. What if someone else died on his watch because he wasn't willing to push his limits? He didn't consider Francois or Carmel part of his duty, but a killer on the loose endangered the entire town—and the people who trusted him.

He was at the shop early and waiting for Hannah when she came down from her room. There were shadows under her long-lashed eyes that indicated she hadn't slept much better than he had. She glanced at him questioningly, then to the dark corners where he'd turned off the damned lights. The sunshine seeping below the boardwalk roof was all he needed.

"I need to start interviewing people," he stated right up front. "We're getting nowhere looking for rocks and things cops can find on their own."

"I thought the crystals were key and police interviewed suspects." She didn't sound argumentative but. . . neutral, as always.

"*People* are key. The sheriff has no reason to suspect individuals like Lance. They can't see inside our heads. And they don't comprehend the history of the crystals or why it's important. Lance and Val once lived at the commune. Xavier and Cass knew the artists. Harvey's grandfather gave him a cache of crystals that may have come from the same place as the ones the commune had, since he owned land up the mountain. Even Walker doesn't have any idea why he should talk to Lucys and their friends, and he'd probably scare them into silence if he tried." Aaron had spent the night thinking about this and had his plan in place, he hoped.

Hannah nodded thoughtfully. "You want me to run the shop while you talk with them?"

Here's where the *faex* hit the fan. He tried not to clench his fists. "No, I would like you to go with me." He didn't want to command her to do this. Even he was uncertain of the efficacy or wisdom of his plan, but he could not sit back and do nothing. "If what you're doing is *enhancing* my ability and not time walking, then it should be safe if we need to get to the truth."

"I think you better let me have breakfast before I consider all the ramifications of that request," she said dryly, heading for the door.

Faex. Of course, she hadn't spent the entire night dreaming this up. "Bring it back here so we can talk, and I'll pay for it. Just tell Fee to put it on my tab."

From beneath that cap of honey-gold hair, she gave him a wide-eyed look that shivered more than his timbers. He was treading dangerous territory. Natalie had got under his skin. Hannah was inside his damned brain.

"Shall I bring you back anything?" was all she asked.

He could almost love a woman who asked about food and not if he was crazy. "I've eaten. I'll fix coffee. Fee would feed me wheat sprouts."

Her generous lips tilted, and she drifted out, gifting him with the sight of well-worn jeans conforming neatly to a rounded posterior. The loose t-shirt did nothing to disguise her slender waist or the sway of her hips. He should have gone into the city last night instead of working himself into a froth.

He had absolutely zero interest in the narcissistic airheads he culti-vated in the city. That told him right there that he was in a heap of trouble.

Summoning every Latin insult to his intelligence that he could retrieve, Aaron typed up his battle plan in his notebook computer. It wasn't much of a plan, but he phoned his starting point and made an arrangement to meet with him. Lance was a little startled at his request, but he suggested meeting at the gallery instead of his studio at the lodge.

When she returned, Hannah handed him a small paper sack, then repositioned one of the tragic coffee tables and set it in front of the Victo-rian loveseat, oblivious of the history clinging to the furniture.

Rather than watch her sit cross-legged on the velvet while visions of the prostitute who had once used it danced in his head, Aaron examined his bag. "Bacon? You persuaded Fee to fix bacon?"

"She'll do it, if asked. Everyone just gets used to letting her choose their foods. I suspect her choices are healthier, but you're allowed to rot your own stomach lining." She nibbled at what appeared to be a small egg burrito.

Aaron drank his coffee and bit into his bacon. Fee cooked it far better than he did. "Lance has agreed to meet with me at the gallery in half an hour. There is no sense in us second-guessing what Francois was thinking before he died. Let's find out what Lance knows about the stones, his sister, and Francois."

"Word at the café is that Lance inherited Carmel's third of the Kennedy property." She added a packet of sugar to her tea.

"Ouch. That's a slap in her sons' faces after all the work they've done, and that's not all. Did you know that this half of the mountain once belonged to Cass's mother? She married a Kennedy, and he inherited instead of Cass. So Carmel leaving the property to her brother, who has utterly no relation to either Cass or the Kennedys, was a blow to Cass as well."

Hannah nodded. "I've seen the genealogy. It's not pretty. And then there was the feud over the other half of the mountain with the Ingersson and Menendez families and the Kennedys cheating people out of their property."

"So we have a small town seething in old animosities that Carmel liked to keep stirred. Lance can tell us the Kennedy perspective, from back in the days before Kurt and Monty were born."

"If the stones are the reason for Carmel's death, we need the history," she agreed, looking thoughtful. "And Cass isn't likely to tell us."

"I'm more comfortable starting with Lance and Xavier. Cass and Val. . . are laws unto themselves."

"I'm interested," she replied. "But I fail to see how I can help. None of these people know me. They have no reason to trust me."

"They have no particular reason to trust me either." Aaron shrugged and finished his bacon. He had the annoying need for one of Fee's organic, wholesome breads. Grimacing, he glanced in the bottom of the bag. Fee had provided a wheat-sprout bagel. If he were superstitious, he would take it as a sign that Lucys would provide what was needed.

Still, he admitted, "I hate asking this of you even more than you hate being asked."

~

AFTER THAT LESS-THAN-IMPRESSIVE ACKNOWLEDGMENT OF HER POTENTIAL use, Hannah laughed at Omniscient Man's expression at discovering the bagel. "Leaving Comfort Zone and entering the Twilight Zone, Commander. Or in the words of the man you're currently reading, 'no man is an island.'"

She didn't need to be psychic to know how very much Aaron hated asking for help—especially from a woman. She was starting to understand his psyche, or maybe his past lives. The Lucys were right. Aaron was meant to be a guardian—but as much as he would like to be, he was no stone statue.

He glanced down at the John Donne he'd taken off the shelf and bit savagely into his bagel, chewing it thoroughly before replying. "I will not believe the spirits put that book in my hand. And yes, I dislike working with others. But I know how to do it if needed."

"Then start by explaining how I can help instead of why you don't want me." She finished her burrito and glanced at a clock. All Aaron's clocks kept perfect time. It was almost time for the shop to open.

"Because if they stonewall, you might help me catch them in a lie or in a memory they don't want to relate. It might not work, but I'm willing to experiment."

"Okay, who's handling the shop?" Hiding her excitement that he actually thought she might help, Hannah picked up her trash and started for the back.

"Wan Hai," he said grimly. "I may as well hang a CLOSED sign, but rearranging makes her happy, which makes Walker, Sam, and Pasquale happy."

"Hire a real salesperson," she called back. "Give me a minute to wash up, and I'll be ready."

She was shivering with anticipation and terror. Whatever she'd been in a prior life, she'd been sheltered in this one. Investigating murder suspects was *so* not up her alley.

She gave her hair an extra brush and donned a gauzy over-shirt so she didn't look as if she'd just crawled out of a jungle. When she returned to the shop, Wan Hai was already turning on all the lamps and moving furniture so the *chi* energy could flow smoothly.

"Don't scowl," Hannah warned at Aaron's frowning disapproval of his shop's rearrangement. "You feel energy with your stick. The world is full of different energies."

"Yeah, well I like mine and not hers." He held the door open so Hannah could pass by.

He smelled of coffee and a deeply sexy shaving soap that heightened her awareness. *Bad Hannah,* she mentally scolded. She tried to tell herself that Aaron's grumpiness was distinctly unsexy, but she was starting to understand the guardian in him too well. The shop was his fortress, his main line of defense. Wan Hai had breached it. And maybe Hannah had also, just a little, which deserved a happy dance. She restrained herself.

Lance had set up an easel in the old church/meeting house he'd converted into a gallery for local artists. Tall and lean like his sister, his golden hair faded to gray and tied in a ponytail, he glanced up at their entrance with interest.

Hannah knew he'd once been an architect, got involved with drugs and the commune and possibly Val, the Lucy's Death Goddess. He'd probably fallen apart about the same time the Kennedy fortune collapsed. But it appeared he'd turned his head around since then. Hillvale was all about second chances, apparently.

"Aaron, how can I help you?" He nodded genially at Hannah. "You're the new school teacher, right? I've already told Kurt I'd be happy to add murals to the schoolroom."

"Thank you. We appreciate that. A school should be a community undertaking." Having no idea what Aaron wanted her to do, she examined the first painting she came to—Val playing the part of Lady Macbeth would be her guess.

"I need to probe your memory. Where did the commune get the crystals they used in their paints?" Aaron took a seat on one of the benches and pulled his electronic notebook out of his jacket pocket.

Lance snorted. "That was Daisy's doing. She grew up in these hills. Mariah claims she had Ohlone blood, but by the time I met her, she was like all the other young blonde hippies running around the farm. Except she was crazy, of course."

"Fey," Hannah corrected from the exhibit. "Fairy-touched. It sounds as if she was able to take care of herself, so she wasn't mentally challenged."

"Sorry. When you're young, you're not into nuance. She danced around with flowers in her hair and collected pretty rocks and made weird sculptures."

"Where did she find the rocks?" Aaron asked, taking notes.

"She roamed," Lance explained. "I don't know if they were the same rocks the kids found in the waterfall. No one paid much attention until some wiseacre decided to grind a crystal into his paint to make it sparkle. LSD inspired, most likely, but the paintings sold like hotcakes."

"So everyone wanted crystals," Aaron prompted.

Hannah studied a portrait of Val as a teenager standing on a rock in what appeared to be a grotto. Lance had to have been considerably older to have painted this with such talent. Was this the waterfall?

"It became a stupid game," Lance said, waving his brush with impatience. "They followed Daisy to find their own crystals after she raised a stink when they stole hers. And then the kids found a supply in the waterfall. None of them were any more than sparkly rocks, quartz, I think. Keegan can tell you the geology better than I can."

"Except some of them turned out to be valuable?" Hannah asked, curiosity winning over neutrality.

He cleaned off his brush. "I didn't live at the commune and don't know the inside story. Some of the stones may have come from Keegan's cave for all I know. I've been told some they found were semi-precious, but in a raw state, they weren't worth much. What I saw was a bunch of starving artists trading with each other and the town for what they needed. One artist might trade a crystal for a brush. Geoff and the other merchants might take pieces of art if someone wanted a room for the night or groceries."

"Geoff?" Hannah asked, then found the name in her memory. "Geoffrey Kennedy?"

"My brother-in-law, right. He was the only one in town with money before the art started selling. Carmel loved jewelry, so I think Geoff sometimes took stones and had necklaces made up. That was back before she fixated on gold as her signature look." Lance glanced up. "My sister was a piece of work, I know, but back then, she was just a young wife and mother."

"So the stones Carmel kept may have been those Geoffrey traded for favors from the artists?" Aaron asked.

Lance shrugged. "Keep in mind that I worked in the city and got high every time I came here. Carmel and Geoff didn't exactly confide in me. I was just the wastrel baby brother."

"Yet she left you her share of the corporation. Do you think Francois knew that?" Hannah asked, assuming that wild guess might be interesting to confirm.

Lance shrugged. "Francois and Carmel were more brother and sister than I was, so yes, he probably knew about her will. I sure didn't. I can't even say if she thought she was taking care of me or being spiteful."

"Were you aware that your sister tried to protect you by keeping your mail to Val from going out?" Aaron asked without inflection.

Hannah could almost feel the impact of that question on Lance. She winced and glared at Aaron.

Lance looked startled, but he unhurriedly returned his paint brush to its container. "How do you know that?"

"Because we found a letter taped under a drawer in Francois's room. Ask Walker. Would Val know more about the stones in Carmel's possession?" Aaron asked.

But Lance was done talking. Looking dazed, he covered the canvas he'd been working on and departed through a side door without explanation.

"I can't decide if telling him was mean or necessary," Hannah said quietly, watching as Aaron got up to retrieve the paint brush Lance had been holding.

"Hell if I know, but it was probably a mistake. At least we know the concealed letters didn't drive Lance to kill his sister. But all I'm picking up from this brush right now is a flash of anger at Carmel's interference. And an image of Val when she was younger. Want to try?" He held out the brush.

Hannah pointed at the can of brush cleaner. "He held that before you lobbed the bomb. He was talking about the commune, crystals, and Daisy. I'd rather see those memories."

"Okay, how do you want to do this? Touch the can? Let me touch the can and you hold mine?" Aaron waited, not touching anything else.

"If my recollection of various psychometry journals is correct, I'm not sure it matters. Pick up the can, and I'll cover your hand with mine." To touch Aaron's hand, Hannah had to stand close, inhale his spicy scent, sense the tension in his long, lean muscles as she put her fingers over his.

Instantly, she was transported to a different scene.

Grotto. A young Val standing on a boulder like a wet selky shedding her skin. Others splashing in the shallow spring, hunting for pretty rocks. Lance's drug-

hazed desire as he painted the scene. A young and beautiful Carmel gazing at them with contempt.

A uniformed security guard raising a rifle and ordering everyone off the property. . .

Sadness. An image of tumbled rocks, dry and dusty, all the beauty gone out of them.

Aaron returned the can to the table, but Hannah clung to his hand, trying to hold on to the spell.

"We weren't in that scene," she said, finally summing up her interpretation.

"No, you just enhanced what I saw from Lance's memory." He blinked and gazed unseeingly at the can. "That was pretty amazing. Usually, if all I see is a flash of memory, it's faded, unclear, and not necessarily reliable. This was like a crisp color photo instead of a blurred old Polaroid."

"What if he'd been wielding the can as a weapon in rage?" she asked out of curiosity.

He squeezed her hand and let it go. "We might have heard words or sensed his thoughts. Action speaks louder than memories."

"There's no grotto now?" she asked, feeling Lance's sorrow at the loss. She returned to study the painting that almost matched his memory. Had the painting enhanced their vision?

"No. I never knew there was one. Fire roasted most of the Kennedy mountain going uphill. Rocks look like rocks. There's no differentiating them. We may have just seen a source for some of the crystals, but I don't think we can find it from that memory." He came over to study the painting with her. "He's ten years older than Val. He knew he could never have her."

"Especially as he descended into drug addiction while she was on the verge of a brilliant career. But the security guard in that memory—does that mean others might know where the grotto is?"

"We'll keep asking. Let's find Xavier. He seldom strays far from his office. He's closer to Cass's age, but he got his drugs from somewhere. The commune is the most likely source." Aaron started for the door.

"Why do I have the feeling that Cass has all the answers and we should go directly to her?" Hannah asked in frustration.

"Because if she had the answers, the killer would be behind bars by now. And if she wanted to talk to us, she'd find us." Aaron took her hand as he opened the gallery door.

Cass stood framed in the sunlight.

EIGHTEEN

"You are not to disturb Xavier," Cass said sternly. "He has suffered enough under our hands."

"You want to talk about it here or at the café?" Aaron asked dryly. "The boardwalk doesn't seem appropriate."

Cass marched toward his shop. Aware that Hannah gaped with wide-open eyes of wonder stirred Aaron's protective instincts, ones better left buried. She was the all-knowing librarian and no innocent. She knew Cass's psychic abilities. He didn't have to protect Hannah from the old witch, right?

Reaching the shop, Aaron sent Wang Hai away. The *feng shui* expert had already rearranged the furniture into a Victorian parlor. All it needed was Hannah fixing a silver tea tray and teapot to re-create the scene of the early spiritualists who had settled in this town. He refrained from rolling his eyes.

Her long silver hair pulled into a knot, Cass chose a high-backed wooden straight chair with satin padding in the center. Hannah set the tray down on the carved Victorian coffee table that had held a murder weapon and took her usual place on the velvet sofa of dubious origin. Aaron paced.

"Why didn't we go to the café?" he asked while they passed each other sugar and cream.

"Because this involves the Kennedys, which involves Sam, Teddy, and Fee, and I saw no purpose in upsetting them." Cass accepted Hannah waiting on her as if accustomed to servants—as she once had been. Cass's family was wealthy.

"So, tell us about the crystals," Aaron said rudely. This was why he didn't deal in people. He was supposed to murmur platitudes and wait for old ladies to tell him what he wanted. Not happening.

"The casket belonged to my mother, who inherited it from her mother," Cass said, sipping her tea. "The Victorian spiritualist who carried the Healing Stone from England was my great-great grandmother, the one who married the rancher who owned all this land."

"Why didn't she write a journal?" asked Hannah, sounding aggrieved. "It would have solved much."

"Their journals are in my library. Like my mother, I saw no reason to continue sending books to England when they were needed here. I hoped an American librarian would show up. One person cannot be everywhere, and you are already bearing a large load."

"So where's the stone?" Hannah asked, apparently dismissing this insult to her abilities.

Aaron had the insane longing to hold Hannah and protect her from what was coming when Cass hesitated over an answer. He knew Hannah was hoping an old stone would solve everything, maybe even her health. But as weird as Lucy abilities were, they were not magic. Aladdin was fiction.

"Carmel always got everything she wanted," Cass said sadly. "The details are tedious. My stepfather inherited everything and only gave me what he didn't deem useful. He couldn't build on the vortex or the cemetery, so he left me those and generously added an attached plot of land where I could put my house. He never really understood the true value of the things he inherited, and neither did Geoffrey, his son," Cass said sadly, stirring her tea. "I probably should have fought harder, but I was young and still learning the extent of my abilities. Material things were unimportant, and I had the arrogance of youth to believe I would retrieve what was mine when the time came. I didn't count on Carmel usurping them."

"But you've seen the Healing Stone? It does exist?" Casting aside her usual indifference, Hannah questioned eagerly.

Aaron was perfectly willing to let her tackle Cass. He preferred keeping a distance from the Hillvale doyenne, or she'd try to use him as she did everyone else.

"I saw it when it was in my mother's care, but she had it locked up. Her life was an unhappy one, and she preferred not to accept her unwelcome gifts or family eccentrics. I went the opposite direction, but she didn't live to know that. I suppose, if I hadn't gone to live with her sister and rebel against my stepfather's edicts, I might have turned out as she did. My stepfather inherited all her worldly goods, including the casket in the safe."

Impatient with this trip down memory lane, Aaron brought her back on topic. "Do you know if the other stones in Carmel's safe also belonged to your family? She considered them valuable, but the sheriff has them, so we can't test that."

"No, they're not my family's stones. My mother only kept the Healing Stone in the casket," Cass said with a hint of satisfaction. "The rest of the collection didn't look important, and I claimed them when she died. I had them assessed once. There are a few semi-precious stones not native to this area, so I assume she inherited them from the grandmother who brought the Healing Stone with her. Some of the stones are of a type found around here, but they are of no intrinsic value. Teddy or Keegan would have to test them for anything else. I did not inherit my ancestor's gift for crystals."

"Do you remember what the Healing Stone looked like?" Hannah prodded.

Cass frowned thoughtfully. "It was nearly fist-sized, blue-white, very compelling. Not polished, but exposed from the usual rock shape so facets were visible."

"A moonstone," Hannah murmured.

Unfamiliar with crystal types, Aaron stuck to his purpose. "Large enough to crack a skull?"

Cass closed her eyes and nodded sadly. "That was never its purpose."

"Lance said the artists collected crystals from a grotto. Do you have any idea where that might be?" Aaron continued, not knowing where else to take this conversation.

Cass shrugged. "My grandfather had an old cabin where the lodge is now. I wasn't interested in hunting and fishing and never came up here as a child. By the time the Kennedys built the lodge, I wasn't much interested in exploring what was no longer mine. I know my son occasionally went to the grotto with the commune children, but I was assured the water was merely a trickle unless it rained."

"That confirms it was on Kennedy property at least," Hannah murmured. "Do you have any idea what happened to it?"

Cass finished her tea and set down her cup. "Over the decades we've had fires and floods. The mountain changes. It always has. Man was never really meant to live here. Too much blood has been shed over ownership of what shouldn't be owned in the first place. If I can help you contain the evil, let me know. Otherwise, I really have nothing more to contribute."

The instant she left, Aaron reached for her teacup. Hannah's hand covered his.

A blue-white opalescent shimmer reflecting the moon's light—enthralling, compelling.

Rage. Frustration. Sorrow.

A room with a glass roof, looking out at the night sky, singing a prayerful song to unleash the energy. . .

Aaron crashed into Cass's mental wall and dropped the cup. It shattered on the floor. Hannah looked vaguely startled and studied the shards at her feet as he fell down on the sofa beside her.

"Well, we know for certain that the moonstone was here at one time," she said brightly. "And I guess digging up the boulder looking for it is no longer necessary."

"Cass deliberately blocked us," he said grumpily. "Wily old woman came prepared with just exactly what she wanted revealed. She wants that stone back."

"And she won't get it if it's a murder weapon. Besides, it belongs to the Kennedys now." Hannah leaned over to pick up pieces of china. "She was angry enough to kill, you know."

"Yeah, and if the cops didn't have Francois pinned for the job, they'd have a field day with Cass. Guaranteed she has no alibi, and she despised Carmel."

"The sheriff would never learn any of that. The Lucys will protect her. I'm beginning to think Walker has a real problem on his hands here." Hannah stood and carried the tray and the broken china toward the back.

"No question there," Aaron agreed. "The Lucys are a modern vigilante group, and they protect each other."

"Power corrupts," Hannah said sadly from the back. "Balance of power is needed."

"Xavier was there the night Carmel died," Aaron called after her, studying his ceiling to see how Wan Hai had managed to illuminate it without wiring. "Word is, he and Cass were an item once. I can't see him as a murderer, but if Carmel made him angry enough. . ."

"Xavier might have whacked Carmel for yelling at Cass and Cass would cover for him?" Hannah emerged from the back, empty-handed. "We could just ask him where the grotto was and if he knew where Carmel got her rocks. Do you have anything kicking around that you could give as a gift? Tell him Wan Hai is cleaning house and you hated to throw it away?"

"*Damnatus*, you're devious. Cass can't complain if all I do is give him a gift." He stood and glanced around. "He's a lawyer. I don't know his taste in books. He spends a lot of time at his desk going over contracts." His glance fell on a vintage Montblanc fountain pen from the 1930s. It was worth some serious cash, but it had been used by a notorious monopolist who had destroyed families and entire towns with his greed. He hated that piece. Blocking his senses, he retrieved it from the pen display. "Got it."

This interviewing business was feeling a little too real. Did he really want to solve a case the sheriff might be willing to write off? Maybe, if the killer was likely to strike again. They still didn't know for certain that Francois hadn't just overdosed on medication.

"Let's take him a rock to look at, so he can hand it back." Aaron rummaged through an apothecary chest until he found the drawer with geological specimens.

Hannah peered over his shoulder. "Did those come from around here?"

"They were here when I moved in. I can feel the hopes of some poor fool who thought they might be gold. There isn't any energy on them other than his." He selected one with a nice streak of false gold in it.

"You keep *everything*," she said in what didn't sound like admiration. "Ever consider having a garage sale?"

"Not once." Pocketing the rock, he headed for the door, only then realizing he had no one to man the desk. No way was he leaving Hannah behind.

He turned the CLOSED sign and locked the shop after her.

IF SHE HADN'T ALREADY HAD HER HEAD EXAMINED, SHE'D BE WONDERING IF she should.

Hannah followed the talented but obtuse *guardian* across the street to the real estate agent's office. Aaron had a talent that could conceivably save lives. He needed to be out in the wider world, using his power for the good of all.

The things he saw. . . It was the next best thing to mind-reading. She should talk to Amber about how her psychic abilities worked, except they seemed related to tarot cards and not easily used in other situations.

Xavier Black was a tall man with thin gray hair and sagging jowls. His eyes were sad but clear, and he wore a nicely tailored blue jacket and matching tie, as if a Hillvale office was just as important as a city law office. He looked up with interest at their entrance.

"Ready to move out of Aaron's place, Miss Simon?" he asked with a laugh.

"I am, actually, but I can wait until the work is done on the school. In the meantime, I'm trying to convince Aaron to clean out his shop before someone gets hurt." She beamed innocently. She knew how to present a blank slate.

"Between Hannah and Wan Hai, they're cleaning me out. Apparently, fountain pens are bad *feng shui*, but I'm not about to fling out a nice piece like this. Even if you don't use them, it looks good on a desk. Since you're the only one in town who actually sits at a desk. . ." Aaron presented the gleaming, gold tipped Montblanc.

"Man, that brings back memories." Xavier caressed the polished case. "Had a fellow in the office who collected these. You sure you don't want it?" He looked up as if waiting to be told Aaron was just kidding.

"Do you know anyone who still uses fountain pens? It's all yours. And while we're here. . ." Aaron produced the glittery rock from his pocket. "Lance was telling us about a grotto where they collected shiny rocks like this. Do you have any notion where that was?"

Xavier hefted the rock in his palm and shook his head. "I know there was water out there once. Menendez swears there was a spring and a stream that flowed all summer. I thought it was on his land, but it's apparently dried up now."

"Was that something Carmel might have known?" Hannah asked, getting into this detective business.

Xavier frowned. "She knew everything, so yes, she may have. For all I know, she had it blocked to keep anyone from using it. Carmel had a mean streak when she got riled."

"We heard the artists found rocks like this in a stream on the Kennedy property, so we were kind of wondering if that's where she got the rocks in her box. For all we know, they might be valuable." Aaron propped his hip against the battered wooden desk as if he had nothing better to do all day.

"Could be, but I didn't participate in rock collecting. We were all into the drug scene back in college, even Carmel. She could have traded drugs for glittery stones just the way she traded her body for Geoff's land. The town is better off without her." Xavier handed the rock back.

Wow, there was a load of bitterness and cynicism. Hannah waited to see what Aaron would do. Did he have the ability to wait until they were outside to access any memories on the stone? Or did he want to do it now, after Xavier's inflammatory statement?

Aaron clenched the stone as if testing it, then held it up for Hannah to take. The instant she touched his hand, she saw what he saw, in Technicolor.

A young Carmel, naked, in a narrow bed, with a very young, very handsome Xavier kneeling over her, half-dressed—and an even younger Cass opening the door. Loathing crossed her face. She flung a book at the couple in the bed and walked out.

Carmel's expression was triumphant. Xavier's despair was devastating.

Hannah held the rock and closed her eyes for a moment before she followed Aaron out. Xavier's pain was that crippling.

"I'll assume that was from before Carmel married Kennedy," Hannah said quietly as they crossed the road to the shop.

"A very long time ago," Aaron agreed. "And it still hurts him. Enough to kill?"

"No, not if he went on to work with Geoffrey to cheat people with their mortgage scheme. He knows his own guilt. It may have been the point that turned him from being a decent man into the greedy fraud he became, though." Hannah thought about that, how one event might turn a man—or woman's—life in a different direction. "I understand he descended into drugs as the Kennedys accumulated more land. Drugs anesthetize that kind of emotional pain."

"The Lucys apparently punished Xavier for his part in the mortgage scheme by locking him in the cemetery. He kind of lost it that night. That's why Cass doesn't want us bothering him. He's been punished." Aaron unlocked and shoved open his shop door.

Half the newly-arranged furniture had been tossed as if by a giant hand. Aaron's valuable library lay scattered across the floor near the shelves. The wardrobes hung open, their drawers ransacked.

And a pile of rocks lay in the middle of the clutter.

NINETEEN

AARON SLAMMED THE SHOP DOOR CLOSED BEFORE HANNAH COULD ENTER, but there was no keeping the Lucys from picking up on his fear and fury. While he raced around to the back to see if he could catch the bastard, they emerged from every doorway in town. They gathered on the board-walk and waited, forcing Aaron to open the front door when he returned.

Without invitation, the women spilled in, sticks raised defensively, just in case a poltergeist had visited.

The bubbling fountain had been knocked over, soaking the zebra-skinned rug Wan Hai had set in front of the door. The prisms in the window still sparkled a rainbow over the soggy mess.

He knew a ghost hadn't tossed his shop. He'd found the back door jimmied. Someone was trying to make him back off—someone who didn't know him very well.

Wan Hai began to wail at the destruction of all her hard work. Thank all that was holy, Hannah took the *feng shui* expert outside, into the waiting arms of Pasquale, the Italian grocer, who led her away, weeping.

Aaron kept his eyes on the more dangerous women circling the room. Tullah and Amber had arrived first, since their stores were clos-est. The thrift store owner frowned and muttered voodoo chants under her breath. Gentle Amber shook her head and patted his arm comfortingly.

Hannah stood back, observing, like the studious librarian she was. Aaron wanted to tell her to go back to Scotland, except he wanted to join her, and he couldn't leave Hillvale unprotected. He was a selfish bastard, but he needed her here, helping him dig out answers—

And waiting for her to convulse on the floor from the *knot* in her head. Evidently, he had one in his too, letting himself in for that level of pain again. Maybe, if he found the damned stone, she'd go away.

Fee popped in, holding her little dog, which yapped frantically and tried to scramble from her arms. The cook sniffed, muttered *mildew*, and trotted back to her café.

Even Dinah came in from the restaurant. Dinah seldom left her kitchen. She wasn't a Lucy, but the gruff, transgender cook was the heart-beat of the town. Looking appalled, she began reverently picking up old books, until Tullah stopped her.

"We need a circle, girl. We need to find who did this. You go back and cook us some gumbo because we're gonna need it." Tullah seldom descended to dialect. When she did, it was serious.

"There's nothing you can do with a circle," Aaron protested. "This isn't a ghost. This is someone trying to distract me from asking questions. I need Keegan or Harvey to test those stones. Otherwise, I just need to start putting things back in place."

"It ain't just about you, boy," Tullah retorted. "The spirits will tell us who was here."

Teddy arrived. Her jewelry store was on the far end of town and often busy. But he should have known she'd receive word the same way the others did—osmosis, he was convinced.

She held her walking stick over the pile of rocks, shook her head, and crouched down. "I'm receiving few emanations from these. Aaron, have you tested them?"

Hannah stepped in front of him. "Don't. Not yet. Let me experiment with Teddy first. You don't want to touch those rocks if they're loaded with anything bad."

There was an entertaining spin—she was protecting *him*.

"There's no *malum* on them," he told her. But he could see she was eager to test her new-found ability to enhance gifts. He almost felt jealous when she held out her hand to Teddy.

As Teddy picked up one of the rocks, Sam and Mariah arrived from the furthest end of town. It was a damned Lucy parade. Aaron just wanted to toss furniture back in place, but instinct stopped him. He had to remind himself that these people were his friends. They wanted to help. He hadn't had much of that in his life, which meant he didn't know how to handle it now.

"Not evil," Teddy repeated, rolling the rock in her palm. "Not really crystal. I'm no expert. You'll need to call Keegan for that. But I think this one is just granite with minute crystals embedded. The emanations feel spiteful, but that's not my bailiwick."

Hannah wrapped her hand around Teddy's. Both women stood still, then shook their heads. Hannah quietly stepped back to stand beside him. "Nothing," she murmured in disappointment.

Teddy tossed the rock back to the stack. "We need a circle. Sam, will Cass be coming?"

"No, I don't think so. Tullah, what do you think? Anything we can do?" Sam, the environmental scientist, had an unnatural talent for growing things but no ability to summon spirits.

Aaron hadn't realized he was growling under his breath until Hannah squeezed his hand. "Do you want to test anything before they get started?" she asked.

"Yes." While the women discussed their hoodoo, he stalked past them to the rocks. He ran his staff over them, looking for any unusual energy. Finding none, he picked up a handful of the smaller rocks. He found only faint impressions.

Hannah's hand covered his as if it belonged there. The meanness in them exploded.

"Just ugliness," she whispered. "Is ugliness an emotion?"

"Yeah, in this case, it's vicious malice, like Teddy said." He flung the stone back. "I think whoever did this enjoys destruction and was paid to do this."

She nodded. "That matches what I was feeling. I just couldn't translate it. Nothing real but an ugly joy in being destructive, like a vandal who knifes art or tags walls."

Who knew he'd been asking about rocks? Lance, Cass, and Xavier. Lance had had time to tell half the town. Cass wouldn't say a word. And this had been done while they were with Xavier. Anyone else? Or did this go back to his searching Francois's room? Was the killer getting nervous?

Looking as if he'd been dragged from bed, which he probably had, Harvey arrived. Aaron watched as the musician regarded the chaos, picked up the stones, studied them, and widened his eyes. "If they're trying to make us believe these came from around here, they don't know rocks or they think we're idiots. See if Keegan recognizes them."

"He's back in his cave. It will take a while for him to drive back," Mariah said. "I had to leave Daphne with a neighbor. So let's get this circle done with, and he can tell you more when he comes in."

Aaron signaled Harvey to follow him as he backed out to the board-walk, leaving behind Hannah, who was fascinated by the Lucy's spirit circle.

"How do you know they're not from here?" he demanded the instant Harvey shut the door.

"I'm no geologist," Harvey warned. "I don't know proper names for anything. But granite is composed of several basic materials. That one's mostly gray, with very little crystal or pink. The granite up the mountain is heavy with quartz and what Keegan says is feldspar. He can tell you more. It has to do with volcanic action and former ocean currents and whatnot."

"So somebody just unloaded a bunch of stray rock in my store to mess with my mind—or because I've been asking about rocks." Aaron glared down the sunlit street to where tourists roamed the walks, unaware of dangerous shadows lurking. Several glanced at his shop, saw the gathering inside, and hesitated. "*Damnatus*. I need curtains on that window." Inspiration struck. "Do you know anything about a grotto?"

Harvey looked suspicious. "On Kennedy land. My grandfather claims they stole his water to make it."

"Wonderful. More treachery to feed the *malum*." Aaron jammed his hands in his pockets and studied his shop window, looking for Hannah. Then he realized what he was doing and mentally slapped himself.

Let the women do their thing. No spirit would explain this level of stupidity. And the spirits clinging to some of that furniture ought to drive them out soon enough. He had more people to interview while they played.

He'd worked without Hannah all his life. He didn't need her now.

He just *wanted* her, which was a dangerous concept best buried and forgotten.

"Want to talk to Kennedys about grottos and rocks?" He started across the street to City Hall.

"I doubt they'll know anything, but it's a start." Harvey crossed the street with him.

Balance of power, Aaron mused, recalling Hannah's comment: evil versus innocence, spirit energy versus money. Was it even possible to balance those?

HANNAH HAD ATTENDED SÉANCES BEFORE, PERHAPS NONE AS ECCENTRIC OR realistic as this one.

Mariah failed to channel Daisy, as she claimed to have done before. Tullah complained that she needed Val, the Death Goddess, who had mysteriously disappeared. The thrift store owner did contact a spirit who apparently lingered in one of Aaron's chairs and who laughed at their puny efforts.

"We just need to know who vandalized the shop." Speaking to the dismissive spirit, Amber used a hypnotic tone that Hannah hadn't heard before.

"Big burly man," Tullah answered in a husky, dismissive voice not her own. "Wouldn't mind trying him on for size. Mean bugger though. Probably beats women."

Spirits were about as useless as neighborhood gossips, Hannah concluded.

"Is there anyone else here who would like to speak?" Amber asked.

"Honor the dead," Teddy unexpectedly said. "Do not disturb the stones."

Hannah could feel shock vibrating through the hands clasping hers. As far as she knew, Teddy didn't normally channel spirits. But the jeweler had helped Hannah dig up a stone guardian. Was she reaching the natives who had created it?

"Have others desecrated the burial ground?" Hannah asked.

"Only Mother Earth. The evil haunts her still. Return the stones so they may rest." Teddy's hand fell limp in Hannah's.

The circle broke up after that. The Lucys chattered excitedly. Uneasy, Hannah began returning Aaron's books to the shelves. "Does anyone know where there might be an old grotto?" she finally asked, because that had been on her mind when Teddy's spirit had spoken.

"I know where one used to be," Mariah said, helping Tullah right the furniture. "Follow the cottonwoods. There's a valley below the lodge, filled with trees. I was told the Kennedys once attempted to create a pool there."

"And I heard the artists gathered crystals there," Hannah said. "Anyone up for an expedition?"

"I thought their crystals came from Keegan's cave." Mariah sounded puzzled.

"That may be where Daisy found hers, but Lance says some were found in a grotto. He has a painting of it in the gallery." Hannah waited expectantly.

By the time the Lucys sorted their schedules, Sam was the only one free to explore. Just as they debated postponing until another date, Keegan arrived. He glanced at the destruction, checked worriedly on his wife—who was still righting furniture—then turned to the pile of rocks.

"You've started raising rocks instead of spirits?" he asked, crouching to wave his hand over them.

"Straight from hell," Mariah agreed cheerfully. "Harvey and Aaron think they're harmless. What say you, Oh Great One?"

He shrugged. "Granite, not local. Driveway material at best. Someone just making a statement?"

"That rocks are rocks?" Teddy swept them onto a shovel. "Only a Null would do that."

"You didn't really think a Lucy did this, do you?" Keegan stood. "Where's Aaron?"

"With Harvey. Tell him he's talking to the wrong people if he wants to find the grotto." With satisfaction, Hannah helped Mariah stack the coffee tables.

Only when they were almost done did she remember the Eversham painting.

Aaron had stored it in back, hadn't he? She was hunting through the storage area when Aaron returned. Understanding what she sought, he wordlessly reached to the top of the old secretary.

His hand came back empty.

TWENTY

THE MISSING PAINTING WAS LIKE A MISSING TOOTH. AARON FELT THE GAP and kept coming back to it, toying with it, irritating already inflamed tissue.

"How did anyone know it even existed?" He paced his carefully curated living room—because Hannah had insisted he was in no shape to re-open the shop. She was damned right. He wanted to commit murder.

"*I* knew because of the journals," Hannah offered. "The Lucys know because we showed photos to Mariah and Keegan. If someone had you investigated. . ."

Reading old newspapers would tell them he'd once had a valuable Eversham in his possession—but how would they know which one? His shop was full of valuable antiques. Why steal the hidden painting unless it was the painting in particular they were after?

He didn't know why he'd let Hannah follow him home. But she made an excellent sounding board and kept him from swinging from the rafters in frustration. "They might be curious about the painting I purportedly stole, but they wouldn't know where I hid it!"

"That part is troublesome, yes. Even I didn't know where you'd put it, besides in the back somewhere. And the place is packed to the rafters with junk."

Hannah sipped the margarita he'd fixed, tasting it as if it were new to her, which it might be. She'd probably been under twenty-one when she'd left the States. He didn't think margaritas were routinely served in Scotland. An *innocent*, a total innocent. He ought to have his mind washed out with soap for even looking at her.

"Which makes me think either I have spyware in my shop or a Lucy took it. You're the only Lucy I know who could sense it." He watched her reaction mostly because he liked looking at her, not because he believed she'd stolen the painting.

She took another sip of the drink and grimaced. "I only knew where to find it because it glowed. I don't know if others noticed. The Lucys have seen the photos we took of the painting. No one seemed very interested."

He pointed at her as he paced. "But once we showed that photo, word of the painting would have got around. A Lucy mentions it to her Null spouse, who mentions it to someone else. . . Probably didn't take a day for news to spread. Okay, that part makes sense now." He returned to pacing rather than watch her with the drink. He liked his salty. She might have preferred more sweet.

"But that doesn't explain how they *found* it," she argued. "And we don't know for certain that it was stolen during the vandalism, unless you're in the habit of checking on it nightly. I would have noticed if I'd seen it glowing if I came in after dark, I think, and I don't remember seeing it since you moved it."

Aaron grabbed the phone and left a message with Walker asking that he check the storage area for spyware. "Unless that painting is giving off infra-red, I just don't see how thieves could find it," he said when he hung up.

She screwed up her petite nose. "And I don't want to think about people spying on us in your office. So let's go see the grotto. I still think that's central to our understanding of whatever is happening. If you need to punish your feet, it ought to be while doing something useful. Mariah said we need to follow the cottonwoods."

"Harvey would have done that already. He's obsessed with finding water on the mountain." His interview with the Kennedys had been a waste. They'd known nothing about the grotto—it had been before their time.

Still, a fruitless search made more sense than wearing out a priceless carpet. Aaron set down his drink to dig in a closet for a backpack. He wasn't the hiking sort, but he had equipment for everything.

Hannah turned to his refrigerator. They'd grabbed lunches from Fee earlier, but sustenance was always good when on the trail. Aaron liked that Hannah was self-sufficient, not needing to be given instructions—a damned good thing because he wasn't accustomed to communicating.

"You restocked," she said dryly, removing various ingredients.

"I called Pasquale, and Harvey picked it up yesterday. I do eat," he added, filling a water bottle.

"Not a vampire, good to know." She cut a crusty roll and began adding vegetables and cheese, avoiding the lunchmeat he preferred. "How many hours of daylight left?"

"Out in the open, four or five. If we enter the more wooded areas, less. We have time for a quick reconnaissance." He grabbed slabs of lunchmeat and slapped them on one of the rolls she prepared.

He continued packing essentials while she finished wrapping sandwiches and choosing fruit. The quiet familiarity of the preparations reminded him that they shared a commonality in spending time in the sparseness of the Shetlands, where striking out across land meant no McDonalds, no gas stations or mini-marts. The routine soothed some of his restlessness.

They set off in the heat of late afternoon, but there was enough of a breeze to prevent melting in puddles of sweat. Aaron felt better now that he was actually doing something, even if it was pointless.

"I have no idea how this helps find Carmel's killer," Hannah said, reflecting his own thought. "I should think if they wanted her stones, they'd have done more to get them by now."

"By robbing the sheriff's office? Or rummaging the suite after Carmel screamed the house down and brought everyone running? If the stones really are the object, he must be biding his time." Which set off a whole new train of thought.

She hopped on that train with him. "He thinks he can steal them from the Kennedys when the sheriff returns them? Unless you believe her sons killed her." Hannah strode beside him, almost keeping up with his longer strides.

"Her sons were in the bar when she started screaming, or they'd be under suspicion by now. Maybe they hired Francois to kill her, then killed him so they didn't have to pay." Knowing the honorable Kennedys, Aaron played this game with amusement.

"Unless they had some pressing urgency to kill their mother now, they'd have done it long ago if they were murderously inclined." Her voice was tinged with humor that showed she knew they'd reached the ridiculous. She cut away from the path to cross a field toward the largest clump of cottonwoods.

"They were talking about having her committed, so I don't think murder was their intent." He studied the sparse line of trees. "There is a lot of dead wood. Any water in there probably dried up this summer."

"We probably ought to have Keegan with us. Or maybe Teddy. She's sensitive to rock vibrations. Even Sam could probably tell us more about what to look for. I just hate sitting idle, waiting for a killer to strike again." She swiped at a hank of sunny hair adorning her brow.

She'd abandoned her wispy shirt for just the tank top and shorts. Her shoulders were turning pink from the constant exposure to sun since she'd arrived. Aaron tried not to look further down than her shoulders, but he should probably remind her to rub on more lotion. . .

Hannah slid a little on the rocky slope.

Unthinking, Aaron caught her arm. Before he could release her, she halted. She looked blank for a moment, shook her head, then glanced up at him. "Wow. Spooky, but I think I like it."

Slanting him a sideways look that tingled all his working parts, she returned to sliding down the hill.

Given what he'd been thinking right before he touched her, he was *not* going to ask what that was about.

MAYBE SHE'D NEVER BEEN MUCH INTERESTED IN THE MEN SHE'D DATED because she hadn't been able to read how they felt. Or maybe they didn't feel things about her the way Aaron did. Or maybe she was just crazy.

But that jolt of insight into his desire had shredded every last cell in Hannah's body and rearranged them. She thought Aaron had been treating her as a tool to be used as needed. She'd had no idea. . . Well, maybe she'd hoped, but she didn't have radar for that sort of thing.

The surly antiques dealer desired *her*? Admired her? That just did not compute. She was the original invisible librarian. No man noticed her. She wasn't cute, she wasn't animated or vivacious. . . She was pretty much a plain nerd, all she lacked was the stereotypical spectacles.

Maybe she was imagining what she'd felt in his touch. At least she hadn't fainted. Or seen knights in tarnished armor.

Focus, Hannah. Besides, Aaron was the one who was supposed to *feel* things by touching, not her. If he didn't sense her desire, then he was blocking her as he did everyone else. Fine. Getting involved had never been on her agenda. She barely wanted to commit to teaching little kids. So if she wanted to believe that spirits might travel through time together, theirs were eternally doomed.

When they reached the dying grove of trees, she regarded the terrain with disappointment. "Looks no different than anywhere else. Lots of rocks, cactus, scrubby looking plants that probably aren't heather. . ."

"It's pretty in the spring, after a wet winter. That's probably the best time to hunt for water. It naturally runs to the lowest point." He studied the landscape. "The tree line goes both ways. I want to assume that the well to our left is the termination point, and that the mountain on our right would be where the stream flows from, but there's a lower elevation straight ahead."

"One that also has trees and is lower than this band of them." Hannah tried to picture a stream flowing down the mountain to the old well and burial ground. The lower stand of trees didn't fit the topography.

Aaron started down the rocky, dusty hillside to the misplaced trees. "But in a wet winter, with heavy rain flooding down the mountain, water might accumulate down there. If the well sprung a leak, that would be a natural drainage pool."

"And if there had been a landslide during one of those floods. . ."

Hannah slipped and slid down the hill after him. Good thing she'd worn her walking shoes this morning.

"And this is the kind of sandy ground that breaks up if you look at it crooked, so yeah, landslides are a given," he finished for her.

"And if the soldier really did add his crystals to the native stone statues, they could have traveled downward from the burial ground with the landslide." She halted on a large slab of slanted rock. Dead trees overhung it—similar to the living ones in Lance's painting?

Aaron got down on his stomach and leaned over the precipitous edge. Hannah held her breath until he rolled back up. "Broken trees and rock, shifted earth, so yep, landslide in the last century or two. And any *lamassu* crystals washed down there are gone."

That was a serious disappointment, but nothing that shouldn't have been expected. Miracles didn't really happen.

"Until another flood washes away the dirt—which may be what happened the year the commune turned this into a bathing pool." Hannah sat on the rock edge planted firmly in the mountainside. "This could be where Val stood in the painting. Which means Carmel and her security guard came down from over there." She nodded to the uphill slope.

"So if we assume Carmel's rocks came from the hippies who used this swimming hole, we need to convince the Kennedys that they belong to an ancient graveyard, and they should return them? They're teetering on the edge of bankruptcy, from all reports. If those stones are worth cash. . ."

"We'll worry about it when the time comes, I guess. Maybe if they can be convinced the stones are the evil that drove their mother mad. . . Although I'm inclined to believe it was her own greed that did that, enhanced by whatever is in the stones maybe." Hannah swung her legs over the edge of the rock and admired the few trees still struggling to survive. "Water would help a lot of people, wouldn't it?"

"Harvey wants it for a winery. Amber's movie star husband is willing to invest, but without water, it's all dreams. If there really is water underground, it would have to be dammed for them to use it upstream. That won't fix the grotto." Aaron sat down beside her.

"There was enough water for a well once." Hannah removed sand-wiches from the backpack. "I don't know about enough for a winery."

Having a sensible conversation while sitting next to a man exuding power and charisma was an exhilarating experience, Hannah decided, one that amazingly achieved balance—both calming and energizing her.

"If we could find the killer, we might find the Healing Stone." Aaron took the sandwich she offered but didn't unwrap it.

"We need a better way to employ your skills." Hannah sipped her water, trying not to admire the strength in the hands so close to hers. She really wanted to touch him again.

Aaron was *way* out of her league, she told herself. Older, well-trav-eled, better-educated, more talented, too handsome, too sophisticated. . . She'd never even had a real boyfriend. And she shouldn't be thinking of a curmudgeonly ex-con in such a manner anyway. Knights in shining armor didn't exist.

"Your enhancing ability might help." He slugged back his water. "But most gifts have downsides. I'm not sure either of us is prepared for that."

If she was prepared to die, she was prepared for anything. "Practice leads to preparation. I'm just uncertain what I can do. I'm uncertain about everything. I hate living in limbo." There, she'd said it, sort of. He had to translate for himself.

He was quiet for a moment. "I suppose we're all living in limbo. A bomb could drop tomorrow. A crazed killer could shoot up the town. I hate thinking like that."

"Your natural state is to protect," she said with understanding. "You want to throw up a shield to shelter the good and shut out the bad."

"A Healing Stone sounds perfect," he agreed. "Too perfect. Essen-tially, we must fix ourselves."

"Or die trying," she said with a laugh. "I'd prefer doing that for a worthy cause, but I don't even know where to start."

"Yes you do," he said quietly. "Every time we touch, we come alive, even if it's in another time or place."

"Oh." She nibbled an apple and didn't look at him. "I didn't think you cared."

"I'm not stone," he said dryly. "The first time I saw you walk through my door, you lit the gloom like sunshine. I can't say I appreciate having my lack of life thrown back at me. But you make me see color again. I'm afraid if I let myself go, I'll suck you dry."

"Don't think it works that way. Admittedly, we're on tricky ground." Hannah tried to sound casual, but her pulse raced. "But experimentation hasn't killed us yet. I've been living in a dark cave as much as you have. I'm not seeing the light you do."

"I want to brush that hank of hair off your face. Are you willing to see what happens if I try?" He turned the dark wells of his eyes on her.

She felt that look all the way to her toes. Mesmerized, she lifted her face, giving him silent permission to touch.

Brown fingers caressed her straying hair and brushed her cheek. Instead of fainting, she recognized the connection to another time and place when he had done that. The memory replaced her earlier shock, grounding her. Hannah felt the longing deep in her soul, the need for another human touch, this man's touch.

Hesitatingly, she traced her fingers down Aaron's angular jaw, to his lips.

He needed no further encouragement. He leaned over and brushed his mouth on hers. When she didn't topple, he pressed for more.

Her world shivered and quaked, but Hannah clung to the contact, the hard flesh and intoxicating male aroma.

Aaron lifted her across his lap. Their encumbering jeans rubbed where she ached the most. His kiss deepened, distracting her again. His big hands ran under her tank top—she could feel his energy, his desire, as skilled fingers explored her flesh. When he pushed up her sports bra, she was totally open to him.

As he cupped her bare breasts, he opened himself just a little, just enough to sense his genuine awe and excitement and that flickering shared memory of long ago. Here was her knight, the man of her dreams, the one who had awakened her.

She'd been waiting for him all her life and then some.

TWENTY-ONE

WHEN HANNAH'S GENTLE HANDS SLID ACROSS HIS BARE TORSO, AARON almost froze with the desperate need for this human touch. But Hannah's caress was different, not just physical but deeper. He could sense her desire and need and her genuine respect and awe. Another moment, and she'd reach right through his skin and grab his heart.

He pressed his forehead against hers and stopped her hand, nearly stopping his heart in doing so. "We're not doing this here, on hard rock."

Those were probably the most difficult words he'd ever uttered, but this connection was too magical, too rare, to be thrown away on momentary lust.

Hannah moaned a little, a mew that sliced right through his gut and tightened his jeans at the same time.

Pushing upward, he rose with her arms around his shoulders and her legs still wrapped around his hips—like a limpet. He grinned in memory of his earlier disdain. Who knew he enjoyed limpet clinging?

She dropped her feet quickly, but he didn't release her. Now that she'd stripped his wicked soul bare, he needed the human contact a little longer.

"I don't get involved with Lucys," he warned her instinctively, then regretted it when she stiffened and pushed away.

"Probably incestuous," she muttered, groping blindly for the scattered remnants of their meal.

He was still thinking with his prick—not clearly at all. "Muddying the waters, at best." He grabbed her and kissed her again until she landed dizzily against his chest, where he liked having her. "And we're nowhere as stable as Mariah and Keegan."

She reluctantly nodded. "Too true. If we're looking for excuses not to deal with this, you talk first." She pushed away again and started back up the hill, sending sand and pebbles cascading downward.

"I like your pragmatism," he said, following, not really liking her practical response at all. But he'd started this, and she was the only woman he knew who could take his own words and beat him over the head with them.

"I thought we were looking for *cons*, like this damned knot in my brain."

"Let's start there then. I want to curse your knot and get a second opinion. You want to say prayers and find a magic stone." Pervert that he was, he enjoyed watching the sway of indignation in her hips as she climbed.

"My head, my choice. I want to live life fully for as long as I am able." She turned and gave him a stink eye. "And that includes sex on a rock. I thought we were floating with the stars."

"I was on the bottom," he said dryly. "One of us has to be practical."

"No, one of has to be *superior*," she said with indignant humor. "I get that. I'm not a control freak, you are. I can accept that. I accept that I won't live forever and totally understand that is a major stumbling block for you. So just make this about getting our rocks off—isn't that what men say?"

Good thing he stayed behind her or she'd probably smack the smirk off his face. She was good. She was damned good. "Lucys do not *get their rocks off*. They cling, like limpets." He quickly changed the subject before she called him a Lucy. "Tell me again why you decided to have an MRI."

She twisted around to study him, but he wasn't smirking anymore. He was serious.

On level ground again, she fell in stride beside him. "Because that damned painting obsessed me, and I'd never been the least obsessive-compulsive before. I dreamed about it, at first. Then it got worse. I'd sit in the office and imagine it coming to life. When I started fainting if I touched it, I figured it had to be physical. I'd never fainted before, ever. I thought—blood sugar gone awry."

"Then you fainted when you touched *me*," he prodded.

She shrugged. "I now know the problem is literally in my head. When I touched you, I had visions of the knight painting and went down out of habit, I suppose."

"You haven't been fainting lately," he said. "Not unless that flying with the stars comment means you were literally out of it."

She stuck out a plump bottom lip in thought. "True. Maybe seeing inside your head is a new symptom."

"You're *not* seeing inside my head. You're magnifying what's on the objects we touch. Someone else probably had sex on those rocks. What if that knot is where you carry your gift? Or maybe even your library? The brain is made up of masses of similar neurons that congregate in one area for specific reasons. You may have a memory mass that others don't. Maybe the knot has nothing to do with your fainting and everything to do with your memory."

"Wow, big leap." She was silent as they reached the path back to his place. "We can't prove anything," she decided. "I'm not about to have the mass removed to find out. You have to accept me as I am."

"Warts and all," he agreed. "Just as you have to accept that I'm an ex-con control freak who doesn't want to hurt you."

"Wonder how long it will take your painting thief to die if your superstition about not touching it is correct? And if we really want magical thinking, maybe the painting *cured* me!" With an insouciant grin and no hesitation, she marched straight up the path to his house, super-stition be damned.

They were going to do this.

It scared the *faex* out of him.

AARON'S BEDROOM WAS UPSTAIRS, HANNAH DISCOVERED WHEN HE LED HER up. No fancy carved antiques—he favored heavy masculine lines, gray and blue furnishings, and explosively erotic pen-and-ink artwork. His shower definitely didn't reflect the mid-century architecture either. Glass, chrome, and marble with thick white towels she could lose herself in. . .

He casually dropped his knit boxers to join her in washing off the day's grime, and she almost fainted for real. *Stud* was the first word popping to mind. This was no undernourished grad student but a man in his prime. When his dark gaze drifted downward with interest, she almost covered her inadequate breasts with the huge washcloth, but she grabbed the soap instead. If she was doing this, if this was the only chance she might have for spectacular sex, she meant to experience every single—embarrassing—bit.

He took the soap, lathered his hands, and began washing her shoulders, tantalizingly just above her aching breasts.

Daringly, she repeated the favor, swirling the dark hairs on his chest in foam, because they were easier to reach than his shoulders.

"No knights and nuns," he murmured approvingly, dropping his hands to cup her breasts.

"Still a chance of fainting," she admitted, noticing hot water did nothing to diminish his arousal.

"We're doing this in a bed," he said firmly, dropping his soapy hands to caress lower. "In a minute or two," he added when she moaned her pleasure.

She was already half spent by the time they wrapped in towels, and Aaron carried her to the bed. He did things to her that woke her again in record time. And when he donned his guardian shield and entered her, she circled the moon a time or three before exploding like a rocket launcher at the same time he did.

No knight or nun or Spanish soldier joined them. For the first time since her diagnosis, Hannah relaxed. She curled up in strong arms that silently promised everything would be all right, somehow.

Because, at long last, they were together, as they were meant to be.

THE INSISTENT RINGING OF SEVERAL PHONES BROUGHT THEM BACK TO REALITY with a crash a few hours later. Aaron groped for a bedside receiver while

Hannah scrambled up, wondering where she'd dropped hers. She fell back against the pillow again when she remembered her cell didn't work out here. Aaron just had a lot of phones.

He was out of bed and grabbing jeans before he even hung up. His curses had her leaping up to look for her clothes.

She was still juggling her panties when Studly Do-Right flung the phone and stalked half-naked out the door, pulling on a shirt as he went. They might have to work on his communication skills.

She couldn't as easily pull on a tank top and stumble down the stairs in his wake. He was almost out the door before she caught up.

"What?" she demanded, following on his heels to his van.

"Bastard tried to set the shop on fire." He revved the engine as she hurried to pull herself inside the tall vehicle. The chivalrous knight had shifted into battle mode.

"Why?" she cried. "You've done nothing!"

"I had the painting. I've been asking questions. Hell if I know." He took the long, narrow driveway at breakneck speed and accelerated when he reached the highway.

As they drove up, they saw half the town milling about the parking lot beneath the light of Hillvale's lone street lamp. Men were wrapping up a flat fire hose, and the stench of smoke lingered in the air. Apparently the town actually had a fire hydrant and hoses. Who knew? Aaron leaped out, leaving Hannah to find her own way down.

Amber ran up to hug her. "We thought you were inside!" she cried in relief. "The back door was on fire, and we had to break in the front." She hugged Hannah tightly. "Thank goodness you're all right!"

Amber's movie star husband hugged his wife with one arm and held out his other hand to Hannah. "Hi, I'm Josh, and I am forever in your debt for not being dead. I do not want to experience Amber's wrath if she goes after another killer."

Hannah supposed Josh was handsome in a slick movie-star way worth admiring. But despite Amber's effusive embrace, Hannah's concentration fastened worriedly on Aaron. He inspected the front of his shop, shoved open the door, and entered what could have been a blazing building.

If she hadn't been in his bed, she could have fried in there.

"Is it out?" she asked worriedly.

"Whoever did this tried to make it look like a trash fire, so there wasn't much fuel," Josh explained. "Aaron has that placed wired to the hilt. The smoke alarm screamed before more than the back wall was affected. I never even considered what the town used in a fire."

Looking weary and wet, the chief of police joined them. "Monty insisted on the hydrants as soon as the town had enough money. Good to see you in one piece, Hannah. Keegan took out the front window trying to reach you."

Knowing her massive cousin would have taken out windows for a dog, she wasn't as impressed by his concern as she was terrified of what could have happened. She glanced at the shattered plate glass. "And you're sure it's arson?"

"Definitely. Trash barrel was moved and squirted with accelerant. Think big barbecue grill shoved against a wooden wall. It probably smoldered for a while before the heat built and the door caught fire. Had the place been engulfed, we may not have even noticed the barrel." Walker sounded grim. "You wouldn't happen to have any enemies, would you?"

And there it was, the fear that had been niggling at her ever since Amber mentioned Hannah could have died tonight.

"No enemies, no exceptional talents anyone could fear, no nothing but what exists in my head. And my head conjures nothing to explain this," she admitted, sorting through the possibilities and seeing nothing.

A few hours ago, she'd been experiencing the most incredible sex she'd ever had or dreamed of having. She'd been feeling safe and happy for the first time in longer than she could remember. And now, this.

"Well, it's probably aimed at Aaron," Walker said. "He's the one who's been examining stones. And if the killer is after the stones or possesses the weapon that killed Carmel, he may fear Aaron's ability."

"Even I don't understand Aaron's ability," Josh pointed out. "How would a stranger realize he can be dangerous?"

Good question, one none of them could answer.

When Aaron reappeared again, looking filthy, tired, and furious, Hannah took leave of her companions and hurried in his direction. He saw her but didn't seem to want to reach for her. To hell with that. She flung her arms around his waist and buried her face in his smoky shirt. "I'm sorry," she blurted out. "If I need to move out, I will. I'm so very sorry!"

He hugged her then and rested his chin on her head. "This isn't about you. And I may tie you to my side to be sure you're safe. If it's a hired jerk doing this, he probably didn't even know you may have been in there."

But there was something in the tone of his voice that said he'd just thought of something. He set her back when Walker approached. "Hired killer," Aaron said, without explanation.

Hannah watched in puzzlement as Walker nodded. "Doesn't make sense, but yeah, it's occurred to me that there's one person in town who hobnobs with the wrong sorts of people."

"Besides my mother?" Kurt Kennedy asked wearily, joining them. Soaked and filthy from battling the fire and the powerful fire hose, he still seemed alert and functional.

"Your mother might have set a hired killer loose?" Hannah asked in disbelief.

"As you may have noticed, my mother wasn't entirely sane. She could have told anyone anything, for any reason. Someone might think there's ancient treasure in Aaron's shop. Maybe they killed her for something they thought she had, and when Aaron searched her rooms, they thought he took it." Kurt shrugged. "I'm reading a lot of crime novels lately, trying to grasp the criminal mind."

Walker snorted. "Understandable. It's easier than believing *evil* stalks the town. But I was thinking of your mother's best buddy, Fred Roper. He got rich arranging private meetings for some of the most dangerous criminals in the state."

Hannah tried to find the name in her copious memory and remembered Roper was the lodge manager. She tried not to gape. "You hired a *criminal* to run the lodge?"

"He's never been arrested for anything," Kurt said, brushing his hair off his face and smearing soot in the process. "He's always been a high-end hotelier. It's just that wealthy criminals flock to wealthy resorts, and he's very accommodating. We're looking for someone to replace him now that Mom's gone. He's the only manager who stayed longer than two weeks while she was around."

"This is all the stuff of fiction," Walker said. "We have nothing. I'll have the sheriff's forensic team up here in the morning. I need to tape off the back alley." The police chief stalked away, a man on a mission.

Aaron kept his arm draped over Hannah's shoulder, as if he needed the contact as much as she did. "I'll have to hire security, if only to keep the town from burning down. I should stay here tonight to keep guard."

Without caring what the rest of the town thought, Hannah met his gaze. "Then I will too. Maybe we should have a ghost party and spook away any more killers."

He almost grinned at that. "Fee did that once. I think we can do better."

TWENTY-TWO

AFTER RESETTING SMOKE AND MOTION DETECTORS, HANGING VARIOUS contraptions over all the antique shop's entrances, including the boarded window, and leaving fans blowing, Aaron collapsed upstairs beside Hannah. Even the second floor stunk of smoke, but at least the bed was dry.

Sex with Hannah earlier had been. . . a mind-altering experience. Innocent angels—or even librarians—shouldn't be so arousing, but Hannah's eagerness and perceptivity was a potent combination. He craved more.

Pumping adrenaline and seething lust could only do so much against exhaustion and shock. He was wiped.

They both needed rest. He snuggled her into the curve of his body, acknowledged her hum of appreciation and his surge of arousal, and promptly fell asleep.

Her nearly windowless room let them sleep late. Waking in an unfamiliar bed, to the stale odor of burnt wood and the sweet fragrance that was Hannah's own, Aaron lay in muddled confusion. How long had it been since he'd simply relaxed, appreciating the fact that he was alive? He definitely hadn't awakened with a woman in his bed in a decade or more. He always drove home alone.

Hannah had got inside his head in ways that no other woman ever had, not even Natalie. Nat had simply accepted his affinity for antiques as an extension of his past and knowledge. He'd never explained his gift. Hannah had *experienced* it, with an intimacy that bound them in ways that worried him.

She stirred—picking up on his thoughts? He might never understand how their physical contact could create so much understanding. He was accustomed to blocking out people, but his curiosity about the woman in his arms was unendurable—until he opened to her just a little.

The connection was instantaneous—and probably nothing more than normal people recognized. He had just closed himself off for so long that it was almost an entirely new sensation to recognize her interest and arousal and wariness as she edged away.

"Another shower?" he suggested, recalling images from the night before that stoked his engines.

"This one isn't big enough for two," she said with regret. "And we probably ought to save our energy for restoring the mess downstairs."

Faex. Remembering the damage to years of hard work, Aaron fought a wave of rage. Instead of playing, he needed to be hunting vandals who could have killed Hannah or burned down the town. He rolled over and threw his legs off the edge of the bed. "You need to be preparing school lessons and overseeing what they're doing at the school. The mess downstairs is mine."

She remained in bed, stretching so the t-shirt she'd pulled on as nightgown strained over her breasts. She wasn't large, but a nice handful. Aaron yanked on his jeans.

"You're shutting me out again," she said helpfully. "It's understandable but don't think I won't whack you upside the head when you need it. I don't know what kind of woman you've been consorting with, but I'm not her. Want to tell me to back off?"

Yeah, he did, and dammit, he couldn't. "*Cons* to Lucy relationship— we get under each other's skins. *Pro*—I like it. *Con*—it will hurt like the devil when you're gone."

"*Pro*—the sex is good." She swung out of bed and headed for the shower. "*Con*—it's hard to whack you when I understand you."

He almost managed a grin at that—and at the sight of her quite respectable ass outlined by the clingy knit shirt. *"Pro*—there's always someone ready to buy you breakfast."

"Anyone can do that," she called from behind the closed door. "The real challenge is whether or not you're ready to face the other Lucys if we go to the café together."

"Hell, no," he said with feeling. "I'll bring it back here."

He left her imitating a squawking chicken. He needed to confront the disaster that was his once respectable shop.

By the time Hannah came down, garbed in her shapeless denim dress, Aaron had faced the realization that his shop would never be the same—and that he needed help.

"You're scowling and there's no coffee waiting," Hannah said in her schoolmarm voice. "My psychic abilities say you've realized this isn't a one-person job and you're not an idiot."

He snorted amusement at this correct assessment. "You're bad for my ego."

"Your ego survived two years in prison and came out assuming, for whatever inane reason, that you had to protect all of Hillvale. I'm grateful you didn't decide to take on the world, the way your Spanish soldier apparently did. He came half way around the globe to stop evil and give precious stones to natives he didn't even know. And who knows what your medieval knight did to acquire the Healing Stone to stop the plague. Having met you, I understand the paintings better." She caught his arm and tugged him toward the door. "I need tea."

"I can't even save Hillvale, much less the world," he said grumpily. Having a woman who understood him was well beyond ego-deflating.

"Your self-esteem can handle a little Lucy suffocation. You might even enjoy the challenge once you get used to it. I do not expect you to ever be a gregarious person, but you aren't a hermit either. I will even declare I'm ready to move into the schoolhouse if that will ease your terror of personal interaction." She released his arm and strode ahead of him down the boardwalk.

Aaron caught up and nabbed her arm. "I am not normally a possessive man. In your case, I'll make an exception. It's apparent we have unresolved issues over several lifetimes. Let's resolve them so you don't haunt me into eternity."

She laughed. She was so damned far under his skin that he enjoyed her laughter. Aaron knew where that led, and he didn't like it. Torn between a rock and a hard place, he opened the café door for her and entered the fox's den still grasping Hannah's arm—like a shield.

AARON DIDN'T HAVE TO WORRY ABOUT BEING PART OF A COUPLE FOR LONG, Hannah thought with amusement as the men dragged him away to discuss repairs, and the women surrounded her with increasingly creative solutions to finding an arsonist.

She'd never been part of a couple, so Aaron even had more experience in that than she did. And she still wasn't entirely certain if what they had was a real relationship and not just some psychic bond from the past that would evaporate once their task was complete. The world had too many possibilities to label anything after one night together.

"I'm new to this detective business," Hannah said, holding up her hand to halt Teddy's latest idea. She sipped her tea and skeptically eyed the heavily decorated bagel Fee had given her. "I need facts, not theories. Could we line up facts first?"

Mariah swung around her notebook computer. "*Fact*—in the late 1700s or early 1800s, Hillvale had weird crystals and stone guardians purported to protect against evil. *Fact*—at least some of those crystals are no longer in place. We haven't dug far enough to find more statues. *Fact* —Carmel had a box of raw crystals with odd vibrations in a *safe*."

"Those aren't exactly facts," Hannah corrected. "The first two are assumptions based on a painting and a single stone statue. And the *odd vibrations* in the third is a matter of opinion."

Mariah gave her a rude gesture and returned to scrolling through her document.

Hannah nibbled the bagel and decided the taste was more than acceptable. Unfortunately, the list of so-called facts led to less than palatable notions. "Aaron and I checked the terrain around the stone statue. There's been a landslide and probably a flood since the time of the Eversham painting. It's quite possible—if the crystals existed—that they washed or slid down the hill into the area the Kennedys turned into a grotto."

"Back to theory," Teddy said cheerfully. "If the raw crystals became visible after a flood, then the hippies may have gathered them to use in various ways, and Carmel bribed, blackmailed, or seduced them away."

"*Why?*" Hannah demanded. "You saw them. They're entirely unremarkable except for the crystal facets that could just as easily have been found in Keegan's cave."

Samantha carried her glass of milk, toast, and boiled egg to the booth and bumped Teddy to make her scoot over. "Val grew up in the commune. She may know, but persuading her to talk is as painful as banging our heads against brick walls. Walker is trying to persuade the DA to release the crystals. The sheriff is just about ready to send a case to the DA claiming Francois killed Carmel. They're trying to determine if the crystals are evidence, since they were safely locked away."

"The Healing Stone is the one we really need," Hannah reminded them. "We know that the moonstone wasn't buried in the ground with the others because Cass's family had it. But Carmel got her hands on it, and it apparently hasn't been seen since."

"She could have sold it," Teddy said, frowning. "We could be barking up the wrong tree. It may have been gone for decades and that was just an empty impression in the chest."

"Speculation again," Hannah warned. "We know it existed. It would be good to find it. Moving on. . . We have a vandal arsonist on the loose as well as a killer. Did Walker's cameras catch anything?"

Hannah didn't know why she'd suddenly usurped leadership of this investigation. She wasn't a leader. She was an observer. But finding a killer arsonist had become so important that she didn't seem able to step back.

Sam finished chewing before responding. "The camera in the alley was disabled. Someone knew it was there."

"Dang, that means it's someone local," Teddy muttered. "That camera went in only a few months ago."

"I've been trying to establish alibis for everyone in town the night of Carmel's murder, the day Francois died, and the incidents at the shop. It's almost an impossible job, even for me," Mariah admitted, calling up another spreadsheet on her computer and turning the screen to face the table. "We're a mobile lot."

"Cass is almost always without an alibi," Sam said with a laugh. "As is Val. And I'm more than convinced either of them could kill with a look. I obviously did not inherit enough of the family genes."

"And Lance and Xavier are sketchy," Amber noted, studying the chart. "Xavier is in his office by himself most of the day and sleeps alone at night. These days, Lance wanders as much as Harvey, who also has few alibis, since he's almost always alone unless he's busking."

"What about Roper?" Hannah asked, studying the confusing chart.

"He's scum and would certainly know how to hire vandals, but he's always surrounded by people. Besides, Carmel was his bread and butter." Mariah turned the screen around and hit the keyboard. "His association with gangsters has put him beyond bounds for most decent hotels now that Walker has made it known that Roper is a security risk. Roper needs his job and wouldn't jeopardize it, especially after that last incident with the kidnapped kid."

"Charming." Sam sipped her milk. "Now Walker is a target of gangster wrath if Roper gets fired. My husband goes out of his way to make enemies. That doesn't explain why Aaron was attacked."

"What if Carmel fired Roper and warned him that she was reporting his gangster propensities?" Teddy asked, almost bouncing in her seat.

Hannah pointed her finger at her as if she were a misbehaving student.

Teddy grimaced, then looked chagrined. "Theory is so much easier."

"I'll happily slap Roper with ectoplasm," Mariah said. "But if he's not guilty, it would be a little awkward ever visiting the lodge again if I ask him if he killed Carmel and vandalized the shop."

"Well, awkward until Kurt fires him," Teddy acknowledged. "And then there's always the danger of irritating someone who hangs with gangsters. Not a recommended solution. Walker may take care of himself but Baby Daphne needs her mom."

"Even Josh can't write a play to cover this many suspects," Amber said, spreading her tarot cards on the table. "I think our psychic detective agency must admit failure."

"So you're totally giving up on talking to Val?" Hannah asked, watching as the men started sliding from their booth.

"Nope, let's do it." Amber slid her cards back into her purse again.

Sam wrinkled her nose but finished her toast and stood up just as her husband walked by. She fell into Walker's arms, wrapped hers around his neck, and kissed his cheek as if she'd accidentally fallen into his path. The police chief didn't seem to mind.

Aaron looked a bit shell-shocked as the Lucys surged from the booth and commanded their men. Hannah knew her eyes were dancing as his possessive side fought with his loner tendencies. It was a good thing that she didn't have any preconceived notions about relationships, or she'd be destroyed by his reluctance.

He fell in step beside her as the crowd spilled from the café. "Kurt says now that his mother is no longer on the board, the Kennedy corporation is willing to sell its properties. I can buy the shop if I want."

"And pay to replace your own window," she said with amusement. "What do you think you'll do?"

"Own it," he said decisively.

Hannah tried not to ponder the implications of his decision to permanently attach himself to Hillvale. He belonged in larger circles, but Hillvale was good for him. Which meant that if she wanted a relationship, she needed to be a schoolteacher and stay.

"Kurt's insurance will cover the window," Aaron continued. "Mine will cover the inventory damage and loss of sales until I can reopen. What were the Lucys cackling over?"

"They want to tackle Val about the rocks Carmel collected. I'm not sure she can tell us anything new or interesting. I'm still fixated on the Healing Stone, and Cass told us everything she knows about that. I think we've reached a dead end, unless Walker has something." Hannah resisted slipping her hand around his arm. He was walking close enough to do it, but this had to be his choice. She refused to be a Lucy *limpet*.

"If I can touch the rocks in the jewel casket with your enhancement, we might learn more. I've asked Walker if we could have access to it." Aaron brushed his hand against hers, then curled his fingers around it as they reached the boarded-up shop.

She enjoyed the sensation of their clasped hands a little too much.

"Brilliant idea," she admitted. "Or a major plunge into time-travel country, not sure which."

"Madness may be the best way to handle whatever this is between us," he said grudgingly, unlocking the door. "Sanity is overrated."

She laughed. "And if the knot in my head grows, it can make me crazy before it makes me dead. Let's do it."

TWENTY-THREE

Aaron handed the insurance adjuster his inventory list and rubbed his forehead as he watched the man walk out. Reducing years of collecting unhappy antiques to a print-out of numbers slapped his ego around a little more. Yeah, he knew he had warehouses of far better merchandise, but these had been personal. They'd taught him how to block out bad memories and treat them as a professional hazard.

At least the arsonist hadn't burned his first editions. Hannah and Wan Hai had scrubbed his bookshelves with vinegar and used fragrant polish to remove the smoke stench. They'd apparently completed that task to their satisfaction and now worked on the books, using a hair dryer to ventilate and heat them to remove any lingering odor. He was immensely grateful that the water damage was limited to the storage room.

That they'd focused their attention on the part of his shop that he loved most spoke of Lucy sensitivities, despite Hannah declaring she had none, and Wan Hai not accepting the designation at all.

The contractor he'd hired demanded his attention in the back of the shop. When Aaron returned to the front, a cleaning brigade was marching through his front door bearing buckets and supplies. Little

Wan Hai brightened and immediately took to ordering them about like a general.

Even Teddy's interior designer sister arrived—without her two munchkins. She'd kept her distance since she'd moved in. She'd suffered badly at the hands of men, and in her high-end business, she had to stay clear of felons convicted of art theft. Aaron respected her reluctance to work with him. So when Sydony marched right up to his counter, he almost bit his tongue in half.

"I know a little about smoke restoration, but I see you're in good hands with Wan Hai. If you will allow me, I can bring in my crew to clean and repaint the walls. I'll be happy to help you rehang and redecorate after they're done." She handed him her business card.

"Thank you," he said, too shocked to do better.

Hannah appeared like a mythical house brownie to ease the gap. "You're Mia and Jeb's mother, right? Hi, I'm Hannah Simon. I'll be teaching Zeke and backing up Sally for your two. We should all probably have coffee some time to discuss the direction of the school."

She led the nervous young mother away, and Aaron had to collapse in his desk chair for a moment while he digested the unusual activity in his normally empty store. He answered the phone, consulted more with his contractor, and when he looked up again, Hannah had returned. She studied him sympathetically, then glided behind him to massage his shoulders. He nearly liquefied in a puddle of gratitude.

"This inventory means something to you," she guessed.

"Every piece is tragic in one way or another," he admitted. "It's a good collection, decent enough for me to have bought each one, but they're nothing extraordinarily valuable. I just don't seem able to let go of the unhappiness scarring them."

"You surround yourself with tragedy?" she asked in disbelief. "Okay, I suppose that resonates with you, given your history. What happens if we clean and polish and rub our hands over each piece?"

He shrugged. "Nothing much. Polish isn't an emotional element. It doesn't seep into the molecules the way a hand that's committed murder will."

"But if we're happy when we touch a piece or we do happy things with it, the new memories might bury some of the ugly?" she insisted.

"Possibly," he said, screwing up his nose in thought, not wanting to give her reason to stop the massage. "Although happiness is less visceral and focused and doesn't usually leave strong memories."

She swung his chair so he faced the sight of Brenda, the nurse practitioner, and Orval, the vet, admiring the poker table that had been the scene of a bloody gunfight over a century ago. Aaron wanted to leap up and steer them away, to protect them from the ghosts of that past.

"They like putting puzzles together in the evening," Hannah whispered. "As I understand it, they're not rich, but they donate their services to people who can't afford to pay. They are really good people who would put joy into that table. And they're here to help you clean up."

The vet and the nurse had cans of furniture cleaners and were happily working on the battered mahogany. They made an incongruous pair. Orval was big, burly, bearded, and wore his long graying hair in a ponytail. Brenda was petite, wiry, and wore her garishly red hair short. Aaron remembered they'd been together at the lodge the night Carmel had died.

An inkling of an idea formed in the back of his brain. He needed more time to ponder its efficacy, but he could do something positive right now—which was what Hannah was trying to tell him.

"How do you know these things?" he demanded, just to keep her distracted. Reluctantly, he raised himself from the chair, abandoning her soothing hands.

"I observe. It's what librarians do." She stood back and let him do what he needed to do in his own way.

She was telling him that his inventory needed to be given *positive* uses, polished with love, adorned with joy, the ugly past scrubbed away and replaced with happier futures. The same could be said of him, he supposed, but that was a metaphor too optimistic to believe in just yet.

Like the executioner who had once rung it, Aaron tolled a brass gong hanging in a dark corner. The low bong reverberated through the shop, immediately commanding attention of even General Wan Hai. She shut up and glared at him.

"The insurance company will be reimbursing me for clean-up. I don't want to insult your good deed by offering cash, although I can, if you'll tell me that's what you want. But what I'd like to offer is any piece in here that might make you happy. Think of it as a giant garage sale where I get rid of some of my clutter. I truly appreciate everything you're doing today. I'll be able to re-open much sooner than expected this way."

Aaron waited uncomfortably as people he'd known for years gaped at him—in disbelief? Was he perceived as that. . . what, tight-fisted? Standoffish? Yeah, to the latter, he supposed. The incredulous silence was unsettling.

Hannah sidled up to Brenda, whispered something, and nodded at the table.

The wiry nurse brightened, catching on. She waved her hand. "If Orval can haul it in his truck, do you want to get rid of this old table?"

"It would be a pleasure to see it in good hands," Aaron said, feeling an odd surge of. . . relief? Satisfaction? He'd blocked himself off for so long that he was bad at interpreting his own emotions.

Wan Hai grabbed the red Chinese porcelain teapot and held it up without speaking. Aaron nodded. She beamed so brightly with delight that he almost forgot that it had been used to poison someone's mother.

Hannah took his arm. "You're doing the right thing. Quit worrying," she assured him. "Wan Hai will love that pot to pieces. It will become a treasured heirloom instead of whatever image is in your mind."

"She'll dispel the ghost the way Mariah swipes ectoplasm into the ether?" Aaron asked, dubious.

"There is nothing in these *things* that can harm any living soul except you. I'll show you the journals of other psychometrists, if you like."

"I'll believe you. Maybe it's time to clean house. But I still want to strangle whoever set the fire. They could have burned down the whole town as well as you. The things don't matter, but the intent was *evil*." He spotted Keegan polishing the medieval cuirass and pressed a kiss on Hannah's head. "Too many ideas at once," he murmured, not explaining himself as he crossed the shop to talk to the big Scot.

He could find this killer if he just focused on his own ability and not everyone else's.

∽

WEARING HER USUAL LONG BLACK VEIL, VAL APPEARED AT LUNCHTIME, JUST as everyone's energy was flagging. She carried big, scrumptious-smelling sacks from the café. Fee had a business to run and hadn't been able to participate in the cleaning party, but she had still found a way to contribute.

As Aaron's workers descended on the sacks, Val sought out Hannah. "Amber said you have questions I should answer."

"I don't suppose you're keeping a journal for the library, are you?" Hannah asked, leading the theatrical Death Goddess toward the back where Aaron was working.

"Erratically," Val admitted. "Cass keeps insisting."

"She's right. Someday, another singer might come along who won't understand how to control her voice, and your experience may make all the difference. Those of us given special gifts have a duty to pass on our knowledge."

"I will try to do better. As a child, it never occurred to me that my singing was anything unusual." She hesitated at sight of Aaron ripping off scorched drywall.

Any woman would stop to admire the view.

He'd stripped off his shirt to work, and Hannah admired his wide muscled shoulders and lean tanned back. He turned to greet them with a lifted eyebrow and returned to his work.

"The arsonist attacked Aaron's shop for a reason," Hannah said, grateful that Aaron understood that Val might not speak to a man. "What you have to say may affect him more than me."

Val nodded her veiled head but kept her distance. Hannah knew the actress had been badly scarred by a former lover, but this past year or more she'd been emerging from her solitude. Hannah didn't want to do anything to drive her back into seclusion.

"We'd like to know more about the stones or crystals that people collected from the Kennedy grotto," Hannah said, keeping her voice low.

Val shrugged. "I was a kid, and it was all just another game, like following Daisy to find her stash. It had rained all winter, and there was a steady river running off the mountain. The Kennedys did something to control it and created a waterfall into an old sinkhole. We found shiny rocks where the water washed over the boulders. We were like jackdaws, picking up pretty sparkly things, pretending they were gold."

"*Pretty sparkly* doesn't sound like what was in Carmel's closet," Hannah said in disappointment.

"The crystal only shines when it's wet and in the sun. They were just rocks with quartz and pyrite and whatever, completely worthless for the most part. Some of them turned out to be rare and could be sold for a few weeks' groceries, which sent everyone into reenacting the Gold Rush for a few months. But mostly, they ended up being traded and used for sparkly paint."

Hannah knew Aaron had to be listening, so she wasn't startled when he flung his trash outside into a dumpster, then joined them. Val backed off uneasily, but she didn't flee. Behind the veil, she probably watched him warily.

"The rocks in Carmel's closet emanated evil. I can't explain better. She must have thought they had some kind of power if she kept them." He gestured at his coffee pot, offering Val a cup.

She shook her head. "After the way things eventually turned out, I suppose they could have been evil. But I went off to college and theater and didn't look back, except from a distance. I do think that all of the adults back then changed over the years, including Carmel. My parents were once loving and generous and opened their farm to their impoverished friends. By the end, they were grasping and angry and nothing pleased them. I hated to see my childhood Eden become what it did."

"Crystals absorb the intent of the owner," Hannah murmured. "I'm not sure how the Ives scientist came to that conclusion, but it does seem to have some validity."

"Ask Lance," Val said. Without explanation, she departed through the empty shell of the back wall.

Hannah grimaced. "This detective business is tedious. When do we get to the part where we gather the suspects in one room and accuse them all?"

Aaron chuckled around his coffee cup. "I'm working on it. But we need to keep gathering what little information is out there. I don't know what Lance can tell us, but if we can persuade the old boy to talk, then we should try."

"It didn't go well last time," she reminded him. "He looked ready to kill Carmel all over again."

"I suspect he had more reason than most. If he knew he'd inherit the lodge, then he had even stronger motive than romantic interference. Siblings often quarrel. I can't picture it, but he could have smacked his sister with anything that came to hand. What if Carmel had been yelling at Val?"

"Carmel could have been yelling at anyone. She could have argued with Brenda, and Orval whacked her. Carmel apparently had a dislike of Lucys. In which case, I'd be inclined to let the sheriff do his thing and blame it all on Francois, who was probably blackmailing whoever did it." Hannah grimaced. "But someone who has killed twice isn't right in the head. We need to find them." She headed for the shop and lunch.

"*Crazy* covers half the town," Aaron called after her.

"Including us," she acknowledged. "Let's hire an exorcist."

TWENTY-FOUR

GRABBING ONE OF FEE'S SANDWICHES, AARON LEFT HIS IMPROMPTU cleaning crew and departed through the burned-out wall. Guarding Hillvale from the *malum* lurking in the ground had taken strange paths over the years. But mostly, he'd been able to follow those paths in solitude.

Interviewing people had never been high on his list. That's what Walker was for. But Lance had told Walker nothing useful. Carmel's brother was a private person. He wouldn't want his real thoughts on public record—or Aaron hoped that's what Val was saying.

He found Lance rearranging an exhibit in the gallery. Many of the pieces had been given to the town over the years in lieu of payment for services, so the proceeds fed the town, not Lance. The artist and retired architect had been more or less living off his sister and her sons for decades.

"Do you think artwork might sell at the lodge?" Lance asked as Aaron entered.

"With the right lighting and price, maybe." He stopped to admire the painting Lance was removing. "Are you thinking you should get more involved in operations?"

"The boys can't afford to buy me out," Lance said. "It's been my home for so long, I don't know any other. Now that Carmel isn't interfering, I thought I could earn my keep a little."

"The place could use brightening. Roper won't give you any trouble?"

Lance shrugged. "He can't argue with an owner, can he?" He turned to look at Aaron. "You're not here to ask about the lodge. How can I help you?"

Aaron shoved his hands into his pockets and sought the right words. "We're trying to understand why Carmel kept those crystal rocks and if they might be important. Val hinted that you might know more. Someone here has killed two people, and we can't come up with any reason."

"Not the rocks," Lance said with certainty, moving his ladder down the wall. "Geoff and Lars both had them appraised in hopes they'd found gold and diamonds. The rocks aren't even from around here."

"But there's something wrong with them," Aaron said, unused to explaining himself, especially to a Null.

"*Carmel* was what's wrong. She believed the things gave her special powers—like Cass's. My sister wanted anything Cass had. That painting you had? Eversham painted it for Cass, but Carmel offered him a pot of gold and a promise to hang it in the lobby. As soon as Eversham left, she sold it to the first person who promised to take it out of town, just so Cass couldn't have it."

Lance knew about his Eversham? Probably from Val, through the Lucys. Aaron wanted to ask a dozen questions, but he bit his tongue and let Lance ramble.

"My sister was jealous of an old woman who has nothing but land no one wants, and Carmel coveted even that. Cass lost everything and everyone she loved, and Carmel still resented that Cass seemed content. My sister was never happy. She never understood that gold and power weren't the sources of Cass's happiness."

"Was she always that way?" Aaron pressed. He wanted to know more about the painting, but the rocks came first.

Lance wrinkled his nose. "Carmel was older than me. We were never close. From my perspective, she was always bossy, interfering, and controlling, but that's just sibling resentment. She didn't turn mean until after Geoff's death, and given the state he left her in, I suppose she had reason."

"But if she knew the rock crystals were worthless, why did she collect them?"

"Because she could. Because others wanted them. And because of her fixation in believing they gave her power. Superstition, I suppose. She flashed her gem collection when she wanted to influence someone, usually her banker friends, and when it worked, she credited the rocks."

"That's sad, when you think of it," Aaron remarked. "All that beauty and intelligence and she believed *rocks* made her successful?"

"Well, it certainly wasn't her charisma in those last years," Lance said dryly. "She used to turn on charm at will, but the meanness took over."

"Don't ever let material goods mean more than people," Aaron rephrased the old cliché. "I suppose greed could make one mean."

"Lack of compassion will do it," Lance said dryly. "Carmel never had much of that. I think the rocks are a dead end, sorry."

"In Carmel's case, you're probably right. I just wanted a simple solution, and she really loved those rocks." Aaron considered that. He'd been thinking of the rocks as inherently evil, but if they absorbed the owner's intent, perhaps they'd absorbed what little love Carmel had possessed. Probably not good to say that to her brother.

"She had two good sons," Lance said harshly. "I was a lousy substitute for their dad, but I love them as if they were my own. I'll always do what I can to see them happy."

Like kill Carmel to save her sons a problem?

Aaron thanked Lance and walked thoughtfully back to his shop.

If Carmel hadn't been killed for the rocks, could she have been killed for what she had done in the past? Or was her death simply a matter of getting rid of an interfering nuisance?

WHEN AARON TOLD HANNAH ABOUT THE EVERSHAM PAINTING OVER DINNER that night, she wanted to leap up and query Cass immediately.

"I *know* she knows more than she's telling us," she insisted. "She's keeping an entire library from me!"

After a day of scrubbing smoke, she'd decided to treat herself—and maybe Aaron—by visiting Tullah's thrift shop. Tullah had immediately produced a lovely floaty sundress in gold and white, with a gauzy shawl to dress it up for evening. Hannah was pretty sure Aaron was admiring the result of her low neckline and her one and only push-up bra.

He still didn't agree with her argument.

"We can't go to Cass and accuse her of stealing a painting," he insisted. "And we still don't know how dangerous the painting is. We don't need to risk losing our minds with time travel."

"It's psychometry," she insisted. "It's not the same as what Aunt Jia does. We can connect and disconnect at will."

"Can we?" he asked ominously. "Are you sure about that? Besides, accusing Cass of stealing a painting is your bigger obstacle. I think you're more interested in adding to your encyclopedic knowledge than solving this crime."

Hannah wrinkled her nose and dug into her risotto. "But history can tell us how to deal with the present."

"Sometimes, but right now it means angering a dangerous woman over a dangerous painting and using rocks that we don't possess and don't understand. Some things are meant to be left alone." He drank his wine and regarded her with smoldering eyes.

He was twisting her mind with promises of sex. When it came right down to it, she was okay with the excitement his sensual look offered. She could tackle Cass in the morning—as long as a killer didn't try to burn the house down around them.

"You have good smoke detectors in here, don't you?" she asked, glancing at the high-ceilinged front room of Aaron's house.

He looked briefly startled, then managed a dark grin. "Unless our killer is Harvey, there are only two means of accessing this place, and once the system is switched on, both will shriek alarms well before an intruder reaches us. And yes, all the alarms are in good working order."

"And why is Harvey an exception?" She had so little experience with men of Aaron's caliber, that she was in serious danger of being bent to his will out of sheer lust. She had to work hard not to be malleable.

"He doesn't use the driveway or the walking path. Personally, I think he swings through the trees. I'm fairly certain that method won't occur to a killer who hires vandals." Aaron rose to take their empty plates. "Dessert? I always have ice cream."

"Are you keeping me here so I'm in no danger for arsonists?" she asked, because she needed to understand why the unsociable recluse was feeding her.

"I'm keeping you here because my bed is a damned sight more comfortable than the one at the shop. If you prefer to stay in the school-room now that the utilities are functioning, I'll order a decent mattress and you can have your choice of beds from the store. But that has to wait until morning. If we're airing our fears here, would you rather spend the night alone than with me?" Without looking at her, he rinsed the plates and dropped them in the dishwasher.

"*Con* of Lucy relationships, we overthink too much." She carried the rest of the dishes to the sink, set them down, and hugged his waist. "I like being with you, even when you're being disagreeable."

He turned, wrapped her in his embrace, and rested his chin on her head. "I like being with you even when I know I will regret it. That makes me disagreeable."

She snorted into his collar. "Let's make lists of murder suspects until it's time for bed. There's a topic where we can find common ground."

"You don't mind not socializing with your friends after they spent the day helping me out? I can take you into town, if you prefer. I don't expect you to embrace my solitude." He brushed a kiss across her hair, then released her to return to cleaning up, as if he didn't have another thought in his head.

She stood on her toes and kissed his bristled cheek. "I have lived inside my head all my life. Solitude does not frighten me. But I will have to move into town or buy a car when the schoolroom is ready in a few weeks, so there's the term limit to your dilemma. Does that ease your mind?"

"It makes me feel like a Lucy limpet," he growled, turning to lift her from the floor and kiss her more thoroughly.

"Right back atcha," she murmured as he carried her toward the stairs. Understanding this lonely man was digging a hook in her heart so deep that she might never pry it out—unless he ripped it out first.

TWENTY-FIVE

THE PHONE RANG WELL BEFORE AARON WAS READY TO WAKE. HE'D TAKEN Hannah to bed early, but they'd not exactly slept all those hours. Instead, he'd explored his willingness to open himself to her in ways he could only do with someone he trusted. The lessons had been fascinating—and terrifying.

He didn't think he had the strength to watch another woman die. And what if enhancing his psychometry worsened the growth in her head?

Hannah murmured a protest and snuggled her nicely padded posterior against his hip as he reached for the phone. *Dammit,* he'd forgotten how much he enjoyed waking to a warm woman at his side. His life had been a lonely one, and he was accustomed to emptiness. That didn't mean he liked it.

Recognizing Caller ID, he lifted the receiver and said, "Yeah."

"The DA is returning Carmel's box of rocks." Walker seldom bothered with polite preface. "The Lucys will be all over them shortly. Hope you have a plan ready."

Aaron stretched and slid his toes over Hannah's leg. "I've been working on one. Not sure you'll like it. And the Kennedys might raise a deserved objection. But I think we need to re-enact the night of Carmel's death, slowly, with observers keeping an eye on where everyone is and when."

Walker's silence wasn't portentous. The chief was often silent. Aaron waited.

"That's a pretty damned big order. How will you keep the guests from interfering?"

"We'll have to wait for tomorrow, at the very least. The lodge clears out after the weekend. I was thinking we could call for a fumigation party—send everyone into town for a free festival and pretend fumigators are spraying the halls." That wasn't all he had in mind, but a Null like Walker didn't need to know the odd Lucy details.

"We could have done that without a box of rocks," Walker retorted, catching on quickly that he wasn't getting the full story.

"Yeah, but the less you know about that, the better you'll be able to report to the DA, if needed. So stew over how we'll get everyone's cooperation. Just lining up the staff that was there that night is a challenge."

Hannah was awake and sitting up, with the sheet pulled over her breasts, by the time he hung up. "A re-enactment? And the less Walker knows about what? Did the sheriff release the crystals?"

"Breakfast," Aaron growled, tumbling her into the pillows and kissing her before she could protest. He tasted her desire and happiness —and a thin thread of frustration. He laughed and let her go. "I like knowing what you feel. I don't seem to have the ability to judge that without touching."

"Difficulty in nonverbal communication," she muttered, swinging her legs over the side of the bed. "Afflicts a lot of people with complicated wiring. Resistant to change, repetitive behavior. . . You're just stuck in a rut, though. You don't *want* to know what other people feel, so you block them."

"My choice is to block or go insane," he said without rancor, watching her grab last night's clothes and wondering if he ought to encourage her to move her suitcase here. "The result is the same. I can't judge people by their nonverbal reactions. I need words."

He recognized the irony. He preferred silence and not getting to know people.

"Fair enough. Use your words and call the Lucys to a meeting. You can't pull off this reenactment alone." She strode into the bathroom and shut the door.

Watching Hannah naked was a better way to start the morning than phone calls.

"Aren't women supposed to do the communicating?" he yelled at the door, before pulling on a robe and padding downstairs to make coffee.

He texted Keegan to have Mariah set up a meeting. That should cover it. Now, to get his hands on the box of rocks.

When Hannah floated downstairs in her gauzy sundress, Aaron nearly had to whack his head to keep his thoughts on track. With that fringe of hair nearly covering her eyes and her creamy swan neck and shoulders rising above the flimsy gauze, she looked like an innocent schoolgirl. After last night, he knew there was nothing innocent about his guardian angel.

He handed her a mug of tea, having learned her preference. "We need to get our hands on the rocks, see if your enhancement can tell us anything I missed that night."

She sipped her tea and watched him over the brim, looking so sexy in the process that he wanted to forget rocks and haul her back to bed. He was in danger of coming unhinged.

"Are you sure you want that much insight into evil?" she asked. "Don't you fear the crystals will pollute your soul? How do you know they aren't a hundred times more dangerous than the Eversham painting?"

"We'll not touch them directly until we've assessed the energy they're emitting. But if our theories and those few journal entries mean anything, then the crystals are much more likely to absorb what we offer than vice versa." He hoped. He was pretty dubious about the whole idea, but they couldn't continue doing nothing and let a killer go free.

"If you're making this a public spectacle, aren't you worried the killer will escalate his terrorism in retaliation?" Hannah set down her cup to rummage in his refrigerator.

Aaron grimaced and took the bacon package she handed him. "You have a better plan?"

"I wish I did, but the number of people who wished Carmel dead is daunting. And if her death was a spur of the moment thing, that complicates the case even more. It might be easier to go after whoever deliberately gave digitalis to Francois, then sent him out to dig." She scrambled eggs and cheese and shredded spinach in a bowl.

"You're determined to make me eat green things, aren't you?" He zapped his bacon.

Hannah looked briefly surprised, then poured the eggs into a skillet. "I eat green. I always thought of it as feeding my brain, but I suppose a well-balanced diet feeds the entire body, which keeps the brain functioning. Unless someone proves green causes the knot in my head, I'll stick with what works."

He didn't want to be reminded that this gloriously healthy woman could be attached to tubes and life support tomorrow. He glowered and crunched his nuked bacon. "I still think you need a second opinion."

"I'd have to go back to the UK. I can't afford the insurance here." She matter-of-factly divided the eggs between two plates and set them on the counter as if she weren't talking about a potential death sentence. "I doubt Hillvale is in a position to pay insurance for their schoolteachers."

Damnatus. "We don't have proof that the Healing Stone actually heals," he reminded her.

"I know," she agreed sadly. "But I see no reason to fret over what can't be changed. How do you mean to employ Carmel's rocks?"

A much less depressing topic to chew on along with his bacon and green eggs.

Holding a Lucy meeting on a busy wedding weekend wasn't easy, Hannah learned. Under Mariah's organization, she cleaned Amber's tarot and gift shop at the end of the hectic day while Amber counted her cash register and prepared a deposit. Then Amber went to help Tullah while Hannah aided Teddy in putting the jewelry shop back in order. Sam helped Fee finish the baking for Dinah's restaurant.

Aaron's shop was still closed, but he spent most of the day with the contractors and sorting through his smoke-and-water-damaged inventory while fielding phone calls from the Kennedys on organizing the staff for the event.

They all contributed toward a potluck dinner in the gallery that Lance closed up for the evening.

Mariah had been busy while everyone was cleaning and bookkeeping. She had the large screen monitor on the gallery wall uncovered and a map of the lodge and its grounds displayed when they entered.

Along the stage, she'd lined a battalion of small stone statuettes.

"Daisy made these by the dozens and distributed them far and wide. She called them guardians and lamassu," Mariah explained when Hannah asked. "Lamassu are ancient Sumerian deities who guard portals. They look nothing like Daisy's version. She was a time walker who frequently mixed up her travels."

Like Aunt Jia. Hannah winced, hoping she and Aaron weren't heading down that path.

"Why are they here?" Teddy leaned over the battered medieval casket of rocks to examine the small guardians surrounding it.

"To protect the box. I've been working with the crystals all day." Keegan took over from Mariah. "Their energy is different from the ones in our cave. They behave passively—not actively emanating what they contain. They're like sponges. They absorb the energy around them and leak it out over time, if left untouched."

"And if they're all kept in a box, they leak and absorb each other's elements until all the rocks are more or less the same?" Teddy asked, poking gingerly at one.

"That is my assumption based on limited testing. To some extent, they can be pressurized like our crystals—like a sponge can be squeezed. A sponge oozes water. Hillvale crystals transform into other crystals. I don't know where the energy in Carmel's absorbent rocks goes. So I'm hesitant to conduct further experiments until we have protective equipment. We could be playing with nuclear fusion for all I know. Don't let anyone touch them." Keegan stood over the rocks rather than investigate the food table.

Hannah glanced at Aaron across the room. He looked uncomfortable studying Mariah's map of the lodge on the wall. She knew he wanted at the rocks. He'd have to speak up sometime. She carried a meat-loaded roll over to him and figured he was distracted when he bit into it without discarding the tomato or other veggies.

"I want to test those rocks before I decide how to deploy them," he murmured, easing toward the stage.

"Keegan said they could be dangerous and not to touch them," she warned, judging his direction.

"So, don't touch them. Wait for my signal, then just brush my hand."

"You could just say, *hey Keegan, let me see those rocks*," she suggested as they crossed the floor.

"A direct command overriding his orders?" he asked in amusement. "Not unless we want a fight. Men act first and apologize later."

She punched his arm. "Troglodyte behavior. You're too civilized for that."

"Are you sure Keegan is? He's guarding those rocks as if they're his own."

Hannah studied the cousin she'd known for years. "OK, he's a bit of a troll. But he is civilized once you get past his affinity for rocks."

Keegan stiffened as they reached the stage. Aaron simply reached past him and hefted a stone from the medieval casket.

TWENTY-SIX

AARON CRINGED AT THE MULTIPLE LEVELS OF PAIN AND UGLINESS SEEPING from the rock he held, but he couldn't clarify one layer from another. They all blended worse than mud in a swamp. Did he dare subject Hannah to so much negative energy?

Carmel's greed was there, along with her sick beliefs about power. Her love and pleasure in the crystal was also absorbed into the overall energy, as they'd surmised. If Carmel had touched these rocks before she died, he couldn't tell it.

Knowing Keegan was fretting and about to interfere, Aaron gestured at Hannah.

He knew he shouldn't expose her to the rocks. But he'd been inside her soul last night. She was as strong as he was, and to treat her as if she were not would be an insult. She had a choice. She didn't have to add her hand to his.

But she did. The impact was instantaneous. The layers sorted so he could almost *see* what they contained.

The stones were old, extremely old. Flashes of Carmel dressed to the nines rushed by. With Hannah's hand squeezing his, Aaron hung on despite the growing pain the fleeting images inflicted. Faces, a glitter of water and sunlight, a rush of rocks and debris. . . A long period of darkness followed by sunlight again. He forced himself to dig deeper into the stone's memories—an impossibility he would never have considered without Hannah.

And there. . . the vague impression of despair and anger from the man attaching the stone to the carved granite of a rounded boulder. The man's hatred of the priest became crystal clear with a devastating glimpse of a young girl, battered, bruised, and wasted to nothing.

Staggering, Hannah released his hand.

Oh God, *what had he done?* Aaron instantly dropped the rock and grabbed her elbow. She was shuddering and barely able to stand.

Was using her enhancement harming her? He tried not to panic as she swayed and held her head. He helped her to a seat.

"I've read the history but it was no more real than a fairy tale until now," she whispered.

Aaron's instinct screamed to take her home—but what if *he* was the problem?

Mariah took the seat beside her. "History?" she demanded.

Knowing Keegan's wife was descended from the natives of this land, Aaron couldn't shield her from their knowledge. But he didn't want Hannah to suffer more.

He signaled Harvey to bring over wine, then crouched in front of Hannah, rubbing her hand. "I'm sorry. I never should have subjected you to that. I've never seen so many levels at once."

She clutched his hand but shook her head. "No, it's good to know our theories aren't too far off. Make sure you write about this in your journal. It's essential knowledge."

Deodamnatus, did the woman never let up on that library? She could have *died* holding that rock.

"What is?" Mariah demanded. "Did you see Carmel's killer?"

"No, Carmel is no more than a fleeting moment in the rock's timeline. I have a feeling we could have gone back centuries, but it's like watching a bloody violent TV series mixed with hours of static," he said curtly.

When Hannah didn't seem prepared to faint, Aaron took the seat on the other side of her and continued, "We'd have to examine each crystal to piece together an entire history of all they've absorbed. It could take years."

Harvey passed around plastic cups of cheap wine, then leaned against the stage with Keegan.

"What history?" Mariah demanded, not taking the wine.

"Carmel, the commune, the flood—we didn't even reach the medieval. We stopped at the mission, I assume the one that was never quite established here." Hannah sipped the wine and grimaced.

Aaron stiffened, fearing she might be in pain. But apparently she didn't like the wine because she continued in her normal lecturing voice.

"I'd read that the priests considered their converts as slaves. I'm trying to adjust my thinking to theirs, but they considered natives as lesser animals to be trained like dogs, I think. They kept young girls in nunneries no better than pigsties."

"You saw all this?" Mariah asked incredulously.

"No," Aaron responded impatiently, wanting to take Hannah away. "You asked for history. The crystals are living history, but they aren't sentient."

Hannah took another sip. "The rocks seem to absorb their surroundings. We saw mudslides and maybe the waterfall and a brief glimpse of Carmel. It was the man who attached the rock to the lamassu who gave off the strongest vibration. Aaron's psychometry kicked in more strongly with human touch."

Aaron hurried up the explanation. "And the sculptor probably held the crystal longer than anyone else did. Carmel just picked through the box, with nothing more than greed on her mind, so we received nothing from her. Whoever plucked the rock from the grotto didn't keep it long and they left no distinct impression."

"But you saw what the native sculptor saw?" Mariah asked, a little more politely this time.

"His daughter, battered, bruised, filthy, and dead," Hannah said flatly. She turned to Aaron. "I had the impression that she tried to escape her prison and died in consequence, but she was so thin, anything could have killed her. That ancient cemetery could hold dozens of dead girls, or given the history, hundreds of natives dead from the disease the white men carried."

There was the pain shadowing her eyes. He'd done that to her, given her that horror.

Mariah's fingers balled into fists. Keegan appeared distressed but didn't intervene.

"The cause doesn't matter as much as the consequence." Accustomed to keeping his feelings bottled, Aaron shoved them down now and gave the curt explanation. "The natives killed the priests and set fire to the mission. Soldiers were called in to staunch the uprising. The resort property is a burial ground for violence and human evil."

"Latter days of the mission," Mariah interrupted angrily. "By then, California had its own government. The military sent to protect the missions started usurping the land. The soldier in Eversham's painting was probably one of them. The priests first pushed the tribes off their lands. After the military took over the missions, the soldiers offered freedom. But without the lands that had once been theirs, my ancestors had little choice but to starve or work for the soldiers. At least the soldiers paid their workers, in most cases."

"What does any of this have to do with Carmel?" Keegan demanded.

Keeping his eye on Hannah, who was regaining her color, Aaron shrugged off his disappointment. "Very little. Carmel collected semi-precious stones in superstitious belief that they gave her powers over men. What matters is that these stones came from the soldier's collection, that the natives believed him when he said the crystals would guard against evil ever happening again."

"But as a just-in-case, the shaman added his own magic, and they put the stones in the lamassu, essentially, a native version of guardians at the portals of hell. It's hard to register our modern interpretation of their beliefs about priests as demons or evil feeding on the spilled blood of warriors." Hannah nibbled at cheese Fee arrived to pass around. "But stopping evil was the intent."

"But evil did return," Mariah reminded them. "There have been battles here after that period. Fifty years later, miners were fighting over gold in the streams. Ranchers fought over water rights. Blood has been shed on these mountains since the beginning of time. So these rocks are worthless as protection."

"Daisy's lamassu prevented a rockslide from killing you," Aaron pointed out. "They're not worthless. But if our theories are correct, they must be employed with good intentions. If the earthquake of 1812 toppled the statues and floods buried them, then the stones merely absorbed nature, and maybe began leaking the evil from the burial ground."

"So they're not *inherently* evil but might help us if we use them for good?" Hannah asked.

"That's what I'm hoping," Aaron said, more grimly than he'd intended. "If we're to capture a killer, we should surround ourselves with good intentions."

"The way putting your antiques in good hands ultimately replaces bad memories with good ones! The journals say that works." Finishing off her wine, Hannah jumped up and kissed Aaron's cheek. "Brilliant."

He did his best not to rub the place where she'd kissed him. He feared he'd been branded as her white knight, when he was everything but. He almost sympathized with the beleaguered Spanish soldier in the painting.

"No. Absolutely not," Fred Roper, the lodge manager said when Aaron and Walker approached him the day after the meeting about staging a re-enactment. "We have fifty guests staying over until tomorrow. I can't tell them to leave their rooms and not come back for hours."

As always, Roper was freshly shaved and dressed in a well-tailored suit and an expensive tie. His unfortunately small eyes gave him a shifty look. Aaron figured the lodge manger needed glasses and was too vain to wear them.

"The town is preparing festivities to entertain your guests. We should easily be done in two hours. We can set up the cameras as the guests are shuttled into town. Blame it on me," Walker suggested. "Say the police are investigating criminal activity."

Roper looked properly horrified. "I can't do that. We have a reputation to maintain."

"I suppose calling it a Fumigation Party isn't any better," Aaron suggested. "Make up a better name, but we need them out of here tomorrow night."

"This is highly irregular. If Mr. Kennedy has approved this, I must persuade him otherwise." He stalked toward his office as if he had a stick up his rump. Aaron eyed his own walking staff and wondered if he could impale a walking asshole with it.

He wanted this damn murder solved so he could decide what to do about Hannah before life got more complicated.

"Kurt had a call from a client and got held up," Walker explained apologetically after Roper's departure. "I called Monty. He should be on his way."

"Why haven't they covered this place in security cameras?" Aaron swung to examine the lobby ceiling where cameras would normally be installed.

"Roper and Carmel opposed them. Given what we know of their shady affairs, it's understandable. Discreet meetings require privacy." Walker studied the hallway from the restaurant and didn't expound further.

Lance hurried in from the back hall and the direction of his cabin, looking more harassed than usual. "Roper just called. Is this really necessary? Can't we just let well enough alone and move forward?"

Aaron filled a cup with water from the lobby water cooler and handed it to Lance while Walker gave his reassuring spiel.

"Of course, it's up to you and your nephews. I'm not in a position to call it obstructing justice if you refuse. I simply want to take a killer off the streets." Walker nodded toward the front door, where Monty was jogging up the steps. "Have you talked with your nephews about your concerns?"

"Carmel's their mother. I can't talk to them," Lance said in obvious distress. "I don't want them hurt anymore." He handed the paper cup back to Aaron and walked off.

Aaron closed his eyes and absorbed the brief images Lance had left, but they were distorted by too many emotions at once. Lance was a very confused man. Images of Carmel overlaid with those of Val and his nephews and Lance's fears gave him nothing to work with.

"At least I don't see him whacking Carmel," Aaron said grumpily as Monty entered. "Doesn't mean he didn't."

Walker snorted inelegantly. "Thanks for that."

"Your manager objects to our plans," Walker informed Monty the moment he reached them. "So does Lance."

"They're protecting Mom in their own way, but we're doing this. If weird Lucy woo-woo can catch a killer, we want it done. If it doesn't, then we've wasted a lot of energy but nothing is harmed. Fee is already planning a taco cart. Give the woman a stove and she's a dynamo. What else have you got?" Monty practically bounced up and down with eagerness.

"Security cameras. Are you planning on installing any?" Walker pointed at places on the ceiling where he wanted them.

"We can't get them in by tomorrow but they're on our agenda. I told Roper to draw up a list of staff working that night. I'll go throttle it out of him while I'm here. What else?"

Giving Mayor Monty a task was a kindness or the man would pace the town in personal search of his mother's killer, Aaron knew. The Lucy tendency to create community projects worked the same way. People needed to feel useful. He preferred to go his own way, but he understood the need to help—and hated being helpless.

He got permission to explore Carmel's suite again. He hadn't known the woman well and was glad of it by the time he was finished. He found no trace of murderous intent on anything in there, just layers of vanity and spite and a degree of boredom. Carmel had written herself into a corner, apparently, and lacked the imagination or drive to dig herself out of the image she had of herself.

There was probably a lesson in that. Aaron didn't know if he had the incentive to explore it yet.

He paced the perimeter of the lodge, recalling as much of that night as he could. It was up to him to place people on the outside. Others would have to recreate that evening from the inside.

He examined rocks along the path, hoping he might sense the vibrations of a murder weapon, but there was nothing. Frustrated, he traced the path Francois might have taken from Carmel's back door to his rooms. The chauffeur hadn't passed Aaron, so he would have had to have taken a round-about route.

When he arrived at the outside door to Francois's meager room near the kitchen, it was open. Assuming Walker had released it so the lodge could return it to use, he leaned in.

Lance was ripping out the walls.

TWENTY-SEVEN

"I'M A *LIBRARIAN*, NOT A FASHION MODEL," HANNAH TOLD THE MIRROR IN her room over the shop the day after the Lucy meeting. She'd taken her clothes over to Tullah's store to wash them and ended up buying a few more outfits. Trying on new clothes made her feel a little ridiculous. She'd never spent much time primping. Her head had always been elsewhere.

That was the problem—her head was very much attached to her body since meeting Aaron. She had physical needs she'd never indulged before. Hadn't an obsession with a man in a painting started her down this path? Maybe she ought to have her head examined again, as Aaron kept insisting.

She'd have to go back to Scotland to do so. She'd seen Aaron's despair when Carmel's rock had nearly brought her to her knees. For his sake, she'd have to return for medical procedures—and to stay if she really was dying. Only one of them should have to suffer, and he'd already had his share.

She was still the Malcolm librarian. That had been an inescapable fact since childhood. She'd never really known any other task or calling. She had a job for life, just as Keegan had a responsibility to keeping the physical library, and Aaron had a responsibility to protect. It was their nature and couldn't be changed.

And no matter how obsessed she might be with the impossible, librarians didn't allow valuable books to slip through their hands. They just didn't.

She had to face Cass before she could even think of leaving Hillvale.

What she wanted just as much was to find out about the Eversham painting, but that was a little trickier, especially since she couldn't come out and accuse Cass of stealing it. But who else would have been able to find it?

The mirror showed that the retro-shirtwaist she'd found in the thrift shop worked well for her, and the mini-skirt was an added bonus. She preferred nondescript neutrals, not baby blue, but the sparkly belt made her happy—and confident enough to do what needed to be done. Deciding the dress looked appropriately librarian-ish with its upright collar in back and modest V neck in front, she headed downstairs.

The workmen were almost finished with the back wall of the shop. Aaron's inventory was less cluttered, and someone had even returned the fountain to bubbling. She didn't know if those changes had dispelled the gloom of Aaron's eccentric collection, but the morning sun seemed to shine brighter through the new front window.

Guests of the current bridal party spilled through the street, enjoying the sunshine and each other, as it should be. They didn't need to know of the foul cloud looming over the hill.

The tale of Cass's ancestors would fill a gap in Hannah's knowledge and perhaps help with understanding Carmel's death. Hannah needed those journals.

As she determinedly strode up the residential lane toward the cemetery, Samantha leaned over her garden gate and waved. "Want company?"

Courage only went so far, and Hannah almost melted in relief. "If you have time, I'd love it. I didn't want to bother anyone."

Wearing her usual dirty denim jeans and a t-shirt, Sam strolled under her arbor of cascading roses as if she were a princess in royal attire. In Hillvale, as Cass's adopted granddaughter and the Kennedys' niece, that was close enough.

"I was wondering how long it would take you to crack," Sam said with a grin. "Cass is a force to be reckoned with, but she's had her own way for too long. We either stand up to her or become her flunkies."

"I've never been the flunky sort, but I've never challenged authority either. I've simply gone my own way. I'm starting to think that just holding books in my head isn't enough. I need to find the ones that are missing." She hesitated to say more than that. The moonstone's healing properties were mostly a fairy tale that she desperately wanted to believe in.

Mariah emerged from her eccentric cottage wearing a sleeping Daphne over her chest. "I need out of the house. If this is a round of Cass wrestling, I'm ready for some fun."

"Incorrigible," Sam declared, admiring the sleeping babe in her rosy bonnet. "Teaching Daphne rebellion before she can even speak."

"She speaks," Mariah said in an ominous tone. "The child knows how to make her needs known."

Hannah touched tiny curled fists. "This is the reason I do what I have to do. Children need instruction. They need to have access to knowledge. Cass needs to share."

Cass was waiting for them on her wide, shady front porch, a pitcher of lemonade prepared. "It's about time you visited," she said sternly. "I didn't know how many invitations I had to send."

"If your idea of an invitation is to tell me you're keeping a valuable library from me or stealing Aaron's painting, then pardon me, I'm slow." Feeling defiant, Hannah let out all her suspicions while she poured lemonade for Sam and Mariah. Then she settled on a porch swing.

She hadn't meant to throw the Eversham out there.

"The Eversham oil was always meant to be mine," Cass said serenely. "It's a dangerous artifact. The artist had nightmares while he was here and was much happier after he left. The painting was meant to be a warning."

Sam and Mariah sipped their drinks and left the ground open for Hannah.

The wily old woman had apparently stolen the painting as soon as word got around that Aaron had it. Hannah had known Cass was dangerously gifted. She pushed the swing with her toe, warding off the force of Cass's personality. The painting no longer concerned her now that she'd seen the subject. The books did. "It's not a warning if it's hidden, by you or by Aaron. It is a slice of Hillvale history—Aaron confirmed that when he touched the crystals from the jewel casket depicted in that painting. Your journals could tell us more."

"You may peruse the journals, if you wish," Cass agreed with a regal nod. "I do not want them hauled off and lost to a musty old fortress in Scotland. I have a temperature-controlled vault suitable for our American library."

"Thank you," Hannah said with genuine gratitude and relief. She'd been afraid her courage would fail her—but she'd succeeded in bearding the lioness in her den! "They ought to be accessible to everyone. The scanner needed to digitalize the journals is expensive. Perhaps a university would be good enough to allow me to use theirs." *Before she returned to Scotland* went unsaid, because sadly, she knew she had to leave. She couldn't torture Aaron much longer.

"If we can't have our own librarian, then digital scanning is an alternative I had not considered. I'll make a few calls. I still have connections. I'd advise only taking out one volume at a time. There aren't many, but they're fragile." Cass placed her hand on a leather-bound book half-hidden by her skirt. "This one belongs to my several-times-great grandmother."

Success! Reverently, Hannah accepted the aging journal, praying the secret of the moonstone lay within.

"There are so many words in my brain that's it good to have my hands on them too. They become more concrete that way." Holding the book, she absorbed as much knowledge as she could from just cradling it in her palms. She'd never found her ability to assimilate Keegan's magical library odd. It had been there even when she was an infant, words that came from nowhere until she understood her heritage.

She sat silently ingesting the writing, flipping pages, while Sam and Mariah discussed their plans for the fumigation festivities and reenactment. Hannah's gift couldn't pick up the emotion of the written words, just the neat pen-and-ink of a woman with a scientific bent. When she reached the part about the moonstone, she halted to read more carefully.

She hadn't realized conversation had died down until she finished reading. She looked up and blinked to return to the real world.

Guessing they were waiting on her, Hannah explained, "The Victorian writer says family legend relates that the moonstone has worked in conjunction with the other stones, but she has no understanding of how. She had hoped to use it to rid the ranch of spirits, without success."

"Which is why they ended up moving into town and starting a dry goods store to supply the miners and ranchers," Cass said matter-of-factly. "No one knows how to properly use the crystals."

"It should be in some journal somewhere," Hannah said in frustration.

"Your medieval nun is all we have," Mariah said. "I've run every search through every journal that's been uploaded and called for more, but fear of witchcraft drove all knowledge underground."

"If we had the moonstone, Aaron might be able to learn from it." Pushing a swing was no longer enough. Hannah needed to *do* something. She paced the porch—just the way Aaron did when he got restless. She was practically inside his skin now. "Maybe there's something in the Eversham. . ."

"No, dear, you've already learned as much from the painting as you can. The lamassu will tell you the rest. It's the moonstone you need. I don't believe Carmel would have sold it. It was almost worthless in terms of money, but priceless in terms of power. She simply didn't know how to wield it."

"But if it wasn't in her safe, then she'd taken it out for a reason. We just don't know how long ago." Mariah expressed the same frustration as Hannah, causing her infant to twitch and flail a tiny hand.

"You are welcome to stay and see the other books, but they're not as informative in terms of crystals. My mother's family became very traditional and didn't explore their gifts, although they kept their thoughts in their journals. They're not very enlightening," Cass added dryly.

"Thank you." Hannah returned the book to Cass. "I'll come back. Every little bit of knowledge is useful in some way. But it's the moonstone and finding a killer that's on my mind at the moment."

And hoping the stone really could heal was right up there with finding a killer, but even she knew that was like wishing on a star.

"Telling Aaron that everyone must die someday isn't helpful," Cass said sympathetically, standing to see them off.

Despite Cass's out-of-the-blue response, Hannah understood. And it bloody well wasn't helpful at all, especially if Cass thought Hannah was actually going to die.

"FRANCOIS HID HIS STASH IN THE WALLS," AARON REPORTED THAT EVENING, when he finally had Hannah to himself again. "He hid everything he ever stole somewhere in that room, under the carpet, in the ceiling. No wonder the place reeked."

"Anything that someone might have killed him for?" she asked, rightfully dubious.

"The blackmail photos alone would justify that, especially if Francois suddenly demanded more. Walker is investigating the men in the photos to see if any of them were at the lodge that weekend. Carmel had wealthy lovers, so any of them could have hired killers." He set out the cartons he'd bought at Dinah's restaurant.

Hannah emptied them into bowls to nuke them. "And they could have taken the moonstone with them," she said sadly.

"You aren't still thinking the wretched stone will cure you?" he asked incredulously. "I have money. I can pay to have your head examined by the best physicians in the world."

She shot him a look he couldn't interpret. "And I told you I refuse to become a vegetable. But the moonstone might help cure Hillvale of whatever evil lurks in the soil."

Despair whirled through him at her denial. He would have to harden his heart again to prevent sinking into that quagmire, and he didn't know if he could do it. "I prefer to believe that once we clean out the rotten core, Hillvale will heal again."

Aaron watched uneasily as Hannah drifted around his kitchen, gathering utensils as if she were a natural extension of himself. He knew he was building up to disaster and couldn't seem to prevent it. "Francois never allowed anyone in his room except the maids. There was a leak in his roof running down between the walls. The place smelled because the whole back wall is covered in mold. They had to call in a mold mitigation company. Roper is beside himself."

She flashed him an absent-minded smile. "So no one is really lying when we have a fumigation festival tomorrow. They'll just be fumigating mold and not bugs."

Unable to help himself, Aaron wrapped his arms around her waist and held her close before she flitted away. It had been so long since he'd allowed himself to feel. . .

She was practically vibrating with worry—not a good sign. He should back off, but he didn't want to. *Feeling* again felt right. He steeled himself against the inevitable pain. "It's entertaining to think we might cure all Hillvale with a stone, but that's what modern medicine is for. We have to do some things ourselves."

She relaxed against him for a brief moment and then shoved away. "You're not guardian of the world, and money can't fix everything. What are the Kennedys doing with their mother's rocks?"

Rebuffed, Aaron closed up again—where he was admittedly more comfortable. He'd done remarkably well without people all these years. He needed to consider he might be hurting her worse and keep his hands off. How well would that work when she lit his kitchen with an incandescence that sucked him in like an illuminated manuscript?

He poured wine and let her busy herself with putting dinner on the table. "Keegan is still examining the casket. Unless he finds something valuable or harmful, the Kennedys have agreed to let Mariah play her games with the crystals and Daisy's lamassu. Her ghostcatchers have worked well these past years to stop the poltergeists. She's hoping the raw crystals can absorb the negative energy afflicting the lodge. It's not as if we can bulldoze the field and retrieve the original statues, even if we knew they worked."

She nodded and took a seat in the chair he held out for her. "Okay. I think I'm just a little overwhelmed. I should get out of the library more often. I'd really hoped Cass would be more helpful."

"You have a right to be overwhelmed. We've thrown a lot at you in the week since you arrived. It's. . ." He reached for a bowl and stopped in mid-sentence, before he said anything ridiculous, like *It's as if you're a fresh breeze sent to clear out the rot.* Or worse. The image of the saintly nun and the courageous knight was now engraved in his brain.

She glanced at him quizzically, waiting for him to finish. When he didn't, she acknowledged his reticence and raised it a notch higher. "We didn't touch the medieval casket together. Shouldn't we try that? It contained the moonstone at some point. There could be knowledge there."

"*Faex,* no," he said without giving it a second thought. "You nearly passed out examining a single pebble. My brain would probably explode going through five centuries of actual people instead of geological events. I touched the casket enough earlier to assume there's nothing new we can take from it."

"But I didn't touch it with you," she argued. "Maybe you'll see what you need to see instantly. We can't know how deep the knowledge is buried."

There it was—the crisis of decision he'd been trying to avoid. Aaron shook his head. "*No,* we're not doing that anymore. I saw how weak you got that last time. Psychometry drains you—that's probably the reason you fainted when you touched me and the Eversham. No more enhancing."

His angel glared at him. "I'm an adult. I get to make my own choices. If this is the way I wish to spend what's left of my life, that should be my decision."

He flung down his fork and glared back. "I refuse to be the instrument by which you kill yourself. I'll leave Hillvale before I allow that to happen."

"Fine." She flung down her napkin. "Be the damned knight and soldier and put saving the world before saving yourself. I'll leave. I want to go back to my room now."

"I don't need you to save me from myself," Aaron retorted, rising with her.

But she was painfully right about one thing—they had to be separated so neither of them would be tempted to use her enhancing abilities again. Her brilliant mind should be safer that way—and he'd learned to survive with a broken heart. He'd simply have to go back to living a half-life again.

TWENTY-EIGHT

FEELING LIKE CRAP AFTER A LONELY NIGHT OF TOSSING AND TURNING IN HER lonely bed, attempting to rework her argument with Aaron, Hannah tried to find interest in the town's re-enactment of Carmel's murder. Deciding she had to leave after it was over wasn't making life any easier. She'd spent most of the day in her room, scouring a library she knew by heart, looking for information on enhancing psychometry, with little success. Old texts didn't cover modern science.

"Don't you feel a little foolish doing this?" Hannah whispered to Keegan as they set small stone statuettes around the perimeter of the lodge.

Mariah and her friends had devised a means of wiring the Spanish soldier's stones to Daisy's small lamassu. The stacks of three rocks with glittering crystal eyes now had wired arms bearing a pebbly burden, rather like a basket. Having no ability to sense vibrations or energy on her own, Hannah felt as if she were decorating with particularly eccentric garden gnomes.

Aaron had distanced himself all day, rightfully so. He didn't need another dying wife, or lover, on his hands. And she refused to put him—or herself—through that pain.

She'd finally decided that she needed to return where she belonged—to Keegan's library.

"The rocks are nae normal, lass," Keegan said, humoring her with dialect. "There's no harm in testing."

"I wish I believed we'd trap a killer this way, but I think he's long gone. Or maybe the sheriff is right and Francois did it, then keeled over from exertion."

"Except Francois did not try to burn Aaron out," Keegan reminded her.

"I've been thinking about that. What if someone wanted to burn the Eversham? Or some other evidence in there? Although that doesn't explain the pile of rocks." She tucked a statuette under a rose bush.

"We just keep trying until we learn more," Keegan said patiently. "Nothing is ever written in black and white except your books."

Maybe that was her problem. She expected life to be as clear and complete as a story in a book. But it wasn't. Life was messy and unfinished, and it was up to her to make her own story happen. As a dedicated observer, she didn't have much experience at making anything happen.

Walker and Aaron, on the other hand, had spent hours planning this *experiment*. The plans were so detailed that they almost didn't have enough people to oversee the reenactment, plus entertain the guests in town. The lodge was large and sprawling, and they couldn't possibly watch everyone, so Walker had his security firm install cameras from his own funds to catch every angle that observers couldn't. She didn't know what they hoped to see.

Once Daisy's lamassu were distributed, Hannah joined the others who had been inside on the night Carmel died. People who hadn't been there were assigned as observers or left in town to run the festival.

Hannah hadn't known Aaron that fateful night. It seemed weird that they'd been strangers when she was half convinced they'd known each other for eternity—unhappily, apparently.

Looking his sexy, professorial best, Aaron was wearing his tan, tailored blazer over a black silk polo and tight black jeans as he choreographed the milling crowd. Her foolish heart longed for him to turn and smile at her just one more time, but he deliberately kept his back to her.

"We're starting from the moment we heard Carmel raise her voice," he told the crowd. "You've each told Walker where you were at that moment. If you'll all find that place, we'll have someone verify your position in a few minutes. You're all on candid camera, so don't do anything I wouldn't do."

That produced a few nervous titters as everyone scattered.

"We were drinking," Monty Kennedy called as he and Kurt headed for the lounge. "Should we be faithful to history?"

"Let's not," Walker said dryly. "Last time, someone died."

Hannah headed down the hall to the room she'd been assigned that night, trying to remember precisely at what point she'd noticed the loud argument.

Amber and Josh had been in the swimming pool, she remembered. She was tempted to sneak down that corridor to see how faithful the couple was being to the moment. With the heavy door closed and the distance, they'd said they hadn't heard Carmel's screams.

Hannah waved at one of the newly installed cameras as she reached the point where she thought she belonged. It was earlier in the evening than the night of the murder, but this area had no windows. The lighting left a bit to be desired, she noted nervously.

If the killer was a local and not a guest, they were re-enacting this scene with a murderer in their midst.

The recording of Val emulating Carmel's shouts of anger reverberated down the hall. It wasn't as frightening as the reality had been, but Hannah still hesitated as she had that night. The one-sided argument had been loud and ugly and probably not sane. Whoever Carmel had been yelling at hadn't been audible.

Hannah slowly walked down the hall as she had that night, until the shouts became screams that abruptly halted. She had no idea if the timing was correct, but she thought she was in the approximate position she'd been then.

She hesitated as she had at the time, then turned in the ominous silence and fled back to the safety of the well-lit lobby.

She passed the long corridor leading to the swimming pool. This time, she glanced down it to see if anyone else was there. No one.

She remembered there had been running footsteps. She didn't hear those this time. That put her off kilter a little. She'd been running from the footsteps as much as the frightening lack of screams.

Hurrying, she ran into the lobby. There was the desk clerk, looking surprised at her abrupt entrance. He'd said he hadn't heard the argument. She gabbled about the screams, not making much sense. The clerk called for security. There had been inn guests wandering in from the restaurant, she remembered, but there was no one emerging from that direction now.

Roper popped out of his office, signaled by the clerk. Uniformed security raced in through the front door and from the restaurant. At the clerk's direction, they hurried down the hall Hannah had just traversed. Roper followed them. Kurt came in from the direction of the bar. She hadn't known him then, but she'd assumed him to be someone important. As she had that night, she turned to follow the others—

That's when she realized it wasn't just the missing sound of running feet that was off.

Hannah halted to glance from the lobby down the hall that contained the door Roper had just used. If that was his office on the right—*he hadn't emerged from his office that night*, as he'd said. She hadn't known the layout of the lodge at the time, but she could swear he'd come from further down the hall, on the left. She could see now that was where the *guest* business office was, not Roper's private one.

There was no other door except for that computer room on the left side. Abandoning the reenactment, she tested the door, but as with most hotel guest offices, it was locked to anyone without a room key. She held her hand to the window to look in. In the back was a door labeled *Storage.*

Now that she had a better picture of the lodge's layout, she followed in the path of the others down the hall toward Carmel's room. She halted at the long, dim corridor to the right leading to the swimming pool. She hadn't been much interested in it the night she'd discovered the pool locked. It smelled of chlorine and had no guest rooms. If she had to guess, the blank wall on the left might conceal Carmel's private courtyard. The back wall of the lobby and business office was on the right side, so except for decorator artwork, that was blank as well. Slipping down the corridor, she found a door in the approximate area of the business office labeled *Employees Only.* She pushed it open to a stockroom.

In the back of the stockroom she found a door leading to the business office—a shortcut from the pool area to the main hall off the lobby.

She returned to the pool corridor. On the far end near the pool, she located a fire exit on the left. The sign said to open only in case of emergency, so it would probably emit an alarm if she tried it.

But any employee who carried the keys to the lodge might be able to open it without sounding an alarm.

All the Kennedys probably had keys—but she hadn't seen them emerging from an office that had an indirect path to Carmel's private courtyard.

Roper had no motive for killing Carmel. Who else could have come through this way? Not a guest. Staff maybe?

Anxiously, she hurried to where everyone was gathering inside and outside Carmel's suite.

Roper shot her a glare—he'd known she'd been right behind him that night. Kurt didn't notice her delay. He'd been too upset to acknowledge her existence. The security guards were off to one side, where Kurt had ordered them at the time.

Aaron was outside with the others, as before, although this time he appeared to be searching for her and looked relieved when she waved at him. She definitely needed to leave Hillvale or she'd lose her mind just trying to catch glimpses of Aaron as she went about her day.

Walker stood in the closet doorway as an observer. He narrowed his eyes at her dalliance but didn't speak. He had a stop watch in one hand and a walkie-talkie in the other.

Ignoring the reenactment of discovering Carmel, Hannah slipped out of the bedroom, back into the suite living room. A patio door slid open into a small courtyard, as she remembered. Walker and his men had covered all this territory. Fingerprints were useless when everyone Carmel knew had been in here at some time or another.

Hannah didn't want to attract attention, so she didn't open the door. She merely confirmed a wall enclosed the courtyard, *one with a gate in back.* Locked? Probably.

She returned to the bedroom and tried to look faint and ill to excuse her pacing. Walker sent her another hooded glance, then spoke into the walkie-talkie, ending the drill.

Looking annoyed and without waiting dismissal, Roper strode out of the room trailing the security guards.

Aaron and Kurt quit play-acting and joined Walker. The room filled with people. Hannah didn't want to accuse Roper in front of a crowd.

Reporting her findings was all that was necessary, wasn't it? A librarian observed.

While the others discussed their discoveries, Hannah connected to the lodge's wi-fi and began typing.

TWENTY-NINE

THE REENACTMENT HAD ACCOMPLISHED NOTHING. AARON HAD HOPED THEY might trip up the culprit on their story of that night—or more superstitiously, that the soldier's crystals in Daisy's lamassu might absorb enough evil to free the truth. But he knew better than to place hopes on anything but good old-fashioned hard work.

After their argument, he didn't question Hannah's reluctance to join the discussion. She had retreated to full librarian mode, observing but not participating unless she had something to contribute.

She was right to back off. He had to quit caring and let her go her own way.

"The medieval casket is probably worth more than the rocks," Aaron told Kurt Kennedy as they waited for Walker to analyze the results of their exercise. "I'd hate to see it leave Hillvale, but it probably belongs in a museum."

"I doubt museums can pay off our debts," Kurt said with cynicism. "And if the box originally belonged to Cass's family, I'd feel guilty about selling it. Maybe the best thing to do is put it in our town museum."

"Since it's not jeweled and has no particular refinements, that might be the best use. I can clean it up. Hannah can probably write a storyboard to go with it." If she stayed around. He had no family here. Maybe he should be the one to leave—after they found a killer. "We can enlarge one of my photos of the Eversham painting and hang that with it. Tourists will lap it up."

"Socialism," Kurt pointed out with a laugh. "Cass usurps your painting without paying for it—for the common good. I hand over a valuable museum piece without compensation so the town benefits—and ultimately the town's business increases. Not sure that Cass's theft actually benefits us though."

Aaron snorted at this assessment, figuring Kurt needed a little escape from the intensity of what they were doing. "Has the coroner released your mother's remains yet?" Out of habit, he ran his hands near the surfaces he passed as they paced Carmel's bedroom, keeping enough distance to avoid any psychic jolts.

"He has. We've arranged a quiet cremation in the city. I thought we might have a small memorial service here for staff so they have closure." Kurt stared unseeingly at the beautifully curated version of his mother represented by her tastefully expensive décor.

"She was a vital part of this town for nearly half a century," Aaron acknowledged. "We might hold a ceremony too."

Kurt nodded absently. "Just standing here makes me feel as if I'm absorbing her negative. . . *energy.* Isn't that what the Lucys call it? I want to post an admission price outside the door and let the ghouls come in to admire her handiwork."

"I can see the temptation. I suspect if you ask Teddy's sister, she'll tell you the cost of these furnishings. They're quality, probably custom made for your mother. It's quite possible Sydony could sell the furniture to some of her Silicon Valley clients. Even the draperies could be remade for pillows or comforters. I think you might earn more renting the room nightly than as a museum piece." Aaron tried not to sound concerned about Kurt's odd suggestion.

Kurt laughed. "I know. I think Teddy is rubbing off on me. I'm starting to believe in evil vibrations. We'll find a place to warehouse these and I'll ask Syd what she thinks." He looked up and gestured at his uncle, who was hanging around uncertainly outside. "Lance, tell us what you think we should do with all this."

Lance had said he'd been in his cottage when he'd heard Carmel's screams. Accustomed to his sister's temper, he hadn't thought anything of the argument until the screams had stopped. Aaron hadn't seen him in his wandering because Lance's cottage was on the far side of Carmel's room. For the reenactment, Lance could only linger outside as he said he had that night. He'd admitted that he'd had Francois drive him into town as soon as he'd learned that Carmel was dead. Francois had essentially been as close as Lance had to an alibi, and he was dead.

"Sell the furniture if it's worth anything," Lance agreed. "But with our housing shortage, you might want to rent out the suite as a private residence long-term rather than nightly."

Aaron backed away, letting the family decide what to do with Carmel's effects. He'd always found this the saddest part of any death. There were funerals and rituals to handle human remains—but everything the deceased ever touched had the potential to become a sacred memorial. That's where he usually stepped in, putting monetary value on sentiment. It was seldom worth much.

He finally gave in to the temptation to seek out Hannah in the front room. He'd found nothing new or unusual on the surfaces in the bedroom. Perhaps the living area would provide a hint.

Hannah wasn't there. Trying to believe it was best that she removed the temptation of her enhancing abilities, he tested any furniture that might reveal clues to Carmel or her visitors. Anger coated so much of what he felt that it was impossible to sort through any specific memories. Despite all her wealth and beauty, Carmel had been a seriously unhappy person.

Aaron pondered that as he stepped into the corridor. Carmel had family and acquaintances who might have become friends, but her only goal had seemed to be wealth. From things he'd heard, she'd also pushed an old-fashioned notion of social standing and possibly political power. He thought it was the emptiness of her goals that caused her unhappiness. She didn't want wealth or power to improve the town or people's lives. She sought them simply because she knew no other goal.

Life had been sucked out of her early.

Aaron knew how that happened. Life had been sucked out of him for years, until he was simply surviving because he could. At least he'd found goals outside himself, but guarding Hillvale had about as much purpose as gaining political power if he didn't mean to improve himself or anything else.

Hannah had taught him to want more than that—and that shook him to the core.

∿

A<small>FTER TEXTING HER REPORT TO</small> W<small>ALKER</small>—<small>AND TO THE</small> L<small>UCYS</small>—H<small>ANNAH</small> had almost decided to walk down the hill toward town. It might be possible to cut through the landscaping instead of using the dangerously narrow and dark drive. She'd hiked the hills of Scotland, after all. This was nothing.

She just had this itchy feeling in the middle of her back that hate arrows were being aimed at her. Did hate have an energy?

Monty Kennedy emerged from the bar area with some of the other re-enactors. At seeing Hannah standing there alone, he offered a ride back to town. Gratefully, she accepted it. She needed time to think, and it was very difficult to do in Aaron's imposing proximity, especially when he was in professorial mode.

She hadn't sent her report to him. She didn't even have his phone number. What did that say about their relationship? Nothing good.

"Is Hillvale starting to grow on you, or are you ready to pack your bags and run?" Monty asked jovially as they drove down the hill.

Hannah had to think about that too. "I like Hillvale," she decided. "I'm just afraid I'm not suited to be a teacher. And I'm not a very good Lucy either."

"Like Aaron," Monty said with a laugh. "He's lousy at being part of a group. Good man, always there when needed, just not a joiner."

He pulled the car up in front of the antique store and let her out. "Talk to Fee," he suggested. "She had a hard time believing she could fit in too. But now she's part of the clockwork."

"I'll do that, thank you." Hannah waved him off, then let herself inside the shop. The back wall and door had been replaced, so her room should be safe enough.

She stood in the dark shop window for a moment, watching the last of the festival-goers climbing onto the trolley, laughing and holding balloons and flashy party lights. She had no real desire to be part of a noisy group like that. She belonged in empty hills or quiet libraries.

Or a nunnery. Snorting at that, she followed the nightlights through the newly-arranged inventory to the stairs.

She *wanted* to be useful, she knew. She simply didn't know how, other than handing out information from books.

Going up the stairs, she checked to see if Aaron's wi-fi was connected, then read her text messages.

Mariah had written: *What if it's the box that's important, not the rocks?*

Hannah collapsed on the stairs and skimmed rapidly through the responses from other Lucys.

The box had appeared in both paintings. The painters had deliberately displayed the intricate box in more detail than the rocks. Had that been a symbol of what they hadn't dared convey in writing?

Hannah opened the library in her head and began searching on *box* and *jewel casket.*

The front door opened, and she jerked back to the moment. It was dark, but she knew who stood there—Aaron.

His stride was quick and sure as he traversed the shop. He only halted when he realized she was there.

"Why are you sitting in the dark?" he asked.

"I don't need light to read my library," she explained. "The Lucys are asking for information, and I think I've found what they need. Give me a minute."

She hastily texted her findings while Aaron checked his locks and security. He seemed as cool and calm as always, so maybe it was her own nervousness that detected an element of tension. She was very bad at relationships for just this reason. She was too detached and caught up inside her own head. She'd told him she was leaving. Why was he here?

She stood up to indicate she was done. "Did Walker learn anything?"

"Only what you told him. You didn't tell me? Why?" He came to stand at the foot of the stairs.

Ah, male ego, understood. "I didn't have your number," she reminded him. "I'm sorry you didn't learn more. Did the lamassu with the rocks help at all?"

"No one got killed," he said dryly, taking the phone from her hand

and adding his numbers. "I wasn't hard to find. You could have told me you were ready to leave."

"I'm capable of looking after myself. I don't want to be dependent on you." Retrieving her phone, she hated that they were ending the most exciting sex she'd ever known. Relationships needed more foundation than the physical, and neither of them seemed skilled at more.

"Does that mean you're sleeping here again tonight? We still haven't caught whoever set the place on fire."

"The Lucys want to search Roper's cabin," she stated baldly. The idea terrified her, but she'd been the one to suggest it. She wasn't ready to go back to being quiet, unobtrusive Hannah just yet. Before she retired to Scotland, she wanted to *do* something with her life.

She just wasn't certain how to work around the mountain that was Aaron. She wanted him. She'd like to have his approval and his aid. She simply couldn't ask him to ruin his life all over again.

"Breaking and entering is illegal in every state I know of," he countered. "Let Walker do it."

"Walker can't. He has no reason for a warrant. And no reason to believe me that Roper wasn't where he said he was. And he has no motive whatsoever. But if we learn Roper has the moonstone, then we have evidence to convince him there's more to the story."

Aaron was silent for a moment. She knew he was processing what little he knew and rejecting her idea. She would have done the same a week ago. She probably ought to now. But she'd come all this way in search of that stone, and she wasn't letting a killer have it.

If Roper wasn't a killer, then no one need bother him. She'd chalk up the anomaly of his behavior as that of a busy man with no patience for playacting.

"Let Mariah slap him with ectoplasm or Fee feed him truth serum," Aaron said. "There are better ways to find out if he's involved and to find the stone."

"Using enhanced psychometry on the jewel casket is another way," she reminded him. "All our gifts are dangerous—and unreliable. The Lucys will keep guard. Roper never returns to his cabin during the day. He's too controlling."

"The casket has nothing to do with anything except the moonstone.

That's what this is about, isn't it?" Now he sounded angry. "A damned stone won't make you better. I've offered to send you to the best doctors in the world. I can afford it."

"You can't afford being tied to another dying woman," she retorted, not knowing why she was angry but striking out anyway. "I'll find the moonstone and go back to Keegan's where I can pay for my own health-care. *Stop hovering.*"

"You're behaving like a suicidal teenager," he shouted. "You're more concerned with playing magic games than looking for real solutions—solutions to murder as well as to the knot in your brain! Magic won't make either happen!"

"I am not suicidal! I just don't want to be a damned vegetable before I've had time to live. You're already pushing me away with excuses, because you're so terrified of Natalie's ghost that you'll never love another living, breathing woman. So go, leave me alone." So she could cry and start wiping him out of her system.

"Fine. I'll turn on the alarm as I leave. I'll remind you that there's a real killer and arsonist in town." He marched back to the front door, turning his back on her—as he had before.

She stomped upstairs and out of sight of the most intoxicating man she'd ever known and would never know again. She hadn't realized it was physically possible for a heart to break over a relationship that had never existed.

THIRTY

AARON STALKED DOWN THE PATH TO HIS HOUSE, WHACKING THE BUSHES WITH his stick.

Stop hovering.

What the frigging hell did that mean? He was supposed to let her leap off tall buildings in a single bound when he knew she couldn't fly? Hannah had an effing *library* in her brain, not superpowers. She had no business turning into a criminal because he—

Harvey stepped onto the path in front of him, raising his walking stick as if it were a quarterstaff.

Aaron contemplated swatting at him with his own staff and only stopped himself when he realized the ridiculousness of playing Robin Hood and Friar Tuck. He waited to see what the elusive musician wanted.

"You're sending off energy spikes so strong half the valley is shaking," Harvey said. "Do I need to move the lamassu around you?"

"Move the useless shit anywhere you like, but get out of my way." Aaron poked his staff at Harvey's lean chest.

"You're using good old-fashioned Anglo-Saxon. She must have done a number on you." Harvey stepped aside. "While *you* may be vibrating out of control, my stick isn't picking up as much evil as usual. I think the crystals in Daisy's lamassu are working, absorbing Carmel's bad energy."

Aaron wanted to go home and open a bottle of his best wine and celebrate a narrow escape, but he couldn't help looking down at the crystal knob of his staff. He'd chosen his house because it was on the border of the territory that caused his hackles to raise and his stick to shudder. His stick wasn't shuddering now.

Harvey might be able to pick up anger spikes, but all Aaron had ever felt was the land's evil.

"The Lucys have been up at the lodge and all around it and none of them are complaining about evil vibrations," Harvey continued without waiting for Aaron's reply.

"The lodge was never as bad as the woods," Aaron said, deciding he needed to take a look and glancing up the hill to decide on a direction.

"The woods are still bad," Harvey warned him. "It's only inside the circle of the lamassu that the bad energy is clearing. Even Mariah's ghostcatchers are slowing down."

"We need to move the lamassu further from the lodge?" The idea intrigued and was probably more useful than getting drunk.

"The question becomes—how much distance can they cover? I'm not of a scientific mind. Do we call Keegan?" Harvey headed up the hill with the ease of a mountain goat.

"Keegan doesn't sense evil the way we do. Let's just move a few to where the energy is the worst and call him in the morning." It wasn't as if Aaron would sleep tonight anyway. He was a churning mass of fury, angst, and. . . He didn't even know what to call it except a danger to his well-being.

The last time he'd felt like this, he'd buried his wife and recklessly stolen a painting. Best not to repeat it.

~

HANNAH LISTLESSLY WENT TO THE CAFÉ FOR BREAKFAST THE NEXT MORNING. She hadn't slept well. She kept listening for the security alarms to blare and fretting over her choices and wondering if the knot in her head was growing and making her crazy. She'd have to see a physician just to reassure herself she wasn't likely to end up in an institution any time soon.

Breaking into a possible killer's house almost made sense with that ax hanging over her head.

Sam hailed her from a back booth. Fee carried over Hannah's favorite tea. Mariah had her notebook computer open displaying the passages Hannah had sent her last night from the Malcolm library.

"Walker doesn't want us to have the casket, but Kurt and Monty say it's okay," Mariah told Hannah as she took her first sip of tea.

"None of them know why, of course," Teddy said in amusement. "Do you think we can do this before the shop opens? It's been pretty busy lately, and I hate to leave Syd with both the store and the kids."

"Val wants to join us. It doesn't matter if I go in late," Amber said. "Why don't you stay down here, Ted? It shouldn't take a full battalion to search that little place."

Fee brought over a giant, scrumptious-smelling cinnamon roll for Hannah. Everyone at the table stopped talking to gape.

"Did you pack it with seaweed?" Amber asked skeptically.

The petite cook smiled beatifically. "Hannah needs sweetness today. I'm sorry I can't join you, but I don't know what a moonstone smells like anyway." She hurried off to fill coffee cups.

Hannah didn't think the most perfect cinnamon roll in the world could sweeten her disposition today, but she forked off a piece anyway.

Fortunately, the psychic Lucys didn't question why she needed sugaring up. She suspected they were already plotting ways of castrating Aaron. She'd have to stop them. Sometime.

It was good to have friends who understood.

It was a pity she wasn't better at returning that understanding.

"I think I should go in alone," Hannah said after swallowing a little piece of heaven. "I have nothing to lose if I'm arrested for breaking in. I just need backup so Roper can't beat me into a pulp."

"It's still hard to imagine that smarmy little man having enough spine to lift a hand against anyone," Mariah said with disgust. "And he's practically the only person in town who has no motive. We're probably making much ado about nothing."

"I probably ought to be the one to go in," Teddy said worriedly. "He knows Kurt has the ability to fire him, so he won't come after me."

"I'll just tell him Kurt sent me," Hannah said with a laugh. "Don't worry. Can we get the box? If the moonstone really does resonate with it as the one journal said, then I should be in and out in no time."

"I still have the box," Mariah said. "Keegan was testing it to see if it had some ability to control the energy of the stones, but he has demanding principles and hasn't reached a conclusion yet. I'll tell him Aaron wants to look at it."

"You shouldn't lie to your husband," Hannah protested. She feared she was setting a bad precedent by suggesting illegal solutions.

"I'm not. Aaron *does* want to look at it. He just won't admit it. Besides, he told Kurt he'd clean it. We'll only appropriate it for a little while before we hand it over." Mariah finished her juice smoothie. "Did everyone get the same message from these passages Hannah sent us that I did? That the moonstone belongs to the casket?"

"That doesn't make sense," Sam said, nibbling at her toast. "The parts that interested me were when they carried the casket to troubled locations, placed it in a church, and prayed. Do we need an incantation or will just any prayer do? Do we need a church?"

"To do what?" Teddy asked. "I know stones can be powerful. My truth stones have caused no end of havoc without need of mystical chants. So we have to be careful how we wield anything that might be as strong as this one seems to be."

"Let's find the stone first," Mariah said, sliding from the booth. "If the casket will help us, then that's where we start. I'll meet you behind the dumpsters at the lodge at nine. Roper will be safely in his office by then."

Hannah swallowed a lump in her throat as she finished her cinnamon roll without tasting it. She wanted to help Hillvale. She didn't want to be a burden on anyone, least of all Aaron. She simply didn't know what was right or wrong in this case.

Calling herself a spineless wimp, she managed a cheerful farewell and headed back to her room.

The front door was unlocked. She knew she'd locked it. Aaron had said he didn't come in until nine-thirty, but he'd shown up early before.

She hadn't expected to have to face him before she did what she had to do. He would stop her if he knew she meant to risk it.

Here was the perfect excuse to escape the foolishness of breaking and entering in search of something that might not exist. She hesitated. Quiet Librarian Hannah would never have even contemplated breaking the law.

Quiet Hannah had been a lonely useless shadow who had accomplished zip with her life.

Aaron had turned his back on her last night. He'd made his choice. She'd make hers.

Setting her jaw, she crossed the street to the new schoolhouse. Kurt had said the upstairs facilities were almost ready. Maybe instead of immediately running back to the hills, she should try staying. Maybe she'd see Aaron more clearly as the emotionally stunted, over-protective ass he was.

The wi-fi wasn't connected in the schoolhouse yet so she couldn't text anyone and ask for a ride. The water was on at least. After using her finger to brush her teeth, Hannah decided she had some extra time and needed exercise anyway. She would just walk up to the lodge.

She left through the back door. Behind this strip of buildings was a narrow lane edged in by the bluff. She strode past the newly repaired stairs leading up to the old commune, admired the small park Sam had planted, and started up the long driveway to the lodge.

The lane was old and barely wide enough for two cars, she noted. She stuck to the left-hand side so she could face anyone coming down. She stepped off when food delivery trucks chugged past. Maybe she could start a town project building stairs up to the lodge so pedestrians didn't need to walk this dangerous path.

She had utterly no experience in organizing anything, much less stairs. She lacked the arrogance to believe she could do more than research stair construction. Could she change?

A wide white utility van roared down the hill, taking the curve at a dangerous speed. With a steep drop off on her side, Hannah was unable to step aside on this stretch. She waited for the truck to slow down and move over. Instead, it veered right toward her.

Gasping, she used her walking stick for balance and slid off the road, into the overgrown landscaping and down the steep hill, falling to her knees and scraping her palms in an effort to keep from falling further.

The van flew past and into town.

Lodged among the prickly hawthorn bushes, Hannah tried to stop shaking. If she'd had a bad knee like Amber, she'd have toppled over the edge and down the rocks. Even now, she could feel the tug of gravity. It was a struggle to pull out of the bushes and scramble back to the blacktop.

Hiking to a level spot higher up, she stepped off the road and tried to see where the van had gone.

It wasn't in the parking lot—it was driving down the narrow alley behind Aaron's shop.

With no cell service, she needed wi-fi to warn him.

Stumbling on her bruised and shaky legs, she ran up to the lodge where she could find a network.

~

SITTING AT HIS LONELY DESK, DRINKING COFFEE AND WONDERING IF THE damned woman had already packed her bags and left, Aaron worked on his bookkeeping. The sound of a motor behind the shop brought him out of his chair. He didn't have any deliveries scheduled.

His phone beeped with an incoming text as he watched the utility van out his back window. The driver was just sitting there, drinking his coffee and staring blankly at his useless phone.

Aaron pulled out his mobile. Hannah had texted him. To say goodbye? Or to beat him over the head with his failings a few more times before she left?

He started to shove the phone back in his pocket, but he was a glutton for punishment. He opened the message. She'd texted Walker as well. So much for hoping for an apology.

VAN BEHIND SHOP ALMOST RAN ME OVER.

Ran her over? He almost hit panic mode before his brain kicked in.

She was okay, he had to repeat to himself several times as he stared at the screen and reached for his landline. She was telling him she was okay, that she'd reached a safe place with wi-fi—but she wouldn't have bothered telling him that if she wasn't worried about the van.

Walker picked up the instant the phone rang. "Can you see the van?"

Aaron leaned against the wall to one side of his window and kept a wary eye on the driver. "He's just sitting there. If he's planning on blowing anything up, doesn't he have to get out first?"

"Maybe he's just lost and too stupid to know where to go without cell reception. I can come charge him with obstructing traffic and trespass and any other law that comes to mind from Hillvale's non-existent law books."

"Do that," Aaron said abruptly, realizing a utility van would have locked back doors, out of sight of the driver.

It wasn't criminal trespass if the door was unlocked and open, was it? He didn't think he'd ask Walker that.

With red rage rushing through his blood, knowing he was about to do something stupid again, Aaron filled his pockets with the tools of his trade, then let himself out the front door.

Old chests and desks in estate sales often lacked keys, and he'd learned to open locked drawers without harming valuable furniture. Sometimes he purchased estate lots in storage units that contained more utilitarian padlocks. Those, he could saw off, but he enjoyed playing with mechanisms. He knew how to pick those too. Safes were easiest since he could use his psychometry on them, but utility vans weren't likely to have combination locks.

He waited around the corner of his shop until he heard Walker talking with the driver. Then he slipped up to the double doors of the van, examined the basic padlock, and pulled out his tools. He had it open in seconds.

The van was empty except for a bundle of brand new rope still in its package, a few old rags, and a bottle with a scent that drove Aaron's rage —and his fear for Hannah—into the stratosphere.

THIRTY-ONE

"IF THAT VAN REALLY WAS AIMING FOR YOU, WE'RE COMING TOO CLOSE TO the truth," Mariah said worriedly, handing Hannah a protective lamassu to tuck in the pocket of her khaki camping shorts. They were the only two Lucys in the back of Roper's cottage. The others were taking up posts in the shrubbery. "Maybe we better reconsider this expedition."

"No," Hannah said shortly, her terror replaced by rage. She might not be Wonder Woman, but she damned well wasn't Quiet Librarian anymore. She wasn't entirely certain who she might be without Aaron, except furious. Her knees and hands *hurt*. "The way I look at it, next time, he may kill me. Or burn down the town. He needs to be stopped."

"But if Roper is in his office, then he wasn't driving the van. Maybe we're on the wrong track entirely." Mariah continued distributing evil-absorbing stone statuettes around the perimeter of Roper's cabin. In her dappled green shirt and feather-decorated black braid, Mariah managed to blend into the shadowed hedges as if she belonged there.

Hannah set a statue under a pine tree near the cabin's back door. "Only one way to find out. Did Teddy get the master key from Kurt?" Roper's cabin had once been part of the lodge's rentals and was still officially maintained by the inn.

Mariah produced the electronic key card from her jeans pocket. "I've dug into Roper every which way I know how, but he covers his online tracks far better than the sheriff does. I promised Keegan I wouldn't dive into operating systems anymore, and the back doors I used to use have mostly been closed, so I can't do anything in depth these days. I feel like my hands are tied behind my back."

"Roper's obviously clever if he can hang out with gangsters and keep his hands clean. He may be guilty of nothing more than shouting at Carmel when she needed it. Maybe Francois wasn't poisoned. But if we peg him with hiring thugs to commit arson to cover up whatever happened, then he has to be stopped." Taking a deep breath to steady her shaky nerves, Hannah swiped the key over the back-door lock. The light lit green, and she turned the knob. "Give me the casket."

Mariah reluctantly handed over the small jewel box. "I'm not sensing any unusual energy from it."

"We may be wasting our time, but I have to try." Tucking the metal box under her arm, Hannah slipped inside Roper's residence.

She'd never done anything so alarming in her entire sedate life. As much as she hoped the box would lead her directly to the moonstone, she knew not to expect magic. She had to use her wits, if she wasn't scared out of them.

Roper's kitchen looked as if it had never been touched. She'd been told that he'd taken over the cottage Kurt had renovated for his own residence, back when Kurt had been running the lodge. The interior was all gorgeous wood and granite with lots of light and open space.

She hesitated between the kitchen and the front room, hoping for some signal from the box. She desperately wanted Aaron's guidance, but he didn't need to be breaking any more laws, and she had to learn to stand on her own. Except she had no gift without him. She'd been an idiot to suggest this. She could still turn back, but she was desperate and furious. If she had to go back to Scotland, she wanted to know that she'd tried everything to find the moonstone.

She summoned the image from Keegan's painting that had first brought her here. The handsome knight had been holding this very same casket, centuries ago, offering its contents to a woman who might or might not be a nun. The journal said they'd saved a village from the plague. Their intent had been positive. So was hers. She wanted to save

Hillvale from a killer—and perhaps from the evil-soaked ground steeped in centuries of violence. If she could save herself in the process, that was a side benefit.

The journal had mentioned prayer and churches, but the rocks apparently operated on *intent*. Maybe the box did too?

Save Hillvale, she whispered before setting foot in the sun-filled front room.

Did the box vibrate—just a little?

The front room contained nothing that might be a hiding place. Nothing adorned the coffee table in front of the leather chairs. No coffee cups sat about. It was as if Roper did not exist outside his office. Maybe the bedroom. . . She crossed the large room toward the dark hall on her right.

She peeked into the modern glass and granite bathroom. All the towels were neatly folded and stacked. Maybe the maids cleaned here first. Good thing—she'd have a hard time explaining her presence. It hadn't even occurred to her that the maids might come in. She made a lousy burglar.

The box told her nothing.

She crept past the bathroom, into the darkened bedroom. Drapes had been pulled over the windows. The bed was made up in dark blues and browns with no decorator pillows or shams. The double closet doors were closed.

The closet. Carmel had hidden the moonstone in her closet. What were the chances that Roper might too?

As she opened the door, the box in her hands quivered as if in excitement.

~

"BACK AWAY, WALKER," AARON WARNED, CARRYING THE ROPE AND THE bottle toward the front of the van where Hillvale's police chief was making a show of writing a ticket for whatever trumped-up charges he'd decided on. "I'm taking over."

Walker eyed the objects in Aaron's hands, raised his usually unexpressive eyebrows, and handed the ticket to the driver.

"Nothing illegal," Aaron promised, showing Walker the bottle he'd found in the truck. "Go find Hannah and you won't be witness to anything I do."

Aaron knew he looked grim, possibly to the point of satanic. Newspapers had commented on that fact at his trial. He'd kept the goatee as his one act of defiance against the forces that had driven him here. He turned his dark glare on the van driver, who didn't have the sense to look wary, just confused. A shop owner in a blazer was apparently not very alarming.

Walker sniffed the bottle, shoved it in his pocket, and took off down the alley at a brisk pace—smart man.

Once the law was out of sight, the driver turned on the ignition. Aaron opened the van door, grabbed the burly driver's shirt by the collar, and yanked him out. He flung the hired thug to the rocky ground, reached in, grabbed the keys, and pocketed them.

The driver wasn't spry, but he was on his feet in fury, swinging at Aaron before he could shut the door.

"Don't mind if I do," Aaron muttered, catching the wild swing and countering with a blow to the driver's gut.

With an *oomph*, the driver went down again. That was the problem with big men—they got soft. And underestimated less bulky people.

"Who hired you?" Aaron demanded.

"I'm waiting for a pick up is all," the driver complained, scrambling backward in the dust.

"A pick up that requires rope. . ." Aaron flung the bundle at the thug's head. "And *chloroform*?"

"Ain't mine," the driver protested, dodging the rope. "I was just told to wait here and pick up a delivery."

"And you thought you'd just run over a woman on the way down?" Not wanting to hurt his fingers punching the goon again, Aaron stabbed him with his stick when the driver tried to scramble up again. Pity the staff had only a blunt end. He supposed he was breaking enough laws already without stabbing anyone.

"I got rights!" the driver screamed, scooting backward.

"Not with me, you don't. I can throw you down that cliff over there and no one would bother looking for your remains." Aaron followed him down the alley, stick raised. "Give me your phone."

The driver flung the useless cell at him and tried to get up. Aaron pushed him in the chest again with his staff while he retrieved it. He used his psychometry to test for images, then shoved it in his pocket. The phone case wasn't providing any clue of what went on in the driver's empty head.

"You can tell me who hired you or you can sit here and rot until I figure it out myself. Your choice. Don't say I never offered." Aaron prayed Walker would find Hannah quickly. He didn't understand exactly what was happening, but he could connect dots better than most, and chloroform rated way high on his danger meter.

"I'm just a hired driver," the man cried, holding his bruised ribs. "I don't know anything."

"You could have killed that woman!" Aaron unpackaged the discarded rope. Setting his staff against the wall, he began wrapping the cord into a noose.

"I didn't hit anyone!" Eyeing the noose, the driver backed up to the newly restored shop wall and tried to push himself to a standing position.

Losing patience, Aaron cracked his fist against a blubbery jaw and let the jerkwad hit the ground. He trussed him like a chicken and rifled his pockets.

Examining a crumpled photo from the driver's shirt pocket, Aaron's pulse escalated to terror mode. He threw all caution to the wind, leaving the goon lying there as he ran for his own vehicle.

The man carrying rope and a chloroform had a photo of *Hannah* as she walked through the lodge lobby.

He tried texting Hannah—no answer. He tried texting Walker, same. *They weren't safely in the lodge.*

Where were they?

He flew around the shop, castigating himself all the way. Why hadn't he listened to Hannah? She'd warned him what she was about to do, and he'd blown her off, why? He'd called her a *suicidal teenager. . .*when she was only doing what she thought best for herself and him. He was an asshole. If those were the last words they'd ever say to each other—no wonder they'd spent lifetimes apart. He needed to find Hannah and. . .

To his astonishment, Cass waited outside his vehicle.

And a stream of Lucys were walking up the hill to the lodge, staffs raised and. . . *sparking*?

Oh hell and damnation. Heart pounding out of his chest, he flung open the door for Cass and nearly tossed her in. He didn't even have to ask the direction. He climbed in, turned on the ignition, and roared in the direction of the lodge.

"What's happening?" he demanded, swerving past Tullah and Brenda.

"Hannah's light has gone out," was all Cass would say.

Aaron screamed inside his head all the way up the hill.

THIRTY-TWO

HANNAH WOKE UP WITH A POUNDING HEADACHE, CUDDLING THE JEWEL casket. Oddly, the casket felt content. Had the knot in her head exploded?

"I think you made my job easier," a male voice said from above her.

She was lying on a floor. Neat lines of suits hung above her. As weird as Hillvale might be, she didn't think the clothes were talking.

It hurt to turn her head, but she managed to look in the direction of the open closet door.

Fred Roper stood there, gun in hand—unless she was suffering delusions.

"I apologize for intruding," she said shakily, still uncertain of how she'd ended up on the floor. "Kurt said it would be okay to look in here." She remembered having some iffy excuse in case she was interrupted.

Roper didn't appear to be buying it. "And that's why your finger-prints are all over the weapon that killed Carmel. You're not quite right in the head, are you? You might get off on an insanity plea. Most of you women ought to be locked in institutions, if we still had them. Shame that. Get up. I've called the sheriff, not the local yokel."

Her head hurt enough to make her mental, but those statements sounded like someone testing a story rather than stating facts. Clinging to the box, she pushed partially upright. "Sorry. You're not making much sense and the room is spinning. What happened?"

"You broke into my house, planning on framing me by putting the murder weapon in my closet. Your friends aren't the only ones who can plant cameras."

Huh. She made a bad intruder. Cameras had not once occurred to her. Nasty idea, planting cameras in what was essentially a hotel suite. Now she had to wonder if Roper had taken up Carmel's blackmail business. She studied the box in her hands. Was he saying the casket was the murder weapon?

Aaron hadn't noticed anything on it, but she supposed she had no evidence otherwise. How would the murderer have had time to return it to the safe?

The whole scene had an incongruous aspect to it, with a respectable middle-aged man in an expensive business suit and tie pointing a small handgun in her direction while she cradled a medieval box. Roper's receding hairline revealed a line of sweat. He must have turned off the air conditioner before he left for work.

But the real incongruity was the chanting voice on the rooftop.

Now she understood the beads of sweat. The Lucys terrified Roper. And that was most definitely Val chanting on the roof. And maybe Mariah further away? Hannah glanced at her walking stick. The crystal was gleaming. She had no idea what that meant, but it reassured her just a little.

She tucked the box under her arm and grasped the stick to push herself up. Her brain was working a little better. Could she pry the lamassu stones out of her pocket and fling them? "Was that your van driver who tried to run me over earlier?"

She didn't think she had the strength or stability to stand up and swing the stick at a gun. Running wasn't much of an option.

Roper shrugged. "Some of those guys get bored. He may have thought it easier than tossing you off a pier. You were supposed to be down there, not up here."

"No one will believe you, you know," she said, probably unconvincingly since she was leaning on her walking stick as if she were an old lady. He must have hit her hard—as he had Carmel? She was lucky to have a thick head then.

"Of course they'll believe me. You're a mentally unstable stranger. I'm a respected member of the business community. I have witnesses who will testify to anything I tell them. The sheriff has believed me before. No reason he won't now. Besides, your fingerprints are all over the murder weapon, along with bits of Carmel's demented brain, I suspect."

Hannah gagged. Not the box then. Walker and Keegan had gone over every physical inch. "Why on earth would I kill a woman I didn't know?"

Was that more voices chanting? They needed to do a little more than sing, if so. Roper looked less confident than he sounded. His trigger finger might go off if she blinked too hard. Could the metal casket deflect a bullet?

"Who knows what crazy people will do? Maybe the two of you got in a catfight." He shrugged and edged backward, glancing expectantly over his shoulder as if anticipating backup. "Maybe you just meant to knock her down and get her out of the way."

Had the van turned around and that was the backup he was waiting on? Hannah shivered and frantically tried to think.

"She was the only reason you still had a job," she said, searching for the real version of this story as she leaned woozily on her stick. "Without Carmel, Kurt will almost certainly fire you."

"He has no reason not to give me a clean reference. That's all I need. Carmel and her blackmailing partner aren't around to muddy the water."

"Was Francois blackmailing you too? Is that why you killed him?"

"Francois was a pig. He was going after powerful men who wanted him stopped. All I had to do was tell him there were more gems by the old well, drop a few pills in his beer, and suggest we go dig them up. He's not much of a loss to the world."

"And now you have to get rid of me. And next you'll have to get rid of all the Lucys. It's not a good pattern," she warned.

He shrugged. "They'll take my word that you're crazy and killed yourself. No one will believe that I wasn't in my office that night, just as I said. A clever woman would have taken my warnings and kept her mouth shut, but you're not real clever, are you? You had to tell the slant-eyed cop, and he and his buddies are asking too many questions." Keeping the gun aimed at her, he used his other hand to check his cell phone.

Warnings? The damage to Aaron's shop—where she was supposed to be sleeping? The thug in the truck. . . If only she had a brain. What few cells she had left concentrated on the immediate problem.

"I've been told that it takes the sheriff half an hour or more to drive up here. And I'm about to throw up all over your shiny shoes. You might want to let me out of the closet." Hannah was fairly certain she was pale as death. Her normal color wasn't much rosier. He ought to believe her.

Roper grimaced and looked uncertain.

The bedroom door crashed open as if hit by a bulldozer or a battering ram, at the very least. Hannah nearly staggered in surprise. Roper swung around to confront the intruder, gun upraised.

Aaron!—looking like the Hulk with his normally complacent features suffused with rage. He'd shed his blazer and rolled up his shirtsleeves, revealing forearms roped with muscle and tendons.

He came at Roper with his staff upraised.

Wood did not beat bullets. Hannah screamed at the top of her lungs and flung the metal box at Roper's back. She hit him squarely between the shoulder blades. Instead of falling, he turned and fired into the closet.

Hannah slammed back into the wall of suits.

Swinging his stick like a cricket bat, Aaron screamed "Hannahhhhhhh!" as she crumpled. Roper's head slammed against the wall.

The lodge manager slumped and slid down. His smoking gun fell from his hand. Pulse reaching heart attack stage, Aaron kicked the weapon to one side and dived into the closet after Hannah.

She was still clinging to the damned jewel box. That had to mean something. Cursing with more profusion than a stranded sailor, he lifted her from the stack of suits she'd brought crashing to the floor and hauled her out of the closet.

Cass stepped out of the doorway to allow him into the front room. He passed Walker slipping back to check on Roper.

Gently laying his silent burden on the broad couch, Aaron frantically looked for blood. Hannah didn't open her eyes. "Dammit, woman, you're a frigging librarian, not a superhero! What the hell did you think you were doing? I told you there's no such thing as magic. Give me that damned box." He wrapped his hands around the box she held.

And tripped backward to another time and place.

"You came," she breathed in that soft melodic voice that rippled under his skin as no battle cry could do.

She hushed a small yapping dog with a snap of her fingers. It lay down in the dust and waited.

"I said I would," he reminded her. *"Had I died, I still would have found my way to you."* He gazed into wide eyes of molten amber, shielded by the headdress of her order. *"You didn't wait."*

"My place is here," she said sadly. *"My gift is to heal. Yours is to protect the lands. I have no wealth or power to help you in a material way. She does. You must marry her. You know you must."*

"I cannot marry where my heart does not belong," he protested. *"I have gone all the way to the Holy Land for these stones that you said will heal the wounds of war and illness."*

Her gaze fell on the open casket. Her eyes widened even more, and her pale hand covered her heart. *"The moonstone?"* she asked in disbelief. *"It exists?"*

"Along with its guardians. That's as it should be, isn't it? The healer surrounded by her protectors? Let me take you home, where you belong." He'd meant it to sound like an order, but it came out as an impassioned plea.

The sadness in her eyes was so devastating that he almost fell to his knees and wept.

"And that is the same here—I am protected by the power of the Lord, as you are not. Go home, Geoffrey. Go home and save your lands from those who would steal them. And with your aid, I will heal the folk who live upon them. Know I love you more than life itself, more than I should any mortal man, but my vow has been given to the church."

He kneeled and laid the box at her feet, his heart breaking into ten thousand brittle pieces.

Someone removed the box. Aaron jerked back to the moment as hands shoved him aside. "Move over and let Brenda see her."

That wasn't said in Latin.

He blinked, trying to orient himself. Cass was no nun, although she might wield the power of her order. There was no yappy dog. The casket sat on a polished wooden floor, not dirt. The woman he loved lay on a leather couch, wearing one of her khaki librarian uniforms, not a wimple and gown.

The woman he loved. . .

Stirred and blinked her big. . . amber. . . eyes. He hadn't realized that golden brown was called amber. He should have, but Hannah's eyes were the color of the trees in autumn, with golden sunlight hitting them. Amber was tree sap—not the same thing. His mind was reeling, trying to straighten out the juxtaposition of the past and present. No wonder her Aunt Jia wandered around inside her head.

"A lifetime of that would make us crazy," he said aloud.

A slow smile formed on rose lips. Long brown lashes flickered beneath her messy bangs. He knew her hair was a natural blond, but her dark lashes didn't need mascara.

"I'd kind of like a dog like that," she whispered. "Roper called me crazy. Maybe I am. I'm no healer."

"You're no nun either," he said, keeping his voice neutral as Brenda bent over her patient, checking pulse and heartbeat.

She'd been there with him. She'd seen and heard what he had. Goosebumps ran up his arms, and the hackles raised on his neck. He wished someone would tell him what in holy hell that meant.

"But you're my knight, riding to the rescue." She wrinkled up her recently-freckled nose. "He had a horse didn't he? I don't remember."

"Knights always had destriers. I only have a van, but it's a utility vehicle just as a destrier is. I didn't deliver the rocks this time though. You did." He was definitely losing it. He wasn't even sure he made sense to himself.

She glanced around, then grabbed her head as if it hurt. "Ow. Where's the box? He said I was holding the murder weapon."

That jarred him back to reality. Aaron glanced down at the casket she'd been holding, then around at the activity in the cabin. In the back room, Walker had handcuffed the unconscious Roper and left him propped against the wall while he stepped out the back to radio in a report to the county. Mariah was blocking the front door to keep out curiosity seekers. The other Lucys were still chanting outside. Brenda had finished performing her hoodoo over Hannah. Saying she could find no injury, she headed back to check on Roper.

Before Aaron could even feel relief, Cass opened the casket. Inside rested a large grayish rock with tantalizing glimpses of shimmering, translucent white. She picked it up using a handkerchief she produced from her skirt pocket. From that same pocket, she produced a stone lamassu, one without crystal or the guardian rocks.

"Put Roper's fingerprints on it," she commanded, holding the statuette out to Aaron.

And even though he knew it was a criminal act, Aaron got up and defiantly crossed into the bedroom to press Roper's fingers to the stone. Sometimes, the greater good was more important than minor details like which weapon had actually killed. In her own way, Cass was telling him that he'd done the right thing by going to jail for concealing the painting, even though he still had no proof that the Eversham had been dangerous in anything more than his mind.

Brenda returned with him to the front room. Holding the moonstone in a bundle of gauze, she used a sterile stick from her bag to transfer bits of matter from the real weapon to the newly fingerprinted statuette.

Aaron would prefer not to touch a rock that had shattered a woman's skull. But the police chief was an honest Null and only allowed them leeway because Lucys offered information he couldn't find on his own. The fake murder weapon would pass Walker's inspection better if Aaron could offer him the real story of Carmel's death.

Gritting his teeth, he held out his palm for the moonstone. Roper's hate and anger came through clearly, as if the stone wished to reject them. Aaron winced at the negativity seeping into him.

Before he could protest, Hannah clasped her hand over his.

THIRTY-THREE

The lying, conniving bitch!

He clutched the stupid worthless rock she'd claimed would solve all her problems. *"A rock won't force people to pay blackmail. And you can't expect me to give you kickbacks for the guests I bring in,"* he said in the calm voice of reason.

"I can when they're criminals and you're using my property for their meetings!" she shouted back. *"If they won't pay, I'll call the FBI! The moonstone will make it happen, trust me."*

His stomach lurched at her crazy talk, but he'd been in tighter spots. *"This is a free country. I cannot prevent anyone who can pay from taking a room."*

"I know damned well you're taking money under the table for arranging those meetings. I want my share!" Carmel screamed.

Her shrieking made him nervous. He wasn't used to it. The people he worked with had reason to prefer quiet invisibility. His knuckles whitened around the rock. Before he could form a reply, a knock at the door interrupted and Carmel flung it open to screech at the intruder. The woman was becoming more unstable every day.

"Francois, you fool! I told you not to interrupt until I called. Give me those photos."

Photos?

Outside, the dissolute chauffeur mumbled and held out a manila packet.

"Proof!" Carmel shouted, grabbing the packet.

She had photos of the meetings? That would get him killed.

Before he knew what he intended—as if the rock had given him orders—he swung his rock-holding fist at the back of her head and snatched the packet from her hand.

HANNAH GASPED IN SHOCK AND DROPPED HER GRIP ON AARON. SHE WAS back in the barren suite, staring at the ceiling.

Crouched on the floor beside her, Aaron stared at the lump of rock in his hand as if it might bite him. Gingerly, he laid it back on the satin in the casket. "Francois and Carmel were blackmailing Roper," he said decisively, before she could interpret the scene aloud.

Was that what he'd taken from that episode? Not that the moonstone had swung itself? Her brain was too shattered to translate anything except Roper's violent reaction.

"Do you think the photos showed his gangster friends?" she asked, probably irrelevantly.

Chief Walker returned from his phone call to hear the last of their discussion. "Roper probably burned anything incriminating he took that night, but Francois kept the originals of everything. Tell me what to look for."

Aaron looked blank for a moment, took a deep breath, then squeezing Hannah's hand, he offered his judicious version of the tale. "Carmel was blackmailing Roper, asking for part of whatever his gangster friends paid him to hold meetings at the lodge. Francois brought over photos we assume were part of the blackmail. Roper lost it. I don't think you have a case for first degree murder. He just picked up the nearest hard object and whacked Carmel to get at the photos. But since Francois was present and a witness, you have some case for first degree in his death."

"If it helps, I can testify to that," Hannah offered. "He said he put pills in Francois's beer."

"Hearsay and probably not admissible." Walker glanced at the moonstone they'd just set in the box, then to the statuette that Brenda offered to him in its protective layer of gauze. "Right. There are new techniques for lifting fingerprints from certain kinds of rocks. Don't know if this is the right kind." He glanced at Aaron. "Did you leave the van driver alive?"

Aaron shrugged. "He's alive. Not sure he's learned his lesson. Since he's too incompetent to have hurt anyone yet, you may have to offer him immunity and nail Roper that way."

Walker nodded. "Hannah, you okay to testify? Attempted murder will hold him until we have everything we need for the other charges."

She rubbed her head. "Throw the book at him, and I'll be there."

She meant it. Her first attempt to be more than the Librarian had almost ended in disaster, but she'd accomplished her goal—*she'd found the moonstone.*

She couldn't leave soon if she had to stand as witness. Could she learn more courage, be more than a librarian?

She glanced at Aaron, who was regarding her with smoldering dark eyes. With Aaron's impassive, iron-jawed expression, it was hard to tell if he was feeling murderous or lustful. As Nurse Brenda packed her medical bag, Hannah shakily offered him a smile.

He looked as stunned as if she'd hit him. Had no one ever smiled at the glowering tyrant before?

Once Brenda got out of his way, Aaron scooped Hannah up as if she weighed nothing and carried her past gaping, protesting Lucys—her friends, who had come to her aid, however eccentrically.

"I know actions speak louder than words," she said, clinging to Aaron's wide shoulders. "But a whisper of what you're doing might help. I'm not fond of being pushed around at the moment."

"You like being overpowered on other occasions?" he asked consideringly, carrying her down the hedge-lined walk to the parking lot.

"Possibly. I've never tried it in a safe context." He was scaring her and exciting her at the same time. She'd had more excitement in this past week than she'd had in her entire life. Was it possible to become addicted to adrenaline rushes?

"You'll always be safe with me," he said, opening the door to his van and setting her in the passenger seat. "I'm not as positive about the Lucys."

"It was *my* idea." She knew she sounded defensive. She didn't care.

"Roper was our only suspect. And the journals indicated the box and the moonstone belonged together. We needed the moonstone. If he'd been there when Carmel died, then it made sense that he might have the missing moonstone."

"I get all that. I might even get why you thought you had to be the one to go after it." He climbed in the driver's seat and started the engine. "What I don't get. . ." His voice raised. "What I *don't* get is why the hell you thought I'd leave you to face a killer alone!"

"Oh. Huh." She studied the windshield. "I guess because you rejected breaking and entering, and I understood that. It's the same as not telling Walker what he doesn't need to hear because it's easier all around."

"Not acceptable." Instead of stopping in the parking lot, he roared on down the highway. "That's what the damned nun did—went her own way without consulting her knight first. To be fair, he probably went questing for stones without telling her. I'm guessing if we want to believe we're reliving our failed past lives—or other peoples' failed lives —then we'd better accept that going our own way results in never seeing each other again."

"I didn't think you *wanted* to see me again," she pointed out. "I have a knot in my head. I could be dying. I think that makes me do dangerously silly things. I don't blame you for backing off."

"I'm *not* backing off!" he roared as he swung the van down his private driveway. "I just don't know what the hell I *am* doing!"

"And you don't like that," she guessed, considering this new angle with interest. "That's reasonable, I suppose. Will you let me know when you've figured it out?"

He slammed the van to a halt outside the house and flipped off the engine. He didn't look at her. "What if I never figure it out? What if I need a lifetime to figure it out?"

Hannah pondered that. "Can I help you work on it?"

There was that smoldering look again. He leaned over and kissed her this time, though, so she guessed he wasn't about to murder her.

"Yeah, I think that's the key," he muttered against her mouth, cradling the back of her head so he could smother her with more kisses. "I think we need to work it out together. Let's start somewhere easy, like bed. I think we have that worked out pretty smoothly."

"You're skipping the difficult bits, mister," she murmured back, reaching for his neck. "Practice talking while you take me there."

He hauled her out of the seat and kicked the van door closed once they were outside. "The shop opens tomorrow," he said helpfully, carrying her to the door. "I have a buying trip scheduled for next week. I'm thinking I ought to hire someone to handle the shop."

At this mundane speech, she laughed into his neck and tickled him anywhere she could reach.

She loved the hard-headed man, and holding him like this, she *understood* him. She didn't need magic or moonstones or even words. Aaron gave off his own vibrations and they resonated with hers.

THIRTY-FOUR

"Look at them, they're adorable," Hannah whispered as they strolled down the moonlit trail to the vortex, weeks after Roper had been taken to jail. "Hillvale really is developing into a lover's paradise."

Since Hannah was holding his hand and all was right with his world, Aaron was inclined to agree, if he knew what he was agreeing to. He glanced down at Hannah, who still managed to glow like a sunny day even in the moonlight. She was so vibrant with life, she brought him to life again. She was a drug he would take for as long as he could have her.

He followed her gaze to the night-shrouded Goddess of Death clinging to the arm of lanky Lance. . . Now that Aaron paid attention, Lance did seem a little more spruced up than usual, with a determined spring in his step that hadn't been there before.

"Val's veil is short and only gray," Hannah whispered. "I don't know if she'll ever wear color again. The black is too ingrained, and now that she's letting her Nordic-blond hair grow out, she looks good in it. She may still frighten guests."

Aaron puzzled over that as the slow procession of candle-carrying Lucys ambled down a trail heavily scented in September roses. "What guests? Val hides around strangers."

"Lodge guests, silly. You really ought to pay more attention to my email." She nudged his hip.

His last buying trip had been a short one. There hadn't been time to do more than skim Hannah's massive missives in case there were matters he needed to address. But she handled everything so well in his absence that he really didn't need to worry. He just liked hearing her voice, even when it was written.

"You really ought to learn to pick up a phone," he countered. "Then I'd listen."

"No, then you start talking sexy and I forget everything I meant to say. Didn't Kurt tell you that Lance wants to try running the lodge? He's lived there forever, knows the staff, knows the guests and routine. He's perfect."

"Yeah, I vaguely recall something of the sort. He'll probably give starving artists a free ride, but that's better than Roper's gangsters, one assumes." The thug he'd punched had turned out to have a criminal record in a dozen states. With a little effort, the cops had pinned him to several deaths. He was spilling his hefty guts to avoid the death penalty.

"Val is moving in with Lance," Hannah whispered. "Monty and Fee are buying her house."

Monty and Fee were getting married by moonlight under the auspices of Cass, who had little more than an online certificate of divinity. Aaron wasn't certain either the mayor or the cook was sensible enough to care for a house, but he wished them well. Fee had been thrilled with the twelve-place setting of vintage, silver-trimmed Noritake china he'd given them—a set with only good memories on it. He'd had to warn Monty not to put them in the microwave.

"Lance and Val as management will be like having the Addams Family running the lodge," Aaron murmured. "Now that the lamassu are draining the bad energy and the poltergeists are gone, we'll just have our very own local vampires haunting the place."

"Lance and Val are not vampires," Hannah scolded. "Carmel might have been an emotional vampire, but Val is just a wounded actress. She can perform at will. With her compelling voice, she's perfect for handling any guest drama. And Lance will simply let the staff run the operation while he writes checks and paints. It's all good. And bless you for hiring Mariah's dad to work in the shop. Thomas is absolutely adorable."

"Hiring an illegal alien may not be my finest moment, but it beats a few others I can think of. And he's a natural. He can spin a yarn about anything." He was lining up more help while he was at it.

Now that he didn't need to protect Hillvale anymore, he had an entire world to explore. Hannah had already expressed interest. Teaching a single student wasn't challenging enough for her quick mind. Sally could handle all three kids, he'd been assured. He just needed to do this right. . .

"I may have to start believing your lover's paradise scenario." Aaron nodded at another couple already seated in the stadium. "Now that she's rearranged my inventory, Wan Hai has moved into Pasquale's house and is rearranging his life."

"Good for her," Hannah said, beaming.

"Better for Walker. She's quit trying to rearrange his and Sam's place."

As they followed the procession down the aisle between the rows of amphitheater seats, Aaron studied the changes that had been made to the vortex arena while he was gone. He knew several Lucy meetings had gone into the planning. It would take time to learn if they'd made the right decisions, but the energy around Hillvale had steadily improved since the Lucys had begun making changes.

Harvey had outdone himself by carving a redwood totem pole to hold the moonstone and its casket. Cass had agreed that locking them in a safe wasn't the way to heal the community. The decision to place the totem pole in the vortex, near the good energy of Cass's property had been a difficult one. Once the Lucys had decided the lamassu bearing the guardian stones could be safely placed at distances from each other, it had worked out, he thought. At least no one had been murdered recently.

Aaron glanced at one of the stone warriors on its concrete base guarding the pathway to the moonstone. "Is anyone digging up the original lamassu?"

Hannah laughed. "Amber's movie star husband has offered to build a community pool there. He's hoping to find underground water. He and

Harvey really want to build that winery up the mountain, if they can just find where the stream has gone."

"It could happen," Aaron agreed. He was feeling very agreeable these days. "Once the negative energy is recharged to positive, anything might happen." Which gave him freedom to roam the world in search of other people or places that needed a guardian.

They set their candles in the wrought iron stand one of the artisans had created, then took their stone seats near the front of the natural stadium. The evening gleamed with stars and candlelight. Aaron circled Hannah's waist, and she leaned into him as Val began singing and Harvey played his organ.

For the first time in his life, Aaron knew peace. He wasn't regretting the past. He was with a woman who gave him joy just by breathing.

Kissing Hannah's head, he released her waist to remove a small box from his coat pocket.

"I love you beyond reason, Librarian. Marry me," he whispered just as the music reached a crescendo and the bride appeared.

As Aaron slid a ring over Hannah's finger, Val's voice rose like an angelic choir to Harvey's dramatic accompaniment. Stunned, Hannah could only stare. It wasn't a fancy ring, just a sliver of old gold and diamonds, but when he held it against her skin, she could *feel* the love in it. He'd looked for a ring embedded with love. Tears sprang to her eyes, and she pulled his head down to kiss him even as Fee walked down the aisle.

She could see Fee any day. She would only ever have one proposal like this.

"I love you, my knight in tarnished armor. I think I always have."

Aaron hugged her close, returning her passion, and under the starlight, her tears fell faster.

He'd asked her even *before* she'd given him the news. She'd only received it today, and she'd wanted to wait until they were alone to tell him. By asking now, he was risking heartbreak all over again, and she thought her own heart might explode at the realization of the depth of

Aaron's love. She'd known his tough carapace concealed fountains of passion. She just hadn't expected him to ever let down his guard.

"I love you," she murmured against his mouth. "I love you with all my heart and soul and into eternity."

"That's how love should be," he said, hugging her closer. "You're my soul mate, my heart, and we'll never be parted, no matter what this life brings us. I'm learning to accept that we'll always find each other. *Te amo, amica mea.* I love you and I need you in my life, please."

She snuggled against his shoulder and watched the altar as Monty's face lit up at the approach of his bride. "This really is a lover's paradise, isn't it?" she whispered as Fee's face glowed under the moonlight. "There is so much love and joy here."

Aaron squeezed her in agreement.

In silence, they listened to Cass's brief ceremony.

As the couple pledged their vows, Hannah pulled Aaron's head down so she could whisper in his ear. "I had another MRI while you were gone. Brenda insisted. She read the results along with the technician. The knot is assimilating—in a good way. She says I was keeping my enhancing gift bottled up, but now that I'm working with you more, it's becoming a part of me. And you."

Startled, he stared down at her with those black eyes that could suck her down channels of time. She kissed him, and his relief was apparent in his passionate response. Professor Aaron might play the part of cool sophisticate, but inside, he was a churning cauldron of emotion.

"Tripping through time isn't breaking your brain but *curing* it?" he asked when they came up for air.

"If you wish to believe Brenda. I suppose it makes sense. I have all these books in my head, often in Latin and French and in ancient dialects that only I might understand when we're pulled into a memory. You may be reading the images through my mind, and that's why we work together. We may still both go nutso," she whispered with amusement.

"I'm writing that up in my journal for some future librarian to translate," he said dryly. "I proposed to a woman who makes me crazy."

Hannah elbowed him. After the bride and groom turned to face the community as man and wife, she and Aaron stood with the rest of the audience. The new ring on her finger practically vibrated love and hope.

She cried with everyone else as the newly wedded couple walked up the aisle.

Aaron held her as she sobbed. Hannah hoped she could impress this memory in her brain to savor for a lifetime.

And then they went home and made love and maybe babies—while planning Aaron's dream of a network of eccentric guardians who might someday circle the world.

CRYSTAL MAGIC CHARACTERS

Mariah Ives (Zoe Ascension de Cervantes) creates ghost-catchers; married to Keegan

Montgomery Kennedy—Hillvale's mayor, part-owner of Redwood Resort

Orval Bledsetter—retired veterinarian

Pasquale—grocer

Samantha Moon Walker—environmental scientist; wife of police chief Walker

Sydony Devine-Baker Bennet—Teddy's sister; interior designer; mother of two small children

Theodosia (Teddy) Devine-Baker Kennedy—empathic jeweler; married to Kurt Kennedy

Tullah—owner of thrift store; psychic medium

Valerie Ingersson (Valdis)—goddess of death; former actress

Wan Hai—feng shui expert

Xavier Black—contract lawyer, Kennedy property rental agent

MOONSTONE SHADOWS CHARACTERS

Daphne Daisy Ives—Mariah's newborn

Malcolm Eversham—a commune artist; oil painter who paints his dreams

Natalie—Aaron's late wife

Nan—Aaron's late aunt, a Malcolm

Aunt Jia—Hannah's 93-year-old time-traveling great-great-great aunt

Francesca (Frannie)—Hannah's airplane pilot psychic cousin

Jack—Hannah's finder cousin

Sally—elementary teacher and sometime waitress

ABOUT THE AUTHOR

With several million books in print and *New York Times* and *USA Today's* bestseller lists under her belt, former CPA Patricia Rice is one of romance's hottest authors. Her emotionally-charged contemporary and historical romances have won numerous awards, including the *RT Book Reviews* Reviewers Choice and Career Achievement Awards. Her books have been honored as Romance Writers of America RITA® finalists in the historical, regency and contemporary categories.

A firm believer in happily-ever-after, Patricia Rice is married to her high school sweetheart and has two children. A native of Kentucky and New York, a past resident of North Carolina and Missouri, she currently resides in Southern California, and now does accounting only for herself.

ALSO BY PATRICIA RICE

The World of Magic:

The Unexpected Magic Series

MAGIC IN THE STARS

WHISPER OF MAGIC

THEORY OF MAGIC

AURA OF MAGIC

CHEMISTRY OF MAGIC

NO PERFECT MAGIC

The Magical Malcolms Series

MERELY MAGIC

MUST BE MAGIC

THE TROUBLE WITH MAGIC

THIS MAGIC MOMENT

MUCH ADO ABOUT MAGIC

MAGIC MAN

The California Malcolms Series

THE LURE OF SONG AND MAGIC

TROUBLE WITH AIR AND MAGIC

THE RISK OF LOVE AND MAGIC

Crystal Magic

SAPPHIRE NIGHTS

TOPAZ DREAMS

CRYSTAL VISION

WEDDING GEMS

AZURE SECRETS

AMBER AFFAIRS

ABOUT BOOK VIEW CAFÉ

Book View Café Publishing Cooperative (BVC) is an author-owned cooperative of over fifty professional writers, publishing in a variety of genres including fantasy, romance, mystery, and science fiction. Since its debut in 2008, BVC has gained a reputation for producing high-quality ebooks. BVC's ebooks are DRM-free and are distributed around the world. The cooperative is now bringing that same quality to its print editions.

BVC authors include New York Times and USA Today bestsellers as well as winners and nominees of many prestigious awards, including:

Agatha Award
Campbell Award
Hugo Award
Lambda Award
Locus Award
Nebula Award
Nicholl Fellowship
PEN/Malamud Award
Philip K. Dick Award
RITA Award

World Fantasy Award
Writers of the Future Award